*Alanna & Harry*
*Thank you for*
*sctra-thing*
*for Debb*

# BEYOND CONTROL

## THE SEED HAS BEEN SOWN

# LAWRENCE VERIGIN

PROMONTORY
P R E S S

Promontory Press
www.promontorypress.com

ISBN: 978-1-77374-0102

Cover Design and Typeset by Edge of Water Designs,
edgeofwater.com

Printed in Canada
987654321

Also by Lawrence Verigin

# DARK SEED

Winner of the 2014 Chanticleer Clue Thriller Award
for
International Intrigue and World Events

Finalist for the 2015 Eric Hoffer Award Montaigne Medal
for
Thought-Provoking Books That Illuminate,
Progress, and Redirect Thought

# SEED OF CONTROL

Winner of the 2016 Chanticleer Clue Thriller Award
for
Eco/Natural Resources Thriller

First in Category Winner
of the 2017 Global Thriller Award

Dedicated to
my wife, Diana Carrillo.
Thank you for all your love and support,
and for "encouraging" me out of bed
early each morning to write.

# BEYOND CONTROL

LAWRENCE VERIGIN

# PROLOGUE

*Wednesday April 23, 2003*

His father was dead, and now he was going to take control. Hendrick Schmidt V needed a moment to collect his thoughts before joining his guests. These men had to know that he was the best person to oversee Naintosa and Pharmalin and for that matter, to lead *them*. His father had been weak, and Hendrick was strong and cunning; surely, they could sense that. If any of them didn't see it his way, he'd eliminate the ones not loyal to him. *I created this opportunity to seize control, and I must be respected for it.* Hendrick forced a grin. *I'm not afraid of them.*

The funeral had been held at the church past the edge of their property line. The mini-cathedral with its stained glass windows and domed roof had been built by a wealthy baron in 1610. The Schmidt family had made it their own, with multiple generations buried within its crypt.

The estate had been built by the Schmidt family in the mid-1800s as a country getaway not too far from the city. Now it was in a suburb of fast-growing Berlin. The buildings were fortunate not to have been destroyed in World War II, and whatever damage had been caused by the conflict had long since been repaired. The trees of the forest had been replanted, hiding the scars of the shelling and stumps of the old growth.

After the service, many attendees had avoided both the supporters and protestors outside as they adjourned from the church. They were ushered to the mansion to toast the life of the deceased. Now only a select few mourners remained.

The butler balanced an empty silver serving tray in his left hand as he closed the double oak doors to the study with his right hand. As he turned, he paused. "I didn't see you there, sir. Would you like me to fetch you a Cognac as well?"

"Wait twenty minutes and then bring me a full decanter," Hendrick said.

The butler gave a nod and retreated down the corridor.

Hendrick took a deep breath and went into the study. The first person he saw was Carlo Da Silva, a man heavily invested in the shaping of the Internet and chairman of the *Club*. Carlo's eyes were directed toward the dark shelves lined with books on the opposite side of the room, but he turned when he heard the doors close.

There were five brown leather chairs situated around a square mahogany table.

Opposite Carlo sat Davis Lovemark, by far the largest media baron in the world. He swirled amber liquid in a snifter and then brought it to his lips. "Tasty." The light from a fresco table lamp nearby accentuated a birthmark the size and color of a penny between his chin and right cheek.

Between the two sat the banking director Malcolm Carter. His long arms draped over the sides of the overstuffed chair, making him look uncomfortable. He reached forward to take a crystal glass from the table.

Hendrick tucked in his black tie so he could button his black suit jacket over it. He'd had the suit made specifically for the funeral and this meeting days before his father had died. He stepped forward into the room. "I hope you've been treated well." He was trying to speak English as much as he could, and his German tongue had to work hard to make the words articulate.

The three men rose to meet their host.

"Carlo ... Davis ... Malcolm." Hendrick shook each hand in turn. He had always called them by their surnames before out of respect for his elders. But that time had passed; Hendrick was to be treated as an equal now.

He knew the empty chair with the untouched snifter of Cognac placed in front of it was meant to be a tribute to his father, the late Dr. Hendrick Schmidt IV, and that he was supposed to sit in the chair next to it. But he wanted to prove a point, so he sat down in the tribute chair. "Are you hungry? Can I have anything brought in?" He smiled toward Carlo. "Remember how my father used to eat everything you put in front of him with vigor when he visited you?"

The others sat back down in their chairs.

"Yes, he had a healthy appetite," Carlo said in his thick Spanish accent that sounded like his tongue was too large for his mouth.

"Too hardy, yet not so healthy," Hendrick added.

"Our condolences for your loss," Malcolm said in his Texan drawl, stilted by a life in banking. "The service was appropriate."

"Your father was a good man." Davis's accent was American with the slightest hint of British, from his roots. "He will be missed."

Carlo nodded. "Yes, very much."

Hendrick's face went stern. "My father was holding us all back. Now that I am in charge the plan will move forward at a much more rapid pace."

Carlo opened his mouth and then closed it. When he spoke, it was in a placating tone. "Do you think you're ready for the responsibility? We can help you find someone to run the companies until you are. We can look after the project: we're on track, and 2020 is years away.

You have to finish your studies."

"I have my Doctorate in Physics, and my Masters in Executive Business is almost complete," Hendrick said. "I will contact Oxford and make the arrangements to take a leave until I have more time. They are very accommodating to my family."

"Congratulations on the DPhil in Physics," said Malcolm, who instructed countries' federal reserves on how to conduct their business. "But you should finish your MBA now. It's going to be very important."

"I agree, Hendrick," Davis said. "There is no need to rush. Finish your schooling and take time to mourn. This must've been quite a shock for you, your mother, brother, and sister. Your father was only sixty-four. As the eldest son you need to be here for your family."

Hendrick tried to conceal the rolling of his eyes but knew Carlo had caught it. "I know what's best, and I'm taking over now. My father was preparing me and would've wanted it this way."

"Your father would've wanted to stay alive until after 2020 to see the plan fully implemented," Carlo said. "He planned on preparing you for the next ten to fifteen years before you fully took over."

"Now that your father is gone, you need to listen to our advice." Malcolm wasn't being polite anymore. "This is a delicate operation that we're not going to let you be a part of until you're ready."

*Why do they not respect me? I just masterfully killed my father and am going to get away with it. Surely they instinctively recognize that I could and very well may decide on the same fates for them.* Hendrick reached out with stubby fingers for the snifter that wasn't intended to be drunk. When he leaned forward, it exposed that his hair was already receding and a bald spot had formed on his crown, just like his father's. He took a healthy swallow of the Cognac, both for effect and in hopes of calming himself. "I Am Ready ... And my companies are the most important for the cause."

Davis rose to his feet. "We'll tell you when you're ready."

Hendrick stared at him. *Davis Lovemark—done. Why do I need his media spin? In the end the people who survive will know it was me who saved them. The world will bow to me.* "I'll go to the other members if you don't cooperate with me."

Carlo stood. "They'll listen to their chairman—that being me—over you."

Hendrick leaned back in his chair, pushing away the feeling of being chastised. *Carlo Da Silva—finished. What does Internet information compilation have to do with what we are accomplishing? And do I really need other Club members' support anymore?*

Malcolm was the third to rise. "You need to be patient, son. Finish your studies and let us help you get the resources to learn specifically what your father was preparing you for.

Hendrick looked up at Malcolm. *Malcolm Carter, you are through as well. Wait, I need their money. Naintosa and Pharmalin cannot bear the brunt of such a large undertaking alone. I will have to bide my time. But I will begin work right away and show them that I am the leader.*

The butler entered, holding a silver tray with a single snifter and a full decanter of Cognac.

▷◁▣▷◁

The men, all dressed in the most expensively tailored, black suits, paused after walking out into the cool spring night. Only their cars and drivers remained in the large circular driveway. It was quiet except for the gurgle of water from a nearby fountain.

"What do you think?" asked Malcolm, the tallest and oldest of the three.

"He's not ready," Davis said. "And he's got his old man's temper."

Carlo thought for a good long moment. "Yet it's inevitable that we must work with him. We need to find someone we can appoint in the interim, who can also help prepare Hendrick at a more rapid rate."

"If he'll listen," Davis said.

"Did you see his eyes and facial expressions?" Carlo asked. "Something's not right upstairs."

"He acts like a stubborn little spoiled brat, if you ask me," Malcolm said.

Carlo smiled. "He suffers from overactive inner dialogue and self-absorption."

All three began to walk toward their awaiting vehicles.

"What about this Nick Barnes?" Malcolm asked. "Do you really think he killed Hendrick senior?"

"I don't think so," Carlo said. "My guess is they're going to have to end up releasing him."

"I've made sure stories discrediting Barnes are running everywhere," Davis said. "That'll make Barnes's *cause* much more difficult to achieve. It's taking the wind out of his opposition to us."

"So, who killed Hendrick then?" Malcolm asked.

Carlo shrugged. "We don't know yet, but I'm sure Plante will figure it out."

Davis nodded. "And I have a few theories."

"Should we be worried?" Malcolm asked.

"Yes," Carlo said.

"Maybe ask your brother," Davis told Malcolm.

# CHAPTER 1

*April 24, 2003*

Maybe now I'd get some answers as to why they had me here and thought I'd done it. I looked at the wall of one-way glass, wondering who was watching on the other side.

The only door to the room opened, and Chief Inspector Jacques Plante entered carrying a binder and pad of paper. A waft of not-as-stale air came in with him. He placed the contents in his hand on the metal table, unbuttoned the top of his suit jacket, and sat across from me. "Monsieur Nick Barnes."

Chief Inspector Plante had interrogated me twice before about our escape from the cabin outside of Vancouver where three of our group had been killed. When he looked at you, it was as if his eyes bored into your brain and extracted the truth.

I didn't bother holding back my frustration. "Why have I been locked up for days without anyone telling me what's going on? Isn't that against the law?"

He glanced up with his steel-blue eyes over his hook-shaped nose, and said in his French accent, "I had more important things to do, like attend Dr. Schmidt's funeral in Berlin."

"You know I had nothing to do with his death."

Chief Inspector Plante opened the binder. "That's what we're here to determine."

"Why would a Chief Inspector of Interpol be interrogating me and not someone lower down on the food chain?"

He didn't look up as he ran his finger along the lines of a written paragraph. "None of your concern."

"Shouldn't I be allowed to have an attorney present?"

"We'll see. Depends on your cooperation."

"You know I didn't kill Schmidt. And for sure not letting me talk to a lawyer is against the law."

"You left Burford last Thursday, April 17, in the morning and returned late Friday, April 18. Is that correct?" Plante raised his eyes from what he'd been reading.

I'd known he was going to focus on that, but I had an alibi. "Yes, I came here to London for editor interviews, hopefully to find one for my manuscript. I can get you their names and addresses so you can check for yourself. I also kept the receipt from the hotel, and Lorraine was with me the whole time."

"Lorraine Badowski is a bodyguard provided to you by Jack Carter?"

"One of, yes." I raised my hands. "As you can see, there was no way I could get to Lake Como, in Italy, sneak into Dr. Schmidt's heavily guarded estate, kill him, and get back to London without anyone noticing while, of course, simultaneously having meetings with editors."

"How did you know Dr. Schmidt was killed at his villa in Lake Como?"

"I read the newspaper just before you came to arrest me in Burford."

Plante wrote something down.

"Ask Lorraine; she was with me the whole time."

"Madam Badowski corroborates your story; however, she's paid to provide protection, so she's not a reliable witness."

"Why are you bothering with me? Do you have any kind of evidence that makes me a suspect? You should be focusing on trying to find the real killer, not this stupid setup."

Plante released the pen in his right hand. "What do you mean by 'setup'?"

"Well, since I didn't kill him and I'm here and probably the only one being detained in regard to this investigation, someone wants you to think I did it. It doesn't take a detective to figure that out." *I probably shouldn't have said that last bit.* "Have you checked out Peter Bail?"

"And you are not a detective." He cleared his throat and remained calm. "You had the time to get to and from Lake Como. Did you have access to Dr. Schmidt's private e-mail?"

"No." He'd ignored my reference to Bail, the only paid assassin I knew.

"You deny sending him harassing e-mails, saying you were going to kill him?"

"How and why would I do that?"

"We have evidence that you did." Plante kept his focus on my face.

As a journalist I'd been trained to read people's expressions. His face was blank, his voice almost monotone, but his eyes were looking inside of me. "Well, they're not real."

"They are real."

"Can I see them?"

"The e-mails are on your computer that we have retrieved."

*What is he talking about? I don't have Schmidt's e-mail and haven't been sending him threatening messages.* "That can't be."

"But they are right there on your computer."

"I want to see for myself."

Plante turned a few pages and then unclipped the three rings of the binder, pulling out a sheet protector. There was a piece of paper between the clear plastic. "Do you recognize this?" He slid it across the table to me.

It was my London hotel receipt. *How the fuck did he get that?* My hands went to my gray coverall pockets, as if I still would've had the receipt in one of them.

"See your name at the top?" He leaned forward and tapped his finger over my name. "This receipt was found folded on the floor of Dr. Schmidt's villa, next to his dead body. It must have fallen out of your pocket."

*What the hell.* "But I didn't do it. This is proof someone's setting me up."

"You checked out of the hotel at eight thirty, right?"

"I had a meeting with an editor at nine."

"That was your last editor meeting, correct?"

"Yes."

"What did you do after your meeting?"

"I went with Lorraine to the Tower of London. Neither of us had been there before."

He produced another protected sheet from the binder. "This was taken at Gatwick Airport at 11:02 a.m."

It was a profile shot, looking down, of a man walking. The black jacket he had on was the same as mine, and he was wearing jeans like I would've been. He was around my height, thirtyish, and Caucasian, and his facial features were similar, but it wasn't me. His brown hair was balding at the top; mine wasn't. His nose was bigger, and he looked heavier. "That's not me."

"This man, who to me looks like you, used fake identification under the name, Nick Hansen."

*Shit.* That was the name I'd used a few years ago. I'd stored the passport and ID in the hiding place in my San Francisco apartment. It dawned on me that when my belongings were retrieved, the IDs hadn't been there. I'd forgotten all about them. When my place had been broken into by Naintosa's security, they must've taken them. So someone associated with Schmidt's own company had killed him? *Shit.* "That identification was stolen from me by Naintosa's security. You should be looking at Dr. Schmidt's own people."

"Do you have proof of that?"

"The stolen identification is the proof."

Plante raised an eyebrow and then looked down at another piece of paper. "These are the facts I have: Nick Hansen took a noon flight to Milan, arriving at 2:50 p.m., taking into account the one-hour time difference." He looked at me, again, straight in the eyes. "He then rented a car and drove the sixty kilometers to the Schmidt home, killed him, and drove back in time for the 6:10 p.m. flight back. Taking the time difference into account again, he arrived back at Gatwick at 7:07 p.m." He hadn't blinked. "Thus, getting *you* back to Burford at approximately 9:30 p.m., correct?"

"How would I know? I wasn't there." *Why had Lorraine and I lingered and played tourist that day?* "After the Tower of London, we went to see Buckingham Palace, Trafalgar Square, and walked along the Thames."

"Do you have proof?"

"Lorraine was with me the whole time."

Plante shook his head. "Again, not a credible witness."

*This is crazy.* "Okay, how did I kill Dr. Schmidt?"

"By injecting a lethal poison into his neck."

"What?" I squirmed in the chair. Just hearing about someone being killed by a needle brought back too many bad memories. "How would I get hold of something like that?"

"I understand you've had experience with such chemicals that dissipate quickly, making them untraceable, like Cirachrome?"

"Yeah, of finding people who'd been killed by injections, but not of using or even knowing how to find poison like that." *Dr. Schmidt had to have been killed by his own people.*

Chief Inspector Plante's eyes bored harder into mine.

"You really need to be talking to Naintosa's security. Injecting people with untraceable poison is their trademark. Find Peter Bail. He's the first one I'd talk to."

Plante blinked.

"This is a setup."

"Or the truth."

"No; s-e-t-u-p."

# CHAPTER 2

*April 25, 2003*

I looked up in time to see the little red light on the security camera outside the cell on the far wall switch off.

The outside door to the room opened, and a guard I'd never seen before entered with another man in the same gray get-up I had on. He unlocked my cell door and took off the prisoner's handcuffs. The officer smiled at me before locking the door and walking back out of the room.

The guy standing in front of me was huge. And I wasn't small at six feet tall, 185 pounds.

I'd been in this cell for five days on my own. Now I had to share? There was only one bed in the corner.

A sneer of malice was on his face. He cracked his knuckles and took a step toward me. No, this guy didn't want to be a cellmate; he wanted to hurt me. If he connected once, I'd be down and out. He took another step to close the distance.

My mind raced through my Krav Maga training—*disable your attacker and be decisive.* I reinforced to myself the fact that his size didn't matter.

He took another step closer.

I backed up until I felt the bars of the cell.

His feet moved twice more.

My position restricted my movement, so I moved forward and left.

He made a fist and swung his right arm at me in an arc.

It wasn't fast, and I was able to duck.

As I moved past him I pushed my right elbow into his side. It was like hitting a concrete barrier.

I saw another swing coming and tried to spin away. I wasn't quite quick enough, and his fist glanced off my head. That was hard enough to put me on the floor.

He was bending over me, but I managed to scramble to the side while seeing stars. Dizzy, I steadied myself against a cell bar.

He stepped in and took a swing at my face. I shifted just in time, and his fist hit the iron bar with a thud. Pain was visible on his face.

I reached to grab his shoulders and brought my knee up as hard as possible. I couldn't reach his stomach, he was too tall, so my knee missed its intended target and got him square in the balls. No matter how tough a man is, full contact to the groin is going to bring him down, and that's exactly what happened. His eyes rolled back in his sockets, and he let out a squeak. My knee lingered for a second, and I could feel that I'd nailed both saggy nuts.

I almost felt sorry for him.

Chief Inspector Plante entered the room. "What's going on here? Who's this man with Barnes?"

An officer with keys went around Plante and opened the cell. Another one came, and they lifted the man who was clutching his privates.

"What are you doing in here, Chancy?" said one of the officers as he pulled the burly man's hands back to apply the handcuffs. He glanced over at me with an impressed look on his face.

"The bugger 'it me right in the gonads," Chancy said. "Fuckin' fairy."

"I was trying to get you in the stomach."

"Right." Chancy shuffled his feet, still in obvious pain. "Bloody wanker."

Plante waited until Chancy was taken out of the room before he came to the open cell door. "Come here."

A third officer entered the room. He made me place my hands behind my back and handcuffed me.

The officer led me down two hallways and into a windowless gray room. Plante hadn't followed; he'd gone in a different direction.

There was one metal table in the middle and four chairs. The barrister, Mr. Brown, who had assisted me when I'd been questioned in the past, was there. He was dressed in a navy-blue tailored suit, starched white shirt and a blue, patterned tie. He was always very neat in appearance.

Once the officer had taken off the handcuffs, he shook my hand. We were left alone.

"Is everything all right?" Mr. Brown asked. He had brown eyes that radiated intelligence. He was above this type of work and I guessed was only helping me because Jack Carter had specifically asked him to.

"Someone tried to beat me up a few minutes ago."

"Seriously?" Mr. Brown looked concerned. "We'd arranged for a private cell so something like that wouldn't happen." He wrote something in his black leather folder. "I will look into it."

"He wanted to beat me into submission."

"And you escaped unscathed?" Mr. Brown's British accent made the word *unscathed* sound impressive.

I shrugged. I didn't want to tell him how I'd taken Chancy out. Why hadn't I hit him in the nose with the base of my hand and broken it instead?

He was studying my face. "Were you hit on the cheek? It's red and looks bruised."

"He did land one blow, somewhat." I touched my cheek—it was tender and warm. "I'm fine."

"You should get checked by a doctor." Barrister Brown referred to his folder. "Now for the matter at hand."

"You know I didn't kill Dr. Schmidt?"

"Yes, but someone sure wants everyone to think you did." He wrote another line down as if making a "To-Do" list. "First step is to get you out of here. We'll be seeing a Crown Court judge shortly to set your surety. Jack will pay it."

◄▣►◄▣►

It didn't take long to see the judge and for him to determine £100,000 as my surety. It took a few hours for Mr. Brown to complete the arrangements and for me to be processed.

As I waited, back in the jeans and T-shirt I'd been arrested in, I had more time to think. I had changed in the last few years, as had my circumstances, and I needed to play the role I'd prepared myself for. I wasn't a down-on-his-luck journalist anymore—that felt like a lifetime ago. I had to move past this setback and get back to our group's mission. Billions of lives were at stake.

My lawyer walked up the hall, followed by an officer.

"Remember, you can only stay within the grounds of the Burford estate," Mr. Brown said. "Please adhere to it. The judge has been very trusting to let it go this way. The officer will follow you home. The prosecutors wanted you in shackles until the trial. I'll let you know what happens next when I know more."

I stood up. "I'll do what I'm supposed to."

"That way." Barrister Brown pointed in the opposite direction to where he had come from. "Your friends have come to get you."

The officer escorted me to the doors leading outside.

It was a breezy spring day with a hint of chill in the dusty air. Lorraine and Sue were standing on the sidewalk next to the Range Rover. It felt like I'd been gone months, not less than a week.

Lorraine had half a head of height on Sue, a larger bone structure, and fourteen more years of being alive. The only similarities between them, other than their belief in the cause, were that they were both strong and at that moment had concerned looks on their faces.

Sue met me halfway and reached for a hug, giving me a kiss on the cheek. "How are you doing?" She was my best friend since college and always there for me.

"Not bad for a killer out on bail."

She brushed my brown hair back with her fingers. "You have a bump on your face. What happened?"

"I'll explain on the way."

Lorraine had walked up. "I did my best to protect you." I always had to concentrate on what she said because of her heavy Polish accent. "I told them the truth and that there was no way you could've killed Dr. Schmidt."

"I know. Plante said you're not a credible witness because you're paid to protect me."

We got into the SUV. Lorraine drove and the police car followed.

"Where's Jack?" I asked Sue, who was in the back seat next to me.

"He's meeting with a private detective to help figure out who really killed Dr. Schmidt." Sue always looked good, even in jeans and a sweatshirt. "He'll meet us back at the house."

Traffic was heavy getting out of London. During that time, I told them what had happened to me in jail.

"You kneed him in his crown jewels?" Sue snickered.

"I missed his stomach." I knew I shouldn't have mentioned it.

She laughed and then stopped when she saw the look on my face. "As long as you're all right. He had it coming to him."

"I would've done the same," Lorraine said from up front.

After two hours, we turned right and went downhill along the main street of Burford. The village dated back to the thirteenth century; all the stone-and-brick stores were old world and quaint. The modern vehicles driving up and down the street seemed out of place, as one expected horses and carts. After a couple of blocks, we turned left. The entrance to the estate we were calling home for now was straight ahead.

Sam was at the two-story wrought iron gate to let us in. He was a large African-American man who was an integral part of our security. He greeted us and then let us pass.

The police escort turned and departed.

On either side of the driveway was lush grass, and flowerbeds edged gnarled shade trees. The crushed-gravel road became circular, with a fountain spewing forth recycled water in the middle. The white stone house was a twenty-thousand-square-foot behemoth that had two stories above ground and one below. We only used five thousand square feet of it. It had originally been built in the sixteenth century as a hospital or monastery, but of course was a fully modernized family dwelling now.

The evening had turned cloudy. The smell of rain coming mixed with the sweet scent of blooming flowers.

Dr. Ivan Popov opened one of the large double-entry doors and came outside to greet us. The sixty-one-year-old, stocky, bearded Russian scientist had been with us from the beginning of our journey three years ago. He was in charge of all the research and worked closely with the Northern European Council for Ethical Farming, who supported us and provided him with a lab.

The estate was lent to us by a supporter of the Council. We'd lived there for close to a year.

"Nick, you are free." Ivan's accent was heavy. He was built like a bear yet had a soft heart.

"Ivan, I thought you'd be back in Oslo, at the Council's lab?"

"Not with you in custody." He pulled me into a hug, patting my back. "How preposterous, that anyone would think you killed Dr. Schmidt."

"They even tried beating it out of him." Sue had come up beside us. "But Nick took care of the fucker by kicking him in the nuts." People were always taken aback by some of the crude language that came out of the petite thirty-one-year-old, but we were used to it.

"I'm not proud of it, but that's the way it went down."

"I am sure he deserved it." Ivan motioned us inside. "You must be tired and hungry. Rose is making dinner."

There were crystal chandeliers in every room that could accommodate one, some as many as six tiers, and marble floors with radiant heat. The owner had a liking for big white furniture and polished teak tables. Every five days there was a flower delivery, even in winter, so the house looked and smelled like spring year round.

We went through the foyer that featured a dual, spiral staircase with a six-foot statue of a naked woman between them, past the living room with a large fireplace as the focal point, and into the kitchen.

Rose was always there. She'd been Jack's private chef in Dallas but had wanted a change of scenery. She'd become our surrogate mother. Rose was reaching for a pan from the rack that hung down from the middle of the ceiling. There were vegetables on a cutting board sitting atop the granite counter, and steam rose from a large pot on the eight-burner stainless steel gas stove.

"They are back." Ivan strode over to help her.

"Oh my." Rose abandoned her attempt at reaching the pan to let Ivan do it and came at me with arms outstretched. "How are you, son?"

I leaned over and gave the matronly lady a hug. "I'm fine."

She pulled back, hands on my biceps. "You look skinnier and

you need a shower."

Sue smiled. "You are kinda smelly."

"I was in frickin' jail, not the spa."

The kitchen door opened, and a tall, lean Jack Carter entered. Right behind him and always nearby was the imposing and muscular Lee Donald. They both had military-style buzz cuts, Lee's blond and Jack's gray.

# CHAPTER 3

Jack Carter's family had been in the oil business for almost one hundred years and in the cattle business for even longer, based in Dallas, Texas. He had liquidated his assets four years ago. That hadn't sat well with his younger brother, Malcolm, because that meant a loss of power and influence.

Lee Donald was Jack's "personal assistant." Wherever Jack went, Lee went. Lee used to be a sergeant in the United States Marines. He was an imposing figure at about six three, 210 pounds, with barely a wrinkle on his forty-eight-year-old skin.

"How are you, Nick?" Jack said in his southern drawl as he walked up to me. He was holding a number of newspapers tucked under his arm.

Lee nodded at me. He didn't use words unless they were necessary.

"I'm fine."

"Good to hear," Jack said. "We're gonna figure this thing out and make sure they don't pin the murder charge on you. What a load of horse crap."

"Sue said you hired a private detective?" I said.

"Yeah, we're doing our own investigation." At seventy-one Jack showed no signs of slowing down. "We have to find the person who was impersonating you at the airport and figure out who hired him. I doubt he was the actual killer, just an accomplice. Also, how did your hotel receipt get to be beside Schmidt's body and e-mails from your computer to his?"

Sue leaned against the kitchen island. "Do we have any idea or theories as to who is behind the killing?"

"Chief Inspector Plante said he was killed by injection of poison, like Cirachrome," I said. "That sounds like Naintosa security. But who in his own company would give the order to kill the boss, much less someone who would actually execute it?"

Jack nodded. "They had to be close to Schmidt—someone who could get around his personal goons. Apparently there wasn't a security breach."

"So what do we do next?" I asked. "I'm under house arrest."

"We wait to see what the private eye digs up." Jack placed the newspapers on the counter. There looked to be at least ten of them.

"Do those have the stories about you and Nick?" Sue asked.

"Stories about Jack and me?" I was going to the fridge for a beer.

"Lovemark's gone whole hog to try discredit you, whether they find you guilty or not," Jack said. "At the same time, he's decided our association is the perfect opportunity to take a swing at me too. They want the public and authorities to think we're batshit crazy and not credible. You know, guilty in the court of public opinion."

"Yeah, I'm aware of the tactic." My instant reaction was anger, but why should it get to me? It was expected that Lovemark would use his resources to take advantage of the opportunity.

"Unfortunately, the tactic works." Sue reached for a paper.

We all read the articles and passed around the newspapers while eating the beef stew Rose had prepared.

Each article had either the airport picture of the imposter or one of Jack and me talking somewhere—I guessed in London a few months ago. The stories sold me as being a radical and stalker of

Dr. Schmidt. Of course, they didn't mention the 2020 Report—the population control plan we'd uncovered—because they obviously didn't want to promote interest in it. The articles said things like: *"Barnes had been terrorizing Dr. Schmidt for three years," "... Nick Barnes's goal in life was to discredit all the positive work Naintosa has accomplished in the field of genetic food engineering ..." "Dr. Schmidt was a pioneer in solving the world's food and medical problems, while Barnes's goal was to demonise the work of Naintosa and Pharmalin."*

Ivan sighed. "Unbelievable."

"What bullshit," Sue said.

One article had a picture of a group of people standing close together, some holding up signs. The couple I could read were, "YOU HELPED FEED THE WORLD" and "YOU DISCOVERED A CURE FOR CANCER." Apparently, there had been people gathered outside of Dr. Schmidt's funeral, praising him for his work. Dr. Schmidt had preferred to stay out of the media's spotlight during his life, so he hadn't been well known to the public. That article, especially, sang his praises, making him look like a saint.

Four of the papers added Jack in as my benefactor. He was made out to be the eccentric and crazy old tycoon that had lost his companies and was now funding a small group of anti-science, anti-progress, and anti-pretty-much-everything-else, fear-mongering radicals. One writer even went so far as to say, *"... his sanity has been brought into question."*

Being an ex-journalist, I understood what the GM Comm company hacks of these articles were trying to accomplish. They were creating doubt in the minds of anyone that had heard of us and our findings as to what Naintosa, Pharmalin, and the cartel only known as "the *Club*," were really doing.

Ivan's bodyguard, Eugene, entered the dining room with another stack of newspapers and placed them beside Jack. "Here are the independent papers you asked for." His voice was a deep baritone, yet gentle. Eugene was Sam's younger cousin, but other than being an inch taller, they could've been twins.

These newspapers were not mainstream and owned by GM Comm. They had smaller, regional circulation.

As expected, the articles in the independents were more neutral, just reporting what was released by the police and background on me, the way journalism was supposed to be.

"Did anyone know that there were also protestors at the funeral?" Sue held up one of the newspapers with a picture of about ten people holding up placards. "It says they were against genetically engineered food and accused Dr. Schmidt of genocide."

"That had to be because of what we have exposed," Ivan said.

"We've been spreading the word for almost two years," Jack said. "I'm disappointed the group wasn't bigger."

"It doesn't say how big the group was," Sue said. "The picture could only show part of them."

It was good to see that there were people in the public that were taking our findings seriously. We'd been sheltered after the 2020 report came out, so we didn't know to what extent people understood what was going on underneath their noses. There were seven organizations in Europe and North America who had reached out to us in support; they were environmental, organic food, and farming groups. One association had been specifically formed to fight against genetically engineered food. None of the groups were mentioned in any of the articles.

I looked around the room. "Has anyone else noticed that the information released by Interpol is skewed and not correct?"

"If it were correct, you never would've been arrested," Sue said.

"I know what you mean," Jack said. "Some of the misinformation has to be coming directly from Interpol."

"That proves there is someone at Interpol working for Lovemark," Ivan said.

"Why wouldn't the Schmidt family, Lovemark, and Da Silva want the police to focus on who really killed Dr. Schmidt?" Sue's eyes lit up and she raised a finger. "Could they all have had something to do with it? And, of course, what a bonus to blame Nick for it."

"So, why would they kill off one of their leaders, the main guy working on the population control plan?" I thought out loud.

Jack sat quietly, looking in the direction of a landscape painting on the wall.

"What do you think, Jack?" I asked.

He turned toward me. "What would be their motive?"

# CHAPTER 4

*April 26, 2003*

I was using yet another laptop since Interpol had confiscated my last one. I had gone through so many laptops in the last few years it was like they were disposable.

While I waited for Sue to finish the article we were going to post on our website, I got up from my side of the large desk and browsed the literary fiction titles. The study held two walls of shelves filled with rare and vintage books, many of them collectors' items. There were original works by Jane Austen, William Wordsworth, and George Eliot, to name a few, as well as more contemporary authors. We'd spent much time admiring them. I'd be spending even more time here while under house arrest.

"It's not as much an interview as a summary now." Sue leaned back in the black leather chair. "It's longer than expected, since we added the background details."

"Well, this is as good a time as any to recap what happened leading up to now," I said. "Maybe a few journalists will want to interview us once they've read it?"

Sue passed her laptop across the desk. "Here, have a go-through."

## Greed and Control's Cost
### By Sue Clark

*There are still many questions surrounding Naintosa's and Pharmalin's plot to poison vast populations around the world, but many facts have already been uncovered.*

*Contradictory to media reports, Nick Barnes, a member of the group proving the existence of the population control plan, did not kill Dr. Hendrick Schmidt IV, the owner of Naintosa and Pharmalin. Yet Barnes is now under house arrest in Burford, England, for that crime, awaiting an uncertain fate.*

*"It began three years ago in the summer of 2000," said Barnes when I spoke with him at his personal prison. "Dr. Carl Elles approached me to help him write his memoir about his pioneering research on genetically engineered food. His intentions had been good, but Naintosa took what he thought were failures and released them into the world. Long-term consumption of their genetically engineered wheat and soy caused colon cancer. He had proof. Dr. Elles wanted to come clean about what his discoveries really did to people and the environment."*

*Dr. Elles was murdered. There is evidence to prove that he was killed by Sig Thompson, a Naintosa security operative, who injected a fatal and untraceable poison, Cirachrome, into Elles's neck. Naintosa hoped his death would stop the truth from being exposed. Nick Barnes was the one who found Dr. Elles in his office.*

*"Dr. Elles's daughter, Morgan, had copies of her father's research and convinced me to write what turned out to be an exposé about how Naintosa intentionally wanted to give a large part of the population colon cancer," Barnes said.*

*"Naintosa's security was after us the whole time, trying to stop the exposé from being written. Now they've filed a lawsuit to prevent its publication."*

*Dr. Hendrick Schmidt IV was part of a group calling themselves "the Club," which is comprised of the most powerful men in the world, who are now known to be in the midst of creating something even more devastating.*

*Jack Carter, a former member of the Club, put together a team of people to uncover what the larger plan was. The team included:*

*—Dr. Ivan Popov, a chemist and physician who had worked with Dr. Elles on genetic engineering at Naintosa and is working with the Northern European Council for Ethical Farming, proving the validity of the exposé's findings;*

*—Dr. Bill Clancy, a physicist who had also worked with Dr. Elles at Naintosa and then partnered with Dr. Popov to work with the Northern European Council for Ethical Farming;*

*—Dr. Timothy Roth, a geneticist who had been researching the long-term effects of Naintosa's pesticides;*

*—Morgan Elles, the daughter of Dr. Elles, whose knowledge of her father's work and editing abilities were crucial to the project;*

*—Journalist Sue Clark, responsible for the group's research and writing;*

*—Journalist Nick Barnes, who coordinated the team's findings and is the main author of their report.*

*"Our next step was to gather all the new information and put the pieces together," said Barnes.*

*What resulted was the 2020 Report, exposing the Club's leaders, including three of the most wealthy and powerful men in the world:*

*—Davis Lovemark, chairman of Global Mark Communications;*

*—Carlo Da Silva, owner of Huergo Corporation;*

*—Dr. Hendrick Schmidt IV, owner and chairman of Naintosa and Pharmalin.*

*Proof continues to be uncovered that genetically engineered crops sprayed with glyphosate and neonicotinoids cause multiple diseases, including cancers and eventual deaths. Seed drift allows for the spread of genetically engineered seed to infect regular crops. Naintosa was, and still may be, in the process of inserting the Plycite gene into their genetically engineered corn DNA, which would sterilize a large portion of the population.*

*Pharmalin Pharmaceuticals was, and could still be, working on cancer drugs—not to cure people but only to extend their lives for a few years. An actual cure may have been discovered as a byproduct, but unproven at this time.*

*Members of the powerful Club and others of their choosing would survive, living off food grown on large tracts of unspoiled land set aside by the organization. The unaltered, organic seed to grow their food is being temporarily stored at a seed bank in Germany until the permanent seed bank in Norway is complete.*

*The people responsible stand to make a fortune on every part of the plan, including the trading of stocks and commodities.*

*The research shows the illnesses and diseases would develop over time. As people ingest genetically engineered grain, fruit and vegetables or animals whose feed was genetically engineered, their genes would alter. Proteins and enzymes from food people eat have always changed their genes and subsequently their DNA, but the genetically engineered food permanently alters humans' genomes in ways nature never intended. It would take years of consumption for most before symptoms would arise which would make it impossible to trace back to the group responsible.*

*Health care systems would be overwhelmed, which would drain government coffers around the world. Where does money for running the government come from? Taxes. It's the citizens who ultimately pay; governments will have no choice but to devote more and more money toward taking care of the sickened population.*

*"There is an unelected, shadow government within all elected and dictatorial governments. Those permanent control groups have by far the majority of power. Ninety-nine point nine per cent of the world's politicians don't have a clue about who really runs the countries and what's beginning to happen," said Jack Carter. "The middle class will be all but wiped out. All the wealth will end up in the hands of less than half of one percent of a much smaller world population. They'll have total control."*

*Carter is fully dedicated to stopping their plan to control the world. "What has already begun is by far the largest shift of wealth in history, accomplished by some of the people who already have the most wealth and power," said Carter. "We need to get people, organizations and governments to recognize that this is happening."*

*For Barnes, the fight to uncover the truth has already been life-altering. As we spoke, Barnes pointed out a framed photograph on the corner of his desk. It was of a bench in a park in South Africa. There was an inscription on it commemorating Morgan Elles's life.*

*"I really miss Morgan," he said. "Her loss was devastating." Morgan Elles was shot and killed by Naintosa*

*security team leader Peter Bail at Indian Arm outside of Vancouver, Canada.*

*"That bullet was meant for me," said Barnes.*

*Morgan's mother, Dr. Claudia Elles, was the first to be killed by Naintosa's security in a staged car accident after uncovering part of Naintosa's sinister plot.*

*Dr. Bill Clancy died in Amsterdam when he was struck by a car right after he and Dr. Popov obtained information on the sterilizing Plycite gene.*

*Naintosa's security had to try twice to kill Dr. Timothy Roth. They set fire to his lab with him in it after his research on glyphosate didn't turn out the way they wanted. Then they fatally shot him in the woods outside of Vancouver. One of Mr. Carter's security team, Tanner Read, was killed there, too, while trying to protect Dr. Roth.*

*There are other deaths as well. Summer Perkins died in a bar in San Francisco while waiting for Barnes. Brad Caulder, working on behalf of Davis Lovemark, injected her with a lethal poison. Perkins was prepared to share information about the seed bank in Norway. Her ex-boyfriend, Mike Couple, found the information after her murder and passed it on to Barnes. Couple is now missing.*

*This may sound unfathomable, but it is all true. All of this has happened because a few powerful men think they are the stewards of humanity and have taken it upon themselves to decide that the world is overpopulated and they are the ones who get to choose who lives and who dies. With the loss of Dr. Hendrick Schmidt IV, who was an integral member of the Club's population control plan, and with the circulation of the 2020 Report, it is unsure what will happen next.*

*Further updates will follow.*

"Good," I said. "Just needs some tweaking."

"Tweaking?" Sue came over to my side of the desk. "Where?"

We began editing.

My lawyer hadn't said I needed to keep quiet while under house arrest.

# CHAPTER 5

*April 27, 2003*

"Let's meditate first," Sue said, catching up to me. She was in her usual workout clothes—shorts and a T-shirt.

I shook my head. "I don't feel like it."

We were walking down the hall to the fitness room. Working out was our ritual first thing in the morning, five days a week.

"Seriously, I can't remember the last time you meditated." Sue arrived at the door first and opened it. "It's so important to your mental well-being, not to mention the insights you sometimes get." She turned toward me and tilted her head, a consoling look on her face. "Morgan would want you to move forward. You can't stop doing things that really help you."

"I know, but it's just not working for me right now." I'd meditated most days ever since learning Transcendental Meditation in college. It helped calm and center me, and at times I even had visions or perceptions. However, ever since Morgan died, I couldn't shake seeing her being shot in my mind's eye every time I tried to meditate. I didn't want to relive that again. "You go ahead. I'll lift weights or something."

Sue proceeded to the floor mats. "I'll do it later. Let's stretch and go through our Krav Maga drills. Lee said he'll come in twenty minutes."

The room had been a dance studio before we moved in. It was basic, with a mirror covering one entire wall, hardwood flooring, and stretching bars. We added a universal gym, free weights, and floor mats.

Once we'd stretched, we practiced Krav Maga moves on each other. We'd worked on them for a year and had become adept at the martial art.

Krav Maga was perfected by the Israeli military. It focused on self-defence in a way that protected you against an attacker and then immobilized them so you could get away. It wasn't pretty to watch like Eastern martial arts. It was brutal. Its focus was to use the strongest parts of your body to take the person down quickly—the heel of your hand, and your elbow, knee, and body weight.

Lee came into the room in black track pants and a black T-shirt. Whenever he was at the estate, he'd spend time with us, making sure we were executing the moves properly and showing us new ones. "Let's go through the basics, to make sure you haven't developed any bad habits since last time."

"It's only been a couple weeks since you saw us," I said.

"That's plenty of time to develop some lazy movements." Lee didn't smile much, was always watchful, and knew his stuff. If he was on your side, there was no doubt you trusted him with your life. He was the strongest and most loyal person we'd ever met.

"It sure worked in real life when I was in jail."

"You kicked him in the balls," Sue mocked.

"I was trying for the gut." *How many times did I have to repeat that?* "He was huge and built like a brick shithouse." I knew she was just trying to bug me.

"Survival is the key, so what you did was fine," Lee said. "Let's just hone your skills so you have other options in the future."

"Told you." I stuck my tongue out at Sue.

"Stance," Lee barked as if back in the marines.

That meant that we extended our opposite leg to our lead hand—my right leg was forward, Sue's left. Our feet were apart a little more than shoulder width, knees bent, open palms at neck level and our lead hands, my left and Sue's right, extended farther.

Lee pushed each of us to make sure we were stable. "Good." He stepped back, reached for a toy gun we kept as a prop and tossed it to me. "Point the gun at Sue."

I raised the gun level to Sue's chest.

In one fluid motion she lunged forward with her hands outstretched, grabbing the barrel of the gun. Her body weight pushed my arm to the side, and as she stepped forward she twisted her wrists. With forward momentum, she brought her knee up to my stomach. I lost my breath and went down—without the gun in my hand.

"Hands, body, feet," she repeated the order of what Lee had drilled into our brains.

As soon as I could breathe and get up, I said, "Why couldn't you pretend instead of taking me down so hard?"

Sue smiled. "Better practice that way."

"I'll remember that next time I take something away from you."

We went through other steps, including choking and disabling someone with a knife. Then Lee showed us an advanced way of protecting ourselves from being attacked from behind.

After an hour we were sweaty but invigorated.

"You're both progressing well," Lee said as he left us. "Keep it up."

"Let's get showered," Sue said. "My goal is to finish the edit of your manuscript today."

"Great," I replied. "I'll see if anyone's replied to our summary post on the website yet."

"Nick and Sue, you should each call your parents," Rose said when we walked into the dining room. "In case they read any of the papers that ran stories about you in the States. I also saw them talk about all of us on GMNN last night before I went to bed. Your parents would want to know what's going on. They'd be worried."

"Really, on GMNN? Wow." Global Mark News Network was the Global Mark Communications flagship. The cable news station had the most reach around the world and was Lovemark's pride and joy. We were getting coverage, albeit negative, on the big stage. "Yeah, I'll call them this afternoon when it's morning in Tacoma."

Sue sat down at the table. "Me too."

Jack closed the newspaper he was reading and placed it beside his coffee mug. "What did they say? More of the same thing?"

Rose placed the platter of omelettes she was holding at the center of the table. "I wish I'd recorded it."

Ivan came from the kitchen carrying a pot of coffee. He leaned forward to fill cups for Sue and me.

"There was a picture of Sue, Lorraine, and Nick standing beside the Range Rover outside a London police station," Rose recalled.

That was disturbing because I didn't know pictures were being taken of us when I'd been released.

"That's kinda freaky," Sue said.

Rose nodded. "They then showed pictures of each of us, of our entire group. It was a background essay compiled by an East Indian lady."

Jack leaned forward, giving Rose his full attention. "Can you remember details of what was said?"

Ivan sat down to listen.

"She focused on who we are as people, but from the false perspective: Nick, again, portrayed as the ex-journalist with a hatred for politicians, science, and anyone in a position of authority; Jack, again, a billionaire who threw away his businesses after his wife died of cancer and went crazy, now blowing what money he has left on a made-up cause; Sue, an angry journalist with a bone to pick with anyone in the establishment, and an uncontrollable environmentalist; Ivan, a discredited and disgruntled ex-employee of Naintosa bent on revenge; Lee, Jorge, Lorraine, Sam, and Eugene, all thugs who do anything you ask of them. They even mentioned me as a failed chef, bringing up a restaurant that went bankrupt after my husband died fifteen years ago. They said what brought us all together is our common disdain of scientific, medical, and agricultural progress. We are all fanatics."

"Should we sue?" Ivan looked at each of us.

"It is defamation of character," I said. "But do we want even more attention, by suing GM Comm newspapers and television networks?"

"We're not going to sue." Jack looked angry. "But they're hitting below the belt."

The GMNN story seemed to be the tipping point of frustration for us. "They are so over-the-top wrong."

"But accomplishing their objective," Jack said.

"Of driving us insane," Sue added.

I placed an omelette and toast on a plate and stood. "I'll be in the study if anyone needs me."

As I walked down the long corridor, I thought about negative publicity. There had never been that much focus on us before. We were just regular people who happened to be working on exposing the largest planned cull of humans in history. *I guess that's not regular.* In return, we were being vilified.

*Wait.* I stopped walking. *This may not be such a bad thing.* I turned around and walked back to the dining room.

Jack, Ivan, and Sue stopped talking when I entered. They looked concerned.

"You know ..." I said. "We might be able to spin this around."

Sue gave me a small smile, and Ivan and Jack looked interested in what I had to say.

"I didn't kill Schmidt, so we have the truth on our side," I continued. "But the main thing is that people are noticing us more now. Even though the news is negative and the media isn't mentioning anything about the population control plan, people will start looking into it. It's publicity to help spread the word of what we've discovered."

"No publicity is bad publicity," Jack quoted.

"I like where you're going with this," Sue said. "It could backfire on them."

"That makes your website post yesterday even more of a good move," Ivan said.

I turned on my heels back toward the study, feeling better. This time Sue came with me.

"We have to increase our uploads of facts that support our findings on the website," she said as we walked down the hall.

When I glanced at her, Sue had a half smile and looked kind of dreamy at me. It was hard to explain, but I had noticed it more often lately. "What?"

She turned her head forward. "Oh, nothing."

*Okay, back to what we were talking about.* "How about we make a brief summary of the 2020 Report that people can read in a few minutes?"

"I can do that after I finish your manuscript."

"I'll outline the integral points while I wait for you."

When we reached the study, Sue went to her side of the desk, and I went to mine. As we started our laptops I could see out the window that the day looked damp and dreary.

I opened my e-mail and waited for the messages that had built up to load. The first two were junk, so I deleted them. The third didn't look familiar. "Do you know an Ogden Dundst?"

Sue shook her head. "No, why?"

"He sent me an e-mail." I opened it. "Oh shit."

"What's wrong?"

"I'll read it to you. '*Nick* ...'"

"He's on a first-name basis with you?"

"Seems that way. '*PEOPLE LIKE YOU have no business scaring people with your LIES AND MURDURING a scientist who was trying to make the world better! Your the person needs to be TORTURED AND KILLED! Your the one whose SCARING PEOPLE with conspiracies against the advancement of science! Dr. Schmidt deserved to be rich because his genetic food engineering found better ways to FEED the starving people AND he found a cure for CANCER! He was a SAVIOR and your the SCUM at the bottom of a fish tank–YOUR SHITE! I don't believe the court system will do JUSTICE, so I have to take it into MY OWN HANDS to clean the bottom of the fish tank! I know where your and I'm coming to GET YOU! True JUSTICE will be served and people will be HAPPY when they learned of the TORTURE I inflicted ON YOU (I won't tell you what I'm going to do to you, I want it to be a surprise) and that YOUR DEATH came slow. They will CHEER for me! Be prepared, I'm coming for YOU! Sincerely, Ogden.*'"

"What the fuck?" Sue stood up. "Psycho."

"That should not be taken lightly." I hadn't noticed that Ivan had come into the room. He pressed the intercom button on the wall beside the door. "Jack, Lee, can you please come to the study?"

I felt unease about the threat. The guy didn't seem very bright. It was easy enough to get my e-mail address off the website, and we weren't hiding in a secret place; a lot of people knew where we were. Was Ogden the kind of man who followed through on his threats?

Jack and Lee entered the study.

"Nick has received a threatening e-mail, and I think we should take it seriously," Ivan said.

"Let's take a gander," Jack said as both he and Lee approached my laptop.

I stood so Jack could sit with Lee looking over his shoulder.

Lee ripped a page from my pad on the desk and wrote down *Ogden Dundst.*

"Chances are that this guy's just a freak," Jack said. "But I agree with Ivan."

"I'll check him out." Lee was already walking from the room.

"I'll let the others know about this." Jack got up from the chair. "Maybe put an extra person on perimeter patrol."

"Call if you need us," Ivan said as he followed Jack out.

"How do you feel?" Sue asked. "I'm a little freaked."

"I'm starting to get numb about threats. All we can do is be vigilant."

"I don't think I'll ever get used to them."

I went back to checking my other new e-mails. There was another name I didn't recognize. Opening it, I saw it was from a reporter based in London and she wanted to interview me about yesterday's website post. *That's good news.* "I have an interview request."

Sue looked up from her screen. "What media?"

"She's a freelancer and said it was based on our website post." I shrugged. "We just talked about any publicity is good publicity."

"What's the reporter's name?"

I looked at the bottom of the message and compared it with the e-mail address. "Adhira Virk."

Sue started typing and then scrolling. "She seems accomplished. Her work's been in both mainstream and independent media across TV, print, and Internet."

"Okay, I'll do it."

"I want to be in the room with you during the interview."

I responded, asking for her to come at 11:00 a.m. tomorrow. When I went to write our address, I hesitated. Should we have been in a more secretive place?

# CHAPTER 6

*April 28, 2003*

Jorge Villegas was a brash, no-bullshit Latino who was part of Jack's security team. He had a knack for managing people, so he helped on the business side as well. Jorge had served in the Colombian military and then done something secretive for the American side. He'd been assigned to be my bodyguard over a year ago when I lived in San Francisco. He was stocky, broad, and very strong for someone in his late fifties. We had gotten out of some dangerous situations together. Jorge had been helping the private detective working on my case in London and had just arrived at the estate late last night.

Minutes before 11:00 a.m., Jorge escorted Ms. Virk to the main living room where Sue and I were waiting.

"Good to meet you, Mr. Barnes." She had a mix of East Indian and British in her accent. "Thank you for taking the time."

I shook her slender-fingered hand and then motioned to Sue. "Sue will be sitting in."

"Pleasure to meet you, Ms. Clark." Ms. Virk had a pleasant smile. Her features were long, yet she was average in height; waist-length straight, black hair draped over the back of her navy-blue pant suit.

"I've read some of your work. It's very enlightening."

"Thanks." Sue gave a cordial smile. "I've read some of your work, as well."

Ms. Virk turned back to me. "And your writing, Mr. Barnes."

Okay, everyone was familiar with one another's writing skills. I gestured for her to take a seat on the couch across from the fireplace. Sue and I sat in the chairs on opposite sides. Jorge hung back at the edge of the room.

She produced a small recorder and a pad of paper from what looked like an expensive handbag. "Is it all right if I record the conversation?"

"By all means." I'd always found that it was best to record an interview. It was better than just taking notes, because there was less room for misinterpretation and misquotes.

"Have you been contracted by anyone?" Sue asked. "Where is this going to run?"

"There is enough interest in your story right now that it won't be hard for me to sell it."

"What's your angle?" My voice sounded defensive right away. I hadn't intended that.

"Your most recent website post gave a good background of your struggles to find the truth of what large companies are doing to the general population for profit—specifically, Dr. Schmidt's Naintosa and Pharmalin." She shifted in her seat. "Your hard work is helping humanity from being purposefully decimated, and if Dr. Schmidt had to die, then so be it. It's for the overall good of the human race."

"But I didn't kill Dr. Schmidt, and we don't know if the two are connected."

Sue straightened. "You can't write it that way."

"That's the way I see it." Ms. Virk gave a forced smile. "That's what I'm here to prove."

"You want some kind of confession from me?"

"That would make the article the most powerful. I'll show you had justification for what you did. Sometimes people need to be sacrificed for larger purposes. Mr. Barnes, this is bigger than you, but you have to play your part. You must sacrifice as well."

"But it's not the truth." *What did she mean about it being bigger than me?*

Sue was at the edge of her seat, and I could see she was trying to remain calm. "Sure, that would make Nick seem honorable to some, but it would also convict him. And we don't want Nick convicted for the murder, because then he can't continue the fight to stop this genocide. Oh, and the most important thing: he didn't fucking do it, so you'd be lying."

Jorge had come to stand closer.

I hid a deep breath before I spoke. "Have you considered that my being accused of the murder is a setup? Why don't you use that angle?"

"Well, but ..."

Sue cut her off. "That's what you should be investigating and writing about."

"That's not what I determined after reading other articles and what the police have released," Ms. Virk said. "Do you have proof I could use about being set up?"

"We're working on it," I replied.

She was basing her background on GM Comm stories, inaccurate police statements, and her own theories. That was weak and sloppy journalism. I remembered that my editor at the *Seattle News*, Paul Ang, had always pushed Sue and me to get to the truth of the story and only report what happened—never add our opinions or try to read between the lines. It would've been great to have Paul around lately. "I don't think we should continue this interview."

"But I have many questions and want to help your cause."

I shook my head. "Not in that way."

Jorge came to stand next to Ms. Virk.

Sue stood as well. "Did you hear about the protestors at Dr. Schmidt's funeral?"

"I was there," Ms. Virk said. "Some of the protestors in support of genetic engineering attacked the group opposed."

"So?" Sue said. "We haven't seen any articles that mentioned protesters being attacked at the funeral."

"People *are* learning about what you've found out," Ms. Virk said. "They're taking sides. You can be the voice for people opposing the genetically engineered food scheme. I must write it the way I see it."

"I think we already are the voice," I said. "And it's bigger than just genetically engineered food."

⬗⬗⬗

Jack and Ivan were in the dining room when Sue and I entered.

"That didn't take long," Jack said.

I sat down opposite them. "She wanted me to lie and confess to killing Dr. Schmidt for the good of the cause."

Sue took the seat beside me. "She wanted Nick to be a martyr."

"Interesting angle," Jack said.

"Do you think she will make up a story anyway?" Ivan asked.

I shrugged. "Probably."

Lee entered the room. "I couldn't find any record of an Ogden Dundst that could possibly be associated with the e-mail."

"So he's a nobody," Sue said.

"Not necessarily." Lee took a chair next to Ivan. "If we'd found record of him, he would probably have been just some guy making threats and hiding behind his computer, dumb enough to use his real name and e-mail address. Not finding anything on him means he's at least committed enough to make up a fake identity. The message was sent from an Internet café in London, and the PI is going to go see if there is a security camera there."

"Keep us posted, Lee." Jack took the last bite of his sandwich. "Nick, I forgot to tell you. Your lawyer, Kenneth Brown, is coming"— he looked at his Rolex—"in twenty minutes."

Mr. Brown was already sitting in the main living room talking to Jack when I entered.

"How are you holding up, Nick?" he asked in his stiff British inflection.

"Fine. It's only been a couple days, so I haven't had time to go stir-crazy."

"Good. A sense of humor will help you get through this mess."

"So what's our progress?" Jack asked.

"The procedure for finding out why an officer let a violent prisoner into Nick's cell is an internal investigation. They have suspended the officer. That's standard. We have to let the investigation run its course."

Lee walked into the room. "Sorry to interrupt, but we have some new findings from the private investigator."

I'd been standing, so I went to the couch. The chairs were taken by Jack and Mr. Brown.

"Fill us in," Jack said.

"The PI was able to obtain security-camera footage outside the hotel in London where Nick stayed." Lee stood next to the unlit fireplace. "It showed a man picking Nick's pocket for the hotel receipt. That man looks very much like Nick. His name's Dale Samson, and he's low-level Naintosa security. When they checked the footage from the airport against the hotel's, it was a match."

I let out a long breath. "Fast work." Finding out who had impersonated me was huge. "I never noticed him picking my pocket."

"Have your investigator send me what he has, and I'll take it to Chief Inspector Plante," Mr. Brown said.

"Do you think he's the killer, then?" I asked.

"Doubtful," Jack said. "Just paid to play a part. All evidence points to treason from inside Naintosa."

"Nick's not out of the woods yet." Mr. Brown reached for the briefcase at his feet. "We still have the e-mails that were sent from Nick's computer to Dr. Schmidt."

He passed me three pieces of paper that each contained an e-mail message. As I read them I noticed they mirrored my writing style, except for the anger and profanity. "Whoever wrote these studied my writing."

When I looked up, Mr. Brown was staring at me.

"But I didn't write them." I rose from the couch and went to stand beside him to point out the flaws. "Where they slipped up was in their use of the threatening words in phrases like, '... *splatter your fucking brains across the landing.' Landing* is the British word for *floor.* The word *cunt* was used three times—I hate that word more than anything. Just saying it right now bothers me. But I understand in England it's not considered as offensive."

I gave the e-mails back to Mr. Brown. "And who would be so stupid as to have sent these incriminating messages off their own computer? And how would I have gotten Schmidt's personal e-mail address?"

Then it dawned on me. "Couldn't these have been sent after Interpol took my laptop?"

"I don't know if it's possible to change a timestamp." Mr. Brown paused for a second and then raised a finger. "No, the e-mails were found on Dr. Schmidt's computer before yours was confiscated."

I sat back. "Then I don't know how they got there."

"I'll find a computer expert to see if they can explain how it was done," Lee said.

"The main thing is we have that Dale Samson guy on video, picking Nick's pocket," Jack said.

# CHAPTER 7

*April 30, 2003*

When I came through the main living room on my way to have breakfast, Jack was sitting on the couch with a newspaper open in front of him.

He looked up. "Virk's article is in the *London News*, so I assume it'll be syndicated in all the GM Comm newspapers."

I approached Jack. "How bad is it?"

"What you'd feared." Jack motioned for me to take the paper. "But it's not long and way back in the paper, I assume because the story is getting stale."

"The whole thing should've had maybe two news cycles at most. Lovemark sure is dragging it out." I didn't feel like reading any more propaganda, so I didn't take the newspaper.

"She wrote that there were also protestors at Schmidt's funeral and that you're trying to be the leader of a rising movement." Jack shook his head. "However, she thinks you don't have the right temperament to lead people against some of the most powerful companies in the world."

My blood pressure was rising, but I still didn't want to read it.

"Let's go have breakfast."

"If we had birds, this is what I'd line their cage with." Jack tossed the newspaper on the table and picked up his coffee mug.

Ivan, Sue, Sam, Eugene, and Lorraine were all sitting at the dining table. At meals, mainly breakfast, was when most of us were around and had a chance to talk.

Sue must've sensed my lingering annoyance. "That Virk chick must've had the story written before she came for the interview."

I sat down. "Probably."

"It can't get any worse, so it'll only get better." Jack reached for the scrambled eggs.

"I propose we stop reading the negative press and focus on our work." Ivan stood from his chair, having completed his meal. "The most productive response is to continue to provide factual proof. I am going back to Oslo today; the Council has summoned me, and I need to get back to our research."

"The Council wants to talk to you?" Jack asked. "Because you've been gone for awhile?"

"I think they are concerned about the negative publicity." Ivan had a steely glare. "I am going to tell them the exact same thing I just told all of you."

"Go get 'em, Ivan," Sue said.

"Good luck." I took a deep breath and envisioned a duck with water dripping off its back. That gave me an unexpected and sudden urge to meditate.

Ivan left the room, with Eugene right behind him.

"Anyone interested in meditating?" I asked. "I know we used to do it before breakfast, but it'll still work after."

Lorraine glanced at Sam. "We have to relieve Jorge and Lee."

Sue looked surprised. "Finally."

"We haven't done the relaxing mumbo jumbo in a long time," Jack said. "I'm in."

After breakfast, we adjourned to the living room. It was a cool, rainy morning outside, so the fireplace had been lit. We sat down on the rug next to the cozy burning wood.

Jack groaned. "Hope I'll be able to get up again."

We all closed our eyes.

Deep breaths, in and out. Morgan's beautiful face, framed by her strawberry-blonde hair, came into my mind's eye. I tried not to be sad and let the memory pass. I focused on my breathing, but it was hard to clear my mind.

In the twenty minutes, only a few moments were peaceful. That was okay, because at least I was trying to meditate again and I hadn't relived Morgan being shot.

Sue opened her eyes and sat quietly, looking at the fire.

Within a minute Jack opened his eyes. "I remember it being easier to clear thoughts from my thick head."

"Me too," I said. "It'll just take some practice. I want to start meditating every morning again."

"Good." Sue got up and walked out of the room.

Jack and I looked at each other but didn't say anything. Sue could be abrupt, but her facial expression had looked concerned or even scared.

"What's the plan for today?" Jack asked.

"I have to finish going through Sue's edits of my book, but that's not going to take long. Why?"

"I have a meeting here with a man named Tom Crane."

I stood up because my leg was falling asleep. "You mean the billionaire tech guy, Tom Crane?"

"One and the same. He wants to talk to me about Moile."

"He has oil and hydraulic fracturing interests? I thought he made his money in computers, programs, and such."

"Everyone with that kind of money has interest in oil."

"But he's a philanthropist now, spending his time with his

foundation trying to save ..." Then it dawned on me. "... starving children in Africa. Do you think he has anything to do with genetically engineered food? Is he a good or bad guy?"

"Interesting." Jack got to his feet. "We know Naintosa is trying hard to introduce their seed in Africa."

"Did he setup the meeting, or did you?"

"He did. I'm just curious."

"Do you know him well?"

"A bit, not well."

"Is he a member of the *Club*?"

A glint came into Jack's eyes. "He'd been sniffing around before; I bet he wants even more to be a member now and that's part of why he wants to meet. I'm not entirely sure of the angle, but we'll see."

"He'd be better off meeting with the current members or filling out an application form. It won't help his cause, talking to someone who was booted out."

"Application form—good one." Jack smiled. "He's a smart man, so I'll see what he has to say. His problem is that he's a self-made billionaire, one of the richest men in the world, in fact. The *Club* doesn't like new money and isn't looking for new members, especially someone with such a high profile."

"Let me know how the meeting goes." I left Jack and went to the study.

When I reached my side of the desk, I opened my laptop and pressed the start button. While waiting for it to boot up, I went to the window to look outside. There was a persistent drizzle again today that reminded me of Seattle.

Sue entered the study. She'd changed into jeans and a light-blue sweater, her thick, shoulder-length auburn hair pulled into a ponytail. "Hey."

"You okay?" I looked at her for an extra second. She really was beautiful, but not in a way where she had to put effort into it. Her attractiveness was natural and casual. She didn't need makeup to accentuate her dazzling blue eyes, high cheekbones, and cute button nose. Her body was petite and lean, with just enough curve in the right places.

"Yeah, why?" She cocked her head to the side. "Why are you looking at me like that?"

"Nothing." I shook my head. "You left right after meditating and seemed upset."

She sat down in front of her computer and opened it. "There was a weird, ominous feeling while I was meditating. It came out of nowhere, and to be honest, scared me. I guess I needed a few moments to collect myself."

"In the past we've always talked about stuff like that." I went back to my computer and sat down in front of it. "Can you explain the feeling?"

"Like I said, just weird and ominous."

"Did a vision come with it?"

Sue paused. "More feeling."

There was nothing to try figuring out unless Sue had more details. "Okay, let me know if you think of a reason."

She nodded and looked at her screen.

Three of the editors I'd met in London had sent me e-mails. Two were interested in my manuscript; one being the editor I liked the best. She was seasoned, gave off a good vibe, liked my writing, and worked for a big publisher. "The editor I want to work with the most wants the book."

"Great," Sue said. "Her response was quick."

"My guess is that since I'm in the news there's a bigger chance of book sales, even though the novel is fiction ... sort of."

The editor wanted me to get an agent to negotiate the contract and suggested three names. I researched them on the Internet and decided on which one I'd choose first. Then I e-mailed them. Usually, getting an agent was hard, but with an already-interested editor of a prominent publisher on board, a large portion of the work had already been accomplished. What agent wouldn't want easy money like that?

"I forgot to tell you." I looked up from my screen at Sue reading from hers. "Tom Crane is coming here to meet with Jack."

"Billionaire philanthropist Tom Crane?"

"Yeah." I glanced at the antique silver clock on the wall. "He's probably here now."

"What for?"

I told her Jack's theories.

"I've always been suspicious of him and his foundation," Sue said. "You know he's buddies with Davis Lovemark."

"Really? Friends with Lovemark and potential ties to Naintosa in Africa; he has to have something to do with the population control plan. And Jack said he's tried to get into the *Club*. We need to do some digging on him."

Sue wrote on a pad of paper beside her. "I'm on it. It's second on the list. You worry about making sure your manuscript is ready to send your editor. It'll be my pleasure to dig deep into Crane."

Whenever Sue put it that way, I always felt sorry for the person she was going after. "What are you working on now anyway?"

"An environmental opinion piece for the magazine back in Seattle." She shrugged. "Nothing you don't already know."

I was editing, and Sue was writing. The only sound was the clacking of keyboards.

Sue swiveled her chair and looked out the window. "The rain has let up. Let's take a break and walk around the grounds. We'll be more productive after some fresh air."

As I got out of my chair she looked me up and down. "As soon as your house arrest is over, we need to go clothes shopping for you."

"Why? What's wrong with my clothes?"

"I know you hate clothes shopping, but you're starting to look frayed."

I gave a half-hearted smile that was obviously fake. "Let's go for a walk."

We proceeded down the hall and into the foyer.

Jack was talking to a tall, slim man beside the main entrance. Tom Crane was wearing his telltale black-rimmed glasses and a bright-patterned bowtie. He always looked nerdy and unassuming, but underneath his exterior he was known to be crafty and extremely intelligent.

I whispered, "Let's go out the back door and let them have their meeting."

Jack looked our way. "Nick, Sue, come over and meet Tom."

As we approached I tried to look into his eyes. Through the glasses I could see apprehension, and then as if he saw I was reading him, a sharpness of attention.

Jack motioned with his arm. "Tom, these are my friends, Nick Barnes and Sue Clark."

"The infamous anti-genetic engineering duo." His accent sounded neutral, because we all originated from the Pacific Northwest. His main home was still outside Seattle.

"More than just that," Sue said.

He raised his eyebrows at Sue's strong tone yet extended his arm. After Sue shook his hand, I followed. It was firm, but to my surprise, clammy.

"Are you two about to have your meeting?" I wiped my right hand on my jeans in a nonchalant way I hoped no one would notice.

"Finished," Jack said. "Tom is just leaving."

"But I hope to be invited back." Tom gave Jack a questioning look.

"You're welcome anytime, but not to talk about Moile, the seed bank, or our mutual acquaintances." Jack's tone was polite, but his look had an underlying menace.

Tom nodded at Jack and then turned to us. "Maybe you all should find something else to occupy your time."

"Why?" Sue asked. "Have we hit a little close to home?"

I thought of stopping Sue's polite aggressiveness but decided to join her instead. "You're either part of the population control plan or want to be, right?"

I was betting he hadn't expected us to be confrontational, yet neither had I. His face turned a shade of pink. Jack had opened the door for him, and he walked through, not saying another word.

Jack closed the door. "Y'all have a minute?"

"Sure, we were just going outside for some fresh air," Sue said.

Jack opened the door again. "Mind if I join you?"

We walked outside to see Tom getting into the backseat of a black Rolls Royce, the driver holding the door. Tom gave a quick look back at us.

We waited for the car to leave before proceeding to the garden.

The air was cool and the sky still a dark gray. One of my favorite smells was a spring garden after a rain—that and a freshly mown golf course.

"How did the meeting go?" My guess was not very well.

"What did he want?" Sue asked.

"He's shrewd; I'll give him that," Jack said. "He wants to buy a part or all of Moile R&D."

"Did he say why," I asked.

"He said it's because drinking water is now our most valuable resource, and he wants to hold oil companies accountable for their polluting while hydraulic fracturing."

"That's exactly why you started the company," Sue said.

"As you are keenly aware," Jack said. "What a person says is not always what they mean ... or not the whole truth anyway."

We walked to a covered gazebo. My running shoes were damp from the wet grass.

"My best guess is," Jack continued, "that he wants to be part of Moile to generate publicity for another honorable deed his foundation is doing. Then when he gains control, he'll fudge the figures to appease his oil and gas buddies, further trying to impress the members of the *Club*."

I needed clarification. "Your ex-*Club* or is there an *oil Club?*"

"There is an oil Club, but my ex-*Club* is the main *Club*. At this point in his life, Crane's main goal is to join the most powerful men in the world, help steer humanity, and profit in kind. It's an ego thing. He's been doing all he can on his own, but he can only do so much without the cooperation of the top movers and shakers. My guess is he thinks screwing me over would be another feather in his cap toward his case of them making him a member. You know this ain't my first rodeo, and you'd have to get up pretty early to pull the wool over my eyes."

That last comment made me smile and was so telling of the experience Jack had and the fight still in him. I hoped to someday get to that point.

Sue and I sat down on a dry bench with Jack on the one opposite us.

"Tom gave me a not-so-subtle warning about leaving the Norwegian seed bank alone," Jack said. "He's heavily involved with it and doesn't want us messing around. Oh, and, stop all this nonsense about genetically engineered food being bad, because his foundation *is* working with Naintosa to push it hard into Africa, and then India, to feed all the starving children."

"Okay, he admitted it," Sue said. "I'll do some research and then write an article we can post on our website."

"Might as well piss him off," I said. "As long as, of course, your findings prove that he's really profiting from making starving children sick."

"We still don't know for sure why the population control plan is being so heavily focused on North America," Sue said. "But now we can guess their next push is Africa and then India."

Jack nodded. "And I have a feeling there's something even fishier happening at the seed bank."

# INTERLOGUE 1

*May 1, 2003*

The fact that Chief Inspector Jacques Plante was financially and politically rewarded for information and steering certain investigative matters in directions benefitting Davis Lovemark and Carlo Da Silva had to remain secret. He was a valuable asset. Davis and Carlo had men on the inside of most lawful institutions, and Jacques was their main man at Interpol.

Their usual mode of communication was by secure phone, but they did at times meet in person. Since they all happened to be in London at the moment, they thought a face-to-face was best.

Davis kept a row house in Regent's Park for special meetings and encounters. The ownership was so far removed from him that no one could trace it back. There was a unique rear entrance that seemed to go into a totally different home. The exterior was nondescript, looking like every other house on the block, but the interior was lavish.

Davis was sitting in an overstuffed Corinthian brown leather chair sipping Tieguanyin tea when Jacques was escorted into the sitting room by a slim young lady wearing a tight green dress.

"Can I get you anything, sir?" She had a stark Scottish burr.

"What he's having, miss." Jacques almost stumbled on the words. His French accent was quite the contrast to hers.

"I'll send someone in with it." Her long red hair waved when she turned.

Both men's eyes lingered on her as she left the room.

Jacques went to a matching chair on the opposite side of a small teak table and removed his charcoal raincoat, revealing a navy-blue suit. "You always have beautiful women working for you."

"My HR department sends them to me." Davis placed the cup on its saucer that rested on the table. "She's a work in progress. She has special skills in getting information from others, so I may use her in other ways than just assisting me."

"I could imagine." Jacques raised an eyebrow.

"Not in that way. Hmm ... well yes, in that way too." Davis only had a hint of a British accent when he was at his home base in the States, but when he was back in England it was full on.

"And your wife doesn't object to all your sexy employees? Mine would not be happy about it."

Davis smiled. "Frenchmen like you notoriously can't keep their dicks in their pants. Brit slash Americans like me have self-restraint." His wife Gwen never asked, and he never told. In his mind he was totally faithful and dearly loved his wife. The sex he had with the corporate-ladder-climbing female employees was completely at their instigation. It was his weakness, not being able to resist them. He couldn't help that at sixty, being six feet tall and in good shape, women still found him attractive and his libido was strong as ever.

"*Cinq à sept.*" Jacques shrugged and smiled. "Five to seven, and then you go home to your wife for dinner."

The young lady re-entered the room with the Spaniard, Carlo Da Silva, and an older man carrying a tea service.

Da Silva, barrel-chested with thick, wavy dark hair, approached the two seated men. "Good to see you, Davis. Jacques." He sat down in a chair upholstered in a bright flower pattern that in an interesting way made the decor of the room fit together.

The butler poured tea for Carlo and Jacques.

"That'll be all, Daphne," Davis said to the young lady.

All three men watched her walk with confidence, behind the butler, from the sitting room.

"You've remodeled," Carlo said with his prominent lisp. "I like the art."

"It needed freshening." Davis did a quick scan of the room. "It turned out well."

Carlo inhaled. "But the smell is the same."

"It smells a little different to me," Davis said. "The pine has a muskiness in the latest batch I'm not sure I like."

Carlo looked at Jacques. "Davis is obsessed with a pine air freshener—he takes it everywhere."

"I wouldn't say obsessed. I just enjoy the smell."

"Obsessed." Carlo smiled, showing perfect white teeth that must have been worked on, because at forty-eight no one's teeth were that white and perfect. "I just received a Maserati Quattroporte to have as my car in London. It's spectacular. You should get one."

Jacques raised an eyebrow. As if he could afford one.

"I prefer the Bentley and a chauffeur here," Davis said. "Traffic."

"Do you mind if we got down to business?" Jacques asked. "I don't have much time today."

"By all means," Davis said.

"Barrister Kenneth Brown came to visit me," Jacques said. "He showed me video footage from the hotel Monsieur Barnes was staying at. It shows a man named Dale Samson, who looks strikingly similar to Barnes, pick his pocket for the hotel receipt. When you compare Samson's image with the airport's, it's a match."

"Who is this Dale Samson?" Carlo asked.

"Samson works for Naintosa's security," Jacques said.

Davis sat back in the chair. *Well, that did point directly to Schmidt's killing coming from within his own organization.*

"We haven't been able to locate Monsieur Samson for questioning." Jacques looked to Carlo and Davis as if asking for assistance.

Carlo shook his head. "Nor will you ever."

Jacques shrugged. "We have to try to find him."

"He'd be eliminated by now," Davis said.

"So now what?" Carlo asked.

"I must withdraw the case against Barnes, and I need to question Hendrick V," Jacques said. "My suspicion is swaying toward Hendrick having performed a *coup d'état* on his own father, but I'm not sure if he did it himself or had someone do it for him. He did fire Hendrick IV's head of security right away, stating he couldn't trust him anymore."

"If Daimler was fired, who's in charge of security now?" Carlo asked.

"Second in command, Otto Schilling."

"And what of the threatening e-mails from Barnes?" Davis asked.

Jacques opened his mouth to speak, but Carlo interjected. "There are ways ... easy enough to plant."

Davis understood where the investigation needed to go. "When you talk to Hendrick, make sure to point out that Carlo and I know it was an inside job. See how he reacts."

"Agreed." Jacques glanced at his watch and rose to his feet. "I will report back."

As soon as Jacques was gone, Carlo said, "Deep down I'd hoped that Hendrick hadn't killed his father, but the more we get to know him, the more irrational he seems."

"We don't know for sure yet if Junior's hands are bloody," Davis said. "But if it turns out that they are, we have to make a decision."

"It's not the first time a son has killed his father to seize control,"

Carlo said. "You can't begrudge him that. It's actually quite common in our history."

"We can at least hold it over him for control," Davis said.

"The question is, can he take over where his father left off?" Carlo raised his hands and then let them fall to his lap.

"The scientists keep doing what they're doing." Davis reached for his tea. "Dr. Smith is competent."

# CHAPTER 8

*May 2, 2003*

Breathing in and out, my mind went blank. Sweet nothingness as I entered the gap—the void of pure potential that could be accessed through meditation. My inner self was floating in space when an image appeared. *I stood on the wharf in Christina Lake, where Morgan and I hid to write the exposé three years ago. It was a beautiful fall day with not a cloud in the sky, and the lake rippled. Morgan sat on the edge of the diving board, bare feet in the water, brilliant blue eyes looking up at me. Her strawberry-blonde hair fluttered in the cool breeze.*

*"I miss you." She reached her hand out for me to take it. "I'm doing what I can to help."*

*I took her cold hand. How I had longed to touch her. "I miss you, too, more than you'll ever know."*

*"You have to be strong." Her face looked sad and worried. "I can see just around the corner of the future."*

*"Since I lost you, I feel numb to whatever happens."*

*She raised her feet from the water, slid over, and stood on the wharf, still holding onto my hand. "You have to become hyper-focused. Others are going to die. The son is more dangerous than the father. You're going to have to be stronger and fight harder. You'll have to lead."*

*I felt a tear run down my cheek. I didn't care about the warning, I just wanted to be with her.*

*We leaned in to kiss.*

I came storming out of the gap, back to reality, and gasped. I opened my eyes. The tears were real.

Sue was looking at me. "What happened? You ruined my relaxed moment."

"I saw Morgan, and she had a warning."

"Morgan again?" She got up from the couch.

"What do you mean, *again*?"

"Nothing." Sue walked toward the hallway. "I'm going to go have a shower."

Maybe Sue and I had been spending too much time together. We'd both snapped at each other from time to time, but today she seemed especially impatient. I'd purposely tried not to talk about Morgan with her, but it still came up sometimes. Today's message was important. I'd explain it to Sue when she was more open to hearing it. Sue was trying hard to be there for me, but it wasn't in her nature to be nurturing. And I didn't want to be doted on anyway.

After a shower and breakfast, I headed to the study.

There were several e-mails that needed attention. The literary agent I'd chosen had agreed to work with me and had attached a standard agreement that I filled out and sent back to him. The editor was ready for my manuscript. It took me a few hours to finish the final edits, and then I sent it off. Now I just had to wait for the deal the agent and publisher worked out.

Sue came into the study wearing jeans and a tight gray sweater. She glanced at me. "I feel like working outside today. It's nice out."

I glanced out the window and saw the sun shining. "Good idea."

She unplugged her laptop, placed it under her arm, and left the room.

I didn't want to suggest that I join her.

I wasn't sure what to do next. With the manuscript sent to the editor, all I could do was wait, which could take months. I glanced over at my To-Do list; everything was crossed off. This house arrest sucked. I wanted to get out in the field—I wanted to go look at the Norway seed bank.

I needed to use this time wisely. The smart thing was to start on my second book.

I heard the ping of a new e-mail arriving. It was from Ivan, addressed to Sue, Jack, and me.

Ivan had just finished meeting with the board of the Northern European Council for Ethical Farming, and they weren't happy. They understood that the media were trying to discredit us; however, if I wasn't cleared of the murder charge, it could put their reputation on the line by associating with me. Ivan felt it was only a matter of time before they disassociated from us if our credibility wasn't rebuilt.

I didn't want to contribute in any way to Ivan's research being slowed. He was progressing well, currently looking at the long-term effects of Naintosa's neonicotinoids throughout the food chain, from insects to humans. And there was the very private study that had just commenced to determine what Pharmalin's latest colon cancer drug really did. We had Schmidt IV on video saying it wasn't meant to be a cure, but we had to prove it. If Pharmalin found out about the study, it would be shut down because of patent infringement—Pharmalin would have had to give permission for the testing, which they never would have.

I stared at the screen for a while, which wasn't productive, so I closed the laptop.

As I was walking through the foyer, Jack and Lee came through the front door.

"Ivan sent us an e-mail," I said as I walked up to them.

Jack looked like he was expecting bad news.

After I explained what was in the message, Jack said, "I was kinda expecting that. I don't blame them for being nervous."

"What can we do?" I asked. "Ivan has to keep his studies going."

"Brown has met with Plante," Jack said. "Plante had no rebuttal to the proof that you were setup. I'm hoping the charges will be dropped any second."

"That'll sure help," I said. "Has the PI had any luck in finding Dale Samson?"

Lee rubbed his chin. "Naintosa's so tight, if they don't want an outsider finding someone, it's darn near impossible."

I looked down at the pad of paper in my hand. I wanted to be alone to think.

"You hungry?" Jack asked.

"No, thirsty."

I followed Jack and Lee through the main living room and into the dining room. Sam was there, finishing his lunch. I kept going to the kitchen.

Rose, in a cream-colored, knee-length dress with an apron over it, was talking on the phone. She looked concerned. "I understand ... uh-huh ... yes ... okay, we'll see you on the ninth." She glanced my way and looked startled. "Okay, then." She hung up the phone.

I wondered who she'd been talking to, but it felt inappropriate to ask. So I headed toward the fridge.

"You want something to eat?" she asked.

"No, I'm not hungry." I opened the fridge door and surveyed the middle shelf.

"Can I get you anything?" Rose had come up beside me. She looked guilty and was overcompensating.

*What was she up to?* At that moment I wasn't in a mood to ask.

"I can whip you up a mean punch."

"No, thanks, Rose, I'm good."

She relented and went back to tend to something in a pot on

the stove.

We had an assortment of beer, since all of us had unique tastes. We'd been experimenting with different European brands—you know, while in Europe, drink as Europeans. I'd never liked darker beer in the States, but some of the ones I'd tried here were excellent. My tastes were definitely changing. I chose the last two Chimay Blues from Belgium. My plan for the afternoon was to find a quiet place to sip beer and see if I could get any new book ideas.

I went to the sunroom. It was bright and warm there, with the windows curving up at the ceiling to let the sunshine in. I sat down in a wicker chair beside some tall plants. There was a small glass-topped table for me to put my drinks and pad on. I took a generous swallow of the first beer—it was rich and satisfying.

Hours later, I wasn't even sure how many, I heard footsteps and looked up. Sue was in the entryway, twenty feet in front of me.

She held a beer bottle, and her eyes were focused on the table beside me. "What are you doing, sitting in the dark?"

"Thinking about what we'll do after I'm able to leave here." To my surprise I was slurring my words. I tried to speak slower to cover it up. "And also starting on the outline of my next book ... trying to be productive."

"Mind if I join you for a minute?"

"Sure." I reached over and turned on a lamp. It was bright, making me squint. On the table next to me were two empty stubby bottles of Chimay Blue, two drained Duvel Tripel Hops, the pad with some notes, and a bottle of Aberlour Scotch missing over a third of its contents. In my hand was a glass containing half-melted ice and amber liquid.

"Are you drunk?" She pulled a brown wicker chair closer to mine.

I sat up straight. "Getting there, now that you mention it."

"Good idea about starting the new book." Sue took a swig from her bottle. "And as far as our next moves, I thought we were going to the seed bank in Norway and then the lab in Colombia after you're free. Were you thinking something different?"

"No, that's still the plan."

"So basically, you've been sitting here all afternoon and evening, getting sloshed?"

I smiled at her. She'd pointed out before that when I didn't have much to do, I drank too much. I needed to keep busy and have a cause to focus on. "Pretty much."

"Did you read the e-mail from Ivan?"

"I can understand why the Council is getting antsy."

She nodded. "That's what Jack said."

We sipped our drinks.

There was a feeling of unease from Sue. "I'm sorry that I was short with you today."

"It's understandable. We've been spending a lot of time together in this place."

"Yeah, but it's not just that. I feel ..."

"What?"

Sue reached out and took my hand. She opened her mouth to speak and then closed it.

"What?"

She leaned over and to my surprise, kissed me on the lips, lingering. I felt a spark and didn't want her to stop.

She pulled back and paused, as if studying my reaction.

Her eyes narrowed and she let go of my hand. Standing, she walked out, saying something I couldn't make out.

"Wait." *That was unexpected.* "Don't go."

I sat back in the chair. The room took a second to catch up with me. I *was* drunk.

# CHAPTER 9

*May 3, 2003*

I shouldn't have skipped lunch and dinner yesterday, especially with the amount I'd drunk. There was a dull throb behind my temples, and my mouth was dry even after two glasses of water.

I thought about Sue. She'd been grumpy yesterday and then out of the blue, kissed me. I hadn't seen that coming. Originally when we'd met at Washington State University, she'd shut my advances down and we developed a great friendship instead. Since then I'd kept the little flame I had for her buried deep inside me. Had I blown an opportunity with Sue? Was it an opportunity at all? Was I ready and wanting such an opportunity? I'd just seen Morgan in a meditation yesterday. Could Morgan's spirit see what happened? Surely she would want me to move forward with my life ... wouldn't she? I sighed; my thinking was making my headache worse.

When I arrived at the dining room it was empty. Opening the door to the kitchen, I saw Rose in front of the stove. "Good morning, Rose."

"Morning, Nick. Coffee?" She took a mug from the cupboard.

"Great, thanks." I took the mug from her and poured my own

coffee. Then I walked over to the island and reached for the sugar.

"Do you want to eat in the dining room?" Rose was standing in front of me with a plate in each hand.

"No, here's fine, thanks."

Jack came into the room and took a stool next to me.

Rose placed the second omelette in front of him and went to get toast.

"I have to go back to the States." Jack sliced the egg with his fork. "Tests at a lake near a site that was just hydraulically fractured are showing high levels of benzene and arsenic. It's not far from Dallas. There's also been seismic activity in the area the past few days."

"Does that have to do with the hydraulic fracturing?"

"They've never had earthquakes there before."

"When are you leaving?" I asked.

"This afternoon."

I reached for the toast that Rose just placed in front of us. "We'll hold down the fort. Or at least you know I'll be here when you get back."

He patted me on the shoulder. "Lee and I should return in a few weeks."

After breakfast, Jack went to his office, and I retreated to my bedroom. I had an urge to meditate alone, so I crawled under the sheets of my bed and propped up the pillows behind me for a comfortable sitting position.

Breaths in and out, in and out. Let thoughts pass right through my mind and not linger. Before long blackness and empty space, calm.

*Out of nowhere I was on a snowmobile, speeding across a frozen inlet, snow-covered, treeless, mountains rose on either side. I was in the lead with Sue, Jorge, and Lorraine behind me—I couldn't see them because of the limited peripheral vision of my full-face helmet, but I felt they were there. Drifts ranging from two to five feet high like hard icy waves rose over the surface, and our snowmobiles became airborne as we launched off each one.*

*The channel narrowed sharply as the mountains closed in, and we had to take a hard right turn. I released the throttle and jammed on the brake, locking up the tread and skidding to a halt. In front of us was a wall of ice at least a hundred feet high. It was translucent, and I knew the light penetrating through the ice was from the seed bank.*

*We'd all stopped side by side, and everyone's helmeted heads looked from me to the wall.*

*A gush of deep crimson liquid discharged down the ice wall, rolling as it covered imperfections. It oozed thick and bubbling, gaining momentum. Dispersed white objects protruded from the red mass that looked like splintered bones.*

*Where was the blood coming from? There was so much of it. The gruesome scene made me want to throw up.*

*My snowmobile shuddered and dropped a foot, then rose two. The ice beneath us was separating. Suddenly, plumes of water spat between the fissures, and everything broke up at once, hard turning to liquid. It happened so fast we couldn't react in time. Panic. In an instant Sue disappeared, Jorge went down, followed by Lorraine. I was next.*

I was gagging and rolled off the bed, tripping over my duvet as I rushed to the bathroom to puke.

Never had I experienced such an intense premonition before.

I'd decided to keep the experience in the meditation to myself for the time being until I could make sense of it. It was hard to not think of the blood and bone and all of us going down into the cold depths to drown. I knew I wasn't meant to take it literally, but there was certain danger if we were to go to the seed bank.

After seeing Jack and Lee off, I went to the main living room window and looked out at the open expanse of rolling fields and pastures. The antique grandfather clock next to the dining room doorway chimed, announcing that it was four in the afternoon.

I hadn't seen Sue all day. Rose told me that Sue and Lorraine had gone for a long run and then she'd sent them to do some shopping for her.

Jorge walked in from the foyer. I hadn't crossed paths with the Colombian tank of a man much lately. "There's an officer here for you."

I followed Jorge. "Do you know what it's about?"

"We'll soon find out." Jorge opened the front double door.

A female in a gray, knee-length skirt and black windbreaker was walking toward us from a white Peugeot parked in the driveway.

"How do you know she's a police officer?" I whispered.

"She showed her badge to Sam," Jorge replied.

The plain-clothes officer reached us. "Mr. Nick Barnes?"

"Yes, ma'am."

She extended an envelope in her right hand. "Your charges have been withdrawn. You are released to go about your business." She had a serious-sounding voice.

I took the envelope. "Thank you." I was free, finally.

"The one stipulation is that you report any travel outside of West Oxfordshire to Chief Inspector Plante. There is a phone number and e-mail address within the envelope." Without another word, she walked back to her car.

I ripped the seal of the envelope and pulled out the folded piece of paper. It stated that I was cleared of any charges and house arrest. The only other thing in the envelope was Chief Inspector Plante's business card, and I already had one of those. "It doesn't say I have to tell Plante when I go anywhere." I handed the paper to Jorge.

He read it. "Hmm, he wants to personally keep tabs on you."

"Like I'm going to tell him anything." I began walking through the foyer toward the study.

I wrote out a statement that all charges had been dropped. I added that I hoped Schmidt's real killer was found and then posted it to our website. Then against my better judgement I sent an e-mail to journalist, Adhira Virk, basically saying *I told you so*. That felt like closure for me.

Just as I got up to go find her, Sue walked into the study.

"There you are," I said.

"Why?" Sue shrugged. "What happened?"

"I was just released from house arrest." I raised my arms. "I'm free!"

"Really?" She rushed forward and gave me a hug. "Finally!"

"It'll be great to get out there again." I pointed at the window.

"The seed bank?" She pulled away. "Let's go find Jorge and Lorraine. We need to get hold of Jack too."

Going to the seed bank was the logical next move. Could my premonition have been wrong? They were almost always right. Should I say something? I didn't want to worry everyone. I decided that I'd keep it to myself, for now.

# INTERLOGUE 2

*May 4, 2003*

Hendrick V preferred the smaller family estate outside Berlin to the bigger country home that his father had liked. This was closer to the action, and he didn't need to take a helicopter to the airport; he could drive if he felt like it. Besides, the older place reminded him of his father, just like the villa on Lake Como.

He'd already begun renovations to make the Berlin home more to his taste, much to his mother's dismay. He'd allowed his fiancée, Helga, to move in and oversee the upgrades. Hendrick's most pronounced change yet was to move from his smaller office to his father's study; now he had room to run his inherited empire.

Otto Schilling entered the study. "Mr. Schmidt ..."

"Doctor Schmidt." Hendrick didn't much care for the man twice his age standing across the desk from him. However, he was the right man to be chief of security. He'd been second in command and showed a ruthless loyalty to the family. Hendrick had to let the former head of security go for appearances' sake—he'd let someone kill the main man he was sworn to protect.

"Dr. Schmidt ... Jack Carter has left Burford and is now in Dallas," said the tall, wiry man. He'd been with the Schmidt security force for the last eighteen years after retiring from the German military where he'd started as a sniper and worked his way up to an officer. "Lee Donald is with him."

"And why are you bothering me with this?" Hendrick said.

"Should we use this opportunity to take him out?" Otto wore round wire spectacles, had his blond hair slicked back, and was always dressed in a charcoal-gray wool suit.

Hendrick pondered that question. It was an opportunity. He was planning on eliminating every member of that group but had to have Barnes and Carter killed simultaneously for a clean break. After that, Clark and Popov could be disposed of at his leisure. Right then everything depended on Barnes conviction. "Make sure Carter's movements are watched for now. Do you still have someone on the Burford house?"

"Yes, sir."

Hendrick brought up the calendar on his computer screen. "I will be going to Oxford on Monday and then to the Colombian lab ten to fourteen days after that, depending on how soon I can finish this round of my studies." He wished he could be done with school and fully concentrate on his businesses. "You will be escorting me, not one of your lackeys."

"Yes, sir."

"Now send in Chief Inspector Plante. I've kept him waiting long enough."

"One other thing, Herr Doctor."

"What?"

"I thought you should know that a man was in Nordkapp, inquiring about the seed bank and how he could get to it."

"Any idea who he was?" Hendrick asked. "Was he questioned?"

"No, he'd disappeared by the time Naintosa security arrived. We're sure he never made it anywhere near the seed bank. We do have a vague description—a fat American."

"Well then, don't bother telling me unless it becomes important.

I'm far too busy."

The head of security gave a slight bow and clicked his heels before walking out of the room. Otto had a permanent limp after being shot in the right leg ten years ago by Hendrick V—by accident.

Hendrick didn't worry about some fat American trying to get to the seed bank. It had been tried before, usually by renegade journalists or environmentalists, with no success. He sat in his new oxblood leather swivel chair and anticipated why Plante had come. Hopefully it was an update on Barnes and that a trial date was set.

Within a moment, Chief Inspector Jacques Plante came through the doorway. "Monsieur Schmidt."

"Doctor Schmidt."

"Excuse me, Dr. Schmidt. Thank you for seeing me on short notice." Jacques walked around the desk and shook Hendrick's hand. Then he sat down in a brown leather chair on the opposite side.

"What brings you here today, Chief Inspector?"

"We have new evidence regarding your father's murder."

"Good, I want Nick Barnes put away for the rest of his life." Hendrick's eyes narrowed. "It's too bad we can't execute him or put him in a gas chamber."

"None of that is going to be happening." Jacques leaned forward. "We have footage of a man named Dale Samson, who has a striking resemblance to Barnes, picking his pocket for the hotel receipt. And the person caught on the airport camera has proven to be Samson. He's employed by Naintosa in your security division, correct?"

Hendrick hadn't expected this. He thought he'd set Barnes up enough and Interpol wouldn't bother investigating into it further. He tried not to show any emotion. "You are mistaken, Chief Inspector, it *was* Nick Barnes who killed my father, not this other man. A man whom you say worked for Naintosa?"

"We don't have evidence that Samson killed your father; however, he suspiciously seems to be a decoy to set Barnes up. That would mean there was someone giving him orders to be the diversion. That someone planned the murder and likely was the one who injected your father with Cirachrome or hired someone to do it for them. And that someone I suspect is part of your own organization."

"That's preposterous. You think someone inside my father's own company murdered the man responsible for their own livelihood; the man who gave them a reason to exist?"

Jacques leaned farther forward, placing his hands on the desk. "Maybe it was because they were getting tired, in their eyes, of the bad decisions your father was making or the pace of progress. Maybe they wanted control themselves." ·

Hendrick's face heated. He tried to control himself from a threatening outburst that might incriminate him.

"Do you know Dale Samson, Hendrick? Have you had recent contact with him?"

Hendrick tried as hard as possible to act calm, even flippant, but it wasn't working. "No, I don't know the man. I can't know everyone in Naintosa's employ. Chief Inspector, are you accusing me of having something to do with my father's death?"

"Did you?"

Hendrick grit his teeth. "My father, and now I, pay you very handsomely to look after our interests. I do not pay you to accuse me. I pay you to investigate the people who should be investigated ... not me!" He wanted to fire him right there but knew that would give Jacques total freedom to investigate him. Maybe it was time for Jacques to have an unfortunate accident.

"But I have to adhere to the law." Jacques kept his focus on Hendrick. "And don't you want to catch the *right* person or persons who killed your father?"

"Of course." Hendrick tried to keep eye contact but couldn't. "And I think you have that person already. Nick Barnes."

"It's not proving to be him." Jacques leaned back in the chair, as if relieving pressure. "Davis and Carlo know and agree. We've let Barnes go and are changing the course of the investigation."

"Why would you involve Davis and Carlo?" Hendrick didn't want them involved with this in any way. The plan was to have Davis and Carlo respect him and treat him as an equal until the day he'd have dominance over them.

"They, too, want the right person caught for your father's murder. He was their friend and colleague."

Hendrick would have to begrudgingly accept their involvement, for now. "If you let Barnes go, he'll disappear. Then when you finally figure out he really was the actual killer, you won't be able to find him."

"I couldn't keep him under house arrest. You'll have to have your people monitor him."

"Trust me, I will."

Jacques rose from the chair. "We will be speaking more about this soon." He turned and walked to the door.

Hendrick said behind him. "Jacques, investigate properly. It wasn't an inside job."

As soon as Jacques left the room, Hendrick pressed the intercom button on the phone and asked Otto to come see him.

This wasn't easily going away like he'd hoped it would. He didn't have time to be worrying about his father's murder anymore, but he had no choice. He just wanted to move forward with the population control plan, unimpeded. With Barnes free, he'd have to take matters into his own hands and eliminate the paltry, annoying opposition himself.

The chief of security walked into the room.

"Close the door," Hendrick instructed.

Otto did as he was asked and then walked up to Hendrick's desk.

"Where is Dale Samson now?" Hendrick asked.

"He's working at the Colombia compound."

"Eliminate him and leave no trace."

Otto hesitated. "I don't think that is a good idea. You may need him in the future as an alibi."

Hendrick pondered that for a moment. *Scheisse, he's right.* "At least make sure he never leaves the compound."

"Of course, Herr Doctor." Otto turned to leave.

"Wait." Hendrick raised his hand. "Have you located Peter Bail?"

Otto swivelled back. "Yes, in Belize."

"Make contact. I have a job for him."

Hendrick was about to shut down his computer for the evening when an e-mail arrived from his head scientist, Dr. Smith. He looked at the priceless antique bronze clock near the fireplace and did the calculation—it was just after 1:00 p.m. in Florencia, Colombia, where the message had originated.

Dr. Smith was concerned; Hendrick could tell by the choices of words used. Dr. Smith was getting field findings that showed the general populace, especially in the United States, were showing symptoms from the genetically engineered food and pesticides years ahead of when they should be. They were already moving into *Stage 4.* That was not good.

Hendrick opened the attachment and reviewed the data. At the new rate, fatal diseases would reach critical mass five, maybe even seven, years earlier than 2020. They were not prepared. The good seed meant for the seed bank could be compromised, as well as the land set aside to grow the unaltered organic food. The life-extending cancer drugs weren't reacting as they should. They weren't even close with the actual colon cancer cure. The Plycite gene was still years away from being effectively mass produced in corn. Everything was being thrust out of balance.

His father had made a mess, and now Hendrick had to clean it up.

He wrote a terse response to Dr. Smith, asking how this could be happening and not to tell anyone.

# CHAPTER 10

"Feel like a post-dinner drink?" Sue half-smiled.

We cleared our plates from the table.

We'd had a busy day getting ready for the expedition to the seed bank and had decided to meet with the Council in Oslo along the way.

When we entered the kitchen, Rose was talking quietly on the phone. She was doing that often lately; before, she never used to call anyone.

When Rose saw us, she placed her hand over the bottom of the receiver. "I'll clean up. You two go relax."

We gave Rose her privacy and went out to the living room.

"What do you want to drink?" Sue walked over to the bar.

"Aberlour." We always had my favorite Scotch on hand. I hoped no one was keeping track of the amount I'd been going through recently. Rose had to be aware, because she was in charge of replenishing supplies.

"Of course." Sue poured three fingers into two glasses and then added two ice cubes each.

I'd sat down on the couch. Sue joined me, handing over my drink.

Sue hadn't brought up the kiss from the other night, and I was debating if I should. This would be as good of a time as any, but did I really want to talk about it?

The ice hadn't had a chance to cool and dilute the Scotch, so the first sip was harsh, but I welcomed the burning sensation as the liquid went down.

I gazed at her, anticipating what she was going to say, but she didn't say anything. I took another, bigger, drink.

Sue swirled the contents of her glass. "I've been thinking about us."

I paused. "What about us?"

Sue looked at me intently. "Our relationship. Where it could go."

Okay, the kiss would tie into the conversation somehow. "And where do you think it could go?"

Instead of answering, Sue carefully placed her glass on the side table. She framed my face with her hands and pressed her lips against mine. Her mouth was warm and gentle. I could feel a buzzing in my brain that had nothing to do with the alcohol.

After a moment, she pulled back, hands still around my face. "Is that okay?"

I nodded.

She leaned in and kissed me again, this time pulling me in closer. I blindly set my glass down on what I hoped was something solid and held onto her arms. Every nerve in my body was tingling.

Sue pulled away, searched my face for a second, then rose from the chair. I took her outstretched hand, and she led me out of the room.

Neither of us said a word as we walked down the hallway to her bedroom. I was having a hard time forming a coherent thought. Sue's hand was the only thing keeping me on the ground.

As we reached the door, something made me stop. I suddenly felt weird, like all the feelings I'd buried for Sue were rising, uneven and confused, to the surface. I was torn between striding into that room and running back to the safety of the living room with its unassuming Scotch.

"What's wrong?" Sue asked.

"Are you sure you want to do this?" I responded. "I mean, we've been friends for so long … this could change everything."

She squeezed my hand. "Change can be a good thing." She opened the door and pulled me inside.

The two bedside lamps lit the tidy white bed and small pile of books on the nightstand. I'd been inside Sue's room before, but this time it looked different. I never noticed the small bottles of perfume on the vanity or the pale-blue robe tossed casually on the chair. Heels and sneakers sat by the closet like she'd just stepped out of them.

Sue stood by the door, her head tilted to the side and watching me. "What are you doing?"

I shrugged, feeling awkward. "Just looking around."

She walked over and slid her hands around my waist.

This time I used my hands to frame her face. I looked into her blue eyes and noticed, for the first time, flecks of gold around her irises. She held her breath as my thumb ran across her jaw and grazed her lower lip. I leaned down to kiss her, running my hands down her arms and around her waist. She gripped the back of my shirt and pulled me in.

Every time one of us changed the angle of the kiss, Sue would sigh into my mouth. My hands found skin under her shirt, and she shivered. I yanked off the fabric, suddenly impatient to feel more of her body against me. Dark-blue lace appeared under the basic T-shirt. It looked impossibly exotic to me, and I couldn't help but stare for a moment.

Sue laughed at my gawking and reached behind her to unhook the bra.

I stopped her. "Not yet." My voice sounded strained in my ears. "I'll take care of it later."

Her laughter turned into a moan as I set my teeth against her neck and shoulder. I could feel her nails grip through my shirt as I unbuttoned her jeans and helped them slide down her hips. My fingers found the matching blue lace, and I traced the delicate designs just to hear her breath catch in my ear. I'd waited years, deep down hoping someday I'd have this opportunity.

"My turn," she whispered, and reached under the band of my jeans. She found me easily, my whole body going on alert as she used her other hand to work my jeans down my boxers.

I pulled off my own shirt and crushed her to me, desperate to feel her small, strong body against mine.

She hopped up to straddle my waist, diving her hands into my hair. We maneuvered to the bed. She pinned me against the pillows and took her time working my boxers away. Clever hands and soft kisses slowly trailed along my stomach and thighs.

When she reached my mouth once more, I flipped her underneath me. "My turn." I gave her a nipping kiss and fulfilled my promise of relieving her of the lacy underwear and bra.

Sue arched under my touch. I could see the scars the past years had given her. Her strength, her bravery, her intelligence had been amazing. I ran my finger across the uneven skin of a spot on her stomach. She moved her hand to cover it, but I gently encouraged it away. I kissed each mark on her body, making my way back up above her ear to the largest healed wound, hidden by her hair; the one she'd received in Maui.

When Sue guided me inside, she whispered my name. I could only hang on as our bodies quickly took over, finding their own rhythm in the dim lamp light. She wrapped her legs around me, and I lost myself in wave after wave of heat and electricity. I gripped her hips, pushed deeper, hearing her call out and hold me tighter in turn.

I whispered her name as she climaxed, feeling her spine curve up in ecstasy and her nails rake across my shoulders. I came soon after, every ounce of control gone. I buried my face in her hair, letting the cascade of shudders course through my body until I could think again.

"You're squishing me," she said with a grin.

"Sorry." I rolled off, onto the bed.

Sue slid up against my side, her hand resting against my heart.

# CHAPTER 11

*May 5, 2003*

Pins and needles were running through my left arm. I rolled over to change position and opened my eyes. Morning light was seeping through the slit between the curtains.

I was in Sue's room, and she was getting dressed. She wasn't putting on lace panties like she wore last night; these looked sportier. Seeing her reminded me how beautiful my best friend was ... or should I call her something else now? "Where are you going?"

"Good morning." She turned to me as she pulled up a pair of black stretchy workout pants. "I feel like going for a run." She pulled on a white T-shirt over her sports bra and then went to the closet and took out the powder-blue windbreaker I'd helped her buy years ago. "See you in a while."

*Hmm, nothing about last night?* I got out of bed, gathered my clothes, and went to my room. We'd talk about it eventually, and I'd hope to understand her motivation and her feelings now. Last night had been fantastic, but something still didn't feel right. Yet, logically, why wouldn't we be together?

I wanted to start the day with exercise too, so I stretched and then lifted weights for forty-five minutes.

While having a shower, I thought about Morgan and how I had to stop grieving. She would always have a special place deep in my heart, but I needed to move forward. I cared about Sue and wanted to focus on the future with her, in whichever way we chose.

Sam was eating breakfast at the kitchen island when I arrived. "Not often I see you here in the morning."

"Got the morning off for once," said Sam in his baritone. "Jorge's covering for me, so I get to chill ... not that I'm complaining. Mind you, I'm about ready for some action."

"Too bad you're not coming to the seed bank." *Or lucky for you you're not coming.* I pushed that negative thought from my mind.

"Someone's gotta protect Momma Rose." He smiled, showing his white teeth that contrasted with his thick dark lips.

I pulled out the stool next to him.

Rose had come from the pantry. "I always feel safe with Sam around."

"You keep feeding me like this, and I'll protect you up until I can't move anymore 'cause I'm so fat."

To look at Sam, anyone would be intimidated, but on the inside he was a real softy. If there was danger, there was never a doubt that he would protect us. He'd proven that time and again.

"Hey, has Sue eaten yet?" I asked.

"Lorraine went out with her for a run," Sam said, while chewing on bacon.

After chatting with Rose and Sam over breakfast, I went to the study.

While waiting for my laptop to boot, I picked up the phone.

The line only rang once. "Jack, here."

"Hey, Jack, it's Nick."

"How are yah, son?"

"Good, how's Texas?"

"Hot. I'd become acclimatized to merry ol' England. Now I'm walkin' around sweatin' all the time. But enough about me; how's it feel to be free?"

"I was holding everyone back, even Ivan with the Council. There's too much going on to just sit here, so I'm happy we can move forward now."

"So, the seed bank then?"

"It's the logical next move." I hoped my tone sounded convincing.

"Yep," Jack said. "You still need to get the Arctic clothes. Also, I'll e-mail you a few more things I thought of while you're performing the recon. You have the logistics we'd planned, so y'all should be good to go."

Sue walked into the room.

"Think you and Sue are ready for this?" Jack asked. "Lorraine and Jorge will be with you, but it'll still be dangerous."

I glanced at Sue, who sat down at her side of the desk and opened her laptop. "We'll be fine." As we were preparing for the seed bank excursion, I'd repeated an internal mantra—*careful and vigilant, and we'll be fine.* I'd convinced myself the premonition was a warning to be extra cautious.

"I just wanted to hear you say it. I think so too."

I hung up the phone and then said to Sue, "That was Jack. After a few last preparations, we're set to go."

Sue nodded. "Good."

I clicked on the Internet icon.

We should've talked about last night. But at that moment Sue wasn't giving me any indication she wanted to, and I wanted her to bring it up first.

"I'm going to check if any media have mentioned that I'm not charged with the murder anymore," I said.

When I looked at a number of sites, including GMNN, I couldn't find anything about me. "Nothing."

Sue looked up from her screen. "Of course not. A person not suspected of murder anymore isn't news."

"I know, I know. It just sucks that unless someone checks our website, everyone will still think I'm a murderer."

"It'll add to your mystique."

A ping sounded, indicating a new e-mail. That must've been from Jack. When I clicked on the icon, right under his message was one from an address I recognized from before. They must've arrived at the same time. "Ogden Dundst sent another e-mail."

"What?" Sue leaped from her chair and came over to my side of the desk to look over my shoulder. "What's it say?"

I opened it and we read it together.

*Hey Nick,*

"What, you're buddies now?" Sue scoffed. "Hey, Nick."

*I HATE losers like you who just hide behind computers.*

"Which is exactly what he's doing," Sue said.

"This guy sounds childish," I said.

*You better PICK out you GRAVE STONE, because even if you didn't KILL Dr. Schmidt, which I DOUBT, your shite and are GUILTY of so MANY other CRIMES! The people are anxious and want your BLOOD and I'm the one who's going to SPILL it for them! And they will rejoice, cheer AND love me FOR it! True JUSTICE will be served and the people will be HAPPY!*

*THE Time is NEAR. DON'T bother hiding or fighting it. Your TIME IS Up!*

*Sincerely,*

*Ogden (the savior)*

"What a fucking whack job," Sue said.

I swiveled in my chair to look at Sue. "He sounds like a guy who has trouble tying his shoes, let alone killing someone."

"We should still take him seriously, to be on the safe side." She touched my shoulder, just for a second.

I swiveled back and clicked on the "Forward" button. "I'm going to send this to Jack, Lee, Jorge, and Lorraine, so they know. Oh, and Ivan too. Even though I envision a guy in his thirties, who works at a comic bookstore and lives in his parents' basement, you're right—we have to be vigilant."

"I ran into Jorge when I was coming to the study, and he suggested we go to the shooting range today to practice one last time with the guns we're taking with us," Sue said. "What I think Ogden's face looks like will be etched on the target."

▷◁⬤▷◁

After practicing shooting, Krav Maga, and then going over the supply list and plan for the trip, the day was over.

Sue and I walked down the hall to our bedrooms, stopping in front of hers.

"So, what do you think?" I didn't want to wait for her to bring it up anymore. I'd thought about it and knew what I wanted. "Last night was wonderful. However ..."

"I know what you're going to say." She took my hands. "Last night was fantastic and something I really wanted us to do. However, we've got to be on our game and not staring at each other with googly eyes."

She wanted the same thing. That was a relief. "Let's just put the warm-and-fuzzy part on hold."

Sue reached for a hug. "To be continued at a later date."

I hugged back. "I hope so."

# INTERLOGUE 3

The late-afternoon sun had done its job of providing warmth and growth in the rejuvenation of spring.

Carlo looked out over the treetops and building roofs surrounding the river below that had gouged out the gully over centuries. He enjoyed the four-story home built in 1869 that he had purchased and remodeled over a year ago. Luxembourg City was centrally located for purposes of travel and a hub of European banking and politics, yet quiet enough for him to work without much distraction.

The butler, who'd served the Da Silva family since Carlo was a child, entered the study. "Mr. Lovemark has arrived."

"Thank you, Charles." Carlo turned from where he'd been standing at the window. "Send him up. Mr. Lovemark will be staying for dinner, but Mr. Crane will not. Also, make sure the largest guest room is prepared in case Mr. Lovemark decides to spend the night." Carlo walked over to a table between the desk and couch. "I see the wine is decanted; however, where is the charcuterie?"

"It will be here momentarily," Charles said and then exited.

Carlo had been very busy, and the algorithms for gathering personal data on virtually everyone on the planet were ready for implementation.

He was curious about the updates from Davis and enjoyed their occasional evenings together drinking his family's wine, food prepared from his family's produce, and planning. Though he wasn't so excited about first meeting with Tom Crane—it was just a courtesy for all his effort.

As Carlo poured two glasses of rich red 1973 Rioja Alavesa, his guest walked into the study. "Ah, Davis. Perfect timing."

Davis came straight over to take the glass extended to him. "I feel like this is one of my homes, I've been here so many times since you've purchased it."

"Please feel as if it were your own."

"I was in the area anyway. Tomorrow I must leave to go back home to New York where my wife, Gwen, is holding a charity fundraiser of some kind, and then I'm off to the head office in San Francisco." Davis took a sip from the glass. "Mmm, more of your family's Rioja."

"Yes, everything you will drink and eat tonight will come from the Valencia estate."

"Of course." Davis smiled. "It always does."

"Only the best for you, Davis." Carlo raised his glass.

They both sat down at the table as Charles entered the room carrying a large tray. He placed the charcuterie in the middle of the table.

"Help yourself to some delicacies." Carlo gestured to the array of cheeses, cured meats, spreadable compotes, pates, pickles, and delicate crackers.

"Tasty." Davis reached for a cracker, goat cheese, and smoked ham.

"So, you spoke with Jacques?" Carlo reached for a mixture of food as well.

"Yes. He released Barnes."

"Now what do we do about him?"

"I imagine nothing for now." Davis shrugged. "We smeared his

94

reputation quite well, which will hold him and Jack back."

Carlo finished chewing. "That's inevitable."

"I think they'll find their support greatly diminished."

"Good," Carlo said. "What else did Jacques say? Any new developments regarding Hendrick's death?"

"He's quite sure now that Hendrick Junior caused his father's death. Jacques planted a bug when he went to see him. There was a discussion between Junior and his chief of security that, while not directly stating it, pretty much incriminated Junior for killing his father. And Otto played a role too. Also, that chap Samson is alive and at the Colombia compound."

Carlo sat back. "Could Otto have injected the needle?"

"Next to a confession, it would be very difficult for Jacques to prove either of them did it, especially due to the bug being illegal."

"It's the knowing that's most important," Carlo said. "Does a conviction really matter to us now?"

They both pondered for a moment.

Davis took a drink of wine. "If he were coming after us next, that would be a concern, but if it's just young Hendrick killing off his dad to take the power ..."

"Yes, a fact of life with ruling families," Carlo said. "It's natural."

Davis smiled. "How long before young Sergio kills you off?"

Carlo almost spit food out of his mouth and laughed. "Twelve to fifteen years, I gather. You're lucky you don't have sons."

"I don't know about that. Rachael is very aggressive and looking like she'll surpass Emily to take over the family empire." Davis's smile always looked more like a leer. "She's already tiring of me giving orders."

"Yes, women are becoming more aggressive than men now."

"Joking aside," Davis said. "We'll have to watch Hendrick Junior even more closely, knowing that he has the propensity to kill in him."

"Yes." Carlo nodded. "We'll mentor him and see how he turns out."

"I'll tell Jacques to leave it be," Davis said. "If Hendrick V screws up again, we'll handle it ourselves."

"Agreed." Carlo brought his glass to his thick lips. "I see great promise in Hendrick IV's other son, Günter. He's at Oxford and going to be a scientist as well, in physics. He seems more level headed than his older brother."

Davis nodded. "We should cultivate him as a long-term backup."

"I've already begun," Carlo said. "I think he'll surpass Hendrick V in the not-too-distant future."

"Then we'll have a bloody mess when they fight for control."

"It's the interim we have to worry about now."

Davis shook his head. "Convincing Hendrick Junior that he has to answer to someone will be a battle unto itself."

The butler entered the room, carrying a small basket. He placed it on the table and unwrapped the cloth covering to reveal freshly baked bread slices. The room instantly filled with their aroma. "Fresh out of the oven."

Carlo and Davis inhaled deeply.

"From your family's ancient grains, I imagine?" Davis leaned forward.

"Of course." Carlo took the basket and offered it to Davis. "And it tastes even better than it smells. The yeast starter has been in the family for hundreds of years."

"Such long tradition." Davis took a slice and then reached for the loganberry compote.

"Mr. Crane has arrived," Charles said. "Shall I send him in?"

"Please." Carlo was taking a slice for himself.

As soon as the butler left the room, Davis said, "We are in agreement as to how we deal with Tom?"

"Fully," Carlo said.

"One other thing the listening device revealed," Davis said. "Otto has found where Peter Bail is hiding, and Hendrick has instructed him to make contact. Apparently, he has a job for him."

That made Carlo pause from adding savory toppings to his bread. "Really? Peter Bail? That can't be good."

They couldn't continue their conversation, because Tom Crane was escorted into the room by the butler.

Tom was in costume with his usual bright bowtie, black-rimmed glasses and bowl-style haircut. Carlo suspected his look was intentional to throw people off. Otherwise why wouldn't he just get an image consultant since he loved being in the spotlight?

"Are you in Luxembourg City for long?" Carlo gestured for him to take a third chair.

"I have a few meetings tomorrow." Tom sat. "I've just been to Zimbabwe, Ethiopia, Uganda, and Nigeria and am looking forward to getting back home to Seattle. However, thanks to both of you for seeing me."

"Always a pleasure," Davis said.

The butler poured Tom wine and topped up Davis's and Carlo's glasses before exiting the room.

"How is everything in Africa?" Davis asked.

"There is resistance from farmers on the genetically engineered seed and pesticides, but the governments have fallen in line." Tom took a sip of the wine. "Oh, this is very good."

"All the food and wine come from Carlo's family estate in Spain." Davis beat Carlo, avoiding his never-ending gloating.

"So it's safe, then." Tom's cheeks turned a shade of pink. "Of course, it is."

Carlo raised an eyebrow. "Everything is grown from ancient seed, and the land has never been touched with chemical fertilizers or pesticides."

"Even his pigs eat better than we do." Davis smiled.

"All our livestock is happy and healthy, roaming free and foraging. They eat the same quality of food we do."

"I'm sorry for the comment," Tom said. "You of all people would be conscientious of your food and only serve the highest quality. It's just where I've been ..."

Carlo waved it off.

"Did you deliver the Naintosa grants to the governments?" Davis asked.

Tom reached for some cured ham. "That money, of course, sealed the deals."

"I will wait until the crops are ready to harvest and then send a journalist to write stories about how you're helping feed the starving Africans." Davis looked proud of himself. "I'll let you know well in advance, so you can be there for photo ops."

"That'll work," Tom said.

Carlo reached for an olive. "What else?"

"Oh." Tom sat up. "I just forwarded another thirty million to the seed bank fund."

"That will help with the final phase," Davis said.

"How long before it's operational?" Tom asked. "I'd like to go see it."

"It's still a few years before we can transfer the seed," Davis said. "Maybe then you can see it."

"Fair enough," Tom said. "Did anyone ever find the American who was trying to get to the seed bank from Nordkapp?"

Carlo and Davis looked at each other, then at Tom.

"What American?" Davis asked.

By the expression on Tom's face, he was surprised yet happy he knew something they didn't. "A suspected American journalist tried to charter a boat to get close to the seed bank and then hire a guide on snowmobile to get him the rest of the way."

"And what happened?" Carlo asked.

"Luckily, he spoke to the owner of the company that supplies cargo for Naintosa. They tried to stall him, but the American got away before Naintosa's security arrived. He disappeared. The description was vague, because he wore a parka and a scarf that covered most of his face."

"Any idea if he found another way to the seed bank?" Davis asked.

"As you know, Nordkapp is the northernmost town in Norway and the point he'd have to depart from. No one unauthorized has left from there, so I very much doubt it," Tom said.

Carlo made note of finding out more but didn't show signs of concern.

"It's not the first time someone has tried to get a close-up of the construction." Davis reached for his third slice of bread. "I'm sure it's nothing to be too worried about. But thank you for bringing it to our attention."

Tom turned his attention to Carlo. "It's good to see the algorithms progressing so well. I understand you've almost finished the beta testing stage." Tom made his fortune in computer software, so he knew what he was talking about. His people were partnering with Carlo's people to create the programs to collect personal data when people were on the Internet.

"Thank you again for funding your part," Carlo said. "It'll be very useful for your future plans as well."

"Yes, it will." Tom looked determined. "Gentlemen, I know I've asked before and you've turned me down, but I can't leave it alone. I need to be a part of the main group. We would all benefit greatly, working as equals together."

Davis took a drink of wine.

Carlo reached for cheese to put on his bread.

Tom looked at Davis. "You're the past chairman." Then he turned his head toward Carlo. "And you're the current chairman. Surely you two can make the necessary recommendations to make me a member of the *Club*."

"Tom, you know it doesn't work that way and isn't that easy,"

Carlo said. "You can't just buy your way in. And your money is too new. Keep working hard, and maybe your son or his son will eventually become members."

"But with all that's happening and going to happen."

"You're on the preferred list," Carlo said. "You and your family will be fine."

Tom stood, all politeness drained from his face. "But I need more control. I need to be part of the overall decision-making."

Carlo and Davis looked at him, but neither said anything.

Tom cleared his throat. "You may change your minds."

"Keep up the good work and we'll see." Carlo knew he was treating Tom like a subservient employee, dangling a carrot he'd never taste. Just because Tom had more money didn't mean he had more power. Davis and Carlo held those cards.

The disappointment was clear on Tom's face. "I'm not going to let this go."

"I don't expect you to." Carlo rose to shake his hand. "Thank you again for all your funding."

After Tom left the room, Davis asked, "Why do you keep giving him hope?"

"You don't want him to give up and stop doing our bidding and donating money, do you?"

Davis began to laugh and then clutched his abdomen. "Ouch. Don't know where that came from."

# CHAPTER 12

*May 6, 2003*

We were on the road to London by 7:30 a.m. to buy the final supplies. I wanted to drive, and no one objected. Jorge was in the passenger seat of the Range Rover, giving directions, and Sue and Lorraine were in the back seat.

Traffic wasn't as heavy as we'd projected.

The store we'd found was for winter sports, mainly skiing. It was the only one around, due to there being a lack of ski hills in England, let alone deep snow in winter. And of course, it was past the season. The last stretch of our coming journey would be by snowmobile within the Arctic Circle, so we needed special underwear, jackets, pants, gloves, boots, and goggles.

"Make sure everything is white," I said.

Sue nodded as she looked for a jacket in her size and a design she liked.

Jorge and Lorraine looked at me as if they were surprised by the number of orders I'd given that morning. I'd felt clear as to our objective and convinced myself that my premonition meant just to be careful.

It took over an hour of combing racks and shelves, trying things on, before we each had what we needed.

As we loaded the back of the SUV with our bulky purchases, Sue stopped and looked toward the end of the store exterior. "I noticed that pudgy guy over there looking through the window when we were inside, and now he's been watching us ever since we got to our vehicle. He's pretty close to what I envisioned Ogden Dundst would look like."

Everyone stopped what they were doing.

I backed up a few steps from the rear hatch of the Range Rover until I was next to Sue. Between a parked car and the sidewalk, about sixty yards away, stood a man with a round face, long nose, thin lips, and weak chin. He had sunglasses on and was facing in our direction. His hands were in his brown jacket pockets.

He must've realized we were looking at him and took a step back behind the hood of the parked car.

"I'm going to have a word with him." Jorge began walking toward the man.

"Wait for me." I was right behind Jorge.

"Not without us." Lorraine closed the Rover's back hatch and then joined Sue, who was catching up to me.

The man stumbled backward, got his footing, turned, and ran.

"He's guilty of something," I said under my breath and began running after him.

Jorge was going full tilt, but I overtook him. Glancing to my side I was surprised at how fast Lorraine could run. Sue was right on our heels—she was so athletic that her size didn't matter; her legs moved in a speedy blur. We all gained on our target.

His short legs were pumping and arms flailing. At the end of the block he turned right around a three-story building.

When we came around the corner, he was at the end of a short block and went right again.

I kept my breathing steady to match my footfall, remembering the long-distance running tip Sue had taught me years ago.

We all pushed forward, harder. Lucky there weren't many people on the street.

We turned at the next corner and saw we'd gained most of the ground. Our prey was running out of steam. He ducked into an alley. I followed with Jorge behind me. Lorraine and Sue kept going straight to the end of the next short block.

The guy stumbled and stopped running, looking back at us. He was at a dead end and out of breath.

Jorge and I slowed to a jog as we came up to him.

"You've got nowhere to go," I said.

He turned to us, chest heaving, and pulled what looked like a six-inch kitchen knife from his pocket. "This ... is ... for ... you ... you ... fuc—"

Lorraine came bolting at full sprint, plowing into the chubby man. The knife went flying, and so did he. Two garbage cans slowed his momentum before he hit the brick facade wall, and then Lorraine used him to cushion herself from hitting the wall. His body flattened as she pushed into him, and he projectile puked. Fortunately for Lorraine, his head was pointing to the side of her. She let go of him, and he crumpled to the ground.

Lorraine stumbled back, and I ran up to catch her. "You okay?"

"Fine." She wobbled and placed her arm on the wall for balance.

I looked over to where Lorraine and Sue had come from. *Wow.* The alley wasn't a dead end; it took a ninety-degree turn to the next street. They'd taken a gamble at flanking him, and it had worked.

Jorge was on the man, who was groaning in pain. He placed his knee on the guy's right side and searched his pockets. Finding a wallet, he opened it.

"This clown really is Ogden Dundst." Jorge held up his driver's license.

"Too stupid to even change his name," Sue said.

There were sirens, and they were coming in our direction.

"Someone must've called the police," I said.

"Nick, we'll stay here and explain that this asshole was stalking Sue and Lorraine, pulling a knife on us when we confronted him," Jorge said. "You shouldn't be here because you were just released from house arrest. Go the opposite direction and meet us back at the truck."

He was right. "Okay, I'll wait for you there." I jogged off through the alley from where Sue and Lorraine had come.

The sirens were really close now.

It ended up that we had almost gone full circle to the winter adventure store. Luckily, I'd driven and had the keys in my pocket.

How was Dundst able to find us? For sure he wasn't Naintosa security.

I chose the back seat in case I needed to duck down.

▷◁▥▷◁

It had taken almost an hour for the others to return.

Jorge took the driver's seat. "We have to go to a local police station to give statements."

Sue climbed into the back seat next to me. "Dundst needed an ambulance." She gave an approving look to Lorraine in the front passenger seat.

"Are you okay, Lorraine?" I asked a second time.

"He was soft in the middle." Lorraine faced forward. "He deserved it."

"Man, did you plow him," Sue said.

"That was a great flanking move," I said.

Jorge reached over and patted Lorraine's shoulder. "Well done."

Lorraine shook her head. "No one messes with us and then pulls a knife."

The three of them agreed on what to say on the short drive to the station.

⋈

Again, I'd waited in the back seat, as it took another hour for them to give their statements.

"How'd it go?" I asked as soon as everyone was back in the Rover.

"The police checked to see who we were and seemed suspicious of us but didn't have any reason to not believe us," Sue said.

Jorge was driving. "Lorraine caused some damage, so Dundst had to be taken to the hospital. I'll find someone to keep tabs on him."

We had to make one more stop at an outdoor equipment store that sold climbing gear, for two long ropes, carabiners, and ice screws.

On the way back to Burford, we thought of ways that Dundst could've tracked us but never came up with anything conclusive. Jorge was going to have our computers swept for any monitoring software, because that was the most obvious.

Eugene was at the gate talking to his brother Sam, and with a wave, opened it when we arrived.

"Ivan must be here," Sue said.

"Thought he wasn't coming for two more days," I said.

We unloaded the bags full of our purchases and piled them to one side in the foyer.

"This will be our staging area," I said. "We'll bring everything out here tomorrow and check it against the list."

"We're ahead of schedule. Maybe we can leave before Saturday," Sue said. "Let's go find Ivan."

"I'm thirsty," I said.

When we opened the kitchen door, right in front of us were Ivan and Rose in an embrace, kissing.

"What the ..." I stopped in my tracks.

"I guessed that was going on," Sue said. "We'll come back later."

Ivan and Rose pulled apart, both blushing, yet still holding hands.

"Our apologies," Ivan said. "We wanted to keep this private. Everyone has more important matters to focus on."

"We have nothing to hide or be ashamed about." There was defensiveness in Rose's voice. "We're adults."

I was coming out of my initial shock. "Of course ..."

"I think it's sweet," Sue said. "You two make a nice couple."

"Yeah," was all I could think of to say. Sue and I weren't the only ones hooking up.

Ivan brought Rose's hand to his lips and winked at her. "We have things to discuss." He gently let go and motioned for us to follow him out to the living room.

Rose smiled at Ivan. "I'll finish making dinner." She seemed happy no one had objected.

"Thank you, my dear." Ivan smiled back at Rose as if happy that their secret was now out in the open.

It was kind of mushy, but seeing them there together—they did make a good fit.

We went to the living room. Sue sat down on the couch, Ivan and I in the chairs.

"First, I hope you don't mind that Rose and I have a special relationship? She is a wonderful lady, and it truly will not affect my work."

"Of course it won't affect anything. You don't need our approval, even though we fully give it." I took a quick peek at Sue. "As long as you're happy."

Sue looked back at me and then Ivan. "Yes, Ivan, we wish you and Rose only the best."

Ivan paused to glance at both of us. Did he suspect that Sue and I had gotten together?

I changed the subject. "So, what did you want to talk about?" We had nothing to hide, but ... whatever. "Is the Council okay, now that my charges have been dropped?"

"Yes, they are comfortable again," Ivan said. "There have been new developments in the research. First, the glyphosate study is complete, and all our hypotheses are confirmed. It definitely destroys people's immune systems and is cancer-causing—yet another confirmation of Naintosa's plan to hurt the population."

"Is the study written?" Sue asked. "What happens next?"

"It will be finished within a week. Then it will go out for peer review. If all goes well it will be published within six months. I know of a journal that isn't influenced by Naintosa that will cover it; others, I'm not so sure will want to take on the giant. The Council also wants to make a special presentation to the World Health Organization. With Dr. Schmidt dead, we hope they will be more receptive."

"Great," Sue said. "How is the neonicotinoids study coming?"

Ivan leaned forward. "That is urgent, because we are already seeing a strong decline in bee populations in countries that are spraying neonicotinoids. There is a definite correlation between neonicotinoids and the destruction of bees' nervous systems."

"I just can't wrap my head around that," Sue said. "Even if they succeed at wiping out a large part of the population, they're still going to need bees."

"Yes, I am not sure what their plan is there," Ivan said.

Neonicotinoids were a new class of insecticides that hadn't been thoroughly tested yet. Initial findings showed that they weren't only toxic to insects and bees, but trace amounts of ingestion were causing problems right up the food chain to humans. After a period of exposure, neonicotinoids caused immune-system suppression and sterility, just for a start. It was another cog in the population control plan. "When will that study be finished?"

"Six months. Then it will go through the same process as the glyphosate study."

"Okay, you're making great progress." I moved to get up.

"There is another development that I am sorry I had to keep quiet until now." Ivan raised his hand. "Are you still planning on going to Naintosa and Pharmalin's Colombia lab after you come back from the seed bank?"

"Yes," I said.

"When do you think you will be ready?"

"We leave in three days for Norway, so ..." I calculated in my head. "Two weeks, most likely."

"I will be coming with you to Colombia." Ivan looked proud. "I have been able to secure an informant at the lab."

"That's what you've been keeping secret?" Sue said. "That's great."

"We are very fortunate that a scientist who has a conscience and is very concerned about what is happening has reached out to me. It is very dangerous for them."

"Excellent. That's going to be a great help to us," I said.

"I have spoken with Jack, and he and Lee will meet us in Bogota when we are ready. Then we will all proceed to a location near the lab and establish a safe line of communication with our informant." Ivan stood and went to his briefcase, which was standing next to where we kept the liquor. When he returned to his seat, he opened the hard-shell case and pulled out a file folder holding paper. "Here is what we have received, so far." He held out two sets of stapled pages.

Sue and I went to retrieve them.

"This is a summary that I hope to obtain details on when we reach Colombia. Apparently the genetically engineered wheat and soy are having a much faster effect on people than was expected, and the glyphosate contamination is compromising the population more strongly than anticipated. The United States has the largest proliferation and has been hit the hardest."

"Maybe we'll get to find out why the US is the biggest target," I said.

"Yes." Ivan turned to the second page. "Here is a chart that shows stages for their genetic engineering and pesticide proliferation that gauges their progress."

Sue pointed to the lines on the page. "Look how systematically and intentionally they're poisoning innocent people."

"They are at stage four when they should only be at stage two," Ivan said. "That is five to seven years ahead of where they want to be."

"How many stages are there?" I asked.

"I am not sure." Ivan directed us to the next page. "Stage one is the compromise of people's immune systems. Stage two is the large increase of allergies and digestive issues. Stage three is an increase of diseases like dementia, colitis, and Crohn's, kidney failure, heart diseases, obesity, autism, diabetes, etcetera. Stage four is the sharp increase of many cancers, but mainly colon cancer. I hope to find out the next stages from our informant."

"Could it be spiraling out of control?" Sue asked.

"It suggests that they cannot manage what they have created." Ivan stood. "Jack has not seen this information yet, so I must go fax it to him."

"I need to call Jack about a few last seed bank details." I went to the phone sitting on the bar. "I'll tell him it's coming."

# INTERLOGUE 4

Peter Bail had been in hiding. He'd done way worse in his life, so it would be a shame if he went down over killing a not-so-important someone like Morgan Elles. He'd been a soldier, then worked his way up to become Naintosa's chief of security and most recently, a freelance security specialist. Each time killing had been part of the job.

He still wasn't exactly sure how he'd slipped up enough to allow for Hendrick Schmidt V's people to find him. But the offer had been one he didn't want to turn down monetarily, especially since he'd planned to do it all along. Now he was getting paid for it.

Peter wasn't surprised to hear about Dr. Schmidt IV's death. He'd predicted someone was going to take him out. But he'd known Barnes hadn't had anything to do with it, even though Peter wished he had. Peter's ego was still bruised from Barnes kicking the shit out of him in the woods outside of Vancouver; he'd never thought the guy had it in him.

Peter wasn't sure what he thought of Junior taking over the Schmidt empire. He always thought of him as a spoiled, entitled little dick. However, Hendrick V now controlled the purse strings, and they had a just-wipe-all-the-fuckers-out-and-be-done-with-them attitude in common.

After this and the next job were complete, he'd have enough money to retire in Belize for good and live like a king.

This time he was going to complete the assignment his way; he'd been given free rein. Peter had the list of people who had to be eliminated—not that he needed the names written down. He knew all the "soon to be deceased" well. The decision of who would go when was strictly based on geography. The first was closest to where Bail had been hiding; the only one currently in North America. After Dallas, it was on to England, and last, Oslo.

The main house was well inside the white fences of what used to be a working ranch. Peter had spent days figuring out how to get around the cameras on the property. The hardest parts were the open spaces between the rock outcroppings and buildings he used as cover. Luckily the grass was high because there were no cattle grazing. Then he had to navigate the motion detectors and more cameras that would sound the alarm in the house. But he knew what he was doing and was neither seen nor heard.

Peter had dressed in earth-tone camouflage to blend in with the environment and wore a brown Dallas Cowboys cap pushed low over his green eyes. His goal was to be a six foot two, lean and muscular shadow.

The stifling afternoon Texas sun would soon set. Inside the house, the air conditioning made it cool.

He'd made his way to Jack Carter's bedroom and into his spacious walk-in closet. He saw that half of the clothes in there were a wealthy woman's. There were jeans and cotton shirts that she would wear on a ranch, alongside designer labels and pastel-colored dresses, silk tops and sequined gowns. Peter deduced that Jack hadn't yet had the courage to put away his wife Connie's clothes after she'd died of cancer four years ago. Love meant weakness to Peter, and he never let it get in the way.

He made sure the silencer was screwed on tight, sat down on a fancy mahogany chair with a blue cushion and placed the gun on his lap. Jack would be coming home at any time.

Jack was responsible for the deaths of two of his operatives in Maui when Peter had been Naintosa's security chief. He'd also had a part in the deaths of two operatives and Brad Caulder, whom Peter freelanced with when they'd tried to capture the resisters outside of Vancouver. Now it was payback time.

It wasn't long before he heard voices.

"I'm going to have a quick shower." Jack's voice came from the entrance of his bedroom. "Trudging around that fractured site was dirty work."

"Me too." It was Lee, from farther away. "Then I'll send the satellite photo of the seed bank to Nick."

Hearing Nick Barnes's name made Peter's blood instantly boil. It couldn't be soon enough for Peter to look Barnes in the eyes when he put a bullet between them.

"Okay, you do that, and I'll start the watershed contamination report," Jack said. "And we have to eat at some point. I sure miss Rose's cookin'."

"I'm going to get a beer to wash the inner dust away." Lee was almost shouting now, obviously walking away. "You want one?"

"Sure."

Peter had to wait until after Lee had come back with the beer and then went to have his shower. It wouldn't be wise to take on both men at the same time. Actually, if Peter could shoot Lee from a distance, it would be best. He didn't want to get too close to Lee Donald. Jack was different; Peter wanted Jack to know he was going to kill him. He looked forward to watching the life flow out of Jack.

Within two minutes he heard footsteps on the tile floor and then Lee say, "Here you go. I'll find us something to eat after."

"We should be able to scrounge enough for a couple sandwiches,"

Jack replied. "We need to get groceries tomorrow, 'cause now we're going to be here for another week and a half."

Peter heard the bedroom door close and footsteps retreat. Now was the time. He moved in silence to the closet door and slowly opened it. Across the room he could see Jack putting down a bottle on the dresser and then unbutton his shirt.

That's when Jack noticed him in the mirror and turned. It wasn't a fast turn of surprise, but an almost expectant slow motion.

Peter raised his silenced revolver a few degrees higher, aiming to the middle of Jack's head.

Both men took a step toward each other, narrowing the gap.

"You knew this day would come," Peter said.

"Not sure what you mean," Jack replied. "I didn't know if you were dead or alive. Plus, you're hired security, not a cold-blooded killer."

"I've been hired to do this as preventative security." Peter took three steps to the edge of the bed—if Jack lunged at him, it would be in his way.

"Who hired you to kill me?" Jack asked.

"I don't think it'd be too hard for you to guess."

"Why do you bother?" Jack stared at Peter. "Why do you do their dirty work? You know they're evil and don't give a rat's ass about you. Why don't you do some good with your life for once?"

"A man has to make a living. The others are next. You've all made me look bad, ruined my reputation. This will rectify that."

Jack's eyes narrowed, and he took a step forward. "Sounds like this has become more personal for you than just a job."

"Maybe."

"If you kill me and my friends, it's not going to stop the world from finding out what your employers are doing to the population. The information is already out there. It's too late."

"I don't give a shit about that."

"If you get caught, do you think Davis Lovemark or Carlo Da Silva are going to rescue you? Do you really think they care about what happens to you? They probably want you eliminated too because you're a loose end."

"They weren't the ones who hired me."

Jack paused for a second and changed gears. "Ah, it's the little fucker who likely killed his daddy, now wanting to clear out the opposition."

"Now you got it."

Jack stood straighter, and there was a slight movement of his right hand. "He's the one who needs the bullet between the ears."

"Normally I'd ask if you'd pay me more to have the bullet meant for you dispensed into my employer." Peter's finger flinched on the trigger. "But I want you dead."

"I'm at peace with dying." Jack looked calm. "I get to see my beloved, Connie, again. It's you who has to live with what you've done."

"That's nothing that a lot of bourbon, pussy, and a beach won't cure."

"Suit yourself, asshole. I'll take you out when you arrive in hell."

The phone on the nightstand began to ring. That distracted Jack for a split second.

Honestly, Peter admired Jack Carter. He was a tough and smart old guy with a lot of spunk still in him. So, he pulled the trigger twice, before he changed his mind.

Jack fell back against the dresser, the back of his head splattered across the shattered mirror.

Peter sighed and then realized Jack's fall had made too much noise. They'd talked for too long. He needed to get to Lee before he knew what was going on.

When Peter came around from the bed he noticed Jack's right hand—there was a gun in it. How hadn't he seen it earlier? If he hadn't killed Jack when he did, that sly fucker could've taken him out. Peter was tempted to put another bullet into him for good measure.

In a slow motion he opened the bedroom door and peered out into the empty hallway. Peter's rubber soled shoes made minimal noise, but he only took two steps out from the bedroom when he heard the squeak of skin tracking on tile.

Lee, in only his boxer shorts, muscles straining, came flying from around the corner.

Peter raised his gun and fired.

That didn't stop Lee.

How could he have missed at such close range?

All the air from Peter's lungs purged in the instant Lee hit him with full force.

⫸⫷

Lee had gone to the hall closet for a fresh towel. The house was usually silent. Now he could hear faint talking, a phone ring, a muffled bang, and then a thud. Something wasn't right.

Lee walked at a brisk pace down the short hallway to where it intersected—one way to the living area, the other leading to Jack's bedroom.

As Lee turned the corner he saw Peter Bail, holding a gun, coming out of Jack's room. In that instant he knew Jack was dead and only one objective entered his mind—kill Bail.

Lee barely noticed Bail's gun raise and the burst of light come from the silenced barrel.

His target was Bail's chest. It only took a few strides to propel his six-foot-three-inch body with 220 pounds of muscle and bone like a projectile. Lee pounded into his target, raising his right forearm up to Bail's neck as they collided.

Bail was almost Lee's size, but Lee had the momentum. Bail's head hit hard on the solid floor; Lee made sure of it. The gun went flying, bouncing and skittering out of reach.

Both men were experts at this type of combat. There was a flurry of moves by both of them to gain control and inflict damage on the other. Blood mingled, splattered, and ran everywhere as each landed critical blows.

Lee's single objective meant there was no other outcome. He focused, and everything went into slow-motion.

Both were on their knees, each preventing the other from getting to their feet. Lee deflected a left and then a right before seeing the opening as Bail's right arm recoiled. Lee drove the heel of his left hand up, directly into Bail's nose, shattering it. The force of the blow knocked Bail back off his knees and flat on his back.

Lee didn't hesitate. He lunged forward and landed three hard elbows to Bail's midsection, evacuating the air from his lungs and disorienting him. Then Lee wrapped his right forearm around Peter's neck, squeezing as hard as he could and threw Bail's upper body over and around him, twisting. The head stayed straight, but the body rotated 180 degrees. The neck snap was audible.

Bail went limp. He was dead.

Lee lay there for a moment with Bail's body half over him, not relieving the pressure. Then he pushed the lifeless hunk of meat away.

Lee tried to get to his feet and slipped on the bloody floor. He didn't know how much was his and how much was Bail's. He used the wall for support. Looking down he saw a round hole in his skin, on his left side just above the pelvis—blood oozing from it.

He placed his hand over the wound to temper the discharge and with ginger steps went to the bedroom. There Lee saw Jack's body. *I'm so sorry I failed you, my dear friend. You're the best man I've ever known, and I swore to protect you ... yet I didn't.* A tear formed and ran down Lee's cheek, making a clean line on his bloodied face. A tear hadn't made the passage down Lee's face since he was a child; when his own father, his first mentor, had died. *I am so sorry for failing you.*

The periphery of his vision blurred. Gray turned to black from behind Lee's eyes as he collapsed.

# CHAPTER 13

*May 7, 2003*

There had been no answer the two times I'd tried to reach Jack late last night. I saw the Roman numerals on the study's antique clock and subtracted the six-hour time difference. It was 1:00 a.m. in Dallas, so I'd try him again in six hours.

I'd decided to tell Sue about my seed bank premonition. She should know before we went. "Sue?"

There were multiple pops of what sounded like firecrackers going off in the distance.

At the same time, the thin clatter of plastic bouncing off the hardwood floor made me look down.

"Oops." Sue bent to get her pen. "What?"

It rolled toward my side of the desk. "I'll get it for you."

Splinters of glass blew out from the window and the screen of Sue's computer exploded.

I was thrown from my hunched position, all the way to the ground. The top of the high-back chair had a hole in it, right where my chest had been seconds ago. It was propelled backward on its rollers from the impact.

Sue was lying on the floor next to the desk staring at me, looking stunned. There was glass, plastic, wood, and chair stuffing raining down.

"We're under attack!" Sue yelled.

"Crawl toward me." Jorge had come to the edge of the doorway, revolver in his hand.

We could hear movement outside.

Sue crawled on her elbows and knees toward Jorge.

I went to get up on my elbows but slipped. There was a smearing of blood. I felt my ear—it was sticky, wet, and had a gash in it. That was my blood on the floor. A searing pain welled up. I rolled over, pushed off from a desk leg, and dove across the room. On the landing, I caught a piece of glass on my arm.

Sue got up, took a few strides and dove, just as books on the shelf exploded beside us. She hit me, bounced off and landed spread eagle in the hallway.

Jorge reached and pulled me by the arm the last few feet to get me out of the room.

Sue rolled over and sat up. "What the fuck is happening?"

"We didn't see them coming." Jorge sounded winded. "They shot Sam. Then Lorraine shot them. Another must be on the wall outside the study. I don't know how many more there are."

I got to my feet. Touching my ear, I felt the source of the blood—it was a trickle, not a gush.

"Let's see." Sue surveyed the side of my head. "You're going to need stitches."

"I'll worry about that later." I pinched the gash, and it stung but was manageable. "We need guns."

"Ivan is getting them." Jorge began to run down the hall.

Sue and I followed.

There was a washroom on the right, and I ducked into it. I didn't even glance into the mirror, just grabbed a wash cloth on the vanity and ran back out. While I caught up to the others I pressed the cloth to my ear and then my arm.

As we came into the foyer, Ivan entered from the living room. He had a gun in each hand. Ivan passed the Glock 18 semiautomatic pistols to us, the ones we were taking to the seed bank. Then he pulled his own out from the back of his belt.

"Where's Rose?" I asked.

"She's in a safe hiding place." Ivan was already backtracking to the living room.

We followed and went to the window that looked out toward the front gate. The curtains were open, except for the sheer white ones that always stayed drawn. We stood at the edges, Ivan and Jorge on one side and Sue and I on the other, peering out.

I had the gun in my left hand and the wash cloth to my ear with my right.

We could see Lorraine moving low from tree to tree toward the side of the house where the study was.

Eugene had just gotten to Sam, who was on his back near the front gate. Eugene was on one knee, his left hand on Sam's shoulder. Someone moved, and Eugene in a quick motion brought his gun up and fired four successive shots, two ricocheting off the closed gate bars.

Eugene got to his feet and ran forward as someone in black took off down the street along the side of a house. Eugene stopped at the wrought iron bars, just as the bulky person turned into an alley and was gone. He didn't pursue and went back to Sam.

Two more shots rang out. It must've been Lorraine.

"Let's get out there." Jorge ran toward the front door.

We were right behind him.

Jorge was cautious to open the door in case there was someone out there we'd missed. There wasn't, so he pointed for us to go toward Sam and Eugene, while he went right to where Lorraine had gone.

We kept our heads low and went toward the front gate.

Eugene pulled off his shirt, ripped it in half and pressed one piece against Sam's right calf and the other below his shoulder blade.

There were sirens in the distance, getting closer.

Ivan was next to Sue and me. "I had Rose call the police and ambulance."

By the time we reached Sam and Eugene, a police car, then another, and an ambulance turned onto our street.

Ivan went to his knees, skidding on the gravel up to Sam.

I kept going to the locked gate and opened it.

The police cars—now there were five—stopped just outside our property. The ambulance continued inside.

Two paramedics jumped out. Ivan was pointing and giving them orders as they went to the back to get a gurney and medical kit.

I was still holding the gate but dropped the gun to the ground as officers approached me, their guns drawn.

Lights flashed off the shade of a building on the other side of our perimeter rock wall. Lorraine was on top of the wall pointing to the north. Jorge was standing below on the grass, scanning the area.

The thump of a helicopter close by reverberated in the air.

Officers fanned out and three came up to me.

One had a sergeant insignia on his uniform and looked to be in charge. "Did you see where the remaining shooters went?"

At that moment I saw a man lying facedown, thirty feet away. An officer was kneeling down with his fingers on his neck. That must've been the one Lorraine had killed after he shot Sam.

"Sir?"

"Oh." I pointed down the street. "Into the alley." Then my arm went to the right toward Jorge. "Others were on the wall, trying to shoot us while we were in the study."

The two officers ran back toward their cars.

The one in charge asked, "Were you shot in the ear?"

I tried to pull the wash cloth away, but it was stuck to my ear. "I think some shrapnel caught it. I'll be fine."

I went over what happened, and the tall sergeant in his fifties listened, shouting orders a few times to officers that were passing.

Sue had come up beside us.

The helicopter I'd heard was touching down on the pad at the back of the estate; we could just see it go below the tree line.

An officer came up to us and addressed the sergeant. "The deceased has no identification."

"Thanks, Tim," the sergeant said. "A pro wouldn't."

Lorraine and Jorge had walked up to us.

"I shot him," Lorraine said. "I'm licensed to carry."

"Best you hand it over for now." The sergeant gestured with his right hand.

Lorraine opened her navy-blue jacket to show her shoulder holster with a gun in it.

The sergeant took a glove from his pocket and carefully wrapped it around the firearm handle, pulling it free. "Seamus, come here."

A sturdy, red-haired officer, thirty feet away, jogged over.

The sergeant pointed at Lorraine. "Take her and her weapon and process them at the van. Make sure her permit is for real."

The officer nodded and gestured for Lorraine to go to a police van that had just arrived.

Three men in suits came around the corner of the house from where the helicopter had landed. They walked straight to where Sam was being loaded onto a gurney.

"Is anyone else here carrying a weapon?" the sergeant asked.

"I am," Jorge said. "And that big guy, Eugene, over there. We're both licensed."

"Were either of them fired in this altercation?"

"Eugene's," Jorge said.

Mine had been picked up by one of the initial police officers, and I didn't know where Sue's or Ivan's was. Jorge looked at us but didn't say anything, nor did we.

The sergeant motioned for two more officers to come over. He instructed one to take Jorge's gun, the other to do the same with Eugene and take them both to the van.

The paramedics were wheeling Sam to the ambulance, with Ivan next to them.

It started to rain.

✕

Ivan had gone in the ambulance with Sam. All Eugene could tell us was that his brother was still alive.

Eventually another van showed up and transported us, including Rose, to a nondescript building in Oxford. There we were led into a windowless room with cots and an adjacent bathroom with showers and given some stale sandwiches. There we waited.

A woman who said she was a doctor came, gave my ear two stitches and a bandage and wrapped my arm in gauze and tape.

After two hours Ivan joined us.

"How's Sam?" I asked.

Eugene had come over right away. "Yeah, how's my brother?"

Ivan looked thoughtful. "He is in surgery, hit in the leg and shoulder. Sam will be okay, but it will take time to heal."

You could see the relief in Eugene's eyes.

There was nothing on the concrete white walls except for one plain black-and-white clock. It read 4:02 p.m. when seven people came into the room and individually asked each of us to follow them.

I was escorted into a small square room that only contained a rectangular metal table with a chair on either side.

I went to the far chair and sat down. I knew this was just procedure and we were safe, but still felt like I was about to be interrogated.

After what seemed like fifteen minutes, a tall man with dark hair, wearing a charcoal suit, entered the room. He was holding a small recorder and placed it on the table. "Mr. Barnes, my name is Lieutenant Thompson, Special Services."

The hair stood on the back of my neck. I'd met a Lieutenant Thompson with a Special Unit a few years ago. He'd turned out to be a killer for Naintosa. But I'd seen him die by a bullet from Jack's gun, and this guy didn't look like him. I took a deep breath. *The name is just a coincidence.*

"It was unfortunate what happened this morning." He pressed the record button. "Do you feel up to giving your statement?"

I recognized that he was one of the men who'd come to the estate by helicopter.

"I can understand why you'd be shaken up." He had a stiff British accent. "Being shot at is traumatic, and it never happens in Burford. However, what you tell me may help us find who did it and their motive."

I recalled that the first time I'd been shot at was by the now dead Lieutenant Thompson, outside Morgan's townhouse in Seattle. I never wanted to get to the point where someone shooting a gun at me was not traumatic—that could be fatal. Was I in shock? Probably, yet I was calm. I only felt a slight throb coming from my ear.

"Mr. Barnes? Do you understand? Are you all right?"

I looked at the Lieutenant. He had a trustworthy face. "Sure."

"Can you tell me what happened in as much detail as you can remember?"

I told him everything, starting with the window of the study being blown out and ending with Sam being taken away by ambulance.

He listened, seeming sympathetic, and nodded on occasion.

When I was finished, he said, "You've had a considerable amount of ..." He paused, obviously choosing his words. "... run-ins the last three years, including being recently suspected in the murder of Dr. Hendrick Schmidt."

"But I didn't kill him."

"Yes, I understand," he said. "Do you think what happened today was connected to your *activity?*"

"Of course."

# CHAPTER 14

*May 8, 2003*

We were told we'd have to spend the night in that room. The cots were uncomfortable. Meals were bland food out of Styrofoam containers. The stay was supposed to be for our own protection, but we felt like prisoners.

"I think we should just leave," I said.

We were sitting on metal chairs facing each other in an almost circle.

"We don't know exactly who tried to kill us," Sue said. "And at least two of them are still out there. They were pretty brazen, so they could try again, anywhere."

"Maybe because you were not charged with Dr. Schmidt's murder and they wanted to get even," Ivan said.

"That's what I was thinking," I said.

"They were professional and aggressive," Eugene said.

"What do we do when they let us out of here?" Sue asked.

"We go ahead with our plan to go to the ..." I was stopped by Jorge waving his hand.

He mouthed, *bugged.*

When we were first arriving, Jorge had pointed out that what we said could be recorded at any time, so we needed to be careful about what we talked about. It'd slipped my mind for a second.

Ivan looked around the room. "I would like for Rose to come stay with Eugene and me, while you all are … away. Then the next phase, we all go together as planned."

Rose nodded. "I can't stay at the Burford house now."

"We need to talk to Jack," Jorge said. "He doesn't know what's happened."

Both Jorge and I had tried to call Jack on our cell phones many times yesterday and today. We talked to Jack every day, so this was unusual.

An officer walked into the room. "Mr. Barnes, please come with me."

I followed, not knowing what it was about, hoping they were going to tell me we were free to go.

I was led down a hall to a room identical to the one in which I'd given my statement yesterday.

I was surprised to see Chief Inspector Plante come in a minute later. He was wearing a black suit, white shirt, and black tie. That reminded me that I was in the same track pants and T-shirt that I'd been wearing yesterday and had slept in, and that I hadn't had a shower. At least I'd brushed my teeth.

"Monsieur Barnes."

"Chief Inspector."

He took a seat across from me. "You lead a dangerous life and have enemies that obviously want you eliminated."

"Do you know who it was this time?"

"Not exactly, yet."

I sat forward and placed my arms on the table. "I bet you're pretty sure who's behind it."

"I have my suspicions." He leaned forward and placed *his* arms on the table. "Why don't you tell me who you suspect, first?"

"Well, in the past it's been Naintosa's security, but they usually get in and abduct you, not start shooting from a distance," I said. "My guess is that it was freelancers ... hired assassins. Who hired them would be the next question. I don't know if he is less or more ruthless than his father, so I'm not sure if it was Hendrick Schmidt V."

Plante gave me a penetrating stare. "So, who else?"

Him saying that took me aback, but I tried not to show it. "Could be Davis Lovemark, Carlo Da Silva, or all three of them."

"Why would you suspect them?"

"Really?" I raised my eyebrows. "Do I have to explain it?"

He didn't flinch or say anything.

"Then there's that guy, Ogden Dundst. But I don't think he's capable of that, let alone have buddies that could help him." I thought for a second. "Or maybe I'm underestimating him."

Plante's face showed some life. "Mr. Dundst was just released from hospital where he was treated for two broken ribs and a collarbone. He is now in jail on several charges."

"More than just stalking us?"

"Related. Mr. Dundst is an unemployed computer technician who was able to hack into the London traffic cameras. We don't know how exactly he was able to know when you'd be coming into the city yet."

I remembered Jorge had intended to get our computers scanned for bugs but hadn't had time. "Could he have hacked into my computer?"

"Possibly." Plante was staring at me again. "Perhaps you should turn your computer over to us."

I didn't like the way he said that.

He must've read my reaction. "What are your plans now?"

"Does that mean you're releasing us?"

"You will be escorted to the Burford home to get your belongings.

You can't stay there while it's an active crime scene." Plante pulled out a pad from his inside suit pocket, jotted something down, and then put it away again. "My suggestion is that you move elsewhere and lead a quieter life not upsetting powerful people."

"Good suggestion." Yeah, right, like I was going to do that.

"Where will you go ... back to the United States?"

"Probably." I hoped he didn't catch that lie.

Plante stood up. "The contents you all take from the estate will be catalogued. Then before you are released, you will have to tell the attending officer where you will be going. As I stated before, you should always inform me of your whereabouts going forward."

I wasn't going to comply with his request; however, we had to rethink what we were going to do. He'd suspect our intentions when he found out that we took winter gear and supplies.

"Let's go." He walked to the door. "I want to speak to your group."

We went back down the hall to the room we'd been held in.

Sue, Ivan, and Jorge knew who Chief Inspector Plante was and looked surprised to see him.

"If I can have everyone's attention," Plante said in his French accent. He then explained what he'd told me about getting our belongings and letting the police know where we were going.

There were lots of glances at me as the others realized we had to rethink our strategy.

"Also, it has come to my attention and I regret to inform you," Plante's voice became sympathetic and slowed. "Jack Carter has been killed."

"What?" *No, that couldn't be.*

"Oh dear God." Rose looked like she was about to faint. Eugene was next to her and helped her to a chair.

Ivan shook his head and looked angry. "Where did it happen?"

"His home in Dallas," Plante said. "I am sorry."

"Fucking hell." Sue had tears in her eyes.

"Do you know who did it?" Jorge's voice hitched.

Plante hesitated, as if weighing how much to tell us. "He was shot by Peter Bail."

*Fucking Peter Bail finally did it.* I felt hopeless. Why Jack? Bail wanted me more than him. Jack was such a great person.

"And what about Lee?" Lorraine asked.

"Lee Donald was shot in the abdomen," Plante said. "He's in the hospital, and I was informed that he will recover." He paused for a second and then continued, "Lee killed Bail."

"Are you sure?" I blurted out. "They thought he was killed before."

"That is the report I received."

"Bail worked for Naintosa and Schmidt before," I said. "They probably came after us at the same time with the goal of killing every one of us at once."

Plante nodded but didn't reply.

*That fucking Peter Bail and that fucking Hendrick Schmidt and that whole fucking Club of mother fucking rich fuckers that thought they ruled the world.* I slumped down on a chair. *Not Jack.*

I heard sobbing and sniffling. I looked up to see how distraught everyone was, except for Jorge and Eugene, who looked downright menacing.

Plante held out his arm. "No one think of doing anything rash. Let the authorities deal with this."

We all looked at him with contempt, and Plante physically took a step back. "I suggest you stick together and go someplace quiet ... someplace safe, until this all can be sorted out."

"Someplace where we'll be easy targets?" Sue grit her teeth. "All bunched together."

"We're now going to Dallas, of course." We had no choice, and I didn't feel the need to hide that. Everyone would suspect that move on our part. It could've been the most dangerous destination for us, but we had to go for Jack. We'd have to figure out how to disappear from there.

Ivan addressed Plante. "Eugene will stay until his brother recovers. The rest of us are going to Dallas to see our friend laid to rest and help the other friend in his recovery."

It was decided. We all went to stand beside Ivan.

Plante nodded. "We will escort you now back to Burford. From there we can take Eugene to the hospital where Sam is. I was told it will take time but Sam will fully recover."

You could see relief on Eugene's large face.

"The rest of you will be taken to Heathrow," Plante continued. "I will contact the authorities in Dallas, but be very careful, there is no guarantee they'll provide any type of security for you."

Jorge went to hug Eugene, which seemed uncharacteristic until I saw him slip a cell phone into his pocket.

# CHAPTER 15

*May 9, 2003*

I was nervous about being out in the open in Dallas, yet relieved we weren't going to the seed bank.

Sue was in the seat next to me, her face pointing toward the little round window with the shade drawn.

I touched her shoulder.

"Are you awake?"

She turned her head toward me, looking tired and solemn.

"I have to tell you something." I adjusted my hip beneath the seatbelt, to face her. "I have to admit that I had a premonition about us going to the seed bank, and it wasn't good. There was blood, ice turning to water, and us drowning."

Sue seemed to contemplate my admission for a moment, then said, "Do you remember when you, Jack, and I meditated, and I told you I had an ominous feeling afterward?"

"Yes."

"It was about the seed bank too."

Thank goodness we hadn't gone to the seed bank.

We landed at Dallas Fort Worth International Airport at 2:10 a.m. local time.

I didn't think any one of us slept much on the flight. I'd probably slept a cumulative two hours when my brain had shut down, needing rest from the sadness of losing Jack and weighing our next options.

"What's our first step?" I asked Sue and Jorge on either side of me, as the plane taxied to the terminal.

"I guess it depends on if someone is waiting for us." Sue had been looking out the window at the lane lights passing by.

"If we're not detained, we need to rent a van and find a hotel," Jorge said. "It's too early to see Lee, and my condo is too small to fit everyone."

I'd forgotten that Jorge had told us Dallas was his home base. Him saying he had a "condo" sounded too normal for him. "Do you have a hotel in mind?"

"There are a few close to the hospital where Lee is."

"What about nearer Jack's ranch?" Sue suggested.

Jorge shook his head. "There's no way anyone is going to let us near there. There's no need anyway."

"Yeah, you're right," Sue said.

As we disembarked the plane, the six of us stuck together. The first thing that struck me as we walked through the terminal was the dryness of the air. The smell of fried food lingered as we passed multiple, closed eateries between gates.

After we cleared customs and collected our luggage, there was no one there to detain us.

We stood together in a huddle.

"This makes me more nervous than if the police were waiting for us," Sue said.

"Agreed," Ivan said.

The other passengers from our flight had dispersed, leaving few people around.

"I'd bet everything that we're being watched," I said.

"There's no way that wouldn't be happening," Jorge confirmed.

Lorraine eyed the room slowly.

Rose looked as nervous as we must have all felt.

I shrugged. "There's nothing we can do about it."

"Let's go rent a van big enough for all of us." Jorge led the way outside the terminal to where the rental agency shuttles were.

The air was thick, like being wrapped in a warm blanket, even at three o'clock in the morning, not like cool and wet England. Dust stirred in the breeze.

We picked up a gray Dodge Caravan, and Jorge drove us into Dallas.

Ivan, sitting in the middle row, was holding Rose's hand and asked, "Do you have your own home here?"

"I had a suite at the ranch," Rose replied. "I'd like to go back there and pick up my belongings."

"We can see if that can be arranged," Ivan said. "Where do you consider home, then?"

"I raised my children in Savannah, Georgia, and my husband is buried there. My son still lives in our home with his young family." Rose's voice was filled with longing. "It's been over a year and a half since I've seen them."

Sue and I were in the third row and kept watching behind us to see if we could spot anyone following us. Traffic was very light on the freeway, but there were cars behind us that travelled at the same speed. When we exited onto another highway, there were two cars that did the same. As we turned into the circular driveway of a four-story hotel, one of the cars drove by, and one parked across the street.

"I spotted the tail," Sue said.

"Right there." It was a midsize gray Chevy sedan, identical to the one that had followed me after I'd met Dr. Elles. A ripple of unease ran through me at the thought of when all this had started, three years ago.

"I'm sure they want to know where we're staying," Lorraine said from the front passenger seat.

"Most likely police." Jorge parked the van to the side of the hotel entrance.

We all got out, keeping an eye on the car across the street. We couldn't see inside from our distance, and no one got out of it.

We checked in, getting three rooms with two queen-size beds each. We'd decided it was time to start being more frugal with money. We were all on the fourth floor but not next to one another.

The interior of the popular hotel chain was about due for a renovation; everything looked worn from heavy use.

Sue's and my room was standard-looking, with brown furniture and gold-colored fixtures. The beige-and-gold striped wallpaper was beginning to lift at the edges.

"It's seen better days." Sue was looking into the bathroom.

I glanced over her shoulder to see a light-gray toilet, tub, and sink. The sink and tub were permanently stained where the water hit the porcelain, but it was clean. "It'll do."

I went over to the window. We were pointing east, because past the highway, between the buildings, on the horizon the dark sky was turning to yellow. "We should try get a couple hours rest."

⬤⬤⬤

I awoke when I heard pipes complain. Looking over at the next bed, I discovered Sue wasn't in it, and the shower was on in the bathroom.

My back was tight, and I felt fatigued.

Reaching over to the nightstand between the beds for the remote control, I saw the red numbers on the digital clock read 7:47 a.m.

We'd slept only three hours.

I turned on the news to see what was in store, weather-wise. It was culture shock to hear everyone speaking in slower southern drawls, compared to the stiff British accents I'd become accustomed to. There had been two domestic shootings last night—that was also something you didn't hear often on the local news in England.

A middle-aged man with a smile way too big pronounced from in front of a chart that it was going to be sunny with the temperature in the high eighties, with sticky, eighty percent humidity for the next five days.

Sue came out of the bathroom wearing a white bra, panties, and a towel around her head like a turban. She looked good. I pushed away a sudden remembrance of our night together; now was not the time for those kinds of thoughts.

"Get your ass out of bed and go have a shower." She opened her suitcase. "How hot is it going to be today?"

"High eighties."

After my shower, shave, and dual bandage replacement, I was ready to face what the day would bring.

When I came out of the bathroom, Sue was putting on finishing touches of eyeliner at the mirror beside the TV. She wore black shorts and an off-white, thin tank top.

The only good thing about having to come to Dallas at that particular time was that I was able to wear shorts, a polo shirt and not have to wear socks.

"Ready? I talked to Jorge while you were lounging in the spa, and we were all supposed to meet in the restaurant five minutes ago." Sue seemed especially blunt that morning.

"Let's go, then."

We grabbed what we needed, anticipating that we'd leave right after breakfast.

The café was busy, and we were the last ones to arrive at our table. Like the rest of the hotel, the restaurant needed a renovation from years of wear and tear.

A middle-aged woman in a black skirt and a white, button-down shirt was standing beside our group, writing down food orders. She looked to be of East Indian origin. When Sue and I sat down, she said, "Good morning, can I get you coffee?"

That took me aback—a Texan drawl coming from a person of her heritage? I'd never experienced that before and smiled. "Yes, please."

As soon as everyone placed their orders, Sue said, "What's the plan?"

"We go to the hospital, which is nearby," Jorge said. "I think the safest place for us would be in Lee's room until I get some protection. I'll need to go to my place to get it."

I assumed Jorge meant firearms.

"I have friends at the police department who may be able to give us some information," Jorge said.

"I know people at the FBI whom I could talk to," Lorraine said. "They might know something."

Everyone looked at her. She'd surprised us more than once.

"Okay, talk to them, but don't give them anything about us," Jorge said.

"Of course." Lorraine showed an annoyed reaction, which was rare. "You think I'd tell them anything?"

Jorge backed down. "No, of course not."

"We're all on pins and needles," Rose said.

After breakfast no one had to go back to their room. One of the many things I liked about our group was that everyone was organized and planned ahead.

Outside it was already warm and humid. The air smelled of a mixture of bacon cooking and asphalt heating. The Chevy that had parked across the street when we arrived was still there. Its tinted windows made it impossible to make out anyone inside.

Sue and I went to the third row of our rental van and positioned ourselves to look out the back window.

"Maybe they weren't following ..." Sue stopped in midsentence as the Chevy's headlights turned on. "There we go."

"At least we know we're being watched," Jorge said from the driver's seat. "We'll factor that in when we need to disappear."

"We have to find out if they are local police, Feds, Naintosa security, or someone else," Lorraine responded from the front passenger seat.

Rose looked worried. Ivan took her hand.

Another car that had been parked about ten spots ahead of the Chevy pulled out after it passed.

"Are our followers being followed?" I asked.

"Could be," Sue said.

We stopped at a red light. There was a small car in-between us and the Chevy. Our van being taller allowed me a view. From the way the sun hit the Chevy's windshield, I could make out two people inside it. Then there was another vehicle in front of the second car that may or may not have been following us.

We moved like a motorcade for the next long block until we reached the Texas Health Presbyterian Hospital. It was a big brown concrete complex, surrounded by a parklike setting. Jorge knew his way around, taking us straight to the parking garage.

As we turned and stopped at the gate to get a ticket, the Chevy, which I could see now was a Malibu, and the other, which was a Ford, drove by.

Jorge was looking through the rear-view mirror. "I'm sure they know why we're here."

After walking for what seemed to be a quarter of a mile, we asked where Lee's room was at an information desk. We had to go up two floors and follow a yellow line around a maze of hallways.

There were no guards outside of Lee's room like we'd anticipated.

He was the only occupant inside, lying in one of two beds. A tube and monitor cord stuck out of his right arm. Lee was awake. There was a bandage over his right cheek and jaw and black and blue bruises around his eyes.

"Hi, Lee." I'd been the first one to enter the room.

Everyone else said hello as they came in.

"What are you all doing here?" Lee focused on us. "It's not safe."

"You mean not safe in the hospital, or in Dallas?" Ivan asked.

"Neither." Lee tried to prop himself up, but you could tell it was painful. "I failed to protect Jack. I can't protect you either. I can't fucking do anything, lying here. Feds have been here, acting like I premeditated killing Bail."

I wondered if the medication Lee was on was making him anxious. His eyes were dilated and his speech pattern unusual for him.

"You do not think Peter Bail acted alone?" Ivan asked.

Rose sat down in the only chair in the room, looking somber.

"You sure Bail is dead?" I had to ask one last time.

"I snapped his neck myself," Lee said. "And Bail only acted when he was paid, so someone put him up to it."

Okay, if Lee himself snapped his neck, then I finally was confident Bail was dead.

"Some people tried to kill us at almost the same time," Sue said.

"Sam was shot and is in a hospital in London," Lorraine said.

"Fuck." Lee tried to move again but winced. "I hadn't heard."

Jorge and Lorraine explained the Burford attack.

Then it was Lee's turn. He told us what he knew of Jack's death and his encounter with Bail. There was both anger and sadness in the room while we listened.

There was a knock at the open door. "Sorry to interrupt." Two men in navy-blue suits walked in. The one in front was four inches shorter and had a shaved head; the taller one behind had a full head of light-brown hair. Both men were probably in their late forties.

"I'm Special-Agent-in-Charge, Furyk, FBI," the bald one said in a gravelly voice, flashing a badge.

The taller one nodded. "Agent Stenson." His voice was an octave higher.

Why was Furyk "special?" That made me not trust him right away.

Looking directly at me, Agent Furyk asked, "Nick Barnes?" He was thick, with a noticeable gut, and barrel-chested. He reminded me of a bulldog. "Can I have a word with you?"

Agent Stenson took a step forward. "Dr. Ivan Popov. May I please have a word with you?"

As I followed Agent Furyk from the room, a woman in a navy-blue pant suit with short, blonde hair came in and went over to Sue.

Furyk led me down the hall to a small meeting room. Ivan and Stenson continued on. I hadn't seen where Sue went; it must've been in the opposite direction.

The room's main purpose was for doctors to have private discussions about patients with their family members. There were two caramel-colored small couches opposite each other, with a cheap wooden table in the middle and a fake fern in the corner.

I went to sit on the furthest couch and took a good look at the special agent. He seemed serious, and my first impression was that he was a bully. "So you're working on Jack Carter's murder investigation?"

"Yes." He'd sat down on the opposite couch. "I just want to get your perspective on a few things."

"Sure." I wanted to make a conscious effort to lead the conversation as long as I could and get as much information as possible before he turned the tables, which he invariably would.

Furyk furrowed his brow. "I'm aware that your group had multiple exchanges with Mr. Peter Bail."

"Have you figured out who he'd been working for?" I leaned forward. "Who ordered the hit?"

"We're not sure yet." Furyk was stone-faced. "We're communicating with his past employers, but at this time it looks like he acted alone. Do you—"

"That wouldn't happen. Bail's motivation was money. He didn't do anything, especially kill someone, without getting paid for it."

"You don't think he acted out of revenge?" Furyk seemed interested in what I was saying, his face showing slight emotion. "Y'all kept getting away from him."

*How did he know that?* "I'm sure that was part of it, but ..." I looked him straight in the eye, wanting to gauge his reaction. "It couldn't be a coincidence that there were attempts on Sue Clark's and my life at almost the same time. Someone is behind both."

Something I'd said triggered a flash of anger in Furyk's gaze. But why? That made me uncomfortable, because I was just stating the obvious. I pressed forward. "It had to be a coordinated effort. They wanted us wiped out at once."

"That's a possibility."

"What do you mean, 'a possibility'?" I leaned halfway across the table separating us. "Are you in touch with Interpol? Have you talked to Chief Inspector Plante? Have they identified the man Lorraine killed? Who's in charge of this investigation? Can I speak with them?"

My barrage of questions made Furyk squint. "Listen, we *are* collaborating with Inspector Plante and Interpol, and we *are* exploring all avenues, I promise you that. But you and your group got yourselves into this mess, and it's hard to believe you didn't think it was going to end up this way sooner or later."

"Exposing the truth always has consequences, especially when it's a plot that affects the population of the entire world. It's worth the risk. Don't you care what's going to happen to you, your friends, your neighbors, the people you work with ... your family?"

"Of course I care. I'm not convinced you do." He was sitting at the very edge of his seat. "Jack Carter is dead, the entire Elles family wiped out, Dr. Bill Clancy, Dr. Kenneth Roth ... do you want me to go on? Their deaths are because of what you've so-called *exposed*."

Okay, he had a good grasp of what had been going on. "You nailed it! So, are you investigating the obvious suspects—Naintosa and Pharmalin security, Hendrick Schmidt four and five, Davis Lovemark, and Carlo Da Silva? They're responsible!"

"No, asshole, *you're* responsible." Furyk's bald head went red, and he wasn't acting "special" anymore. "You're the ones picking on good citizens and their companies, meddling where you shouldn't be."

"What the fuck are you talking about?" I was ready to nail the guy. "You call the most obvious suspects *good citizens* and then say it's our fault? Do you not know what we're desperately trying to prove? These guys are working on culling the population of the Earth! They want to cut it by more than half and at the same time control everyone!" I caught myself yelling and toned it down. "This affects you and everyone you know ... *everyone*. Only the people responsible are safe. Don't you see? This is really important."

"What I see is a liberal, tree-hugging, anti science environmentalist, trying to spread fear and misinformation." Furyk stood. "You and your kind are against any kind of progress. You think mixing science and food is the Devil's work, that we should leave oil in the ground and all put up windmills. The world isn't going to end just because it heats up a few degrees, and Naintosa isn't killing us with their food. Why would any American company do that? It's absurd. This is America, son, and good, God-fearing people don't put up with your shit!"

I didn't bother taking the bait. "Actually, none of the men behind this are American. Well, Lovemark is now a citizen. Oh, and I didn't mention Malcolm Carter, Jack's brother—he has a role in all of this." Now I knew what kind of person Furyk was. He wasn't an unbiased, impartial, FBI agent—he would've steered our talk in a different direction. With him working on our case, I knew we weren't going to get any help. At least I'd found out quickly that we were on our own. "Well, it's good to know how you feel."

"Opinions aside ..." His head was now turning pink and wrinkles relaxing. "If we find any wrongdoing, there will be justice ... on both sides."

*He hadn't responded to my reference to Malcolm or my comments about the others not being American.* "Are we done?"

He pulled a card from his inside suit jacket pocket and handed it to me. "I want you to inform me of your movements at all times— where you go and who you see."

Great, another officer who was going to be disappointed when I didn't report in to him.

# INTERLOGUE 5

Davis sat at his desk, deep in thought. The ever-present pine scent from the air freshener wasn't relaxing him as it was meant to.

Being at the top of San Francisco's Transamerica Pyramid, Global Mark Communications US Media's head office was in the clouds or sometimes above them. Davis didn't often bother to notice the view of the city below, or of the Golden Gate Bridge in the distance. Today, at least, his gaze was pointed toward the floor-to-ceiling window on the west side of his large office.

Davis had needed to become more personally involved as of late in all aspects of his business interests. There was union unrest at two of his major presses. The war in Iraq wasn't going to be won as easily as Bush and his buddies thought. Too many reporters were trying to skirt the direction of the news Davis demanded. Thank goodness his wife and daughters were all happy and content—one less distraction.

Russell Norman, his second in command, had just broken his leg in a late-season skiing accident in Whistler. He'd been trying to keep up with his new twenty-three-year-old mistress—the idiot. Davis had wanted Russell, in the interim, to oversee operations of the genetically engineered food, pesticides, and cancer drugs.

Pharmalin and Naintosa were not Davis's companies, yet Russell could've relieved Hendrick on the business side; surely there wouldn't have been objections to that.

Davis had heard that young Hendrick was on his way to the lab and planned on working from there for the foreseeable future. Hendrick himself hadn't been communicating with Davis or Carlo much in the past few weeks. Their last conversation had ended with Hendrick telling him to back off, that he was going to prove to them he knew what he was doing. That's why Davis needed someone to watch over Hendrick. That and the obvious fact that Hendrick was ordering hits on people without consulting with anyone. The assassinations and attempts were drawing far more attention to all of them and could hurt the execution of their plan.

A sharp pain came from Davis's abdominal area, and he winced, placing his hand on his stomach, which seemed distended. He'd felt the pain on and off for months, and now it was happening more frequently and increasing in severity. He hated having his doctor come to see him except socially, but maybe it was time to check whether anything was wrong.

The sudden change in the light of the room distracted him from his many thoughts. A cloud was passing right in front of the window, blocking the sun's rays.

One of the large double mahogany doors opened, and his latest secretary entered, carrying a tray with tea and an afternoon snack. She'd only started two weeks ago. Davis was going through a big-breast phase, and she fit the bill.

The secretary placed the tray on his glass-topped desk, giving him a view of her assets as she bent forward. He couldn't remember her name ... no matter. He called her "Tits" to everyone but her.

"Can I get you anything else?" She parted her plump, bright-red lips to form a smile and show her perfect white teeth.

The private secure line that sat on the desk rang.

Davis ushered her away with a flip of his hand but waited to get a peek at her round butt under the tight skirt as she departed before picking up the receiver.

"Davis, it's Carlo. Is this a good time?"

"I've been expecting your call."

"I'm on my way to London and then Dallas tomorrow. I thought we should talk before the funeral."

"Let's have dinner after the funeral."

"Sure, but we may not be alone, so let's catch up now."

"Fair enough." Davis leaned back in his black leather and chrome swivel chair. "Have you spoken with Jacques again?"

"Yes," Carlo's voice was strained. "He's very frustrated and wants to pursue Hendrick for giving Bail the order to kill Jack."

"But like Jacques told us, the bug is illegal."

"He wants to investigate, to see if he could find any legal evidence that it was Hendrick behind it," Carlo said. "Why else would Hendrick have had Bail found and contacted shortly before Jack's murder?"

"We can't risk the public exposure, even if I black out my media from covering an investigation," Davis said. "More people than just Barnes's group will put two and two together. If we want to do something about Hendrick, we have to do it internally."

"That's basically what I told Jacques, but you know he's an officer of the law through and through. He's having difficulty leaving it in our hands." Carlo cleared his throat. "And maybe we need to get control of Hendrick instead of just thinking about it. Look at what he's done in such a short period of time, and he hasn't even started managing Naintosa and Pharmalin yet."

"I agree. We'll have to figure out what to do. Let's make sure we put some time aside in Dallas to talk privately." The conversation wasn't helping with Davis's abdominal pain. "What about the attack at Burford? Was it, for sure, Hendrick's doing as well?"

"As you know, none of this is a hundred percent certain." Carlo's voice faded for a second, then came back strong. "According to Jacques, the man who was shot in Burford by Badowski is not known to Interpol. There were, from the looks of it, two more men on the property, but no evidence as to their identity. The security-camera footage shows them in masks with no close-enough angles to see any features. It was a targeted hit, but not an efficient one."

"Who was watching the estate at the time?"

"Naintosa security, I assume."

"Uh-huh." Davis scratched his birthmark. "Currently not credible."

"Agreed."

Carlo sighed. "What else? Has your man established contact with Barnes and the others in Dallas?"

"He has two of his men doing it; he said he gave them orders to scare and cause uncertainty in Barnes."

"Good."

"Things have changed now that Jack is dead," Davis said. "This could be the breaking point for Barnes and his group."

"Yes, no more resources and money," Carlo said. "I doubt the muscle would stay on without getting paid."

"Especially with two out of commission already."

"Let's hope," Carlo said. "Anything else?"

"Tom Crane has begun the takeover of Moile R&D." Davis sat up straighter, having trouble ignoring the pain that persisted.

"Malcolm will make sure the sale happens."

# CHAPTER 16

Jorge and Lorraine were helping Lee sit up in his hospital bed with an extra pillow at his back.

Lieutenant Furyk hadn't followed me into the room, and I didn't bother acknowledge him leaving.

Ivan was standing beside Rose, who was seated and still looking concerned.

Sue came in and closed the door. "What a bitch."

"Yeah, mine was a confrontation," I said. "That was the FBI, for Christ's sake. Granted, I was trying to control the conversation, but what happened to professionalism?"

"That seems to be the tactic they are using," Ivan said. "They want to scare us and hope we disband."

Jorge put his finger to his lips. "Bugged?"

"No offense, Jorge, but I don't give a fuck anymore. I've had it." Knowing that Ivan and Sue had similar conversations pissed me off even more. I took a deep breath—I had to control my emotions.

Jorge and Lorraine glanced at each other, and I could almost see smiles cross their lips. I'd expected Jorge to be concerned about my comment, not approve.

"They figure since Jack is dead ..." From the look in Lee's eyes, I could tell he was going to feel responsible for a long time, probably the rest of his life. "We're done."

I forced myself to calm down. My focus went from Lee, to Jorge, and then to Lorraine. "Technically, you all worked for Jack. Now that's over, so you're free to go at any time. You're not getting paid anymore."

Jorge reached toward the table near him, where he clicked on a clock radio and turned a dial to the right. Country music hissed and rasped out of the small black box. "If you won't listen to me about the bug, this will help."

We all huddled around Lee's bed.

"What are everyone's thoughts going forward?" Lee asked.

"I'm continuing," I strained to whisper. "But that doesn't mean anyone else has to."

"Count me in," Sue said.

"What about the financing?" Ivan said. "I am fine, and with the Council's help will be continuing. However, we do not expect you, Rose, Jorge, Lorraine, and Lee to do the same."

"Fuck that." Lee's tone was higher than a whisper. "I'm helping as soon as I'm able. Jack would be even more pissed at me if I stopped. You're going to need protection now more than ever."

I was happy to hear Lee wasn't quitting. "I'll use my own money. Jack was very generous in paying all the expenses until now and gave me more than needed for any work I did for him."

"Jack recently updated his will, and everyone in this room has been taken care of," Lee said. "Not sure how long it'll take to be executed and if it'll be contested, so in the meantime there are two operating accounts I have access to that can't be frozen. There's plenty in them, and that's what Jack intended them for."

Jorge jabbed Lee in the shoulder. "You're the one who needs protecting right now." Then he looked at Sue and me. "You two couldn't survive a minute without me. So count me in."

"I really respect what you're doing." Lorraine's shoulders went back, and she stood straight. "It's not about the money; it's about helping to do the right thing, and even if my role is only security, I'm happy to play my part."

·Even though I'd said that I'd understand if anyone didn't want to continue, I sure was happy with their responses. "Everyone has many roles. We're a team, and I'm so grateful we're moving forward."

Rose cleared her throat. "I'm sorry, I can't."

Ivan looked down at her and squeezed her hand. "We understand."

"I'm just a cook," Rose said. "I'm too old and not built for this running around."

"You're tougher than you think," Sue said.

There were tears in her eyes. "I'm truly sorry, but this is too much for me."

"It's okay, Rose." I was going to miss her mothering and fussing.

"How about this," Ivan said. "Once things stabilize and we are safe, hopefully in a place like Oslo, we will send for you?"

"That sounds fine." Rose perked up. "Maybe I just need to go to Savannah to see my children and grandchildren for a spell."

Ivan brushed his hand across her cheek and gave a sympathetic smile.

"Okay, it's settled," Lee said. "The money in the accounts will cover all our expenses. But it's not a limitless reserve, so we need it to last for who knows how long until the will is divvied up."

"We should consider pooling the money Jack left us too," Ivan said. "When the time comes."

Lee adjusted in the bed. "Jack had more money than anyone thought. Other than his son and daughter, there's no one else he wanted to give it to. He didn't want either of his brothers to get any; they have more than enough already. So his kids will get half the money and the property. That leaves a good chunk for all of us."

"How big is a *chunk*?" Sue asked.

"Tens of millions, each."

Everyone's eyes lit up.

*What.* "Each?" *Holy shit!*

"What a generous man," Jorge said.

"I wish I could thank him." Softness showed in Lorraine's tough exterior.

"Yeah, I wish I could give him a really big hug right now." Sue was getting emotional.

"Dear God," Rose said.

"*O Bozhe.*" Ivan repeated Rose's words in Russian.

I missed Jack more than ever in that moment. I knew everyone else felt the same—it wasn't the actual money; it was the thought behind it. His reasoning was to make sure we could continue to expose the population control plan with whatever resources we needed.

Everyone took a moment.

I let out a deep breath. "Okay, let's plan."

"We will place Rose on a plane to Savannah after the funeral," Ivan said.

Rose looked grateful.

"Everyone should come with me to get the security devices at my home," Jorge said. "I now don't feel it is as safe here."

"I will stay with Lee," Lorraine said. "He's too vulnerable in his incapacitated state."

Jorge nodded. "We will keep Lee company in shifts."

Lee looked put out that somebody had to protect him but didn't protest.

"After the funeral tomorrow, we have to figure out a way to disappear from anyone who's watching us." I tried to whisper even quieter. "I assume our next destination is the lab in Colombia now?"

"Yes, we need to get to our informant," Ivan said.

"I'll stay with Lee until he is fit enough to travel," Lorraine said. "Then we can meet up with you."

"We can look after Jack's estate while we're here," Lee said.

"Jorge, contact Eugene, explain what's going on, and see if he and Sam still want to participate," I said. "They can meet up with us as soon as Sam is able."

Jorge nodded. "I'll handle it."

"We just have to figure out how to disappear and get to the lab," Sue said.

"That will be the challenge," Ivan said.

"We'll pull it off somehow," Jorge said. "I have connections here in Dallas and in Colombia."

"Okay, let's go," I said. "Lorraine, when you check with your friends at the FBI, ask if they know a Lieutenant Furyk and Stenson."

Lorraine gave me a thumbs-up.

"I think I should stay here too," Rose said. "I don't feel right about going outside again."

"I'd rather we stay together as much as possible." Jorge was opening the door to the room. "Lorraine doesn't have protection yet ... not that she needs a weapon."

Rose remained seated and looked up at Ivan, pleading, still holding his hand.

Ivan nodded. "I will stay here as well. It will be okay."

Jorge exhaled. "Fine, I'll go alone."

Sue was already at the door. "Nick and I will go with you."

That's what happened when you had a group of strong-willed people. "Separating in half for a short time is okay." I wanted to see what Jorge's place looked like and what *protection* he was referring to.

We took the long walk back to the parking garage with no apparent followers. Yet a block after we left the hospital, the two cars from before fell in line—the Chevy three vehicles behind us and the Ford two vehicles behind it.

Sue and I had taken our posts in the very back seat and were watching the cars.

We drove along a freeway; on either side the grass was dry and brown. After around ten miles, we exited into a residential area. A few blocks farther, we turned into a complex that had three medium-rise relatively new buildings, all the suites having balconies and the grounds well maintained.

I'd pictured Jorge living someplace different from this middle-class, sanitized neighborhood—somewhere tougher.

We pulled up to a gate that led us to the secure, underground parking of the middle building.

The Chevy parked just past the driveway and the Ford carried on.

Sue turned forward in the seat. "Do they think we're stupid enough not to notice them following us?"

"The Chevy isn't trying to hide," I said. "The Ford, maybe, and I doubt they're together."

"I agree." Jorge used a fob on his keychain to open the garage gate.

Once inside we waited for the timed door to close so no one could enter behind us. Then we proceeded to an empty parking spot next to a navy-blue Ford F150 pickup that looked brand new.

"Is that your truck?" I asked.

"Yes, I have two parking spots." Jorge was cautious when backing in.

We took the elevator to the top, the eighth floor. The concrete building had to be less than five years old.

Jorge unlocked the door to his suite and let us in.

The inside of the condo was of good quality and sparsely furnished. There was a bathroom just to the right of the entryway and a kitchen with granite countertops. Beyond the kitchen island was a dark-stained, wood dining room table with nothing on it. The open floorplan continued to a dark-brown couch and a glass coffee table, situated across from a TV. Patio doors opened onto a sizable but empty balcony. The light-brown walls were bare. Looking closer I could see a film of dust everywhere.

"Jorge, you're obviously not married, but do you have any

154

children?" Sue asked. "I feel bad that I never thought to ask before."

"I have a grown daughter. She lives with my parents in Colombia."

"Are you going to see them when we go?" Sue asked.

"I hope. We'll see." Jorge changed the subject. "I'm barely ever here, so it doesn't have a homey feel. Jack encouraged me to have a home base and to start thinking about retirement someday. But I could never just sit here and do nothing."

Sue looked thoughtful. "You need a place to call home and escape to from time to time."

Jorge nodded. "True."

"When was the last time you were here?" I asked.

"About a year ago. I'd come to Dallas with Jack that time Lee was busy in London."

"I remember that," Sue said.

"I'll only need a few minutes." Jorge turned and walked into another room.

I glanced to where he went and saw a corner of a bed.

Within minutes Jorge came out holding a black duffel bag, which he left on the floor as he went back into the bedroom.

I went to the patio and scanned for the vehicles that had followed us. They were half a block apart. The doors of the gray Chevy were open, and as I watched, two men in suits exited. "Sue, come see this."

Sue joined me at the railing.

I pointed to the men walking below on the sidewalk. "They got out of the Chevy."

We watched as they passed the building's main entry and kept going.

"They seem like plain-clothes police or FBI, just by the way they walk," Sue said.

It was hard to see any distinguishing features from our angle and distance; however, one had a bald spot and the other, short, curly hair.

They kept walking until they arrived at the second car that had been following us. The one with the bald spot motioned with his hand, and the doors of the Ford opened. Curly reached into the inside of his suit and held his hand there.

Two men from the Ford stood facing the two from the Chevy. One had on a light-colored, short-sleeved button-down shirt and his head was shaved; the other wore a blue polo shirt and had dirty-blond hair. The men from the Ford were larger in build.

Jorge came out onto the patio. "What's going on?"

"We're watching the guys who were following us," Sue said. "It doesn't look like they know each other."

Bald Spot showed something that looked like a badge; there was a shiny glint when the sun hit it. Dirty Blond gave him what looked like a business card. Then they talked, Bald Spot doing most of it.

"Confirmed that the two suits are officers," Jorge said. "The bigger guys are private. The question is, working for who?"

After another minute of talking, the two men from the Ford got back in their car and drove away. Curly took his hand out from the inside of his suit, and then he and Bald Spot walked back to their car. All of a sudden, both men looked up.

All three of us stepped back.

"Time to go." Jorge headed back inside.

We followed as he went over to a second, identical duffel bag near the entryway. It was open, and he pulled out two handguns. "Here are Glock 18s, just like you practiced with." He passed one to each of us.

It felt comfortable in my hand, but I always felt a tinge of nervousness whenever I handled a gun, knowing there was the possibility I'd have to use it against someone. That feeling could cause hesitation, which was life-threatening for me and the team. Yet I hadn't been able to shake it, no matter how much I practiced.

"Neither of you is licensed to carry in the US, and we don't have time right now to register you," Jorge said.

Sue and I nodded.

"I have full trust that both of you can handle them safely and effectively." He surveyed us. "Nick, hide it behind your back under your shirt and belt. And you, Sue ... why do you barely ever carry a purse? It would be much easier to carry it in one. Your shirts are always too short."

Sue's T-shirt barely reached the top of her shorts, which had pockets, but too small to conceal a gun.

Jorge took the gun back from her. "I'll give it to you after you change or get a purse."

"Jeez." Sue looked annoyed. "I never thought of that when I got dressed this morning."

"You'll have to start thinking about that from now on," Jorge said.

# CHAPTER 17

*May 10, 2003*

Yesterday evening Lorraine had gone shopping with Sue for a purse that she could conceal her Glock in.

I'd done a shift with Lee, and then Jorge relieved me at 2:00 a.m. Everyone wanted to attend Jack's funeral, but we always needed to have someone with Lee at the hospital, so Lorraine volunteered.

The rest of us, dressed in black, filed into the rented minivan when Jorge pulled up to the hotel entryway.

My suit was too warm for the hot day. Too bad; I'd have to suck it up.

We traveled south on I-75 in late-morning traffic.

"I didn't know Jack was religious," I said to Ivan, who was sitting next to me.

"I never thought to ask," he replied.

Rose turned her head toward us from the front passenger seat. "Jack's family is Catholic from way back, but only his late mother practiced."

"The gray Chevy is back there again," Sue said. "No sign of the Ford."

It took us about twenty minutes to get to the Saint Thomas Aquinas Catholic Church. The closest parking spot we could find was two blocks away.

The humid heat on the street made everyone perspire. There was no sign of where our shadow had parked, or of where they were watching us from.

Along the way we passed news vans setting up—three were local and one was from GMNN.

We stopped across the street from the church, taking shelter under the shade of a large oak tree. Sunday mass had just ended, and worshippers were exiting the front doors.

"They'll be setting up for the funeral now," Rose said. "It'll take a few minutes."

I wondered if Rose was religious. Probably. After the time we'd all spent together, we still didn't know many personal details. I blamed it on the circumstances.

The church was a large four-story structure made of limestone. In the front there was a round, ornately patterned window set into the façade, and at the very top of the steep roof stood a cross. Between the two sets of double, wood-stained doors was a statue of Jesus. The church wasn't the size and grandeur of Europe's cathedrals, yet it was still impressive.

Out front on the street was a hearse and a row of black limousines stretching down the block. It made me feel out of place and outclassed, thinking of us having to park our minivan far away and wearing regular off-the-rack clothing. That feeling faded when I reminded myself as to how most of the people in the limos made their money.

"I hope the church is air conditioned," Sue said.

"I doubt it." Rose pulled a paper fan from her brown purse, unfolded it with a flick of her wrist, and waved it in front of her face. "But it'll be cooler than out here."

"Good idea to bring a fan," I said.

"A southern woman must always be prepared." Rose gave a coy look.

Sue smirked. "A Pacific Northwest woman comes only with a rain jacket."

People began approaching from both sides of the street to congregate at the front entrance. A group of reporters stood on the left, half with cameramen at their sides.

After about ten minutes, a man in a dark suit opened the wooden front doors to let people inside. Wealthy people poured out of the limousines and approached the church. The reporters sprang into action, but few stopped to talk to them.

We waited for the line to end before we entered.

It was cooler inside. There were long rows of wooden benches that faced a pulpit with gold etching. Above was a large statue of Jesus on a cross and three men kneeling at his feet. Tall spindly iron stands held white candles. On either side were alcoves with sculptures and stained glass windows depicting angelic scenes.

At the foot of the pulpit was a black casket, closed, with a framed picture of a younger Jack, smiling.

It hit me even harder that we'd never see Jack again. Why did awful things happen to such good people?

We sat down in the second-to-last row.

By the time the priest appeared, the church was packed with hundreds of people. The latecomers had to stand at the sides and back. Everyone looked solemn.

"Do you recognize anyone?" I asked Jorge, who was to my right, next to the aisle.

Jorge half stood to look forward. "I can see Jack's son and daughter at the front, and Malcolm and his sister."

"I didn't know Jack had a sister."

"She's the youngest, in her early sixties," Jorge said. "I've never met her, only seen pictures at Jack's place."

Sue, who was on my left, took my hand. I glanced at her, and she seemed about to cry, which added to my fighting back tears of my own.

The priest talked about Jack's life and about God. I was only listening to parts, fading in and out of my own thoughts of Jack. He'd been a unique individual. He tried to make the world a better place and fight the greed and corruption that had given him power in the first place.

As for me, I wouldn't be alive if it wasn't for Jack. I squeezed Sue's hand—her either. Jack had provided us with protection, resources, and information. Even in his passing he was providing for us. I was going to miss the guidance he gave me.

I focused on what was going on. Jack's son was talking at the front about a childhood memory at the ranch he grew up on. He was a younger version of his father; tall, lean, standing very straight, a full head of hair, but not a buzz cut. He must've been in his mid forties. He had an inward smile as he shared with the mourners how his father had taught him how to rope a steer and how terrible he was at it. Then he told a story of Jack's compassion for animals and about their family dog. His face turned to grief when he ended, saying he hadn't seen much of his father the last few years and regretted it. He'd been working with his uncle Malcolm and hadn't always seen eye to eye with his dad. He loved him. "Why was he taken from us in this way?"

Jack's son saying he was working with his uncle Malcolm in the banking industry answered a lot of questions as to why we'd heard very little about him.

Malcolm was next at the pulpit. He was four years younger than Jack with similar features, an identical buzz cut, but a stiffer cadence to his Texan drawl. The way his suit hung, his look and posture reeked of power and wealth. Malcolm spoke of Jack without emotion, as if he were just an acquaintance and nothing more. He recited Jack's accomplishments throughout his life but stopped short of the last few years. Malcolm didn't mention anything like he missed his brother or was sad that he'd been killed. He ended with, "He had a prosperous life."

The priest came back and begun to speak in religious terms.

I zoned out to my own thoughts again. Had Malcolm had a part to play in the ordering of Jack's death? He was in tight with Schmidt IV, Lovemark, and Da Silva, just not as much in the forefront as them. He was at the top of the World Bank and the US Federal Reserve. He controlled the flow of money, thus needing to stay in the background and look legitimate in every way—even more so than the other *Club* members. But could he have secretly allowed or even ordered the killing of his brother?

After two more relatives who spoke kindly of Jack and a last psalm reading from the Bible by the priest, the ceremony was over. Everyone stood as they wheeled the casket past on the way to the hearse. Jack's son was one of the pallbearers.

Since we were at the back, we had to wait for all the rows in front of us to clear. The crowd was older, with only a few small children visible. Two of those children were with the woman who had been seated next to Jack's son and therefore, I assumed, were his family. Behind them walked an elegant and well-groomed lady in her forties. She had a Carter family resemblance, so she must've been Jack's daughter. She was holding hands with a heavyset man who had to be several years older than her.

Malcolm was next in line with a classy-looking woman beside him. The pearls around her long neck stood out against her sleeveless, knee-length black dress.

Four people behind Malcolm and his wife walked Davis Lovemark.

"Didn't think he'd show up," I whispered to Sue.

"Look," Sue whispered back. "That's his wife?"

Beside Lovemark was a short, pudgy woman, who wore a calf-length black dress and an array of glistening jewellery. Even though her clothing and accessories had to be expensive, she looked frumpy and walked in an awkward fashion as if not used to the heels she had on. Her face was stern, accentuating wrinkles around her eyes and forehead. She stumbled, and Lovemark placed a stiff hand against her back. She said something to him—I couldn't make out what—but I caught a New York accent with a high-pitched, nasally tone. He seemed annoyed.

At that moment Lovemark and I made eye contact. He sneered and gave me a slight nod of acknowledgement.

Jorge tensed as Lovemark passed by.

"That's not at all what I'd expected Lovemark's wife to look like," Sue said.

Next was the suave-looking Carlo Da Silva, facing straight ahead. I'd never met him and only seen pictures. He had strong features—prominent nose, thick lips, and a cleft chin with a dimple. His thick, wavy dark hair that was graying at the temples was somewhat unruly. The woman beside him had to be Spanish, too, and she was stunning. She was tall and slim with long, straight black hair and flawless, tanned skin. She carried herself as if she knew she was very beautiful.

"I'm surprised Da Silva came to the funeral as well," Sue said, as it was finally our turn to leave the church.

"Yes," Ivan said behind her. "Yet I did not see Hendrick Schmidt's son."

*Interesting.* I wondered if that meant anything.

Outside, Lovemark was giving an interview to the GMNN crew, and a few others were talking to the media.

The hearse was preparing to leave, and occupants were gathering at their limousines to join the procession.

We hurried our pace to the minivan, so as to not get too far behind everyone else.

As we drove, Jorge explained that the cemetery was small, old, and private. Jack's wife and her family had all been buried there. He wanted to be next to Connie. Jack didn't want to be buried with the rest of the Carters in Houston.

It took ten minutes to get there, parking behind a long row of cars.

The afternoon sun bore down. Luckily, there were large trees to provide shade. We followed others toward the gathering in the distance. Turning onto a path, the smell of dust came up from the fine gravel as everyone walked on it. The earthen particles mixed with the moisture being sucked from the grass by the heat. I stepped on an underground sprinkler head. They had to use large amounts of water to keep the well-manicured grounds so green.

We came to stand at the back of the crowd of about a hundred people gathered in front of a family crypt of around five hundred square feet. It was made of weathered concrete and covered with ivy that had spread up the sides and top, making it look creepy.

"Jack's wife's family must be rich too," Sue said, from beside me.

"That's obvious." I could see the edge of the open door from our angle but couldn't make out the surname etched in the stone above it.

"I'm going to do some research on her family when I have time," Sue said.

Rose and Ivan moved close to us. Jorge stood a few steps back.

"Do you recognize any people here, Rose?" I asked.

"Just the whole family over there." Rose nodded toward the side of the crypt entry.

Ivan motioned to the right with his head. "Next to Lovemark and Da Silva over there are Ivgeni Svetlov, a Russian banker, and Thomas Crane."

"Sue, did you ever have time to do some in-depth digging on Crane?" I asked.

Sue shook her head. "It was the next thing on my list the day we got shot at in Burford."

The priest, followed by the pallbearers, approached the crypt. The priest moved to the side as the pallbearers continued taking Jack's encased body inside.

That was it. It felt like one more shining light had been extinguished by unscrupulous powers as the world inched closer to darkness.

After the pallbearers came out, the priest said a prayer from scripture and a few final kind words. The crowd was stoic, with some audible grief being shed.

Sue and Rose had been weeping. There were two tears running down Ivan's cheeks, and I felt one run down mine. Jorge stood straight and grit his teeth.

As people began to wander away, through a gap in the mourners I saw the FBI officers that had interrogated us at the hospital. *Interesting.*

"Hello, Mr. Barnes."

I hadn't noticed the two men come up. Blood flushed my face. "Mr. Lovemark."

"You haven't met my colleague and friend in person, but I believe you know of him, like he knows of you." Lovemark placed his hand on the shoulder of the slightly shorter yet stockier man next to him. "May I introduce Carlo Da Silva."

"We finally meet." Da Silva had a very strong Spanish accent and a noticeable lisp. His dark eyes were intimidating. "However, in unfortunate circumstances." He extended his right hand.

I didn't know what to do, so I shook it. "Nice to meet you." *Nice! Why did I say 'nice'?*

Jorge stood so close to me our shoulders touched. Sue was next to me on the other side, and Ivan right next to her. Only Rose took a step back from us.

"Ms. Clark, we haven't been formally introduced," Lovemark said, and then he looked at Ivan. "Dr. Popov."

Da Silva nodded at both of them.

"So what will all of you do now that Jack has passed?" Lovemark said. "You don't have the money or the means to fight us any longer ... nor, I bet, the motivation."

"Why? Do you have a confession to make?" Sue growled.

"My dear girl, we had no part in Jack's death," Lovemark said.

"He was our friend," Da Silva said. "Even though he was causing us ... trouble, as you all have been."

"But Bail worked for you and Schmidt," I said.

"*Had* worked for me, and before that, Dr. Schmidt," Lovemark said. "He had not been in either of our employs for some time. I think he acted alone. Unless, of course you managed to annoy others?"

I wasn't going to bite on the last comment. "You know Bail wouldn't act unless somebody paid him to do it."

Lovemark looked at Da Silva.

"Jack did have old enemies in the oil industry," Da Silva said. "His anti-hydraulic fracturing company wasn't helping."

"Then why were we attacked at practically the same time Jack was shot?" Sue asked.

Da Silva and Lovemark looked at each other again.

"It had to be connected to us trying to stop your population extermination plan," I said.

"Extermination is not the right word," Lovemark said. "It sounds awful."

"But that *is* what you're doing," Sue said.

It was interesting that with all of us standing there and no one else close by, they didn't deny it.

"It's time you stop meddling in something that's not your business," Lovemark said. "Now with Jack gone, you have no choice."

I didn't want to reveal anything about what we were going to do next. No one in our group answered.

Lovemark addressed me. "I can get you and Ms. Clark a job at any of my newspapers."

"Not a chance." Sue balled her fists and looked like she was restraining herself from decking him.

Lovemark ignored Sue's rejection. "Dr. Popov and Mrs. Dean can finally retire." Then he gave Jorge a look of distain. "And you could go be an assassin for any criminal organization."

Jorge didn't show any emotion, say a word, or move. I wondered if they had a history with each other.

"Thank you for your concern," Ivan said. "But we will all manage just fine."

"So, then ... what will you all do now?" Da Silva asked.

"Let's keep that as a surprise." Did they actually think we'd confess our next move? Did they honestly think we'd give up? "I'm sure the second we do something, someone will tell you ... literally."

They looked at me for a moment without speaking. All I could see were two arrogant, overconfident, too-rich pricks, and I wanted to bring them down, now more than ever.

"Well, it was nice chatting with you," Lovemark said. "Let's hope it's for the last time."

Da Silva gave a nod. "Literally."

Lovemark and Da Silva turned as the women who'd accompanied them to the funeral walked up to them.

Lovemark's wife's heels were not cooperating with her on the grass, and she was dangerously close to turning an ankle. Da Silva's wife glided along as if on a catwalk.

"Davis, let's go," She had a grating voice, with the same nasal pitch I heard at the church. "This heat is killing me. How can anyone stand it out here?"

"Yes, dear," Lovemark said.

"Could you imagine listening to that voice all day?" Sue said loud enough for everyone to hear.

Lovemark glanced back at us, the politeness of his expression replaced with contempt. With a dismissive flick of his hand he went to his wife. "Let's go back to the hotel, Gwen, where you can rest."

# CHAPTER 18

As we were leaving, we overheard a snobby-sounding woman say to another that the reason Jack was killed was because he had gotten brainwashed by some radical ecoterrorists who had convinced him the world was ending.

The second woman replied, "Poor Jack, maybe he was getting *the All-zimers.*"

Sue opened her mouth about to speak. I poked her and shook my head. She actually did what I asked and didn't say anything. It was sad to hear how out of touch with reality those ladies were, but the fact was that they were in the majority.

We didn't go to the reception; instead we drove to the hospital.

The air conditioning couldn't overpower the smell of antiseptic in the hallways.

Lee was sitting up in his bed when we arrived. Lorraine was in a chair, talking on her cell phone.

"How are you feeling today?" Sue asked.

"Tired of just lying here," Lee replied. "How was the funeral?"

Lorraine stood and walked out of the room, still talking on her phone.

"Very sad," Ivan said. "We lost such a good man."

A sniffle came from Rose, who went to sit in the chair Lorraine had vacated. I observed that Rose had really started to look frail the last few days.

"I wish I'd been there." Lee's head hung low. "I really miss him."

"Best man I ever knew." Jorge cleared his throat.

That was a lot of emotion for Lee and Jorge as well.

There was a knock on the door. Special Agent Furyk and Regular Agent Stenson didn't bother for an invitation to enter.

Furyk was holding a paper pad and ballpoint pen. "Now that the funeral is over, it's time to know where you'll all be going."

We'd known the question would be asked, so we decided on the answers we'd give when we were driving from the cemetery.

"I'll be right here for you to visit anytime," Lee said.

"Yes, I understand you'll be laid up for a while yet." Furyk flipped to a blank page on his pad and started writing names on it.

Lorraine came back into the room. "I'll be staying to look after Lee until he's recovered."

We hadn't had a chance to agree on our responses from Lee and Lorraine, but their honest answers worked.

"Are you two a couple?" Stenson asked.

Lorraine gave him an annoyed look that seemed to be a satisfying answer to him.

Furyk looked to me next.

"I'm going home to Seattle," I said. "Sue too."

"Can you give me your addresses?" Furyk poised the pen on the pad.

"I'll stay with Sue until I find an apartment."

Sue gave her address.

"I will be going back to Oslo," Ivan said.

"Why would you need to go back there now?" Furyk watched Ivan. "It's all over."

"I have other research to conduct. Then I will retire back to

British Columbia."

"I'm going to stay with my family in Savannah." Rose gave him her address.

"I'm already home," Jorge said and then recited his address.

I wondered if Furyk would be suspicious of us giving him the information so freely, but he didn't seem to catch on.

"Now, I'll need all your cell phone numbers," Furyk said.

I assumed he wanted them for tracking purposes but hadn't figured that all but Lee's had British numbers. We had to get new SIM cards or new phones with US accounts. Therefore, we had no problem giving them to him.

In quick succession Sue, then Rose and I recited our digits.

"You don't have US of A numbers?" He looked up from writing.

"Nope," I said.

Everyone but Lee shook their heads.

Furyk reached in his pocket, produced business cards, and passed them around. "Everyone call or e-mail me your new numbers when you get them."

I took the card to add to my collection. "Of course." *Like that was ever going to happen*—I liked saying that to myself every time someone in law enforcement made a demand. We were going to get disposable, prepaid phones as soon as we could.

"All right, then." Furyk flipped the pad closed. "I'm glad you're all being smart, going your separate ways and hopefully staying out of trouble."

*Did he actually believe that?* "Good luck in your investigation. I hope you get to the bottom of who all were involved in Jack's killing. Will you let us know when you find out?"

Furyk looked right at me. "No. You'll know when the general public knows."

*Asshole.* I tried to say that with my eyes as I stared back at him.

Furyk turned and walked out of the room with Stenson following.

Lorraine stayed by the door to watch them leave, with her hand raised.

"Come with me," Jorge said. "You too, Lorraine. Lee, we'll be back in a bit."

Lee nodded his understanding.

Lorraine lowered her hand. "Okay, they're gone."

Jorge led us to the elevator that took us to the ground floor. There we found a door that would take us outside. We crossed a street to a park that was on the hospital property.

It was getting close to sunset, and the day was cooling. The grounds smelled of freshly cut grass and a nearby white flower I didn't know the name of. We found a spot under a dogwood tree where there were two wooden benches.

Jorge looked around. "It's safer for us to talk here."

There was no one else around, other than a linen truck driving up the street that we'd just crossed.

"Does anyone have any bright ideas of how we can get away without being seen?" Sue asked, as she sat down next to Rose.

"As planned, let us get Rose on a plane tomorrow," Ivan said.

Lorraine was standing. "I was speaking to my FBI contact, and he doesn't know a Lieutenant Furyk and Agent Stenson, but he's looking into them. Also, by tomorrow morning he'll find out about what's happening with Jack's case."

"My main local police contact said the same." Jorge stood between Lorraine and me. "So in the morning we should have a better idea of what's happening."

"Okay, so after that we need to become invisible and escape." Part of an idea came to me. "Could we go on a boat to a Caribbean Island and then fly to Colombia from there?"

Sue tapped her index finger against her chin. "I like that idea."

"We are expected to fly," Ivan said. "So, they will be watching the airport."

"I've already started the process of getting new IDs and passports, which will be ready in three days," Jorge said.

"We will need head shots," Ivan said.

"I'm using the ones we took last year," Jorge said.

"We need to find a boat," Sue said.

I knew someone who owned a boat down south, but I couldn't remember who. The answer would come to me.

# INTERLOGUE 6

Davis surveyed the private dining room, with only one table in the middle—the one they sat at. "This place is too tacky."

"It's okay and gives us privacy." Carlo reached for butter. "However, I could only find one wine that is worthy of us."

On cue the waiter, dressed in a tuxedo with tails, brought the bottle of wine, opening it in front of them.

"You know this place used to be the private home of a cotton baron," Davis said, still looking around. "The family name doesn't ring a bell, though."

"Hmm." Carlo tasted the wine after swirling and smelling it. "It will do."

A second waiter brought two plates of small appetizers.

"I want a salad." Davis shifted in his seat, in obvious discomfort. "The food in Texas is too heavy."

The waiter nodded and departed.

"Are you all right?" Carlo asked. "You seem uneasy."

"I've had these aching pains lately." Davis shifted again. "They come and go. I'm having my doctor see me as soon as I get home. I'm sure it's nothing."

"You'd better take care of yourself. We have much work to do."

Davis nodded and reached for the wine. "Malcolm is going to join us after he finishes playing the grieving brother."

"Good," Carlo said. "Why wouldn't you let Tom join us?"

"Crane's such a suck-up, and I wasn't in the mood for ass-licking tonight." Davis rolled his eyes. "Besides, we have business to discuss with Malcolm that's not for Tom's ears."

The waiter came with Davis's green salad.

"Was this premade?" Davis looked up at the slim, middle-aged attendant. "It came out very fast."

"The chef works quickly."

"I want fine, not fast, food. It looks boring."

The waiter nodded and took the plate away.

Carlo chose a canapé. "You're in a state tonight."

"I'm still annoyed by our encounter with Barnes and his group. You know they're going to continue somehow. Maybe Jack left them some money."

"I wouldn't doubt it."

Malcolm Carter entered the private dining room. He had changed from his black suit to a brown sport jacket. "Gentlemen." He looked at the server standing in the corner. "What's the best whiskey you have?"

The man had to raise his voice. "Michter's, sir."

"That'll do. Get me four fingers with two ice cubes."

When Malcolm took the third seat, Carlo said, "It was a very nice service."

"As funerals go."

A large man in a black suit and shirt came into the room and stood in the doorway.

"Is there a need for protection so close?" Davis motioned to the man.

"Jack's murder has made me nervous," Malcolm said.

"It was Baby Hendrick who contracted Bail," Davis said. "Surely you don't think he would send someone after you?"

"Are you positive?" Malcolm asked.

"Pretty sure," Carlo said.

"Well, until we know a hundred percent for certain, I'm taking extra precautions," Malcolm said. "And you should too."

Malcolm's drink was brought to him, as was Davis's spruced-up salad.

"Not that my brother didn't have it coming, but if it was Hendrick, we need to rein him in." Malcolm held the glass and sniffed the contents. "Who's next? I don't want anything coming back at us. Mind you if he'd succeeded in taking Barnes and his group out of their misery, that wouldn't have been such a bad thing."

"Agreed," Davis said. "On all points."

Carlo reached for another canapé. "I think it's time we stop talking about controlling Hendrick and actually do it."

"You two will have to be in charge of it." Malcolm took a generous drink of his whiskey, draining half of it. "I have to stay far away from the population control plan."

"We'll figure it out," Carlo said.

"Have you been able to see Jack's will yet?" Davis asked. "And do you know how much operating money there is in different accounts?"

"Jack's estate lawyer is loyal to him, so I won't know everything until the reading. Yet I have my suspicions he left Barnes and the group money." Malcolm swallowed the rest of the drink, leaving only the partially melted ice cubes. He raised the glass to the waiter in the corner, who nodded and left the room. "His several operating accounts have substantial amounts in dollars, euros, krone, and pesos."

Carlo reached for his glass of wine. "Which country's pesos?"

"Colombian."

Carlo's eyes narrowed. "And krone?"

"Norway."

"That's what I was afraid of." Davis plunged his fork into the salad. "Their destinations being the seed bank *and* the lab."

"To do what?" Malcolm said. "No one could get close to either."

"Remember, Lee Donald had infiltrated the Bolivian lab," Davis said.

"And Barnes is getting craftier as he goes," Carlo said.

Malcolm thought for a moment. "It would be very possible that they have access to the accounts ... Donald especially."

"Can the accounts be frozen?" Carlo said. "Something to do with the will or estate?"

Malcolm swirled the ice around in the liquid-less tumbler. "If they're straight business operating accounts, then no."

The waiter brought Malcolm's second drink and asked, "Would you like anything to eat? Perhaps a look at the menu?"

Malcolm took the glass and gulped some whiskey back. "No, I'm not hungry."

"And how's the acquisition of Moile by Tom coming along?" Carlo asked.

"He'll be able to take it over," Malcolm said.

# CHAPTER 19

*May 11, 2003*

I'd stayed at the hospital until two in the morning. During that time, I'd written down a draft of our still-developing plan and given it to Lee. He, in return, gave me some good suggestions.

Jorge had come to relieve me. Lee and Jorge needed to discuss the operating bank accounts. At the moment only the two of them had access, and a portion of the money had to be transferred into accounts harder to trace.

In the morning, Lorraine took her turn with Lee, and the rest of us drove Rose to the airport. The Chevy tailed not far behind, which was welcome to provide proof that we were doing what we said we were going to do.

"Sure am going to miss your cooking," I said as we escorted Rose to domestic-departure security.

"And your looking out for us," Sue added. "My mother's probably still going to call you all the time. Do you mind giving her your number in Savannah?"

"My mom too," I said.

"Of course." Rose had tears in her eyes. "I'm going to miss y'all so much."

I tried to smile. "It's not the last you'll see of us. And Ivan will keep you posted."

"I will be in touch whenever I can." Ivan held Rose's hand.

I was happy Rose was going to stay with her family. She deserved a quieter life. Plus since Jack had died, the will to fight had left her.

Ivan wrapped his arms around Rose and gave her a long kiss.

"They're so cute." Sue's eyes were all misty.

We all gave Rose a hug and waved as we watched her proceed to security.

"Do you see anyone watching us?" I asked Jorge as we began to walk back to the van.

"No, but they're out there," Jorge said. "There are cameras everywhere."

I looked up and saw a security camera on the wall to our left.

Sue had her hand on Ivan's shoulder as we walked. He was visibly sad to have let Rose go. It made me think of Sue and that we needed to give our relationship a chance once this was all over.

Sue looked my way and gave me a sad smile, as if thinking the same thing.

The Chevy again followed us back to the hotel.

As soon as we climbed out from the van in the parking lot, Jorge motioned to the Mexican restaurant adjacent to our hotel. "Let's go have lunch."

It had been decided yesterday that we only talked about what we were going to do in public places in case our rooms and the van were now bugged.

As we walked toward Pedro's Cantina, Sue surveyed my ear and touched it. "Does it hurt at all?"

Today was the first day I'd gone without a bandage over it. "No, it's fine."

"I think that notch is permanent." She made me stop so she

could get a better look. "Like a mouse took a nibble. Ivan?"

Ivan nodded. "I'm afraid that your ear will always have that small portion missing."

"I know ears don't grow back." I didn't really care. It could've been worse. "Whatever."

"It gives you character." Sue patted me on the back.

The restaurant was busy, but we managed to find a table for four. One wall had a mural of a brown, mountainous desert with cacti and a low scrub. Live cacti were in pots in the corners. The tables were made of light-colored wood with blue-and-white tiled tops and the chairs were wicker.

It was nearly impossible to avoid genetically engineered food ingredients in the States when eating out unless you were in a place that expressly served organics. We didn't know how much exposure it took to genetically engineered food to start getting sick, because everyone's body was different. We did know that long and continuous consumption was the main factor, so we took our chances when we had to. The only other option was starving.

"Any more word from yours or Lorraine's contacts?" I asked Jorge.

"We should hear later today."

"Are we still on schedule to leave in two days?" Ivan was looking at Jorge.

"Yes." Jorge nodded. "After lunch, I have to do the banking as per Lee's instructions."

"I can go to the banks with you, Jorge," Ivan said.

"Good." Jorge nodded. "As soon as the passports and IDs are ready, we can leave. I like Nick's idea of taking a boat to an island in the Caribbean and then flying from there to Bogota."

"We probably need to get to Florida, right?" Sue said. "From Texas it would take forever to get to an island."

As soon as I heard Florida again I realized who I knew there. "Didn't Paul, our old editor from the *Seattle News*, retire to Key West?"

"That's right." Sue's eyes lit up. "He was from there, and when his father died, he inherited the family home and *fishing* business. Fishing means boat."

"Yeah, he was really into boats. He even had one in Seattle," I added. "Remember that time he took us out? We went up to Port Townsend and did some fishing."

Sue gave a slight memory smile. "You fished. I drank."

"That's right; you got seasick on the way back."

"Do you think you can find him?" Ivan asked. "Even if he cannot help, maybe he could introduce us to someone who could."

"Shouldn't be too hard," I said.

"Do you trust him?" Jorge asked.

"Definitely," Sue said. "And as a bonus, he hated Davis Lovemark and GM Comm."

I remembered. "That was part of the reason he retired early— the ethics of the company. He would definitely sympathize with our cause."

▷◁▥▷◁

Ivan and Jorge were going to stop by the hospital before they went to the three banks. We hoped that the men in the Chevy would follow them, leaving Sue and me to do what we had to.

When we arrived at our hotel lobby, Sue and I hid behind a pillar and watched our rental van drive onto the street. Two seconds later, the Chevy pulled out and followed.

"Step one complete," Sue said.

I pulled the napkin with the address Jorge had given me out of my pocket. "Let's get a cab." My other pocket contained the wad of hundreds and twenties he'd given me at the same time.

We walked out to the street, crossed it, and started heading south. Within a block we saw a cab and hailed it.

It took twelve minutes to reach our destination.

Once out of the cab Sue pointed toward the end of the block. "There's the store with the phones and the Internet café two over from it."

Just then the Ford that we hadn't seen in days pulled up right in front of us. We were standing at a bus stop, so there were no parked cars. Before the sedan even stopped, the passenger door opened.

"Run!" I pulled Sue around by her arm but was too late.

A large man with hands the size of baseball mitts grabbed her other arm and twisted her toward him. "I want to talk to you two."

I'd lost my grip on her.

"Let go!" Sue swung up so hard her feet left the ground and nailed the man with her palm between his eye and nose. "I don't want to talk to you!" Then she kicked him in the stomach.

The man fell back, hitting his head against the open door of the car.

Sue lost her balance, and I caught her just before she landed on the sidewalk. Pulling her to her feet, I propelled her away from the car. We both bolted.

We sprinted around the block away from the store and café we needed to visit. It was a busy sidewalk, and we had to dodge and maneuver around pedestrians.

As we came to the corner at the next street, I slowed and glanced to see the big man half the block behind us. He wasn't agile; he was lumbering.

Sue stopped. "Look, the Ford's coming toward us."

*They're trying to box us in.* I saw a restaurant to our left. "In here."

I opened the door and let Sue go first. We tried to look casual, walking slow while catching our breath. Sue went straight toward the back of the informal eatery. We came out into a patio courtyard landscaped with high shrubs to block the view of the back alley. The tables were half full of patrons. I spotted a break in the bushes with a gate. Sue was already heading toward it. She threw the latch and headed out.

"Excuse me."

I turned to see a server holding a tray coming toward us. I didn't bother explaining and went through the spring-loaded gate that was closing.

We were in the alley and running. Sue had a head start and her legs were in full motion, so I had to give it all I had to catch up.

We turned onto the other side of the block from where we'd first come, back toward our original destination. Luckily the light was green, and we didn't have to stop before crossing the street.

I'd caught up to Sue as we arrived at the store, and we went in one after the other. It sold phones and the gadgets that went with them. We stopped at the window display and looked back outside.

After a long thirty seconds, Sue said, "I think we lost them."

"Stand watch and I'll get the phones." The handgun I'd hidden behind my back under my belt had ridden up from the running and was about to fall out. I lifted my shirt and pushed it down to the point where I could feel the barrel between my butt cheeks. Then I turned and walked farther into the store.

It was a small shop with no one else there but a teenage guy behind the counter.

I realized that when I'd pushed the gun back into place, it had been in full view of the teen.

He was watching us carefully and looked nervous. I'd be apprehensive too if someone barged in like we had and was carrying a firearm. He probably thought we were going to rob him.

"Hi." I tried to look and sound friendly. "I need six prepaid, disposable, cell phones—basic ones, nothing fancy."

"S-sure. You need burners." He came around the counter to a display on the wall and pulled off a phone wrapped in a plastic case. "How's this?" His hands were trembling as he handed it to me, and his face was red, accentuating his acne problem.

I wanted him to feel more at ease, so spoke softly. "Six of these would be fine. Can I get two hundred dollars put on each of them?"

"Yes, sir." He took six phones back to the counter and unwrapped them.

It took over ten minutes for the phones to be ready and then another minute for him to instruct me on how to add more minutes. After that I counted out the cash, he placed the phones in a plastic bag, and we were done.

"Anything?" I asked Sue when I came up to her.

"Nothing. They must've thought we went the other way."

"Good. Let's go."

Two businesses over was our next stop, the Internet café. It was basic and clean with three desktop computers in front of the window and a row of them on long tables against a wall. There were only two people in front of computer screens. On the opposite side was a bar where you could get drinks, sandwiches, and desserts.

We went to one of the computers in front of the window so we could watch for the Ford.

"It shouldn't be hard to find a family of Asian heritage in Key West, especially when they own a fish market." Sue had a tone of confidence.

She was right as the search only took one try. Within thirty seconds the screen showed a website titled Ang's Fish Market. Sue clicked on the "About" button, and a photo of a family standing in front of a store loaded above text. There was Paul, his wife, and two grown daughters, smiling.

"He looks the same, but his daughters are totally grown-up ..." I was distracted by a dark Ford passing by on the street outside, but it wasn't the same model.

"It's been ... what?" Sue looked up at me. "Five years since we last saw him?"

"Yeah, about that." I noticed a link. "How about 'Charters' at the top of the page?"

Sue moved the cursor up and clicked.

The screen slowly loaded, revealing pictures inside and out of two sizable boats. "They're plenty big enough."

Sue copied down the address and phone number on a receipt lying next to the keyboard. "Let's head back to the hotel before we call him."

A person was getting out of a cab right in front of the café, so we asked the driver if he could take us to the hotel.

When we arrived, there was no sign of our rental van or any of our followers.

"Let's call from over there in the shade," Sue said.

We strode over to a bench on a patch of dry grass that the shadow of the building shielded from the afternoon sun.

"Can you hand me the number?" I opened the bag in my hand. "Now's a good time to use one of these phones."

Sue pulled out the piece of paper from her shorts pocket and gave it to me, her hand having a slight shake.

"You okay?" I realized that I was jittery as well.

"We were almost abducted ... again."

"Thanks to your quick moves, we got away." I placed my hand on her back to reassure her.

"Every time they interrogate us I get the shit kicked out of me," Sue said. "I don't want that to ever happen again."

She was right, and I needed to move faster to help make sure that never happened again in the future.

"Call Paul."

There was an answer on the third ring, "Ang's Fish Market and Charters," said a male voice.

"Is this Paul?" I was pretty sure I recognized his always calm voice.

"Yes, speaking."

"Paul, it's Nick Barnes. Remember me?"

"Of course. Nick, how are you?"

"Um, pretty good. How's life with the fishes?"

"Can't complain. Love the freedom."

"Great to hear." I felt an urge to get to the point. "Listen, Paul, Sue Clark, some friends, and I are in Dallas and were wondering if we could come see you? We'd like to charter a boat to take us to a Caribbean island."

"Say hi to Sue for me. Is she still cute as a button and feistier than shit?"

"She'll never change in either of those departments."

Sue looked at me and I shrugged.

"Sure, I have a boat for that," Paul said. "Will you need a captain?"

"Yeah, and it's a one-way trip."

"Oh."

"I'll fill you in when we get there."

"Nick, I've read everything on your website and know you've uncovered some scary things. And I know about your battles with Davis Lovemark, the late Dr. Schmidt, and your connection with Jack Carter."

"Wow, I didn't think anyone in the States even knew what we were doing because we didn't get much media coverage over here."

"With the Internet, you can find information from anywhere. On a whim one rainy day last year, I wanted to know what you were up to and did a search. From there my old investigative-reporter habits took over, and I've been reading what I could find about you ever since."

"Well, that'll take care of all the explaining I thought I'd have to do." I was impressed that he was keeping track of us. "We're in Dallas because we attended Jack Carter's funeral."

"Right." There was a pause on the line.

The thought crossed my mind that with him knowing so much he may not want to help us. Maybe he was getting cautious as he aged. He must've been around sixty by now.

Paul cleared his throat. "I'm guessing you're in some kind of trouble?"

"I'm not sure if trouble is the right word ..."

"I could use some adventure. The fish business can be a little stale at times. I'll help you get to whatever island you want."

*Phew.* "Great. We should be there by the end of the week."

"I'll be ready for you."

❈

We met at a bistro two blocks away from our hotel. Sue and I had scoped it out when we went for a walk after talking to Paul.

They advertised using fresh local ingredients, and the menu sounded good. The restaurant was bright with two walls of windows, clean, and modern, with glass table tops and generous amounts of chrome. There was an open kitchen and a bar where patrons could sit and watch the food being prepared. All types of ingredient aromas mingled together.

Ivan had stayed at the hospital to take a shift with Lee.

"I heard from Eugene today." Jorge was the last to join us. "Sam needed a second surgery on his shoulder. He's going to be out of commission for a while."

Sue and Lorraine looked concerned.

"So for sure we'll be down four security people in Colombia."

"Maybe I should come," Lorraine said.

"No, someone needs to stay with Lee," I said. "Hopefully you two can join us when he is better."

"We'll be okay," Jorge said.

Sue said to me, "Tell them the details of your call with Paul."

I went through our conversation.

"I like that idea," Jorge said.

"Ask your friend if Lee and I could use a similar route once he's able to travel," Lorraine said.

We paused when a young server with red hair and freckles came to take our order.

As soon as the server left, Lorraine looked at Jorge. "We should tell Nick and Sue what our contacts told us."

"Of course, I was just getting to that," Jorge said.

Lorraine leaned toward Sue and me. Cleavage was showing above her white tank top, so I consciously focused on looking her in the eyes.

"We found out that the men in the Chevrolet are FBI, working with Interpol to keep tabs on us," Lorraine said.

"Which is actually a good thing, because the men in the Ford are Naintosa security," Jorge said. "So with the FBI around they can't just abduct us."

I never thought of it that way. The FBI was actually protecting us.

"The guys in the Ford tried to snatch us today when we went to get the phones," Sue said.

"What?" Lorraine looked surprised.

"We lost them, though," I added.

"They still tried to abduct you?" Jorge said. "That's brazen if they tried to grab you right on the street. Splitting up wasn't a good idea."

I didn't want to make a big deal about it, but he was right—if there had been four of us, they wouldn't have tried to grab us. "Did you find out anything about Agents Furyk and Stenson?"

"That's a bit of a gray area we're not positive about yet," Lorraine said.

"My local police contacts say they're FBI," Jorge said.

"My FBI friends say they're CIA," Lorraine said, "but have some kind of special status, like counterintelligence."

"What kind of special status is that?" I asked. "And how does that work with the FBI, if they're CIA?"

"That, we don't know yet," Lorraine said.

# CHAPTER 20

*May 12, 2003*

We all did a shift with Lee at the hospital that day and otherwise laid low. There wasn't much to do until our IDs arrived tomorrow. Our plan was to rent a second minivan, distract the men in the Chevy, and then make a run for it to Florida.

Sue and I were each sitting on our beds as the credits rolled of the movie we'd just watched on the hotel pay-per-view.

I clicked the TV off. "It's getting late. We should get some sleep."

"Nick." Sue bit her lip. "I know we decided to wait until this was all over, but ..."

I knew what she was getting at and had an instant urge. It was an opportunity to release the tension of what was coming in each other's arms, if only for a few moments. I jumped from my bed to hers and came almost close enough for our noses to touch. "Yes?"

She smirked. "Well, that didn't take any convincing."

There were three successive knocks on the door.

Sue fell back against the pillow. "You wanna get that?"

"Why did I know that was going to happen?" I got up from the bed.

"Because we're supposed to wait." Sue sat up.

Looking through the peep hole, I could see it was Jorge, so I opened the door.

He didn't say anything, just handed me two manila envelopes and a piece of paper.

I nodded, and he walked away down the hall.

I brought what he gave me to Sue's bed and opened the first one. In it was a passport, driver's license, credit card, and an inch-thick stack of cash for a Susan Saprovich. I passed it to her.

The second envelope had the same but for Nick Scott. And on the piece of paper was written: *The IDs came early. We leave tonight. Meet at the back entrance of the hotel in ten minutes.*

I passed the message to Sue and then went to pack.

It only took us five minutes to shove everything into our suitcases, so we left early, the whole time not saying a word.

The hotel was quiet that late at night. Once on the ground floor we went down two halls and found the back door. As soon as I opened it and took one step I stalled. Agent Stenson was about fifty yards away, walking right toward us.

I stepped backward and bumped into Sue. "Get back," I whispered. "Stenson."

She turned and started walking back up the hall. I followed, looking for a place to hide.

"Nick." Sue motioned with her head.

I saw the door to the men's washroom and followed her inside.

"Oh God." She put her hand up to her nose.

It reeked of someone having a nasty bowel movement. I nearly gagged and tried to hold my last breath in.

"It smells like …"

"Sue, is that you?" A familiar voice came from one of three stalls.

"It smells like Mike Couple." She shook her head.

"Wait a second," said the voice from the stall. We heard toilet paper being unraveled, a faint butt wipe and the toilet flush.

Out came our friend, Mike Couple, whom we hadn't seen for a year. Our last contact had been at the cabin north of Vancouver. His khakis and shirt were hanging off him; he must've lost twenty pounds yet looked as disheveled as usual. "I was about to find you two, but nature called first." He walked toward us.

"Wash your hands," Sue said.

"Oh yeah." He turned abruptly toward a row of three sinks. "You need to learn how to hide better. It wasn't hard to track you down."

"We're not really trying to hide ... except at this second," I said.

He wiped his hands dry before coming over to us. He gave me a hug, which was not in his character. Then he moved over and embraced Sue.

Sue took a step back. "Jeez, Mike, no offense and it's great to see you, but you smell as bad on the outside as you do on the inside."

"Sometimes it's hard to find time to shower and change clothes when you're on the run." Mike cocked his head to the right. "How'd you know it was me, Sue?"

"Everyone has their own scent, and you've farted around me enough times in the past that I know your stink."

That grossed me out, but actually, she wasn't wrong. I focused on Mike. "Who're you running from?"

"I've been running since I last saw you, but that's a long story for later," Mike said. "I picked up a tail at the airport when I came into town three days ago. I thought I'd lost them, but I think they followed me here."

"Hmm," I was still standing next to the door and opened it a crack. I could see Ivan and Jorge standing in front of Agent Stenson. I motioned for Mike to take a look.

After he had a peek, I gently closed the door. "Is that your tail?"

"Yeah, and there's another guy who looks like a frickin' bulldog."

"Furyk," Sue said.

"You know them?"

"Yeah, they're FBI or CIA, we're not quite sure," I said. "You two wait here. I want to go help Ivan and Jorge."

I walked out into the hall. "Oh, there you are. I had to take a quick detour."

Ivan caught on right away. "We were wondering where you had gone."

Stenson glared at me with suspicion. "Where were you going? I saw you come outside and then turn around."

"I needed to relieve myself."

"We're meeting for a drink," Jorge said. "They have nothing to do until they fly out tomorrow night."

"Why are you going for a drink with your suitcases?" Stenson pointed toward Jorge and Ivan's feet. Then he looked back at me. "You had a suitcase when you came outside. Where is it?"

"No, I didn't." Denial was the best I could do at that second.

"Ivan was helping me with my bags," Jorge said. "I'm going to sleep at my own home tonight. Then I'll pick everyone up tomorrow and take them to the airport."

"Where is everyone going?" Stenson asked.

"We've already told your partner," I said.

"Just checking if anything's changed." Stenson looked from Ivan to me, focusing on our eyes. "Have you booked your flights?"

"Of course," I said.

"Do you have the tickets?"

I shrugged. "Not on us."

"What are you doing here, Agent Stenson?" Jorge deflected.

"Just passing by."

Jorge's eyes narrowed. "Uh-huh."

"Let me remind you that you need to contact Lieutenant Furyk or myself once you settle in and give us your phone numbers for future contact."

"Yes, sir." I said.

Stenson looked over our shoulders. "Where is Badowski?"

"Keeping Mr. Donald company," Jorge said.

"What about Ms. Clark?"

"Probably waiting for us in the lounge," I said.

"Fine, then." He turned and started walking toward the back exit. He stopped at the men's restroom door and hesitated, then opened it.

My heart skipped a beat, and I wondered if I should go tackle him.

He poked his head inside and then pulled it back out before continuing outside.

I exhaled.

We waited a good minute, not saying a word. Then Jorge went to the back door and peered out. Walking back to us, he said, "Get Sue and let's go to the lounge to have our drink. We can't leave right now. He's standing by his car."

I went to the restroom and walked inside. "Sue? Mike?"

There was a thud in the closest stall as my suitcase hit the floor. "Fucking heavy." Then Mike had to fight with the door, because the suitcase was jamming it from fully opening.

I went to help him.

Sue stepped down from the seat of the toilet in the second stall and came out. She dropped her suitcase and went straight to the sink to wash her hands. "Who knows what's been going on in there?"

"The coast is clear," I said.

Ivan and Jorge's eyes both went wide when they saw Mike.

"Very interesting to find you here," Ivan said.

"*Carajo*," Jorge said.

Mike shook both of their hands. "Nice to see you gentlemen again."

"And you," Ivan replied.

For some reason Jorge didn't seem impressed at Mike's arrival. "The bar is down there." He pointed back to where we'd originally come from.

The lounge wasn't very big. It was dark with shadowy lighting, and there were worn burgundy cushioned chairs around six square tables. A server was talking to the bartender on the other side of the bar. Two middle-aged ladies occupied a table, chatting and laughing.

We went to the back corner and pulled up an extra chair. The server noticed us right away and came to take our order. No one really cared what we drank, so we ordered a bottle of Malbec to share, except for Mike who had to have a Budweiser.

"So what brings you here?" Ivan asked Mike.

"He's been trying to find us." *That's not right.* "Actually, he's found us."

"Right." Mike settled back in his chair. "You know I've been trying to do my own thing lately, to create perceived distance from you."

Sue raised her hands and shrugged. "No, we didn't know what you were trying to do lately."

"Yeah, all right, I'll give you the whole story later." He still had traces of his Rhode Island accent, where he'd grown up. "But I knew you were in England and getting heat from the 2020 Report. By the way, it was very well done."

"Thanks," I said.

"Anyway, since the focus was on you, I was hoping all the bad guys would forget about me so I could move around freely."

"Go on," Sue said.

"When the fucker, Schmidt, got wasted and they were blaming Nick, I thought for sure it was the perfect time to go to the seed bank and see firsthand what was going on."

The drinks came and we paused while the server unscrewed the cap and poured wine into our glasses.

When the server left, I said, "We were going to try getting close to the seed bank ourselves. How'd you do?"

"Not even close. I didn't have the resources. I drew attention, and now I'm being tracked. I made it back to where I'd been laying low in Amsterdam ..." He took a long pull of his beer.

I watched Mike. His wavy brown hair always looked unkempt and his clothes wrinkled. I remembered some of the questionable past events of the man Sue and I had known since college and thought Amsterdam was a good fit for him—what I'd heard about the place anyway.

"Then I heard about Jack's death by fucking Peter Bail," Mike continued. "I knew I had to get back to you guys. You wouldn't quit, and I didn't have the means to do anything on my own. I'm obsessed about getting these fucking world-wreckers."

You wouldn't guess it about Mike, but he was smart and passionate when there was something he believed in. The seed bank had become his focus after he'd discovered information obtained by his short-term girlfriend, Summer Perkins.

"How did you find us?" Ivan asked.

I noticed Jorge watching Mike, not saying a word and not drinking his wine.

"I got a fake passport and headed for Dallas because I knew you'd come here. I hung way back at the funeral and then followed you to the hotel. That was something—you actually talked with Lovemark and Da Silva."

"Yeah, that was unexpected," Sue said.

Mike nodded. "Then I waited awhile before I tried to come find you, because I didn't know what rooms you were in. Luckily, we stumbled upon each other. Did you know there's a gray car following you guys?"

Jorge finally spoke, "Yes."

"What is the plan now?" Ivan asked. "We may have to fly out to the destinations we told Agent Stenson and Furyk and then regroup."

A sudden plan with potential crystallized in my head.

# CHAPTER 21

*May 13, 2003*

Last night Ivan, Sue, and I booked evening flights with the same airline. That way we could stay close together when we checked in. Ivan chose a one-day layover in New York, so he'd have to leave from the domestic terminal as well.

We'd been able to get Mike to our room without anyone noticing. I'd given him my bed, and I shared Sue's. We both made a big deal about me staying on my respective side so Mike wouldn't suspect that we'd become "more than friends."

Mike had started snoring within seconds of us turning off the lights. He was six years older than me and seven older than Sue. After we'd met at and attended Washington State University together, Mike had followed a journalism career also and worked for GM Comm companies, the last two being the San Francisco News, and then KLU-TV, where he had become a producer. He and I had played golf regularly when we were both living in San Francisco. He became wrapped up in all this when, after dating Summer Perkins, he'd discovered that she was gathering information on the Norway seed bank. The documents she possessed had gotten her killed by Brad

Caulder, Lovemark's private henchman; Summer had come too close to discovering the truth. I was the one who'd found her in a seedy bar where she'd wanted to meet and share what she had. Combining our information on genetic engineering and pesticides with what Mike was able to obtain of Summer's hidden seed bank research had helped fit the pieces of the puzzle together. After we'd escaped from the Naintosa thugs in Vancouver, Mike had disappeared. I'd been worried about him and was glad he'd come back to us.

We checked out of the hotel by eleven in the morning.

Jorge picked us up in the potentially bugged rental van, and we went to the hospital. As we drove, Sue, then Ivan and I each read the details Jorge had written down of the escape plan we'd formulated last night.

Mike had waited behind until the coast was clear and then was supposed to get a cab to go pick up his belongings. The plan was to go to the hospital and wait for us near where we'd parked in the garage. The van would be backed into one of the stalls we were sure we could get.

Lorraine was standing at Lee's bedside, adjusting his pillow when we entered the room. Lorraine's face blushed as she stepped back.

"We've arrived," Sue said as she locked eyes with Lorraine for a second.

"Good news." We were used to Lorraine in jeans and T-shirts, but today she wore a skirt and tight mauve blouse. She even had makeup on. "Lee gets discharged tomorrow."

It was nice to see Lorraine paying so much attention to Lee. "That's great, Lee. Are you well enough to travel?" I wondered if we should postpone our plan by a day.

"No. It'll be at least a few weeks until I have enough strength to be of any good."

"Maybe a month," Lorraine added. "We'll start his rehab right away."

"We'll need ..." Sue caught herself. "Great that you'll be able to start the next part of your life."

Lee almost smiled.

Jorge passed Lee the instruction sheet he'd given us, so he knew our plan.

I also gave him a piece of paper on which I'd written down Paul Ang's contact information and what we hoped would happen in Key West. "Here's our contact information in Seattle. Make sure to keep in touch."

"Sure will." He took both pieces of paper and placed them under his pillow.

There were chairs for all of us that we'd collected from previous visits. We had an hour to kill, so attempted to make small talk. Most of it was lies in case anyone was listening. We were anxious, hoping we could pull off losing our tails and escape.

I was surprised we hadn't seen the Ford since the men in it had tried to abduct Sue and me, but sure they were still lurking.

"I'm meeting with Jack's lawyer and the bank next week to start getting everything sorted out," Lee said.

"Will you be able to have any authority?" I asked. "Other than on the operating accounts?"

Lee raised an eyebrow. "I'm the executor."

"You never told us that," Ivan said. "That would not make his family happy, especially his brother, Malcolm."

"Jack was aware of that, and we made every provision we could."

I didn't know why I was still surprised at how close Jack and Lee had *really* been. And Lee was much more than just muscle; he had keen intellect. I remembered Jack had told me one time that Lee had great business sense.

"Rose arrived at her daughter's and is settling in," Ivan said.

"That's great to hear," Sue said.

We'd run out of things we could talk about without giving anything away, so we sat in silence and twiddled our thumbs.

Finally, Jorge looked at his watch and said, "Time to go. We don't want you to miss your flights."

Ivan, Sue, and I shook Lee's hand and gave Lorraine a hug.

I had to purposely take deep meditative breaths and walk slow, because I wanted to race to the van, get to the airport, and get this over with. I attempted to clear all the anxiety from my mind. Sue and Ivan looked equally as antsy.

As we came out of the elevator in the parking garage, I could smell a cigarette burning. When we arrived at the van Jorge pressed the fob that unlocked the doors. Sue stood beside me and the car parked next to us, cutting off any view toward the concrete wall. I opened the side door and Mike appeared with the two black and two gray duffel bags. He jumped into the van, going straight to the back, sitting down on the floor between the seats. Sue and I sat in the middle row. Ivan closed the side door and then climbed into the front passenger seat.

Within two blocks of the hospital, the Chevy pulled into its usual position behind us.

Traffic was heavy with people going home from their day's work. It was good that we'd given ourselves extra time.

The sun was setting behind us when we arrived at the airport and drove straight to Domestic Departures. The area was busy, but Jorge managed to wedge us into a spot out front. The Chevy wasn't so lucky and had to proceed forward.

Ivan, Sue, and I took our luggage from the back and said goodbye to Jorge. Sue even gave him a kiss on the cheek for effect. Mike stayed hidden in the back of the van.

Inside the terminal we found the airline we'd booked with and entered the line that snaked back four long rows. The time it would take for us to get checked in would give anyone following us ample time to find us—we'd anticipated that.

It took twenty-five minutes for us to reach an airline representative that gave us our tickets and checked our bags. Ivan had gone to the attendant two stalls to the left of Sue and me. As our luggage disappeared on the conveyor belt, I wondered if we'd ever see our suitcases again.

We waited a minute for Ivan to join us before proceeding toward security. There was a steady stream of people all walking in the same direction. That was good.

Ahead of us was a janitor fiddling with his cart of cleaning supplies on the left side of the corridor. As soon as we were a few feet away he locked eyes with me and opened a door next to him. We walked through, and the door closed behind us.

We were in a supply room. In front of us hung three sets of airport janitorial outfits clipped to a rack of industrial cleaning products. Each had a short strip of masking tape with the letter S, I, or N written on it. We each took the one meant for us and pulled them over our clothes. The navy-blue pants had stretchy waistbands, and the navy-blue smocks had a yellow strip on each side. Ivan's and mine had padding sewn in the front to give us the appearance of having sizable guts. There were caps as well that we pulled down low. Sue's hat had a black wig sewn into it, and she put on platform shoes that gave her four inches of extra height. A mirror on the wall allowed us to make any needed adjustments.

"Good to go?" I asked.

Ivan and Sue nodded. Their disguises looked effective.

As we'd read in Jorge's note, there was a different exit to the room. As we approached, the door opened and a Latino man in the same clothing we had on walked in. We hesitated. He held out a ring with two keys on it. That was the next step of the plan, so I walked forward and took them from him.

Proceeding out the door, we turned left as per our instructions. I didn't bother looking around to see if anyone had spotted us or if we were being followed; this was either going to work or it wasn't. Our heads were down and forward, like three airport janitors just doing their job.

The corridor was crowded, and we had to weave around people. We turned the corner, and the door with the correct number on it was to our right. I used one of the keys to unlock it. It led to an employee changing area with lockers along one wall. No one was there. We discarded our disguises, shoving them into an empty locker.

Sue pointed to the opposite end of the long room. "There it is."

I used the second key to open that door. We walked out into a small courtyard with a slightly ajar gate at the end.

We paused to look around before opening the gate. Jorge stood fifty feet away next to a nondescript gray cargo van.

We ran in a crouch and jumped in the back.

Jorge was in the driver's seat in a matter of seconds and we were off.

There was a wooden bench with cushions on either side for us to sit on. The only window was the front windshield. The duffel bags were there, next to a couple of rolled-up lengths of foam and thin blankets.

Mike was sitting on the bench right behind the front passenger's seat, smiling. "We did it."

I didn't want to celebrate yet and moved around Sue to sit right behind the driver's seat. I watched as Jorge maneuvered the bigger van out of the airport and onto the road leading to Interstate 20.

"Notice anyone?" I finally asked to the back of his head.

"So far, so good." Jorge was checking his mirrors constantly.

Ivan had moved up to the opposite bench, next to Mike. "How long will it take us?"

"More than twenty-four hours." I'd been the one who'd mapped out our route. "Fifteen hundred miles, give or take."

Ivan leaned his head back against a metal rib of the unfinished van. "Might as well get comfortable."

Sue reached for a duffel bag and started rooting around until she found a sweatshirt.

"You cold?" Mike asked. "I'm warm."

"I have less fat than you," Sue prodded.

"Hey, I've lost a bunch of weight." Mike showed a bicep and flexed. "I'm lean."

Sue smiled. "You're lean ... er."

The duffel bag switch was a good idea. They were Jorge's. We'd transferred our warm-weather clothes and toiletries to the duffels. We'd left our bulkier clothes and a few hotel towels for weight in our suitcases.

"Jorge, you must thank your custodial friends for the help," Ivan said.

"They owed me a favor." Jorge glanced back at Ivan. "Come sit in the passenger seat. It's more comfortable."

Ivan took him up on his offer. "It's not going to take long for the authorities to figure out we didn't get on the planes, but we have a head start."

"And they have no idea which way we're going," I added.

We entered onto I-20, heading east.

Everyone settled in and got as comfortable as possible.

I rummaged around the duffel bag containing my belongings and found the only bulky article of clothing I'd kept, a sweatshirt. I used it as a pillow against the metal wall.

With idle time I was curious about Mike's last year. He was sitting across from me. "So what happened to you after getting away from the cabin outside of Vancouver?"

Mike looked like he was dozing off. "Oh, um, it seems so long ago already." He sat up straighter. It was like his mind went away for a moment and then came back. "It really freaked me out, seeing

Tanner and Dr. Roth get shot right beside me. It fucks you up ... you know."

I knew the feeling.

Sue was next to me. "Yeah."

"I felt like I needed to get far away and regroup. Jorge and Lorraine wanted me to stick with them while they figured out how to hook back up with you all. At the time I thought the farther away I was from you guys the safer I'd be. I realize now that I wasn't thinking straight."

It was rare to hear Mike talk about how he felt. His usual response to everything was, "Whatever, fuck it."

"I figured that since I was a bit player, I could get away and the Naintosa thugs wouldn't track me. And it worked for a while ..." He zoned out again and then came back. "I rode a bus east to Kelowna. Not a bad place to lay low—desert, big lake, fruit orchards, and wineries. A guy I grew up with, Bob, married a Canadian, and they lived there, so I stayed with them for a few months. They had two annoying young kids and a small place, so I couldn't stay with them indefinitely. Plus, I was scared to access my bank account, so I worked with Bob in construction, banging nails, which sucked."

"I don't see you doing manual labor," I said.

Sue pushed up against the side of the van for support. "What happened next?"

"Bob's wife had a cousin who was a pot grower. He had a supply line to get his product to the US. There was a border exchange point in the middle of nowhere at a place called Midway."

I remembered driving through Midway when Morgan and I went to Christina Lake to hide and write the exposé. A lump formed in my throat at the memory.

"You could only get to the place on dirt bike at night. I had to be doubled on the bike by some big smelly fucker. I got across and was given a ride by the US pot bandits all the way to Wenatchee.

Those guys were serious grease balls—missing teeth, tattoos, Pantera blaring from the cassette player of the pickup. I had to pound Jack Daniels with them and chain-smoke Camel un-filters, just to fit in."

The way he said it made me think of a number of sarcastic comments, but I wanted to be supportive of Mike because it wasn't funny for him. I glanced at Sue and her jaw was clenched, most likely feeling the same way.

Mike looked from me to Sue. "It was serious. I was scared."

"Sounds serious," I said.

"What happened then?" Sue added in a reassuring tone.

"I caught a bus to my sister's place in Bellingham and lay low there. I didn't go out for the longest time."

Bellingham brought back another memory of when Morgan and I passed through there on our way to and from Vancouver. "I didn't know your sister lived there."

"She married a wildlife photographer, and they moved there. Cool guy. And Bellingham has a big arts community. Anyway, I kept up with what you put on your website, including the final 2020 Report. After a while I realized my life was worth nothing just sitting around hiding. That encouraged me to want to get back on the trail of the seed bank, but I thought I'd be best flying alone under the radar. So I planned my expedition to Norway. You know the rest already—almost got caught, was chased, got back to Amsterdam, and then came to find you guys. Barf. The end."

# CHAPTER 22

*May 15, 2003*

We'd all taken turns driving. The only times the van would stop was for gas, restroom, and food breaks, or the number of occasions when there was heavy traffic in larger cities.

Everyone else was asleep. I checked the rear-view mirror out of habit. We hadn't spotted anyone tailing us the whole way. There hadn't been many cars on the road overnight since I'd taken over driving, and this stretch was long straight bridge, after long straight bridge, with some land occasionally thrown in. What I could see of the scenery in the dark was beautiful—vast ocean and then white sand beaches, palm trees, and cute villages, on almost every island.

The sky was beginning to lighten, and it promised to be another sunny day. I glanced at the clock on the dashboard—it had taken us seven hours longer than I'd thought it would.

More vehicles were now on the road as we passed by a naval air station that practically took up a whole key.

"Are we close?" Ivan had awoken in the passenger seat.

"I think so," I said.

"There's a map in the glove box." Jorge knelt between the seats.

Sue and Mike were awake too and crouched behind Jorge to look out the windshield.

Ivan found the map, and I reached into my pocket for the paper with the address.

None of us had been to Key West before, except for Jorge, who'd been once.

We crossed another long bridge, and at the end was a sign that read, WELCOME TO KEY WEST.

"I just might retire here," Mike said. "Let my hair grow, stick my toes in the sand, listen to Jimmy Buffet songs all day long."

"I could see that," Sue said.

Following Ivan's directions, we turned left onto White Street.

A block before a marina we turned onto a boulevard lined with palm trees and shops on both sides. At the corner of the next block, we found what we were looking for. It was so early in the morning that we were able to park right out front of Ang's Fish Market and Charters.

Everyone got out and stretched their legs. It had been a long thirty-two hours in the cargo van.

The air was refreshingly cool with flat light as the sun was just beginning to peek over the horizon. The smell of the ocean surrounded the island. Yet a sudden waft of dog poo overpowered all other scents.

"Don't people clean up after their dogs around here?" Mike asked no one in particular. "That reminds me, I need a toilet. Nature is waking up."

"Don't draw attention," Jorge said.

"From whom?" Mike asked. "The place is deserted."

Cries of seagulls could be heard, yet otherwise all was quiet.

The fish market wouldn't be open for another two hours. We noticed a popular chain's coffee shop down the street and decided to go there. Its green mermaid logo beckoned us.

As we walked a street sweeper rounded the corner, its sound

overamplified due to the lack of background noise.

Only a few patrons were inside the shop. The restrooms could only hold one person at a time so we alternated, making Mike go last. Everyone ordered variations of coffee. There weren't any specific breakfast foods, so we settled for muffins.

Once back outside, we strolled back to the fish market.

At the end of the block Sue pointed to benches one street over on a promenade. "We could wait there."

As the sun rose higher, a breeze was kicking up, intensifying the salty tang in the air.

Past the buildings the view opened up to show the ocean beyond a decent-size marina. There were boats of every size and shape. On the promenade we sat down on two side-by-side, metal-ribbed white benches.

"Nice place," Ivan said.

"Very chill," Mike said.

"Look at that beach over there." Sue pointed to the right.

I turned my head in the direction Sue had drawn our attention to and noticed a man walking toward us. I recognized him. It was the man we were looking for.

"There's Paul." Sue stood up.

Paul saw us, too, and quickened his stride. Next to him and keeping pace was a chocolate Labrador retriever, tongue lolling.

Sue and I stepped forward to greet him.

"You made it," Paul said as he came up to us.

I went to shake his hand, but he embraced me instead, then Sue.

The muscular dog sat down on his haunches a few feet away and sniffed the air.

Sue introduced Paul to the others. Paul and Mike had remembered meeting before.

I patted the dog on the head, and he looked up at me, eyes approving.

"This is Tao," Paul said. "He's our family protector and guide ... very wise."

"He's beautiful," Sue said.

"He goes where I go," Paul said.

Paul was small in stature but had a large energy about him. I'd always seen him in button-down shirts and dress slacks when he was the editor of the *Seattle News*, but now he looked right at home in a T-shirt and cargo shorts. He'd aged since we last saw him, his tanned skin taking on a leathery texture with wrinkles setting deeper. However, the black-rimmed glasses were the same.

"I see you've all got coffee," Paul said. "Let's go to my store and figure you out."

We followed Paul and Tao across the street and into an alley, passing a loading bay to reach the back entrance of his fish market.

There were two men—one younger, the other more elderly, both of Asian descent, filleting fish on a stainless-steel table. The room had a concrete floor and white tiled walls. We kept going and walked down a hall with boxes piled on one side until we reached an office. One wall had a window that looked out into the store, where we could see refrigerated displays, a glass-fronted freezer, and shelves running down the middle of the room that contained canned and packaged goods. The office's white walls had several pictures of boats moored or out at sea. The room was set up in the way Paul kept everything—neat and orderly.

Paul took a seat behind the old chipped-and-scratched desk in a well-worn chair on casters. He motioned for us to sit in five similar chairs, less the casters, across from him. Tao went straight to a tan dog bed in the corner.

"So, you need me to take you to a Caribbean island, where you can get a plane to somewhere?" Paul restated from our phone conversation. "I'm assuming it's because your movements are being tracked and you don't want certain people to know where you're going."

Ivan gestured with his hands. "You see, we have been conducting experiments and have made findings about ..." He stalled midsentence, as if not sure how much to divulge.

"I've kept up with as much as I could find about what you're all doing." Paul slanted his head toward a desk top computer. "Rest assured, Dr. Popov, I believe in your findings and want to help in any way I can."

Ivan looked visibly relieved.

"You're an upstanding guy," Mike said. "Always have been."

Paul smiled at Mike. "And from what I remember, you like to get into trouble now and again ... but your heart is in the right place."

Mike visibly blushed.

Paul had never been afraid of fighting for causes he believed in. He was a man of integrity, and his word meant everything. It was known that his retirement from the *Seattle News* wasn't just because his parents were elderly and someone needed to take over running the family business, but because of an ethical issue with GM Comm. What that exact ethical issue was, he'd kept to himself.

"As I mentioned to Nick, I have a boat big enough to take you, if you can spare the time it would take."

"Getting away unnoticed is the most important objective," I said.

Paul nodded. "Do you have a particular island in mind?"

"Saint Thomas, US Virgin Islands, would be ideal," Jorge said. "That's where the individual who's going to help us on the next leg of our journey is based."

Jorge had told us that he had an old friend there who was a pilot and had two planes.

"You see, we'll be going to ..."

Paul cut Mike off. "I don't need to know your final destination. It's better that I don't."

Mike nodded in acknowledgement. "It's just that we trust you."

"You're dealing with ruthless organizations, and I don't want to have where you're going beaten out of me." Paul stood and took a framed map of the Caribbean off the wall and placed it on the desk.

We all huddled closer.

"I've chartered to most of the islands before." Paul put his finger on Key West. "Our starting point." He moved his finger down and around Cuba. "We can't stop to refuel in Cuba, so it'll have to be Puerto Plata, Dominican Republic." His finger moved again. "From there, we can get to Saint Thomas."

"How long will the voyage take?" Ivan looked worried. "We might not have that much time."

Paul took his finger off the map and opened a drawer in the desk. He pulled out a chart and started writing calculations on a pad of paper. "It's eleven hundred and seventy miles as the crow flies. So approximately ..." He made more calculations. "Two and a half days, give or take, depending on the weather."

Ivan seemed to relax. "That's manageable."

"Even though, hopefully, you weren't followed here," Paul said. "This is a good plan, because it definitely throws off any pursuers by taking you off the grid."

Everyone was in agreement.

Paul nodded. "How about you go wander around for, let's say, two hours, while I get things setup?"

"Thank you for doing all of this, Paul," Sue said. "I'm sure you have a lot of other stuff you need to be doing."

"For you, anything." He stood up. "You all have to try to stop this population control plan ... and whatever I could do to make Davis Lovemark's life more difficult, I'm for."

We found a place to have breakfast and then took a walk along the promenade, admiring the warm sea air and the ocean we would soon be on.

We wondered out loud about what Paul had said regarding hopefully not having been followed to Key West. Could the Naintosa men in the Ford have been a mile behind us and now lurking somewhere? I was confident they weren't because of the long straight bridges across the Keys—I would've noticed.

Using the burner phone I'd given him, Jorge called his pilot friend on Saint Thomas to confirm he could fly us to Bogota in three or four days. "All set," Jorge said as he pocketed the phone after the call.

We turned around to head back to the fish market.

"I apologize, but I have to ask again," Jorge said. "You trust Paul with your lives, right?"

"Yes," Sue said. "As much as I trust you."

"Me too," I added.

"I'd vouch for him," Mike said.

"He seems to dislike Davis Lovemark," Ivan said.

"Yeah, but he won't tell us why," Sue said. "There was some sort of ethical dilemma."

"Which isn't hard to find with Lovemark," I added.

We turned off the promenade at the spot where we first met Paul.

This time we entered through the front door of Ang's Fish Market and Charters.

Mrs. Ang was behind the counter, helping customers. She was a petite woman with an easy smile and personality to match. She acknowledged us and bobbed her head to the left toward her husband's office.

Paul was hanging up the phone when we walked in. "Perfect timing."

We filed in and took seats.

Tao was in his bed and got up to a sitting position, his thick tail thumping against the wall.

"We're all set to go," Paul said. "We leave tomorrow just before sunrise."

"What can we do to help get ready?" Jorge asked.

"Miguel, my trusted second in command, is gathering supplies," Paul said. "You can help him load. Then we'll all spend the night aboard the boat."

"How much do we owe you?" Jorge asked.

"Well ..."

"Paul, charge us what you would a regular charter," I said.

"We can afford to pay you," Sue added.

Paul reached for his dated desktop calculator and began to punch in numbers. "All right, you can pay for the food, supplies, fuel, and Miguel's salary, but I'm not charging you my fee."

I opened my mouth to tell him to include his time and effort.

"No discussion on that." Paul took out a receipt book and wrote out prices and what they were for, then ripped out the white page and passed it to Jorge.

Jorge nodded. "You may want to get rid of the yellow copy so there's no record of this voyage."

"Good point." Paul tore the second page from the book, took the sheet he had given Jorge and placed them in the shredder next to where Tao was. The dog leaned away from the short burst of noise. "You'll pay in cash?"

Jorge lifted the edge of his shirt and unzipped a pouch that was attached somehow to the inside of his jeans. He retrieved the appropriate amount of hundred-dollar bills and passed them over.

Paul swivelled in his chair to a cupboard behind his desk and pulled a knob, exposing a safe. He turned the dial three times to open it and deposited the money inside. "Okay, let's go help Miguel."

He led us to the rear processing area again, where next to the two men who were still gutting fish a slim young Latino man was loading boxes onto a pallet resting on a manual hand forklift.

"Miguel, this is our charter group," Paul said. "They're hands-on people and want to help us get ready. Show them what to do."

"Hi, Miguel," Sue said.

He blushed and pointed toward the corner of the room. "You can bring those coolers and put them on this empty pallet." His accented Mexican voice cracked. He had brown tanned skin, curly black hair, and traces of acne scars on his face. His sharp-brown eyes avoided contact with ours.

Paul gave a broad smile. "I hope you all like to eat fish."

After the pallets were filled, we loaded them into a trailer that was attached to a pickup truck. Jorge brought the van around to the loading bay, and we took our belongings out, adding them to the trailer. Jorge gave Paul the van keys and the name of the trusted owner that would pick it up in seven days.

It was a short distance to where the boat was docked at the marina. Jorge, Mike, and I rode in the trailer, while Sue and Ivan were in the cab of the truck with Miguel. Paul would join us later.

When Miguel opened the trailer door to let us out, we saw that he'd been able to come up right beside the boat. Actually, it was a hundred-foot, three-level yacht, with a clean, white fiberglass hull glistening against dark varnished-wood accents.

"Holy shit," Mike said. "This ship is sweet."

Miguel looked proud. "It has everything you need to be comfortable on open-ocean voyages."

We formed a loading chain to place the supplies on board.

The interior featured wood-paneled walls around large windows. Wood beams ran in parallel lines across the off-white ceiling. Brown-and-white furniture sat atop plush beige carpet. The word that best described the ship's appearance was "stately."

"Follow me," Miguel said. "You each get your own room."

He led us down a level, and we each picked our own bedroom. Mine had a queen-size bed with a brown duvet, white walls, a round window a few feet above the water level, plus my own bathroom with a shower.

Half of what we brought on board went into a storage room; the other half went into a full-size galley that had clean granite counters and stainless-steel appliances.

Once everything was stored away, we settled in the living area.

"After being on the run for so long, sitting here on this awesome ship makes me think of just going out to sea and waiting everything out." Mike placed his beer atop a coaster on the glass coffee table, leaned back, and stretched his arms above his head.

Sue sat across from Mike in a matching brown leather chair. "Nice thought, but you know after a week we'd all want to get back after the fuckers."

"I know, I know. It's nice to dream about escaping all of it, though." Mike stood up. "Time for a smoke."

"I haven't seen you smoking much since you've returned," Sue pointed out.

"I'm trying to cut back and hopefully quit." Mike walked toward the sliding door to the rear outside deck. "Besides, I'm tired of you giving me snide remarks that I stink."

Sue smiled. "That's good. My comments are having the right effect, then."

❀

We'd offered to help Miguel prepare dinner, but he declined, telling us to enjoy the down time. No one complained.

Paul arrived at dusk. "Everyone all settled in?" He went straight for the bar fridge and grabbed a beer.

"Hey, where's Tao?" Sue asked. "I thought he was always with you."

"Always with me on land." Paul twisted the cap off the bottle. "He gets seasick."

Our meal consisted of tacos with fresh-caught flounder and *pico de gallo*, refried beans, and salad. The food disappeared in no time.

Ivan finished chewing. "Miguel, you are an amazing cook."

Everyone nodded and raised their wineglass or beer bottle to him.

I was surprised at how much everyone was drinking; even Jorge had a couple. I guessed it was because we felt safe for the moment and we knew we were going on a boat trip tomorrow. I decided to stop drinking at that point—someone had to have their wits about them.

I was sitting between Sue and Paul when I thought I'd give it another try. "So, Paul, you never did tell us what your problem with Davis Lovemark was."

"Yeah, what did he do to you?" Sue said. "You know about what he did to us."

Paul seemed to ponder for a moment, before saying, "Remember, Nick, when Senator Lawrence gave you false information, then you wrote about it, it was published, and then he referred to it as factual?"

"How could I forget the information laundering incident; it screwed me up for a long time."

"I practically had to talk him off the ledge," Sue added.

"Well, it wasn't the first time Lovemark had helped his causes and cronies by encouraging it," Paul said.

I hadn't known Lovemark specifically had something to do with it. Another piece fit into place.

"I was tired of the bullshit." Paul finished the remainder of his beer. "The last straw was when I caught him and his right-hand man, Russell Norman, gaslighting."

"What's 'gaslighting'?" I asked.

Mike came over to listen, bringing a fresh beer for Paul. "That's an extreme bullying tactic."

Paul welcomed the new beer. "Gaslighting is used by unscrupulous people to gain power over others. It makes the victims question their own reality. The bully tells blatant lies and then denies them, even if the victim has proof of the lies. They keep doing it until they wear their target down. Then they throw in positive reinforcement to confuse and weaken the victim. Finally, they project whatever the victim thinks the bully is doing back onto the victim. The bully tells the victim and the people around them that they are crazy. It's a long game, takes time, and can be performed on a large scale."

"Is that ever manipulative," Sue said.

"Lovemark has no fucking scruples," Mike said.

I thought of a specific dictator, and gaslighting fit with what he was doing to his people. "And you found Lovemark and Norman doing that to someone?"

"Not to *someone* but to *everyone*—multiple times and on a huge scale for oil companies, Naintosa, Pharmalin, and others." Paul looked frustrated. "I couldn't take what they wanted us to publish anymore. And when I had the opportunity to call him on it to his face, he said I was overexaggerating and then tried to bully *me*. I quit the next day. I guess I could've fought him, like you are, but I didn't have it in me anymore."

Sue patted his lap. "Now we know."

"That's why I want to do at least this little part for you now."

# CHAPTER 23

*May 16, 2003*

I was awakened by footsteps running on a wooden surface. There were loud whispers that I couldn't understand. My stateroom was on the dock side. Sitting up, I could see out the porthole. It was still dark outside, but there was a lamppost nearby, illuminating the area. Nothing out of the ordinary was in my view.

The big boat shuddered as the engines ignited, followed by a faint, consistent vibration.

I jumped out of bed, grabbed my T-shirt and shorts off the floor, and went out into the hall. I caught a glimpse of Jorge as he climbed the stairs. Sue came out of her room at the same time but fully clothed; I was still fumbling to pull my shirt on.

"Something's going on," I said.

We followed to where Jorge had gone.

Sue reached the stairs first. "We were planning on leaving at five, but it's only three thirty."

At the top of the stairs, we went to the window of the living area and saw Jorge outside, his handgun drawn, moving starboard and out of view.

Sue and I went out the back sliding door.

Jorge was untying a thick rope. He saw us and motioned for us to do the same at the bow.

We ran the thirty feet. Sue pulled up the bumper, and I undid the knot.

There was a young Asian male standing on the dock looking from us to the shore. *Is the kid with us?* I followed the direction his head pointed and saw two figures running toward where we were. They had to be three hundred yards away but closing.

A whistle from above caught the boy's attention. He loped up the gangway and then retracted it electrically.

The stern line was off, and I'd just dislodged the last part of rope around the cleat when the boat began to move. We were thrown off balance.

Jorge was running toward us and practically picked up the boy and pushed him forward. "Inside!"

We followed.

The yacht began to turn.

We were about twenty feet from the dock when the two men ran up and stopped. They both had guns in their hands.

I recognized the big guy immediately. He was the one who tried to grab us in Dallas.

"The Naintosa fuckers from the Ford," Sue said.

They held their guns up and seemed to be searching for someone to shoot at. They scanned from starboard to bow and we made eye contact.

Sue and I immediately ducked, not wanting to give them targets.

Jorge was in-between the windows, peering around the sill, gun drawn.

"They've found us," I said.

Ivan was standing at the top of the stairs, and I motioned with my hand to stay put. He nodded.

The boy, who I guessed was around thirteen years old, had obviously been standing watch. He was now cowering behind the bar.

Miguel ran up the stairs to the bridge.

The boat had completed the turn away from the dock and was now in the channel exiting the marina.

Jorge went to the other side of the room to watch the men on the pier. Sue, Ivan, and I followed. They were now just silhouettes.

"We made a mistake somewhere along the line," Jorge said.

"Or they did follow us from Dallas," I said.

"No, they would've grabbed us yesterday," Jorge said.

Paul came down the stairs from the bridge. "Everyone all right?" Everyone acknowledged that they were.

"Good. This means we leave ahead of schedule." Paul looked toward the bar. "Ji, thank you for being so fast and watchful. Since you'll be coming with us, you might as well do some work. I'll call your mother and let her know you're helping me on a charter."

The short teenager, Ji, who had a slight build, stood up and followed Paul, who led him toward the galley.

"What's going on?" Mike's voice was hoarse. He stood at the top of the stairs that came up from the cabins.

Sue exhaled. "We just had a close encounter of the Ford kind."

Mike's eyes were bloodshot and the skin around them puffy. He'd gotten drunk last night and had been chain smoking, lighting one off the other.

〓〓〓

The day was clear and the salty breeze warm. Black-backed gulls floated on the thermals, diving down to the water when they spotted meals, a few alighting on our railing for a rest. The waves were high enough to keep the boat swaying and rolling.

Sue and I sat on reclining chairs on the starboard outside deck.

"Did you notice how Mike looked this morning?" she asked.

I nodded. "Yeah."

"He's been drinking every chance he gets since he met back up with us," Sue said. "This isn't the time to go on a bender."

"He's a good guy and has flaws like the rest of us, but I've noticed a change since he's returned," I said. "Either something more happened in the last year that he hasn't told us about or this being chased is affecting him harder."

Sue sat up. "We should talk to him. I wouldn't hold it against him if this is too much for him to handle."

Mike came out the sliding glass doors.

"What's that?" Sue asked.

"Bloody Mary." He sat down next to us on a reclining chair. "Takes the edge off." Mike licked the salt and pepper rim and then took a sip. "It's really good. You should get Miguel to make you one—he has many talents."

"I think I'll wait." Sue said.

It was as good a time as any to talk to him. "So, Mike ..."

Sue got right to it. "We've noticed you haven't been yourself since you've met back up with us, and that you're drinking harder than usual."

"Is there anything you missed telling us about?" I sat up and turned to face him. I was the last person who should criticize someone's drinking, because I was known to drink too much. However, that was during downtime. I was always conscious about not consuming too much alcohol when we were in the thick of things and I needed my mind to be sharp.

"It's understandable if this is too stressful for you," Sue said.

"I told you what happened." Mike turned stubborn. "I drink when I'm nervous, and being chased and having my life in danger makes me plenty nervous. You two can't say that you aren't scared too, and you're the last ones to counsel me on drinking."

With his guard up, this discussion wasn't going to go anywhere.

We'd have to try when he was more receptive.

"Okay, if you ever want to talk more, we're always here to listen." Sue looked over at me. "We should meditate."

"Oh gawd." Mike got up and walked back inside.

"That was easy." She smiled. "Let's just keep an eye on him."

"Agreed. I'm sure he'll snap out of it." I lowered my sunglasses and adjusted my baseball cap so it wouldn't fly off in the wind. "And just mention the word meditation, and he gets all freaked out."

"We haven't meditated since we were in Burford." Sue was also wearing a baseball cap and sunglasses. "Want to?"

"Sure." I always found a woman in a baseball cap with a ponytail sticking out the back sexy. I wasn't sure why, but I did.

A plane with pontoons flew low overhead. We watched to see if it would turn back to us, but it didn't. There were other boats on the water that we could see, but none seemed to be following or paying any attention to us.

"Okay, see you in twenty minutes." I closed my eyes and focused on my breathing, in and out. The sound of the wind and the wake provided a good background and the swaying back and forth lulled me, so I was able to clear my mind. I went to my inner room, sliding without effort into the gap. In my mind's eye I was in a jungle. *Sue was beside me. We were making slow progress, because of the thick underbrush. There were faces, watching us. The people had deformities and their eyes and mouths showed great sadness and fear.*

"Get you anything?" said a voice with a heavy Chinese accent.

That brought me out of the gap. I took a deep breath and opened my eyes. Young Ji was standing in front of us. Since we had our sunglasses on, he wouldn't have known that our eyes were closed.

"No, thank you," I said.

"I'm feeling a tad peckish," Sue said. "I'll come inside in a moment."

"I have put out some snacks on the bar." Ji gave a slight bow and then went back in through the sliding doors.

"Well, that was short-lived." Sue leaned forward. "How was it? Did you see anything?"

"I did, actually." I explained the jungle and the people.

Sue was smiling the whole time. "Cool, I love it when we're in sync. I had almost the identical vision."

It never ceased to excite me when we were in the flow together. It was good reinforcement that we were on the right path. "What do you think it meant?"

"Well, we are on our way to the Colombian jungle."

"The deformities and sadness must be from the people being experimented on," I added. "Pretty self-explanatory."

"Yep, I agree." Sue got up and stumbled from the rocking. "I'm going to go have a snack ... and make sure Mike isn't getting shit-faced again." She bent over and kissed my forehead. "Want anything?"

"That was nice."

"Just felt like it."

I liked the little gesture. "I'll join you in a bit. I'm going to go up to the bridge."

We both went inside. Mike was sitting at the bar munching on some snacks set out in bowls. His drink was almost empty.

I climbed the stairs, holding onto the railing for support.

Paul had his hands on the large chrome spoked ship's wheel and was sitting on a raised, amber-colored chair. The enclosed bridge had windows on all sides. Jorge was next to him in a matching chair, and Ivan was standing behind them.

We hit a set of larger waves, direct and hard. My shoulder bounced off the wall, and I grabbed the railing that ran around the perimeter of the bridge.

Ivan had to grab the back of Jorge's chair to steady himself.

"Here, take this seat." Jorge stood and gestured to Ivan. "I'm going to go get my binoculars."

"There are binoculars here." Paul pointed to the corner where a pair of Bushnell Marine's hung on a hook.

"That's okay, I prefer my own." Jorge walked by, swaying. "Hi, Nick." He continued down the stairs.

"How are you, my boy?" Ivan perched on the chair Jorge had surrendered to him.

"Fine." I replied. "I just wanted to see how you're doing up here."

"Sea's a little rough today," Paul said.

# CHAPTER 24

*May 17, 2003*

E veryone but Ji was on the bridge as we idled out of the marina in Puerto Plata. We were all staring at the black screen with green dots everywhere. There was one dot in particular we were concerned about.

"I first noticed it leave Key West fifty-five minutes after we did," Miguel said.

"It could be just another boat on the same path we're on." Paul was steering us out into open water.

"Or it could be the Naintosa thugs," I said.

"That boat is traveling a little slower than we are, but they made up time when we just stopped to add fuel," Paul said. "However, chances are they'll have to stop as well."

"If they have radar they can track us like we're tracking them," Jorge said.

"Yes." Paul pushed the throttle forward. "We can't go much faster than we already have been, but I'll increase our speed by three knots."

"And we'll keep watching," Miguel said.

No one could keep their eyes off that little dot.

# INTERLOGUE 7

Carlo pressed the red "Kill" switch and kicked the stand out on his orange-and-black KTM 640 Enduro. It was way more motorcycle than he needed to get around the family's large tracts of land, but it made him feel virile. He was proud that he could still handle such a powerful machine at forty-eight. Usually he had a rush of excitement when he rode, but not today. This evening he was angry.

Davis sat in his New York office at GMNN, which he used when he was home on the East Coast. Office staff would be leaving for the day, but he was stuck to his oxblood leather chair, not wanting to move, unwilling to accept what his physician had told him moments ago.

The intercom sounded and a sultry female voice said, "Mr. Lovemark, are you there?"

Davis didn't want to speak, but with reluctance said, "Yes."

"Mr. Da Silva is still waiting on line one."

"Fine." Davis took a deep breath and picked up the receiver. "Carlo, sorry to keep you waiting."

"We have a real problem." Carlo's voice was an octave higher than normal. It was rare that he was outwardly upset. "A different strain of wheat has materialized on my most eastern field—Naintosa's genetically engineered plants are taking over my ancient grain."

"Could it be seed from a nearby field that's drifting onto your land?" Davis said.

"There are no fields next door, only mountains. It was either drift from a long way away or someone purposely spread the seed."

"Hmm ... sabotage?"

"Also, the vines growing on the north side of my property have died."

"The genetically engineered wheat wouldn't cause that."

"Of course not. They were killed with glyphosate."

"You don't use glyphosate. You brag about that all the time."

"Of course we don't."

"Then it was sabotage," Davis said. "I remember seeing a fence, does it go all around the perimeter?"

"Yes, it's more of a wall and hard to get over."

"Do you have cameras?"

"Not everywhere; it's a tremendously large property. Yet I will have them installed, even though the damage has already been done. This is not good, Davis."

"I know." Davis took a second to think.

"I feel like we're losing control." There was no trace of Carlo's cool and calm demeanor; only frustration and anger. "Not just my farm but the whole plan."

"I've decided to go to the Colombian lab personally," Davis said. "We need to know what's happening."

"I tried to call Hendrick but couldn't reach him."

"I know he's at the lab now. He won't talk to me either." Davis had additional motivation—his health diagnosis.

"Do you want me to join you?"

"I'll let you know if that's necessary after I get there," Davis said.

"But you should plan for it."

"As we agreed, I've met with Hendrick's younger brother," Carlo said on the other end of the line. "Günter is receiving the same education as the Schmidts before him, seems brighter than Hendrick V, personable, and even-tempered."

"That's positive," Davis said. "Can we speed up his education?"

"Possibly by a year, maybe two. I've already begun the process. Also, I spoke with Ivgeni Svetlov, and his brother might be able to help in the interim. I have arranged a meeting in Moscow."

"Very good." Davis felt the recurring pain in his intestinal area but didn't let on to Carlo. "I'll see what Hendrick's progress and stability is."

"Keep me posted," Carlo said. "And ask Dr. Smith if he knows of any way the damage could've been caused to my wheat and vines without sabotage."

Davis had a sudden intense need to relieve his bowels, and sweat formed on his brow. He had to cut the call short. The thought of seeing blood in his stool again scared him.

# CHAPTER 25

*May 18, 2003*

We came around a protrusion of land on either side and through a channel that brought us into the natural harbor of Saint Thomas. Sailboats were anchored nearer land, and two cruise ships were moored along a long pier. White buildings with orange roofs populated the shoreline and dotted the steep mountainside. The air was warm and smelled of the tropics, brought on by the breeze.

We had skirted charcoal clouds of rain on our voyage, and now one seemed to be following us into Amalie harbor. The sun disappeared and droplets of water bounced off the window of the bridge next to where I stood.

The dot on the radar had made a brief stop last night and then continued on our same course. Paul had calculated that the boat had sped up even more than we had and was an hour behind us if it came to Saint Thomas.

The marina could easily handle a yacht of Paul's size, and there were a few open slips.

As we idled in, Paul said, "To the right is the charter and cruise-ship terminal. That's where you'll find your pilot friend's office."

Jorge scanned to where the cruise ships were docked.

"Straight ahead is a duty-free mall," Paul added.

There were a number of two-story white stucco buildings with orange tile roofs, all with prominent retailer logos displayed.

"Is that round cabana a bar?" Mike pointed to the right.

Not too far away on an adjacent pier set on pilings was a sizable, round, open-air restaurant with a patio surrounding it and a metal roof painted the customary orange.

"That would be a good place to wait, so you could watch boats coming in," Paul said.

"Good idea," Jorge said. "You can all wait for me there."

Once docked, we departed the boat with our duffel bags, giving a wave to Miguel and Ji. The shower had stopped, and the sun was coming back out.

"Okay, then." Paul gave Sue a hug and shook the men's hands. "Best of luck."

"We really appreciate what you did for us," Sue said.

"Thanks for everything, Paul," I said.

He patted me on the shoulder. "Stay in touch when you can, and let me know if I can help in any way."

"It would help if you published the story of Davis Lovemark gaslighting," I said.

He paused. "Let me think about it. Maybe I should at least write it out so I don't forget the details."

"That's a start."

"Try to leave within an hour, just in case that boat is who we suspect it is," Jorge said.

Paul waved as he went back up the gangway. "That's the plan."

We walked along the pier for about a hundred yards until we reached land.

"I shouldn't be very long." Jorge strode away toward the cruise ships.

We continued along the edge of the mall until we reached the pier that lead to the circular bar and grill. As we stepped atop the wood slats, on either side the water glimmered where the sun's rays hit the ripples.

My shirt was already soaked through with perspiration. It was a relief to step into the shade of the covered patio. A refreshing breeze blew in off the water.

The cabana had seating around its perimeter, with the kitchen and bar in the middle. We found a table that looked out at the cruise ships on the left and the marina on the right where we could see Paul's yacht and the bay in front of us—a perfect spot for boat-spotting.

"I could hang out here," Mike said, lighting a cigarette.

A pretty waitress with large dark eyes, wearing a floral, sleeveless dress covering ample hips, came over to take our drink order and provide us with menus.

A black cloud rolled in across the harbor with an opaque liquid wall below it. The breeze intensified.

Sue gestured. "You all notice what's coming?"

Within a minute, it was raining so hard that we could only see twenty feet beyond the cabana. Even though we were under a roof, we were getting wet from the rain ricocheting off everything. It was refreshing, but the inundation overwhelming.

As soon as it came, it was gone. The sun was back, bringing with it intense humidity.

We passed the time sharing appetizers and looking out at the bay while chatting about the view, along with the past and future.

Jorge had been gone for close to an hour. We hadn't thought it would take him that long.

Mike ordered another beer and lit a smoke.

Boats were going in and out of the harbor, a few coming into the marina. None of them looked suspicious; however, we didn't know what we were specifically looking for.

The sky was taking on shades of yellow and orange. Another dark, possibly rain-soaking cloud that was the shape of a meringue approached.

"Mr. Nick Barnes?"

I turned to see a woman standing behind us. It took a second to recognize her. "Ms. Virk?" It was the reporter who had tried to interview me in Burford and then written a story anyway—Adhira Virk.

"Who's asking?" Mike said.

"What are you doing here?" Sue asked.

"I could ask the same question," Ms. Virk said. "I'm on vacation."

"So are we," I responded.

"Oh? Where are you staying?" Ms. Virk asked.

I hesitated for a split second, but I knew it was enough to cause suspicion in my answer. "We're in transit."

Sue pivoted. "Isn't Saint Thomas a long way from London to come for a vacation?"

"Oh, I've accepted a position at the *New York News*," Ms. Virk said. "Thought I'd take a little break before digging into my new job."

"That's a GM Comm paper," Mike said.

Ivan wasn't saying anything; just watching.

"GM Comm is the biggest media organization in the world." Ms. Virk frowned at Mike and then tried to recover. "A girl's got to make a living. It was hard, freelancing." She turned her attention to me. "How's it feel to be free?"

"I was innocent all along and not a martyr like you wanted, so of course it feels good."

"What's it like to intentionally write misinformation?" Sue wasn't holding back. "I hope your new job is to write opinion pieces and not to be concerned about facts, because that's what your story about Nick was."

Virk's eyes narrowed. "You all need to be careful about what you're saying and doing ..."

We all stood at once. That made Virk take a step back.

I hadn't noticed the two large East Indian men a few paces back until they took a step forward.

Was she really a reporter on vacation? Maybe not. I wanted the conversation to be over.

A boat's horn sounded. It was nearby and kept going in a steady drone.

We all turned to where the noise was coming from. It blared from Paul's yacht that was pulling away from a fueling station along a long dock not too far out. As if he saw that we'd noticed him, the horn stopped.

We'd been distracted by Virk and hadn't seen a large white boat pull into the slip we originally docked at. Leaping onto the pier was the big Naintosa thug from the Ford and another man who I assumed was his partner, because I'd never really gotten a good look at him before.

"Fuck," Sue growled.

"The bad guys?" Mike asked.

"Depends on your perspective," Virk said.

Virk's comment raised my suspicions higher—she may have been there to find and distract us long enough to be caught. We weren't going to wait around to find out. I reached into my pocket, grabbed enough cash to cover our tab and dropped it on the table.

Sue pushed Virk aside. "Excuse us."

I thought we may have to fight the two big guys with Virk, but they parted when all four of us stormed at them. One man bumped into a chair that a lady sat in, spilling her drink. The shaved-head man with the woman who now had green liquid down her cleavage stood. He had a sizable gut but big arms and wore a Hell's Angels wife beater.

We proceeded past, not waiting to see the outcome of the

inevitable confrontation.

When we came out into the open I looked to see where the thugs were. They were standing, looking out at Paul's boat as it was now just out of reach for them. As if on cue they looked in our direction.

For a split second everyone hesitated. They looked to shore. We looked to shore.

We were closer to land and began bolting down the pier.

The thugs took off as well.

As soon as we reached the promenade we veered right, away from where the Naintosa men would be coming from. We were a couple of hundred yards ahead of them. Sue and I were holding back, making sure we stayed at the same pace as Mike and Ivan.

I saw Jorge turn a ninety-degree corner on the promenade from where the nearest cruise ship was and start walking toward us.

We were coming into a congestion of tourists making their way back to their ships as the sun was setting. They would soon be departing back to sea and on to their next port of call.

Mike was breathing hard next to me. Ivan had slowed some to make sure we didn't abandon Mike.

Jorge saw us and stopped. He peered beyond our trajectory and then waved in a circular motion, encouraging us to hurry up.

I snuck a look back and saw the thugs approaching the crowd of tourists. They'd made up ground on us.

We weaved and zagged around meandering vacationers.

Just before we reached Jorge, he turned and started running, leading us. No one said a word and just kept pushing forward.

Turning the corner of the promenade, there was a row of kiosks and single-story storefronts—selling travel excursions, charters, ice cream, and confections, and then a restaurant.

Jorge took a sharp turn into a narrow alley between buildings, and we followed. I brought up the rear, put my hand on Mike's back and nudged him forward; he'd run out of steam but not given up.

We turned left again behind a store, then went to the other end of it and stopped next to a dumpster. We were just in time to see the thugs pass on the promenade. As soon as they were out of view we ran in the same direction.

Just before we entered the crowd again, Jorge opened a door to a business.

The only person inside seemed to be getting ready to leave. It was a charter company, and he was coming from around a desk. He stopped when he saw us, with a short skid on the concrete floor.

"Ricardo, you need to hide us," Jorge said.

"Sure, Jorge. Follow me." Ricardo was a tall, hefty, middle-aged Latino with curly hair cut short. He led us past four desks, down a short hall, and into a supply room.

"The reason we needed anonymity found us," Jorge said.

"How many?" Ricardo asked.

"Two," Jorge said. "One big and one average. White, American."

Ricardo nodded. "Do you have protection?"

"Just me," Jorge responded.

He was the only one who'd kept his gun, as he had a license. The rest of us had left ours with Paul, who was going to place them back in the van in Key West for pick-up. We were going to receive new protection in Colombia.

"Stay here. I'll go watch for them." Ricardo left the door ajar.

We were all catching our breath. Mike had his hands on his knees and was bent over, panting.

"They were on the boat we were suspecting?" Jorge asked.

I nodded. "Had to be."

"Now what?" Sue asked.

"We wait here until we think we're in the clear, and then Ricardo gets us to a safe place until he flies us out in the morning," Jorge said. "That was pretty much the plan anyway."

The room was small and crowded, with office and cleaning

supplies and scuba gear. We had to stand shoulder to shoulder.

Within a few minutes we heard the front door open and Ricardo say, "How can I help you?"

"You charter planes?" a baritone voice asked.

"We have two single-prop island-hoppers and a jet for longer distances." Ricardo had a similar accent to Jorge's. "Unfortunately, they're all booked for the next few days."

"Could they have been booked by two Americans, a short woman, a Colombian, and a Russian?" Baritone asked.

"That sounds like the beginning of a joke," Ricardo said.

"No joke."

"No. My planes are reserved for a pop star, businessmen, and a couple politicians. That *could* be the beginning of a joke."

"Uh-huh."

There was silence for what seemed to be a minute.

"Mind if we look around?" asked Baritone.

"No."

"No, you don't mind that we look around?" a third male voice said.

"No, you can't look around," Ricardo said. "Why would you need to? There's nothing here. Do you think the planes are parked out back?"

Another moment of silence.

"Do you want me to book you a charter later in the week?" Ricardo asked.

"No, thanks," Baritone said.

We heard the door open and close.

# INTERLOGUE 8

Hendrick V wiped his face as he walked into the lab, partly from perspiration and partly from skirting the downpour outside. Drying his wet hands against his white lab coat, he continued past equipment, stations, and scientists until he saw Dr. Daniel Smith sitting on a stool reading a printout.

"Dr. Smith, what are the results?" Hendrick's well-spoken English had a heavy German accent.

Dr. Smith looked up and pushed his wire-framed glasses higher on his nose with his right index finger. "Still not enough reaction." He dug into his lab-coat pocket and produced a pen. He placed the long paper perforated at the folds on the stainless-steel counter and pointed at numbers.

Hendrick bent forward to read the results. "Why are they still not reacting?"

"The adjustments in composition and dosage were promising on the rats but not on the human subjects." Dr. Smith scratched his temple below graying blond hair.

Hendrick moved his stubby finger up the page and then folded it over. He kept tracing until he reached a specific formula result. "These numbers are close with the life-*extending* drug. We could almost be there." He went to another printout on the table. "Your adjusted theory makes sense. So why, then, do your alterations to this life-*saving* formula not rid the cancer?"

"That's the question we keep coming to." Dr. Smith tapped the pen on his front tooth and thought.

Hendrick turned his attention to the white board that had writing in blue marker that only a scientist would understand. He studied it again. "The life-extending drug is based on the current immune-suppressive principles. The cure is based on immune-enhancing principles."

"What if ..." Dr. Smith swiveled on his chair. "The problem could be that the test subjects we are using for the cure have genetically engineered food and pesticide contamination."

Hendrick stared at Dr. Smith as what he had just said registered. "Fuck!" He picked up a blue marker and flung it as hard as he could across the room, narrowly missing an assistant. "Tell the missionaries we need a fresh batch of homeless. And not more deformed ones, they're hard to look at. *Scheisse.* Why didn't you think of that before—like years ago?"

Dr. Smith glanced at the printout and then at Hendrick. "It just came to me, and it makes sense."

"Years my father was trying to make the cure, only to be sabotaged by his own designs."

Dr. Smith cleared his throat. "Actually, he never wanted a cure; I did. I thought we'd found it too. But after what I thought was the initial breakthrough something always wasn't quite right. This makes sense. The genetic engineering and or the glyphosate could be altering genes in more ways than we know."

"Really." Hendrick looked for something else to throw. He was sure people in the lab were hiding throwable objects from him so he'd stop breaking things. Maybe he should punch Dr. Smith for disrespecting his late father. He took a deep breath. "Now we have to retest everything for different parameters. It's going to take so much more time."

"First, we must confirm that the contamination is the problem with new test subjects, starting from the beginning ..." Dr. Smith did a calculation with his pen on the printout. "If everything goes well ... hmm."

"Fuck!" Hendrick didn't wait for Dr. Smith's answer. He knew any further delays were bad. "We're already behind a year as it is."

"We've exhausted pretty much everything else." Dr. Smith shrugged. "We have no other choice."

"*Scheisse!* Get back to work."

The other technicians, scientists, and assistants avoided Hendrick as he walked through the lab. Slamming the door behind him, he continued down the hall to his office.

Otto, chief of security, looked out the window. His tall, slim form was straight, his long arms at his sides.

"Why is it so hot in here?" Hendrick went to the thermostat next to the door. "The lab was cool. Why isn't the air conditioning working in my office? This place was built by idiots."

Otto didn't turn around, instead adjusting his round glasses. "We have a visitor who is now peeking into all the goings on."

"Who?" Hendrick walked to Otto's side to gaze out the window.

It had stopped raining. Tom Crane was standing next to rows of test corn. The stalks were only two feet high. For some unknown reason, after the Plycite gene was spliced into the DNA of the corn, as it grew it was dwarfed and unable to reach maturity.

"What's he doing here?" Hendrick banged on the window.

"He arrived about an hour ago," Otto said.

"Why didn't you tell me?" Hendrick slid open the window and yelled through the screen. "Tom! This way, come here!"

Tom waved and walked from the test plot to a near door of the prefab building.

"Make sure, for however long he's here, Tom has an escort and is not allowed to see any sensitive areas," Hendrick said as he went over to the computer on his desk. "Hopefully he'll only be here for five minutes."

"I don't know why he doesn't have an escort already. He should've been assigned one at the gate." Otto was stern. "I will have to do it myself."

"Well, hello there." Tom entered the office. He wore a teal button-down, short-sleeved shirt, sans his trademark bowtie, tan cargo shorts, and brown socks and sandals.

"Tom, how are you?" Hendrick motioned for him to sit down on a metal chair at the opposite side of the desk. "I don't remember inviting you here."

"I thought I'd come have a look at your operation." Tom sat. "There seem to be some problems. I told Carlo and Davis. I'm sure they've mentioned them to you."

"I'm too busy to speak with them. Don't ever communicate challenges to them. Come directly to me."

"The Africans and Indians are having difficulty growing the soy and corn we gave them."

*More problems.* What had he inherited? If he could kill his father again, he would, but he'd make him fix everything first. "What, exactly?"

"The yields of soy are lower than their conventional counterparts, and there is a high degree of dried-out pods, they think due to the climate. They are asking for a variety that grows better in hot weather. The corn ears are smaller than they're used to, and frankly they say the corn doesn't taste very good—it's dry. Animals don't even like it."

"Both the soy and the corn are grown in Texas, and they're fine," Hendrick said. "It can't be that much hotter in India and Africa."

"In some places, yes," Tom said. "What about soil composition?"

"Yes, that definitely plays a role."

Tom pointed to the window. "Is that corn out there the same variety?"

"No, that has the Plycite gene."

"What's a Plycite gene?"

Hendrick realized he'd slipped up. "It's not important."

Tom gave Hendrick a quizzical look.

Hendrick wasn't going to explain how the Plycite gene created antibodies that attacked sperm, causing infertility in people, and that the corn was the delivery system—another step in mass population control. "I will send people to India and Africa to look into the issues."

"What about going back to a previous generation of seed that you know worked?"

"That's not an option."

# CHAPTER 26

*May 19, 2003*

Yesterday we'd waited in the charter store for two hours until we were sure the coast was clear before Ricardo drove us to his family's home to get some sleep.

⋈⬤⋈

As I climbed the six retractable stairs to the plane, I had a sudden urge to look back at the hangar we'd walked through. As I stopped and turned I caught a glimpse of a person standing at the outside edge of the oval-shaped building a few hundred yards away. It was Adhira Virk.

Ivan was behind me, so he had to stop. He turned to see what I was looking at.

That made Jorge at the foot of the stairs swivel around as well. "We're not leaving unnoticed."

"Too late now." I proceeded into the cabin.

Once we were all seated in the comfortable caramel chairs of the well-appointed jet, I asked Jorge, who was the only one still standing, "Is there any way Virk could find out where we're heading?"

"I'll see what I can do." He went to the accordion doors of the cockpit.

"What?" Sue sat in front of me.

Mike was across from us and looked out the window. "That bitch from the restaurant yesterday is watching us from the edge of the hangar. And look who just came up beside her."

Sue and I jumped over to the seats on Mike's side.

"Shit," Sue said.

The big Naintosa security thug was standing next to Virk. He was writing down what could only be our plane's call sign. He then turned and walked out of sight. "That guy and his partner are literally only one step short of catching us."

Jorge came out from the cockpit.

Sue pointed out the window. "Did you see ..."

"Yes," Jorge said. "Ricardo has tricks to throw them off our scent."

⬛◀▥▶⬛

The weather was good, and it took just over three hours to touchdown in Bogota, Colombia.

I had researched Bogota on the Internet when I was under house arrest. It was situated in a huge valley on a high plateau, 8,700 feet above sea level. With six and a half million inhabitants, Colombia's capital had been founded by the Spanish in 1538.

I was looking forward to seeing the country, even under the circumstances. It wasn't so dangerous now, because the Farc guerrillas weren't as active as they'd been in the past, and there wasn't the drug bedlam of the Pablo Escobar era. However, I couldn't deny that I was nervous about the danger we'd face in the jungle, getting close to the Naintosa/Pharmalin lab. First, we had to get to Florencia without being caught by the Naintosa thugs.

Walking from the plane to the terminal, the smell was unique—a mixture of dust, jet fuel, and something sweet I couldn't recognize.

I felt like I'd just chain-smoked a pack of cigarettes and couldn't catch my breath. Jorge had warned us that at that altitude we might experience some breathing difficulties until our bodies became accustomed to it. Puffy white and gray clouds were dispersed in the brownish-blue sky. The temperature was comfortable—I'd read that it averaged sixty-five degrees Fahrenheit year round—it seemed right on that number. You'd think that being so close to the equator that it would be hot, but because Bogota was so high up, it remained cool.

Our new passports worked well, and we had no trouble clearing customs.

As we walked through the terminal, I said to Jorge, "How much time do you think whatever Ricardo did to throw the thugs off gave us?"

"A couple hours," Jorge said. "It'll be hard for them to find us in the city."

"But they would suspect we would be coming here," Ivan said.

Jorge nodded. "Yes, they would have eyes and ears here. We must stay vigilant."

We could see the exit doors in the distance and signs in Spanish pointing toward them. People were going in different directions—a sea of black-colored hair.

"Does it feel good to be home?" Sue asked Jorge.

"Yes." Jorge took a deep breath. "There's no place like it on Earth. You'll see that the people are warm and inviting, the food spectacular, and the scenery ..." His accent had thickened.

Jorge stopped walking and looked at all of us. "But you have to keep your wits about you. We must stick together at all times. There are still kidnappings, and *gringos* like you are thought to be easy prey for the not-so-virtuous of our society. Then there's the jungle we're going to, but we'll deal with that later." He began to walk again.

As we walked out the exterior terminal doors, we had to maneuver around clumps of people on the sidewalk. On the covered street were tour buses, shorter bright-colored buses, and small yellow well-worn cabs, all in a congested mess. Then among them were passenger vehicles. Thick exhaust fumes in the air mixed with the altitude made it even harder to breathe.

Jorge led us to a car rental agency where we picked up a navy-blue Hyundai Santa Fe.

Jorge drove, Ivan was in the passenger seat, and Sue sat between Mike and me in the back.

Driving in Colombia was like driving in France but even more chaotic. There were no lines on the roads for the most part, and where there were, no one paid attention to them. Cars and buses weaved everywhere. The multitude of little yellow cabs seemed especially pushy. And then there were motorcycles riding along the shoulders. The only saving grace was that traffic wasn't moving fast. When we stopped at a red light, motorcycles moved around and in-between the cars to get to the front of the line.

"*Como cucarachas*; motorcyclists are like cockroaches." Jorge glanced at me through the rear-view mirror and must've noticed that I was shaking my head at the commotion of motorists. "It's lucky that most cars and motorcycles here don't have as much power and are smaller; otherwise everyone would kill themselves."

He was right, the Santa Fe we were in was the biggest vehicle I could see except for buses, and it was considered midsize in the States.

"Colombians are generally nice until they get behind the wheel," Jorge added.

We all watched to see if anyone was following us, but in the congestion, no one could tell.

Along the sides of the road were all sorts of businesses from auto repair shops, to electronics and clothing stores to supermarkets, from newer concrete buildings, to dilapidated brick-and-tin structures that had precarious electrical wiring hanging off the side. Behind them were blocks and blocks of high-rise concrete-and-brick apartment buildings.

Jorge swerved around a pothole but wasn't fast enough to miss the second one that made our vehicle shudder and vibrate.

"They could use some roadwork," Mike said.

"I remember some of these potholes from last time I was here, and they are twice as big now," Jorge commented. "If there wasn't so much government corruption, there'd be money for many improvements, not only the roads."

I noticed a hole that someone had thrown a bunch of rocks into to lessen its severity.

Ivan was looking to the left. "Those buses are interesting."

There were long, red double buses in the median between the lanes of traffic, traveling at higher speeds. Every mile or so there was a station and overhead walkways for people to safely get to them.

"That's the main transit system," Jorge replied. "There isn't enough money to build a proper metro, even though the government keeps talking about it. Again, maybe if they weren't so busy lining their own pockets ..."

A few miles later we turned left off the major thoroughfare and came into a quieter area that had brick façade structures and thick leafy trees along the sides. There were high-rises among two and three-story older buildings that had more architectural character.

Even with lighter traffic, we still hadn't noticed any suspicious vehicles following us.

"This is the North Side where it's quieter and safer." Jorge turned the steering wheel to the right at the end of a block. "It's the richest area, and many people speak English. I think it's the best place to stay."

"You aren't going to take us to stay with your parents?" Mike said. "I heard it's an insult to come home and not stay with family here."

"My parents are old and live in Ibague, which is three hours from here. I'm not sure what they'd think of the likes of you. They'd definitely be out of *cervezas* right after you arrived."

Mike licked his lips. "A *cerveza* sounds good about now."

Jorge hadn't mentioned his daughter to Mike, so I didn't want to say anything. Also, Jorge hadn't said anything to any of us about the mother of his daughter.

We pulled up beside a nine-story building with a lighter brick façade that looked as if it had been sandblasted to appear dated and classy; the Embassy Suites by Hilton Bogota–Rosales.

"Rosales is the part of town we are in, just in case you ever need to know." Jorge opened his door. "Let's grab our luggage and check in."

Glass doors led into a brick archway. A set of stairs brought us into an atrium where each floor's hallways and room doors could be seen above.

Jorge strode over to the front desk to talk to the young lady in a navy-blue suit.

The floor and walls were light marble with gray veins. Above the arched entryway were five sandstone slabs with running horses etched into them. On the other walls hung framed, charcoal sketches of dated buildings that I envisioned as 'old Bogota.'

A bellhop brought a trolley and piled our duffel bags onto it. He then led us to one of the two elevators.

Our suites were adjoining—Sue and I in one, Jorge, Ivan, and Mike in the other.

Right inside the entrance to our room there was an inset bar with a mirror over it. To the left was a desk and a black chair, next to a sitting area with a brown couch.

The bellhop took our bags down a short hallway and into the bedroom. Sue and I followed. There was a queen-size bed with a taupe, patterned cover and five white pillows in the center, propped against a dark wood headboard, with a colorful flower painting above it.

When the duffels were placed on the bed, Sue said, "We don't have any pesos. Would US dollars be okay as a tip?"

The bellhop extended his hand and took the ten-dollar bill. Looking at it, he nodded and smiled before leaving us.

I went to the window to check out the view. Below was a fenced outdoor parking lot paved in brick. Beyond were more brick buildings, with a few white stucco ones thrown in. In the distance, a lush green steep mountain rose below a cloudy gray sky.

There was a knock on the door between the sitting room and bathroom. Sue went to open it.

Jorge poked his head into our suite, from theirs. "When you're ready, let's eat and then go for supplies."

"We're ready," Sue and I both said.

The three of them came into our room, and then we all filed out to the elevator and down to the lobby.

We peered into the combination bar and restaurant, Alta Cocina 7-70. The walls were dark, and there was a seating area in front of us and then stairs down to a bar at street level. Orange and green fabric chairs added color.

There was a menu behind glass on the wall. The food choices, being at a Hilton, seemed pretty standard.

Jorge stood behind us. "Do you want to eat here, or would you like to taste authentic Colombian food?"

"Colombian food," Sue said.

"I am up for an adventure," Ivan said.

I wasn't sure if Ivan meant the food or was psyching himself up for what was to come.

We retrieved the Hyundai and drove five blocks to a retail area and parked in an underground parking garage.

"This is the mall where we can get most of our supplies," Jorge said. "The restaurant I want to take you to is a block away. We can walk there first."

Mike's stomach growled loud enough for everyone to hear. It'd been more than five hours since we'd had breakfast.

We followed Jorge to a cobblestone plaza, where people were milling about. Small children played while their mothers sat on concrete benches, keeping a close eye on them. The sweet scent of orchids overpowered the underlying acrid smell of pollution.

Still being vigilant, we watched for anyone shadowing us.

Across the street and one block away, we descended five stairs to a small café. It was as if we were entering someone's home that had tables in the living room.

A stout older woman with dark features and a shine to her skin greeted Jorge with an enthusiastic hug. She placed her hands on either side of his head, encouraging him to lower it and kissed his forehead. They spoke for a few seconds, and then she pinched his cheek. It was endearing, seeing Jorge blush.

"Come. Sit." She motioned us to a table. Her accent was thick, but she spoke in English.

"This is my Aunt Clara," Jorge said. "She is going to make us an authentic Colombian lunch."

"*Hola*, Clara," Sue, Mike, and I said at the same time.

Ivan gave a gentlemanly nod.

She smiled and then exited to the kitchen.

"You don't have to worry about the food being genetically engineered or pesticide laden," Jorge said. "All my aunt's produce and meat come from two farms my uncle owns."

There was only one other couple seated at the nine tables, being that it was between lunch and dinner time. We were at the table right in the middle.

"What's the plan after we eat?" Sue asked.

"We go buy the clothes, boots, and backpacks from the list we made on the plane," Jorge said. "Then we get a good night's rest and leave for Florencia in the morning."

Jorge's cell phone rang. He proceeded to talk in fast, rhythmic Spanish.

I should've paid more attention in high school Spanish class. I still remembered some words, but very few.

I studied a framed black-and-white photograph on the flowery wallpapered wall across from our table. It was of a boy standing next to an aged man holding a pitchfork. They were in a corn field. I wondered if they were relatives of Jorge's.

"Colombia seems nice so far," Mike said.

"I will admit that I was nervous to come here, taking into account Colombia's drug-cartel history and their war with the guerillas," Ivan said. "But what we are doing is worth the risk."

"I did some reading before we came," Sue said. "The bigger cities are as safe as any others now; however, there's still drug and guerilla activity in the Caquetá region where we're going."

"I also read that the jungle right outside of Florencia has been one of the areas heavily sprayed with glyphosate," I said.

"Why, specifically?" Mike asked.

"To kill the plants and trees and expose the coca plantations and cocaine labs," I replied.

"They sprayed whole villages in the process and now there are many deformities of the people living there and their offspring," Ivan said. "It was a joint project by the Colombian and American governments, with the help of Naintosa. It is an indisputable example of how toxic glyphosate really is."

"I'm interested in seeing that firsthand," I said." We'll have to write about it and take pictures, so we can post the proof on our website."

The others looked at me. I knew they were thinking—*if we get out of there.*

Jorge closed his phone. "I have confirmation that the safe house outside of Florencia is ready for us. Also, we'll have a vehicle switch on the way."

A pretty girl in her late teens with shiny long black hair accompanied Clara. Each of them held a platter.

Jorge explained the first dish they placed on the table. "These are *arepas.*"

"*Yuca arepas con queso,*" Clara clarified.

"These particular *arepas* are buns made from yuca flour and have cheese filling," Jorge translated and then pointed from platter to platter. "There are *rellenas*—a blood sausage. Chorizos. *Chicharron*—that's the skin of the pig and part of the meat, my personal favorite. Rice. And to start *ajiaco*—a corn and potato soup with chicken. Avocados go good with it."

"Not a lot of *just* vegetables here," Sue said.

"The animals who provided the meat ate vegetables," Jorge said.

*Holy crap, Jorge just made a joke.*

Jorge's eyes went wide. "Sue, I'm sorry, I totally forgot you're a vegetarian." He said something in Spanish to Clara.

"*Si, si.*" Clara rushed back to the kitchen.

I really liked everything but the blood sausage, which was too weird for me. The yuca buns and the fried pig skin were my favorites—I could eat them all the time.

Clara brought Sue some steamed vegetables in a sauce and encouraged her to put it over the rice. Sue seemed to like it.

We washed down our meals with *Club Colombias,* the country's national lager.

After a great lunch, we thanked Aunt Clara and went to do our shopping.

The mall was like any other mall, this one having many high-end stores, being in the wealthy part of the city. The retailers were the same as the ones you'd find in the US.

It was busy. The vast majority of people were casually dressed, with jeans being the most popular attire.

All the time, we kept looking over our shoulders. If we were being watched, they'd blended into the surroundings.

It took a few hours to get our clothes and supplies. We were prepared, as much as we could be, for our expedition.

# CHAPTER 27

*May 20, 2003*

Sue and I had awakened at four and tried to meditate, but couldn't with so much nervous energy flowing through us. We ended up talking about what to expect in Florencia and worked ourselves up even more.

We checked out of the Hilton by 6:00 a.m. and headed to Clara's café for breakfast.

The restaurant had opened early just for us. Clara served us *tinto*—small portions of strong Colombian coffee and *tamales*, which consisted of a yellow corn paste with chicken, pork skin, carrot, split peas, and potato, all wrapped in a banana leaf. Sue had scrambled eggs with tomato and green onions. For dessert Clara had prepared *bunuelos*, cakey balls mixed with a feta-like cheese that were deep fried. It was all delicious and the perfect energy source for the day ahead, yet the anxiousness we all felt made it impossible to savor.

As we were leaving it was heartwarming to see how caringly Jorge acted with his *tia*, as he embraced her and spoke softly in Spanish. She wiped tears from her eyes when she wished us a safe journey.

He'd never admit it, but was Jorge worried about going into the jungle as well?

"It's going to be an eight-hour drive," Jorge said as we sat down in the Santa Fe.

Traffic was already heavy at seven thirty, and we inched along, trying to get out of the huge city. It was easier to maneuver around potholes at five miles an hour.

Again, we couldn't see anyone tailing us.

Sue was twisted around in the back seat between Mike and me. "Wish we had radar."

Eventually the snarl of vehicles lightened as we distanced ourselves from the center of Bogota. On the left was a treeless mountainside with tightly packed dwellings that for the most part looked hobbled together.

"Is that a *barrio de invasion?*" Ivan asked from the front passenger seat.

"Yes, it is a shanty town." Jorge put both hands on the steering wheel as we passed a truck carrying goats.

Along the side of the road at about one-mile intervals, soldiers stood holding automatic rifles.

Eventually the buildings disappeared as the road started to climb. The landscape on the edge of the valley where we travelled consisted of yellow-orange dirt and little vegetation; across on the opposite side, it was lush and green. We passed several colorfully painted small buses spewing black exhaust and well-worn cars you wouldn't think would be able to make the climb. Then out of nowhere, a Porsche blew by us.

At the summit was a checkpoint with soldiers and large army trucks, but we weren't stopped.

"The roads where there are soldiers are safest to travel," Jorge said. "They keep people safe from guerillas and bandits."

His comment made me feel more comfortable. Before that, the soldiers were making me nervous.

The descent took at least an hour on a steep and winding highway.

We reached the *Desierto de la Tatacoa*, which was a low, flat, desert. The road was straighter. The ground surrounding us was brown with a yellow tint to it, and the foliage minimal.

Eventually we were past the desert and the highway wound around as we drove down into valleys and back up into mountains. Every so often we'd go through a small town. Soldiers on the side of the road became less common.

Six hours after leaving Bogota, we arrived at a particular village. Cinder-block houses originally painted white with red clay tiled roofs sat next to the road, most having storefronts or selling fruit. We pulled off and drove around the back of what appeared to be a car repair shop.

"This is where we change vehicles." Jorge turned off the Hyundai and opened his door. "Everybody out."

Mike stretched. "Remind me why we didn't fly?"

"Because flying into Florencia would make too many people aware of our arrival," Ivan said. "We can drive in without being noticed."

When we exited from the vehicle, the heat was wilting. The buzz of insects could be heard past the small clearing in the forest beyond.

Jorge went to talk to a man covered in grease that had come out from the back of the shop. They embraced, and Jorge gave him a strong pat on the back.

Mike lit a cigarette. "It's hotter than fucking hell." He walked over to a large tree with long branches that provided shade.

The rest of us followed.

It felt ten degrees cooler in the shade. The ground was dry and dusty, and from the tracks it was obvious that many cars had parked there. We stood beside a mid-90s red Jeep Cherokee that had a layer of dirt on it, making it a rust color.

The man Jorge had been talking to gave him a black duffel bag. Jorge walked over to us and opened the back of the Cherokee. He put the bag down and unzipped it, exposing numerous guns and ammunition.

"Who was that?" Sue asked.

"My cousin," Jorge replied.

Mike's eyebrows rose. "Uh, that's a lot of firepower."

Jorge gave each of us a Glock 18 9 mm pistol and a clip of ammunition.

I was happy we were sticking with Glocks—at least the grip felt familiar when I wrapped my fingers around it.

Sue and I checked that they were in good working order, as we'd been taught.

Jorge was cautious with Mike because other than a few basic lessons at the cabin up Indian Arm, he didn't have any experience with guns.

"I will spend some time with you once we reach Florencia to make you more comfortable with the weapon," Jorge said.

Mike took the pistol from Jorge. "Sounds good."

"In the meantime, don't shoot any of us or yourself," Jorge said. "If you do I will kill you." He wasn't joking.

"Ha." The gun looked uncomfortable in Mike's hand.

We all put the pistols behind our backs under our waistbands.

The duffel still contained a few rifles and quite a bit of ammunition. Jorge zipped the bag back up and pushed it forward into the cargo area. "Let's get the rest of the stuff and get going."

As soon as we got back on the road, Jorge said, "Keep an eye on the green car behind us, just in case. It pulled out behind us just as we left the auto shop."

We all turned and made note of the small sedan.

"Also, my cousin is going to follow a few minutes behind and then stay outside the safe house overnight to watch for any activity,"

Jorge said.

"Great thinking." I was more comfortable knowing Jorge was able to provide added precautions.

It was uncomfortable sitting with the gun in the small of my back between my ass cheeks when I sat back against the seat, so I kept adjusting its position.

There was no air conditioning. We had to roll down the windows, making it windy and noisy inside the vehicle.

The mountains were higher now, and the jungle thicker on either side of the winding road. Traffic was steady with transport trucks, buses, and military vehicles in among the cars. We passed our fourth checkpoint, but none had been stopping vehicles.

"There is still guerilla activity around here." The urgency in Jorge's tone made us all take notice. "When we get to Florencia, don't ever go out on your own."

"No plans to go sightseeing," Mike said.

We came around a switchback and saw a long valley with a river winding through it. A city sprawled, carved out of the vegetation.

"That's Florencia, right?" Sue asked.

"Yes," Jorge said.

"I hope so," Mike said. "My ass is sore from sitting on this hard seat."

"Do you know the area well?" Ivan asked.

"Yes." Jorge nodded. "I have relatives here, and I was stationed in Florencia for two years when I was in the military."

"I read that the population is one hundred sixty-five thousand and the average temperature in May is eighty-six degrees." Sue pointed at the rain drops beginning to hit the windshield. "And it rains more this time of year."

Traffic thickened, and there were people walking on the sides of the road. Buildings appeared—houses and businesses.

We didn't drive into the center of the city. We turned onto a side road with pavement crumbling at the edges.

"The green car kept going on the highway." Mike turned to face forward.

"I wasn't too worried but thought we should watch it, just in case." Jorge had to slow down and constantly dodge potholes; not all were possible to avoid, sending hard jolts through the vehicle.

"This road leads to the Naintosa-slash-Pharmalin compound," Jorge said. "My sister lives a few kilometers away. We're going to stay with her and her family."

"That's the safe house?" I asked.

Jorge nodded. "Yes."

"How convenient," Sue said.

"Yes, it is," Jorge replied. "They've been doing some reconnaissance for us already."

I wasn't sure if involving more people, especially his family members, was such a good idea; now they were in danger as well.

Land had been cleared for farming on each side of the road. Not big industrial farms but what looked like ten to twenty-acre lots with modest homes set in the center.

The road cut into the jungle. The foliage was lush and green, with palms breaking through to the sky.

We turned left onto a one-lane path that had a metal, slatted gate eighty yards in. A closer look revealed that there was a rock wall on either side that was camouflaged by ivy and other growth.

"Nick, can you open the gate?" Jorge asked when we stopped. "It should be unlocked."

I got out and almost flipped—the ground was hard clay, wet from the shower that had just passed, and greasy slick. From a distance the gate blended into the environment, but up close I could tell it was new and on rollers. It opened easily.

The air was intensely humid, and there was no breeze. Sweat soaked my T-shirt within a minute.

I let the Cherokee pass before closing the gate again.

Jorge leaned out the window. "Lock it."

There was a heavy lock hanging by the latch. It took both hands to close it.

Once inside the property I saw that the yard was well manicured. The thick-bladed grass was cut short around many palm trees. Numerous patches of red, yellow, and blue flowers stood out, adding a floral, clean aroma to the heavy air.

I decided to walk and stretch my legs.

The house was set back about a hundred yards from the property entrance. It was a single-story, brick rancher with a green metal roof. It suited the landscape.

In the driveway was a small red Toyota pickup and a white, late-model BMW 323i.

I came up to our vehicle as everyone was getting out.

"My brother-in-law is ex-military and an engineer," Jorge said as we gathered around him. "My sister is a lawyer, and their two girls are both in university. You can trust them."

"Thanks for setting this all up," Sue said.

"Well then, let us go meet your family." Ivan began walking up the pathway.

There was a red brick entryway that matched the house facade.

The front door opened as we approached, revealing a strong looking man about six foot five with dark mustache and hair, wearing silver-rimmed glasses. "*Hola!*"

Jorge said some quick words in Spanish and embraced the man. He was a head taller than Jorge, yet their girth and age were about the same.

"These are my friends." Jorge introduced us. "This is Enrique."

We each took a turn shaking his large hand.

"Welcome to my home; please come in." Enrique's English was understandable.

Entering, we immediately got a waft of something baking that smelled appetizing. The floor was clean white tile, and various vivid landscape paintings hung on the white walls.

"My wife, Monica, has painted all the pictures in the house." Enrique appeared proud.

I looked closer at the painting nearest the doorway. I wasn't an expert in any way, but Monica had real talent.

Sue studied one of a jungle hillside. "Amazing detail."

We walked into a two-step sunken living room. I figured the home had been built in the seventies but definitely updated since then. The furniture was dark, like stained teak, and the sofa and chairs had bright red, yellow, and green cushions. There were big windows but not an immense amount of light because of all the trees outside—it gave a feel of privacy. A dusky-orange brick-faced fireplace was the focal point but looked never to have been used. *Why would anyone have a fireplace here?*

"*Como estas,* welcome." A very attractive lady, most likely in her late forties, with auburn-streaked hair, came out of the next room. She wore a white, thin cotton dress and a flower-patterned apron.

"This is my sister, Monica." Jorge went to kiss her on the cheek.

I looked from Enrique to Monica. She was just over five feet tall—they were a contrast in size.

Jorge introduced us. She had a warm sparkle in her light-brown eyes.

"I hope you are all hungry?" Monica was well spoken in English. "Enrique, show our guests their rooms so they can settle in and wash up. Then we can have something to eat."

"*Si, mi amor.*" Enrique motioned toward a hallway.

The feeling was of visiting a friend's relatives while on vacation, not the real reason we were there.

The house was larger inside than it looked from the outside, yet most of the rooms seemed to already be in use. Sue and I shared a bedroom again, and so did Mike and Ivan.

As soon as we were alone, Sue looked at the one queen-size bed and said, "Does everyone think we're a couple already?"

"If anyone asks, let's say our relationship is 'special'." I was happy to be sharing a room and bed with Sue, even if nothing *special* was going to happen. I wanted to keep her close and safe.

The white tile floor and white walls ran throughout the whole house—it must've been for a cooling effect. The color was all in the details, like the thin flowery bedspread, the additional landscape paintings, and the vase of freshly cut flowers on the dark wood dresser.

We dropped our duffel bags on top of the bed and went back to the living room. Ivan and Mike were right behind us.

Enrique emerged from a doorway. "Come with me."

We followed him into a dining room that had a long country-style table. There were two young ladies standing at a doorway at the opposite end.

"These are my lovely daughters." Enrique gestured. "Olga and Esmeralda."

"*Hola.*" They both came over to us.

My guess was Olga was nineteen and Esmeralda twenty-one. They each received height from their father and beauty from their mother. Both had shiny black hair, infectious smiles, and flawless light-brown skin. They were very polite and fluent in English. Olga's almond-colored eyes portrayed shyness, and Esmeralda's had a glint of mischievousness.

"I hope you all found your rooms to your liking?" Monica entered from the door that the girls had been standing next to, carrying plates.

Everyone nodded and thanked her.

Sue and I sat in the empty chairs between Mike and Ivan.

"Enrique, girls, can you please help bring out the food?" Monica said as she retreated.

"We're going to compensate your family for all of this, right?" I asked Jorge, as soon as our hosts had gone into the kitchen.

"Yes, of course."

Enrique came back, carrying bottles. "You will find that beer best quenches your thirst in this climate—better than water. It's not strong, so you'd have to drink much to be drunk. Your body perspires it out as quickly as you put it in."

"I'm all for that." Those were the first words Mike had uttered since we'd arrived.

We'd been followed from Dallas to Key West, and then to Saint Thomas. Hopefully we had thrown off the Naintosa security thugs in Bogota, but there was a chance they knew exactly where we were now. "I don't mean to be impolite, but shouldn't someone be on guard in case we were tracked here?"

Monica and her daughters came in with trays of food.

"Our cousin has confirmed that he's hidden beside the turn-off from the road to the driveway," Jorge said. "And nothing suspicious has happened so far."

"We have a perimeter alarm and cameras," Enrique said. "Yet you are right, we must be extra vigilant, and I will go check them."

I exhaled. *Of course, they'd be on top of security.*

"You've all had a big journey and need to eat and at least rest for a minute." Monica helped her daughters place the food on the table.

Enrique passed the bottles around and then left the room.

The meal consisted of thin steaks covered in *chimichurri* sauce, fluffy little potatoes that we were supposed to cover with a spicy tomato-and-green onion salsa, ripe plantain, red beans, and rice.

Enrique came back and informed us that all security functions were operational.

While we ate everyone was asked questions about their backgrounds. We found out that Enrique, Monica, and their daughters had read our reports and were totally onboard.

By the time we were done with dinner the sun had set, and we adjourned to the living room. It became cooler as the ceiling fans circulated air coming in from the open windows.

"Let's go over the first part of the plan." I sat between Ivan and Sue on the couch.

Esmeralda came and squeezed in-between Ivan and me.

I looked at Enrique. "Are you sure you want your daughters involved?"

"They will be our couriers, nothing more," Enrique said. "I want them to play a part. They have to know the realities."

"But this is going to be dangerous," Sue interjected.

"This means our future," Olga said, standing behind her father's chair. "It's more important to help you than anything I know of."

"The world can be a dangerous place," Enrique said. "There is much injustice, and I want my daughters to fight for the things they believe in. And what you're fighting is the largest injustice of all."

Monica looked worried but didn't say anything.

Put that way, we couldn't argue. I'd make sure to watch that the girls would in no way be placed in jeopardy. "Let's talk about our initial steps."

"In the morning I will need to get a note to our informant at the lab," Ivan said. "I will tell him we are here and want to meet."

"The girls can deliver the note to the established spot on their way to class," Enrique said.

"Yes, no trouble," Esmeralda said.

"That is how the notes have been going back and forth?" Ivan cleared his throat. "I did not know how it was being done."

"Ivan told me what he needed, and then I instructed Enrique to take care of it," Jorge said.

"And the spot is safe?" Sue asked.

"I set it up." Enrique had a glimmer in his eyes. "It's perfect— people around but not too crowded, and a safe place to leave things that no one would steal."

"We've been monitoring the lab ever since they started building it," Monica said. "Anything Naintosa does in this country is suspect."

"We've been keeping tabs of the comings and goings," Enrique added. "And some spying."

Mike sat quietly, following the conversation, drinking his beer slower than usual.

"I have only one engineering project, and it's near completion," Enrique said. "So I am available to help as much as you need."

"I've made sure I have a very light caseload right now," Monica said. "We have a communications room assembled with secure Internet and phone for you to use."

"We can contact Sam, Eugene, Lee, and Lorraine; plus Ivan, you can communicate with the Council," Jorge said. "By the way, Sam called. His recovery is slow but progressing. He and Eugene still hope to join us when he's able to travel."

That was promising news about both Sam and the communication room.

Mike perked up. "We could use the extra muscle."

"I would like to contact the Council and update them, then," Ivan said.

A cautious feeling came over me. "Ivan, maybe you should remain quiet for a little longer ... just in case."

# CHAPTER 28

*May 21, 2003*

I woke up with Sue snuggled right next to me. It was cool in the bedroom. The window was open, and a fan rotated above the bed.

Last night before we fell asleep, Sue and I had talked about the nervous feeling we both had when Ivan mentioned contacting the Council for an update. We didn't know what it meant, but better to be silent for the time being. Thankfully, Ivan hadn't objected.

Anxiousness of being so close to the Naintosa and Pharmalin compound and the eagerness to get going on what we were there for had awakened us all at sunrise.

On our way to have breakfast, as we walked past the living room, I noticed a blanket and pillow on the couch. Next to it was Jorge's backpack. "Jorge's sleeping there."

Sue stopped. "We should tell him to take our bedroom; he's worked so hard, getting us here safely. He deserves it. I can sleep on the floor, and you can have the couch."

"You actually think he'd take the bedroom and have us sleep out here?"

Sue didn't hesitate. "No."

As we came into the dining room, we heard Ivan say to Monica, "You cannot be cooking for all of us on your own; that is too much."

"I have someone helping me with the cooking and cleaning," Monica replied. "She lives in the back suite and has been with us for many years."

Esmeralda and Olga left for school at the *Universidad de la Amazonia*. They promised to drop off the note Ivan had written in the designated location. It consisted of one sentence: *We are here and would like to meet as soon as it is safe for you.*

Monica led Ivan, Mike, Sue, and me to their office. The room was large enough to have two desks, a bookshelf, various electronics, and a couch. On each desk sat a computer monitor. Through the window was a view of a vegetable garden.

Jorge was working at the desk on one of the two laptops we'd brought but had avoided using since England. "Everything seems to be operational."

Monica looked at us. "I do a fair amount of government work, so they've set me up with a secure server. However, it's not tied to the government."

She then stepped over to the table that had a TV monitor on it with a split screen. "We have two cameras hidden in a tree next to the road. We're able to see vehicles coming to and from the Naintosa compound and Pharmalin lab. It's the only road. We record twenty-four hours a day, so we can play back all movement and don't have to be watching all the time. It has slow motion and still functions, as well as photographic capabilities, so we can focus on who is in the vehicles. For example, Hendrick Schmidt V arrived a few days ago."

Ivan looked at me. "It is interesting that he is there personally."

"He's been there before, as was his father before he died," Monica said. "Also, Tom Crane was there the other day."

"What would that guy be doing at the lab?" Mike asked.

"He's been their advocate to get genetically engineered seed into Africa," Sue said. "That shows how tight he really is with the Schmidts and Naintosa."

"Sad," Mike said. "I used to think he was one of the rare good guys that helped humanity with all his money."

"I don't think there are any of those left," I said.

"Jack was one," Sue said.

We all paused.

Ivan cleared his throat. "And maybe the last."

"How far, exactly, is the lab from here?" I asked.

"Two kilometers west." Monica had picked up three manila envelopes. "Why don't we look at the recon pictures we've taken?"

Sue, Ivan, and Mike sat on the couch. Monica, Jorge, and I brought over chairs to face them on the other side of a rectangular coffee table.

Monica began pulling eight-by-ten photographs from the envelopes. "These are from the road, showing the daily movement of supplies."

I was next to her, so Monica passed the photos to me first, one by one. Then I passed them along. They were mainly covered cargo trucks, some with refrigerator units, and one open, with lumber. They all had DON CHUCHO TRANSPORTE written on the driver's door. Then there was a picture that I stopped to take a closer look—an old school bus full of people. The occupants looked solemn, of different ages, and mainly indigenous.

"Do you know what this is about?" I asked Monica.

"Yes, we were curious and did some inquiring," she replied. "A group of American missionaries have been rounding up poor people, promising them food and shelter if they come to live at the Naintosa compound. They've been doing this every couple of months since the camp opened."

"The human guinea pigs," Sue said, taking the photo.

"Yes, that was exactly what they were doing at the Bolivia lab,"

Ivan said. "They are the disposable human test subjects."

I had a sick feeling in my stomach. I would never get accustomed to seeing what they did to people and their disregard for human life in the pursuit of power and what they deemed progress.

"Most of these people die, right?" Mike studied a second picture.

"It depends on what stage they are at with their testing," Ivan said.

"Fucking Nazis," Mike added. "And what's with these missionary conspirators?"

"We found it strange that they were here, trying to convert people to their born-again Christianity, when the country is ninety-five percent devout Catholic," Monica said. "But they aren't actually real missionaries, that's their cover."

"Obviously they get paid per head by Naintosa to bring people to the compound," I said. "Like we found out they did in Bolivia. It's a business to them."

"Human traffickers," Sue said.

Next was a photo of a Mercedes G55 SUV, but without the tinted windows they had in the States. Clear as day, Hendrick Schmidt V was in the back seat looking directly at the camera. He had a scowl on his face and looked older than the last picture I'd seen of him. "Are there any shots of Schmidt V leaving?"

"No, just the one going in." Monica placed pictures on the table for all of us to take.

"Nick." Sue turned a photograph around that was almost identical to the one I was looking at. "The driver looks like you."

Jorge reached his hand out, and Sue passed the picture to him. His eyes grew wide. "That's Dale Samson—the one who picked your pocket for the hotel receipt to frame you for Dr. Schmidt's murder."

"Really?" I hadn't looked at the driver until then. "Oh yeah."

"Holy shit," Sue said. "He really does work for Schmidt junior!"

"*Hospadi*, dear God," Ivan said. "Our theory was right."

"What?" Mike perked up.

I looked at Mike. "Someone tried to frame me for the murder of Dr. Schmidt."

"Yeah, I know," Mike said.

"That's the guy who was impersonating me. Interpol couldn't find him after they figured it out." I held up the picture. "That makes it pretty obvious who's responsible for the murder."

"Junior was responsible for his old man's murder." Mike had caught up to the rest of us.

"We should contact Chief Inspector Plante," Ivan said.

I thought about it for a second. "Contacting Plante would reveal that we're here, and I don't trust anyone right now."

"Yes," Jorge said. "Now's not good."

"Let's wait, then," Sue said.

I felt relief and foreboding at the same time. Tying Samson to Schmidt junior would erase any lingering doubt that I'd killed Dr. Schmidt. However, knowing that Schmidt V killed his own father reinforced how dangerous he was.

I picked up two pictures of the same Mercedes with a different driver and Tom Crane in the back seat. One was of him coming and the other going.

When we were done, Monica placed the contents of another envelope on the table. "These pictures, Enrique took at the perimeter fence of the compound."

The ones I picked up showed about a ten-foot-high, barbed-wire fence around a large clearing with a number of wooden and cinder-block buildings. Rows and rows of plants were growing along the edges and through the middle. Some trees remained inside the compound. Near the gate was a parking area that had an assortment of supply trucks, SUVs, and cars.

"Do you know what these buildings are for?" I asked.

"I can tell you what we think," Monica said.

I held out the pictures so everyone could see.

Monica leaned forward and pointed. "These are barracks to house the test subjects. Beside that is the common area with kitchen, showers, and toilets."

"At least they don't live that bad," Mike said.

"All around are test plantings." Monica's finger moved around the pictures. "Over there are accommodations for the scientists and people working for Naintosa and Pharmalin and their eating area, etcetera. Schmidt has an apartment there too. That side of the cinder-block building is the lab. Near the middle is the infirmary."

"The infirmary is large," Ivan said. "That says something."

"To be able to further test after the people are sick," I said.

Ivan nodded. "They had anticipated it."

"What's that gray metal building back there?" Sue asked.

Monica hesitated. "We think that's an incinerator."

"What?" My heart jumped.

"Like a fucking Auschwitz incinerator?" Mike looked disgusted.

"They have to discard their failed experiments somehow," Jorge said.

That did make terrible, sickening sense on Pharmalin's end. I wondered if the innocent people being tested on knew that was their fate?

"Those poor people," Sue's expression showed revulsion.

"We've never seen a bus with people ever come out of the compound." Monica held up a zoomed-in shot of the incinerator.

The building itself gave off a devilish vibe, not to mention the broad, bald guard standing at attention in front of its double steel doors.

Monica pulled out more pictures and distributed them.

They were of various people in lab coats. In one of them, a fair-haired man with glasses looked familiar. I gave that picture straight to Ivan. "Is that the scientist from Dr. Roth's video? You know, the head Pharmalin guy who said he found the actual cure for cancer and Dr. Schmidt IV became mad at him." After we'd escaped from Vancouver and made it to Paris, we'd discovered that video on Dr. Roth's laptop.

Ivan studied the picture. "Yes, Dr. Daniel Smith."

The next were long-distance shots of guards with rifles, dressed in camouflage, all big and Caucasian. There was a heavy metal front gate with a guard house next to it. "Not exactly easy to get in there without being noticed."

"Enrique thinks he may have found a way," Monica said. "He will show you."

The last set of pictures was of the test subjects—people with noticeable deformities: men and women with burn scars on their arms, legs, and heads, some with missing patches of hair. There were small children with misshapen facial features: small noses, ears, and lips, and oddly-shaped arms with missing stubby digits on their hands. "So sad."

"That's not the result of the current conditions. That is the result of glyphosate poisoning," Monica informed us. "Enrique wanted to get pictures of people going in and out of the infirmary but couldn't."

Ivan nodded in recognition. "From the government spraying."

"Yes." Monica nodded. "Since 1994, the Colombian government, with funding from the US government and glyphosate from Naintosa, have been spraying from airplanes vast areas where coca was suspected of being grown. The rationale was to kill the plants that produce cocaine, but there's been no regard for the poor farmers that had been forced to grow the coca by the drug traffickers. In some cases, they sprayed whole villages. The adults with the burn scars were directly in contact with the glyphosate, and the children with deformities were the result of their mothers being poisoned internally."

I remembered us talking about it. Naintosa still denied that glyphosate was toxic.

Ivan shook his head. "Further irrefutable evidence."

"This is evidence you guys were right," Mike said.

When Enrique came home in the afternoon, we asked if it was possible for us to take a closer look at the compound the next morning. Jorge, Sue, and I only, would go with him, because we didn't want too many people wandering around in the jungle at once.

The girls came home after school and said that the drop had gone well.

Sue and I hadn't checked our e-mails since we'd been shot at in Burford, so that was our task after dinner. I was surprised that there weren't too many messages.

My publisher had written to inform me that my book was coming out at the end of June as a "Summer Read." They'd mailed ten advanced reader copies to me at the Burford estate. *A lot of good that's going to do me.*

"My book's coming out in five weeks," I said to Sue.

"That's exciting." She looked up from her screen. "You should be really proud. I'm sure it'll do well. Maybe we'll be back in time for you to promote it?"

That last sentence hung in the air.

# CHAPTER 29

*May 22, 2003*

We were up before dawn. Monica had given Sue, Jorge, and me dark-green, long-sleeved shirts and camouflage pants to wear. Each of us was equipped with a backpack that held food, water, binoculars, two extra ammunition clips, a flashlight, and emergency kit.

Enrique brought out a cardboard box containing used holsters and helped Sue and me choose ours. That day we'd wear ones that went around our belts and strapped to our thighs. For the future we chose holsters that would conceal the guns under our clothes inside our back waistbands.

I couldn't keep down more than half an *arepa* and a cup of coffee yet was trying not to show how nervous I was.

Sue was having a pickle dipped in peanut butter.

"What are you eating?" I asked. "You hate pickles ... and peanut butter?"

"I don't know. I had a sudden urge. It tastes pretty good." She swallowed the last bite. "Let's go."

As I holstered my gun and placed my arm through the backpack strap, I noticed Sue giving me an approving look. "What?"

"Nothing." She cinched her backpack. "I just had a flashback. It's amazing how far we've come in the last three years, especially you. Think back to when you were a disillusioned journalist fighting your internal struggles, and now look at you, in camo, packin' a gun, and going to spy on the villains. You've grown a lot."

I took a second to remember. "Yeah, right. You too ... except for the internal-struggles part." It was true, I felt like a different person.

Sue went to push my shoulder, and I stiffened at her impact.

"You're in better shape, that's for sure." She put some extra weight behind her arm to show she could still move me.

That little exchange with Sue loosened me up, and I wasn't as nervous about going into the jungle.

To our surprise there was a tunnel beneath the floorboards of the laundry-room closet. Enrique said that the last owners had been in the drug business.

The passage was cut through the dense soil, reinforced by plywood on the ceiling and two-by-fours along the sides. Roots grew down that we had to maneuver around. In two places there were wooden doors blocking access to what I assumed were other passageways. The confined space was claustrophobic.

After two hundred yards we reached a makeshift door made of palm fronds. Outside was a burned-out shell of a cocaine lab, already almost all reclaimed by the environment.

We moved along a faint path.

It had rained less than an hour ago, and the leaves dripped moisture, wetting our clothes even more than our perspiration. You could taste the water evaporating, and the scent was of orchids and disturbed, decaying vegetation. Birds chirped in the branches above in a jumble of song, and insects double the size I was used to hummed and swirled around us.

I was second from the back, in front of Jorge, who was carrying a scary-looking automatic rifle. Enrique led the way in silence with Sue right behind him.

Walking was slow because of the density of the foliage, downed trees to climb over, and slippery roots hidden under leaves. It took about an hour before Enrique raised his hand in a motion for us to stop.

Moving up, I could just make out a wire fence about thirty yards ahead.

"Let me go see where the nearest guards are." Enrique snaked around ferns and vines, making his way forward.

When he was a few feet from the fence he stopped. In slow motion Enrique dropped to his knees, and then he rolled under a wild fruit tree.

I tensed in anticipation and strained to see what he was watching. Memories surfaced of bullets flying through the air past us. I felt the notch in my ear.

Beams of sunlight broke through the canopy above as clouds parted. Natural spotlights illuminated bushes and trees, their moist leaves glistening. Jorge motioned for Sue and me to move back for more cover.

Enrique waited a few more moments before rising back to his knees and then to his feet. He moved with ginger steps to the wire fence. We saw the back of his black-haired head move from side to side. Then he looked up and we noticed a camera on a high fence post next to him. Once it panned away, he motioned us forward.

I should've felt relieved that he thought it was safe, but I didn't.

We snuck to the fence made of razor wire, tightly woven. There was no way of separating it and climbing through. If we cut it, it was so taut that the vibration would sound around the whole perimeter. The fence was twelve feet tall, with a *V* at the top—too difficult to climb over.

Enrique pointed out another set of wires strung along the inside of the main fence about a foot apart, up to seven feet in height. A large mosquito went to land on the wire in front of us at eye level. It was fried to a crisp before it even landed. That made us aware of zapping sounds all along the fence line. I didn't know how strong the voltage was and had no desire to find out.

Enrique gestured up the pole we were standing next to. The camera, red light on the side, moved in slow motion from left to right. "We're in a blind spot," he whispered. "They're more concerned about people getting out than in."

The corn stalks on the other side were taller than us, so we couldn't see anything past them.

"Those plants have grown quickly," Enrique said. "Follow me and I will take you to a better vantage point. Stay low."

We waited for the camera to be angled directly away from us before moving back into the jungle.

There was no path this time, and we had to be careful not to disrupt leaves and branches that would show movement. We came to an opening between rows of vegetable plants that gave us a view inside the compound. It was just like the pictures we'd seen.

Each motion, sound, and breath we made seemed amplified in my ears.

We pulled out our binoculars; Enrique produced a camera with a sizable telephoto lens.

There were several people in white T-shirts near the barracks, sitting at three picnic tables in the shade of an oak-like tree. Sadness ran through me as I saw their forlorn faces. There were children around them, playing, oblivious to what was really happening. Scanning right, I saw two men and a woman in white lab coats talking under the awning of a building. That had to be the infirmary. A limping man with lesions on his face approached them. The woman looked perturbed but took the man inside.

Scanning farther right, the dark-gray metal building came into view. It gave off an ominous feeling. *How many people have been cremated there?*

A figure in white passed my view. I followed with my binoculars to see a stocky man with broad shoulders and short legs walking with a confident stride. It was Hendrick Schmidt V, going from the infirmary to ... what must be the lab. *There's the little fucker.* Anger rose inside me as soon as I realized it was him.

"Everybody down," Jorge said in a strong whisper.

I was pushed to the ground from behind, as was Sue. Jorge landed on top of us.

Leaves and branches shredded above and all around, as bullets tore in. Sudden chaos enveloped us.

Jorge rolled off and we crawled as fast as we could back into the jungle.

There was an explosion of sound right behind us. Jorge had let loose with his automatic rifle, sending a spray of bullets into the compound, taking out the guard that had shot at us.

Yelling came from a distance.

"Go!" Enrique practically lifted Sue and me to our feet, and we stumbled and ran.

Jorge sidestepped behind us, rifle pointing back at the camp.

"We don't know if they'll follow us," Enrique said. "But we're not going to wait to see."

Within a minute we could hear voices behind us. They *were* following, but we had a lead.

Jorge tripped and went down because he kept looking behind us, but was back up immediately.

Enrique was in the lead, guiding us.

We kept slipping on roots and scratching ourselves on branches as we stayed away from paths.

Sue twisted and flipped onto her back trying to get over a fallen log. I landed right on top and winded her. Getting back on my legs as fast as I could, I pulled her up and helped her along until she caught her breath.

Enrique stopped and pointed. "Keep going straight ahead another two hundred meters."

*How far are two hundred meters, again?* I'd go by yards, because that's what I knew from playing so much golf in the past, and hope that was close enough.

After a few steps Sue and I looked back to see Enrique, with Jorge's help, pull on a rope that lifted three bed-spring frames with metal spikes, into the air. They slid them onto springs and pulled the frames down against the tension, latching onto a thin one-foot-high rebar pole. From there Enrique unwound thin wire just above the ground eight feet in front and about thirty feet across and tied the end to a thick bush.

Before then we hadn't noticed any of that apparatus on the jungle floor.

Jorge came at us. "You have to keep going."

"What is that?" Sue asked.

"A trap, in case they come directly in front of where we're going." Jorge motioned us forward.

Within seconds, Enrique was back with us, taking the lead. His legs took one stride to Sue's two.

He made an abrupt stop at a stump, and we all came skidding to a halt behind him.

Jorge grabbed a dried palm frond and started wiping away any obvious tracks we'd made.

"Where is it?" Enrique stepped around the stump to a bush. Neither were what they appeared to be once he reached into a hole in the bush and the stump opened. "Flashlights on."

As we piled inside and Jorge pulled closed the stump door, we heard agonizing screams. More than one man had been following right behind us and gotten caught in the trap.

Our flashlights bobbed as we ran through the dirt tunnel. I hit my head multiple times, filling my hair with dirt.

We continued forward until we reached stairs.

Enrique pushed a trap door up and we came out into a dimly lit, dusty room. As soon as we were all out, Enrique let the door fall back down and latched two bolts across it.

There was one door, which led us out into an alley.

Across the hard-rutted dirt was a door to another house. Enrique gave the peeling painted wood a hard rap and then opened it. An old man and woman were sitting at a kitchen table. The gentleman nodded and raised his beer bottle as we raced by.

In a bedroom there was another trap door, under a thin rug, leading to another tunnel. Flashlights back on, we kept running. The ceiling was higher and the passageway better kept than the last.

At the end we exited through a cover made of intertwined branches. That brought us out into the jungle again and then eighty yards later another altered stump and yet another tunnel.

We pushed on for a few hundred yards until we reached a padlock that was in a hole with a metal rod between it and a rusty door. Enrique reached into his pocket and produced a set of keys. He unlocked the partition, and we passed through.

A passage went in either direction—we went right.

This route seemed familiar. A couple of minutes later Enrique lifted yet another trap door, which opened to his laundry room.

Sue and I leaned against the washing machine to catch our breath. Even Jorge looked tired. Sue had dirt all over her face—mine was probably worse.

Monica rushed into the room. "What happened?"

"We were fired on and had to do the multi-tunnel escape," Enrique wheezed.

"I see," Monica said. "Is everyone all right?"

Mike and Ivan came into the doorway.

"What the hell," Mike said.

"We were shot at and chased," Sue said.

"I doubt they knew it was us," I said. "And there's no way they could trace us back here through that labyrinth."

"We're safe." Enrique took a deep breath. "What's for lunch?"

"Go clean up while Maria finishes making lunch," Monica said. "Bring me back your dirty clothes, so I can have them washed and ready again.

I gathered Maria was the helper that we hadn't seen yet.

Sue stripped down to her underwear as soon as we came to our room. On her way to the shower, she turned and said. "The men impaled by that bed-spring trap thing, and the guard shot at the compound ... we took more lives."

"I know." I knew what she was getting at but wasn't sure what to say. "It was them or us."

She watched me for a moment as if waiting for more of a reaction and then went into the bathroom.

I was feeling numb. Had I become accustomed to all the violence? Had I stopped caring about other people? No, that wasn't it—it was survival, for the greater good.

Everyone was in the living room, discussing what we'd seen, when the girls arrived home.

Esmeralda went straight to Ivan. "We have a response for you."

Ivan took the piece of paper she handed him and read it. "We have a meeting tomorrow. We have to go to this address."

Enrique rose from his chair and retrieved the paper from Ivan. "It's close by, in an industrial park."

# CHAPTER 30

*May 23, 2003*

"So, what's up with you and Sue?" Mike asked.
"What do you mean?" I was cleaning my gun in the laundry room. There was dust and moisture in it from yesterday.

"Are you officially a couple now?"

Had Mike come to talk to me purposely about that?

A sudden roar of drumming vibrated the house. We both looked out the window in the back door to see a heavy downpour of rain.

I had to raise my voice. "It doesn't just drizzle here. It's all or nothing."

"At least it goes by quickly, not settle in for days like back home," Mike said. "So, what about you and Sue?"

"Our focus is on what we're doing here." I decided not to deny the future possibility. "We'll see afterward."

"Good for you. She's a keeper ... even though she's frickin' sarcastic and bossy." He gave me a thump on the back. "I oughta find me a nice *senorita* when this is over."

"That's a good idea. You deserve some lovin'." The gun was clean, so I loaded a clip, placed it in the holster under my waistband, and pulled my shirt over it.

"It's weird that we're all packing heat now," Mike said as he followed me to the communication room.

The fact that I was getting used to it made me uncomfortable.

Sue and Jorge were sitting in front of the screens, and Ivan was at a desk.

"We just saw Davis Lovemark in the Mercedes, going to the compound," Sue said.

"Really?" I said. "He's here?"

Ivan placed the pen on the pad he'd been writing on. "Something especially important must be happening."

"What, I wonder?" I said.

"Dr. Smith drove by toward town as well," Jorge said. "If that makes any difference."

"It could. He's important," I said. "In the future, we should tail Dr. Smith. His movements may provide information."

Jorge nodded agreement.

Ivan looked at his watch. "We have to go."

Enrique walked in, a set of keys dangling in his hand. "Ready?"

We'd decided that Enrique would take Ivan, Jorge, and me to meet with the informant.

It only took ten minutes to drive to an area with rows of warehouses.

Enrique held up the piece of paper with the address on it. "That's it, to our right." He turned the car around, in case we needed a fast exit and parked it a hundred yards away from the building we were looking for.

Steam was rising from the pavement as the sun shone, evaporating the burst of rain that had fallen. The gray warehouse still had water dripping from a drainpipe in the corner.

Jorge pulled out his gun, and we stood opposite the dirty white door. Enrique opened it slowly and as quietly as he could. Jorge leveled his Glock and peered around the doorway. Satisfied no one was there to greet us with a hail of bullets, we entered.

It was an office, next to a large storage room filled with boxes.

A figure stood to the side.

Jorge aimed his gun at the person.

They raised their hands. "I'm unarmed, and no one else is here, so put the gun down." It was a man with an American accent. He turned on a lamp that sat atop the desk beside him.

"You are Dr. Smith," Ivan said.

"Yes," Daniel Smith said. "I'm sure you can understand why I didn't want to reveal who I was until now."

"Of course," Ivan said.

Our informant was the head scientist for Pharmalin. *Shit. Good work, Ivan.*

Dr. Smith was dressed in shorts and a lilac polo shirt, not the lab coat from the pictures and video, so of course he appeared somewhat different. In his hand was a thick manila envelope.

Ivan pointed at each of us. "This is Nick Barnes, Jorge Villegas, and Enrique Bautista."

Dr. Smith nodded. "Nice to meet you all."

"I don't want to sound rude," I said. "But do you mind telling us why you're meeting with us and supplying information? I doubt Hendrick Schmidt would be very happy."

"It's my conscience." Dr. Smith leaned on the desk. There was a slight twitch in his hand when he pushed his glasses farther up the bridge of his nose. "I don't want to be a part of the scheme anymore. But I don't have any other options. I can't just leave. I'm hoping you can help stop these premeditated atrocities."

"But you're the chief designer," I said. "Your creations made it possible."

"That wasn't my intention, and it's gone too far."

He was willing to give us information now, and maybe it wasn't too late, so I decided to stop the sudden hostility I felt toward him.

"I have limited access here to the outside world," Dr. Smith said. "So I don't know the full extent of what's happening. But I do know from overheard conversations that you have Hendrick V and the others worried because you're on the right track. I want to support you. I know you're affiliated with the Northern European Council for Ethical Farming, and they have the ability to verify what I'm giving you."

"We appreciate the risk you are taking," Ivan said. "We will do our best to verify the information, and when we make it public, we will not divulge the source."

"I trust you." Dr. Smith held out the manila envelope. "This is what I could get you right now."

Ivan took it from him.

Dr. Smith exhaled and seemed to relax somewhat. "Will you be in Florencia long?"

"We can be if you'd like us to," I said. "Do you want us to get you out?"

"Like I said, it's too late for that." Dr. Smith frowned. "The best I can do is forge ahead in the positive areas and slow the progress of the negative. If you stay at least another week, I can relay more documentation. What I'm giving you now is just the portion I was able to slowly compile without drawing suspicion."

Ivan looked at me and then Dr. Smith. "We will wait for it. And if you change your mind about leaving, we will help you."

"At least ..." Dr. Smith sighed. "Let me get you everything I can first. Then maybe I'll reconsider escaping." He seemed to ponder what he'd just said. "If I were to run away, Schmidt V would have me hunted for the rest of whatever life I had."

"Join the club." I didn't have much sympathy. "How bad is it, really, in terms of the plan's progress?"

Dr. Smith took a deep breath. "The genetically engineered

seed is spreading and infecting traditional crops at a much higher rate than was predicted. And it's out of control—we can't stop it. Glyphosate, and following close behind, neonicotinoids, are leaching into ground water in higher concentrations and not diluting as anticipated. It's happening in every country that allows their use. So yes, it's probably worse than you thought. The only positives, if you can call them that, are that it seems to take longer for people to develop cancer, and plants and insects are becoming more resistant. Also, the Plycite-spliced corn doesn't produce ears big enough for commercial growing, and a solution hasn't been found ... yet."

The words *spreading out of control, faster* and *not diluting* were bad. Even though we pretty much had known all of that already, it was harsher coming from his mouth. "What about the cancer drugs? We saw a short video from over a year ago. You were telling Dr. Schmidt IV that you may've found the actual cure for the colon cancer the genetically engineered food was creating."

Dr. Smith looked surprised. "What video?"

"Someone, we don't know exactly who, shot a video of you and Dr. Schmidt IV talking at your Bolivia lab. You said that you may've found the actual cure for the cancer. Dr. Schmidt got angry and said you were only supposed to extend people's lives, not cure them."

"I remember the conversation, but I didn't know someone had taped it."

"How are the cancer drugs progressing?" Ivan looked down at the envelope in his hands. "Did you provide us with information?"

"I can try to copy that data next." Dr. Smith brushed away sweat that had formed on his forehead. "We decided to work on both. Life extending works on immune suppression and actual cure works on immune enhancing. But we're having challenges with both and haven't found solutions yet."

"I heard on the news a while back that Pharmalin was releasing a new drug that was a breakthrough in the fight against cancer," I said.

"That drug is a step forward but only meant as a stop-gap measure until life expectancy can be extended three to four years. That's what Dr. Schmidt, and now his son, have been trying to achieve. To them, that length of time gives the most profit potential."

Enrique gasped. He had not been exposed to as much information as the rest of us.

"And you're just feeling guilty now?" I couldn't hold back my re-emerging contempt. "It's because of your talent that you've given these destructive tools to the Schmidt fuckers. And it's just starting to bug you now?"

"I know ..." Dr. Smith hung his head. "There's no excuse."

Ivan touched my arm and shook his head. I knew he didn't want me to scare Dr. Smith into cutting off the flow of incriminating information.

"I was on a few days' break in Bogota." Dr. Smith was almost cowering. "That's where Jack Carter found me and talked sense into me. I'm very sorry to hear about his death."

So Jack had turned Dr. Smith but kept it secret that it was him. "Jack Carter was a fantastic individual, and yet he wasn't the only one who's died exposing what you're aiding. For example, the whole Elles family was wiped out."

"Yes, I know." Dr. Smith did look remorseful. "Without Dr. Elles's research, all this wouldn't have been able to happen, yet that wasn't his intent either."

In that moment, his words hit me so hard I had to reach my left hand out to brace against a metal rack—if it weren't for Dr. Elles's research and what Dr. Smith had done with it, how much different our lives would've been.

Ivan raised his hand. "What is done is done. I had a part to play in this mess too. Now we must join together to do what we can to stop it."

"The best we can do now is develop real solutions to counteract the conditions people and the environment will develop," Dr. Smith said.

There was finality to Dr. Smith's admission. *Shit.*

"So be it," Ivan said. "We must work within the confines of the new reality."

"I must go. I can't be gone from the lab for too long, or they'll get suspicious. Everyone there is paranoid—it's the culture Hendrick V is breeding." Dr. Smith walked toward the exit. "Check the drop-off spot starting in three days. As soon as I've compiled more, I'll signal you to meet again." Sunlight spread into the room as he opened the exterior door.

We followed and paused outside our vehicle to watch Dr. Smith drive off in a Mercedes-Benz SUV. Just as he passed the last warehouse and turned right onto the road, a small gray sedan came out from around the shadow of a warehouse and turned right as well.

I jerked. "He's been tailed!"

"Everyone get in." Jorge opened the back-passenger side door. "If it's Naintosa security, they'll have our license number and possibly pictures of us."

Enrique got in and started the engine. "If we have someone following us, I'll lose them before we go home. I don't want anyone knowing where we live."

"And you can't use this car again," Jorge said.

Jorge and I watched from the back seat as we turned left onto the road. When the warehouses were almost out of sight, a dark-colored car came out and turned our way.

"Do you see it?" I said. "It's quite far back."

Everyone said, "Yes."

"Our cover's blown now for sure." What were we going to do? Was Dr. Smith going to be eliminated? Was Naintosa security going to come at us in full force?

"They're too far behind." Enrique sped up as we entered an area of stores and cafés. "They'll be easy to lose."

We took sharp turns into alleys and streets. We raced past blocks of middle-class homes before driving back into the farm area.

After fifteen minutes, we drove down a long straight stretch. No one was behind us.

# INTERLOGUE 9

Otto escorted Davis to Hendrick's office. The two men Davis had brought with him waited outside the door.

Hendrick didn't get up from behind his desk. "Davis, you didn't need to come all this way to check on me. You could've just called."

"I wanted to see this place for myself ... and I did call, but you didn't answer." Davis pulled a foldable chair to the desk. "You could splurge for some decent furniture."

"What's the point? We're in a jungle in the middle of nowhere." Hendrick turned over the pad in front of him, hiding what he'd been working on. "How long will you be staying?"

"Until I don't have to be here any longer." Davis didn't mince words. "I saw someone who had a striking resemblance to Nick Barnes outside. Who was that?"

Hendrick squinted. "His name is Samson. It's hard to get good security down here, so I've had to bring men from Europe."

Davis knew that was the man who'd impersonated Barnes when they tried to frame him for the murder of Schmidt IV. Why would he keep such a liability, and so close by, for further incrimination?

"In the last three months we've had three occasions when intruders tried to breach the compound, including yesterday," Hendrick continued. "Each time gunfire was exchanged, keeping them at bay, but no one was caught. Someone hostile is out there, trying to figure out what we're doing here."

"Can't you get assistance from the Colombian military? We pay the government enough."

"I don't want them getting too close. The Colombians think this is a test lab for glyphosate. We were asked to make adjustments because they don't want so much damage to the villagers; they're getting too much backlash."

"Are you figuring it out?" Davis winced and changed position in his chair.

"We have one scientist working on it in case government officials want to see a progress report. But who cares, because all the villagers will be eliminated as the population control ramps up."

Davis winced again. He was feeling sharp stabs of pain from his abdomen, most likely his condition aggravated from the flight.

Hendrick studied Davis's face. "You don't look well. You're very pale and sweating. Have you lost weight?"

"It's like an oven in this place."

Hendrick looked toward the window where the air conditioning unit was. "I find it quite cool in here."

"Is Dr. Smith here?" Davis looked serious. "I'd like to speak to him."

"He should be in the lab. How about I take you for a tour around the compound?"

"After I talk to Smith."

"Very well." Hendrick rose from his chair. "I'll take you to him."

"Just point me in the right direction. I can see him on my own." Davis didn't want Hendrick overhearing the conversation he wanted to have with Dr. Smith.

"Nonsense, I will take you."

Davis faltered as he stood and had to steady himself against the desk. He didn't have the strength to argue with Hendrick. "Take me to him if you must."

"Are you sure you're, all right?" Hendrick asked. "Maybe you'd like to lie down for a period? We have visitors' quarters."

"No." Davis took a deep breath. "I need to see Smith."

At the office doorway, Hendrick didn't acknowledge the two men standing there.

Davis nodded for them to follow. Stenson and Furyk, both counterintelligence officers, were on loan from the director of the CIA. Davis had incriminating information on the director that he used every time he needed services from him. He'd worked with Furyk before and found him competent. Davis had no background with Stenson. Davis felt he might need them in case he had any trouble with Hendrick. Also, he planned on leaving them after he left, to keep an eye on things. He didn't want to spare his own people.

Davis found it hard to mask his frailty while proceeding down the hallway, needing to place his hand on the wall for support several times.

Hendrick narrowed his eyes in suspicion but didn't offer assistance.

They passed Otto talking to a muscular man in a T-shirt a size too small for him.

From around the corner came Dr. Smith carrying a cardboard box.

"Where have you been?" Hendrick came up beside Dr. Smith.

"I had to go to the warehouse for more test tubes." Dr. Smith walked through the doorway to the lab.

Before Davis entered the lab, he looked back at Stenson and Furyk and raised his hand for them to stop and wait there. He knew they didn't like acting the part of bodyguards, but he didn't much care what they thought.

Dr. Smith set the box down on a stainless-steel table and then reached for his white lab coat hanging on the back of a chair. He turned to look at the men. "Mr. Lovemark, I didn't know you were here. Welcome to our lab."

Davis lowered himself onto a stool. "I wanted to see for myself how everything was progressing. This is quite the state-of-the-art facility. How *are* things progressing?"

"Well ..." Dr. Smith glanced at Hendrick. "You always hope that everything moves faster, and we've had our fair share of setbacks, but I'm confident that we'll find our desired solutions. It's just taking longer."

"What exactly do you mean by 'taking longer'?" Davis asked.

Dr. Smith hesitated before saying, "I'm working on the cancer drugs, and both the life-extending and cure formulas need adjusting. We're just not quite sure which way to adjust at the moment."

Davis grit his teeth and took a deep breath. When he thought he was sufficiently calm enough to sound the part, he said, "How long before the actual cure is ready?"

Dr. Smith looked toward Hendrick as if for support. "The life-extending is much closer to being ready. The cure may be a while, but our team feels like a breakthrough is imminent."

Davis could sense Dr. Smith was just trying to sound optimistic. The reality must've been that they weren't even close. "You said a year ago that you'd found the actual cure."

"I thought I did, but not quite."

Davis pulled out two folded pieces of paper from his linen pants pocket and handed them to Dr. Smith. He wished even more that Hendrick wasn't present to hear what he had to admit. Davis saw what he had as a weakness and hated it. "I have advanced colon cancer; the kind we were supposed to be protected from."

"Really?" Hendrick looked surprised.

Dr. Smith unfolded the papers and read.

"How could that be?" Hendrick asked. "You knew what foods to avoid. Could it be from the environment?"

"I don't know. I eat in the finest restaurants; however, they aren't always immune to genetically engineered food. Maybe I should've been more careful." Davis stared right at Hendrick. "Or maybe what your father unleashed is deadlier than anyone thought. Which means we're all at grave risk."

"I'm sorry, Mr. Lovemark," Dr. Smith said. "This is severe."

"So what are you going to do about it?"

Dr. Smith looked down at the papers for a long moment. "Why don't you stay here for a while and we can run more tests. There's a chance we may be able to help you while you help us with the cure."

"You want me to be one of the guinea pigs?"

"I don't see any other option," Dr. Smith said. "There is no known cure at this time. We are the only ones who are close. However, your cancer is quite advanced ..."

"I can't believe this." Hendrick took the papers from Dr. Smith. "Who gave you these results?"

"My personal physician. I assure you that the testing was conducted by experts."

"We were supposed to be protected from this." Hendrick read the summary. "If it could happen to you, it could happen to all of us."

"Didn't I just say that?" Davis crossed his arms. "The plan's not working so fucking well."

Otto approached. "Dr. Schmidt, may I have a word in private?"

# CHAPTER 31

We sat in the living room. As Ivan finished reading each page of Dr. Smith's information, he passed it onto Sue, Mike, and me.

There were a lot of formulas and numbers, so it was hard to understand, but I could get the underlying theme and it wasn't good. It reinforced what Dr. Smith had told us at the warehouse. Unaltered fields were being cross-pollinated with genetically engineered seeds from up to a hundred miles away, and at an alarming rate, much higher than anyone had predicted. That was the case with every type of crop, but especially with wheat, soy, and corn—the most prevalent crops. Then the newly infected crops spread their seed in another large radius. The only way farmers could know what was happening was either to take samples to a lab for testing, which was expensive, or to spray them with glyphosate—if the plants lived they were genetically engineered.

Then there was the rapid contamination of ground water with glyphosate and neonicotinoids. That dramatically increased the subsequent build-up and detection in peoples' bodies. Naintosa had hoped the gradual increase of the poisons would not be noticed in people or the environment. However, the much faster rate was beginning to cause alarm in the scientific and medical communities.

In the spectrum of Naintosa's plan, the first two stages of weakening immune systems and allergies were increasing exponentially, but the third stage of increased diseases had not jumped at the same rate yet. Maybe people's immune systems were fighting back? But for how long?

I saw why Dr. Smith had admitted that the focus now had to be on how to save people from the sickness that would follow. It was sad to think that it was time to admit defeat and focus on a future of having to live with the consequences.

Ivan stood and collected the papers. "I must get this information to the Council." He looked upset, and rightfully so.

Not knowing what else to do, I followed Ivan to the office. Sue and Mike were right behind me.

Jorge was watching the monitor and had his cell phone to his ear. There were now four split screens. Enrique's face was in one of them, adjusting a camera.

Ivan had gone straight to one of the desktop computers.

"You have more cameras?" Mike asked Jorge.

"Yes, we placed one up on the fence before the driveway and one in the backyard, in case someone comes at us from the jungle."

Ivan began scanning the pages of information. Sue and I went to help.

# CHAPTER 32

*May 28, 2003*

It had been five days since our meeting with Dr. Smith. The girls had checked for a message each of the last two days. Jorge and Enrique went with them to watch from a distance and see if the drop spot had been compromised. We had no way of knowing what had happened to Dr. Smith after he returned to the compound.

Jorge had been spending much of his time watching the cameras and reviewing footage from when he was unable to be in front of the screens. The Mercedes that was used to transport more important people had made two trips, but we hadn't recognized the passengers. The men that had followed us all the way to Saint Thomas were now at the compound and very active, we assumed looking for us.

Sue, Mike, and I had written a partial report on Dr. Smith's information. We'd finish it when we hopefully had all the data. The final report would be posted on our website and released to our media contacts.

Ivan was in contact with the Council on a daily basis, doing what he could to oversee the verification of the supplied research.

Sam had to have another surgery on his shoulder, so he was

going to be out of commission for a while yet.

Lee was well enough to travel, so he and Lorraine, with the help of their contacts, were on their way to Bogota. From there, Jorge had arranged for his cousin to drive them to Florencia. If all went well they'd arrive tomorrow in the late afternoon. The reinforcements were welcome.

# CHAPTER 33

*May 29, 2003*

Sue and I had decided to meditate every morning as soon as we woke up, to help us stay centered and keep our minds clear. We'd just finished and were on our way to have breakfast when we heard activity.

Monica came into the living room wearing a colorful flowered dress and walked to the laundry room door. Out of curiosity, we followed.

Jorge and Enrique were standing there, wearing camouflage and muddy boots. Enrique had a black canvas bag in his hand. Night vision goggles were sitting on the washing machine.

"What are you doing?" Sue asked.

"Enrique was able to borrow explosives from the construction site of the engineering project he is part of," Jorge said.

"We have a hidden compartment in the tunnel." Enrique's hands were dirty. "I think that's the best place to store them."

"I want to see where it is, so I'll come with you," Jorge said.

"What are you planning to do with the explosives?" I asked.

"Nothing specific," Jorge said. "Just in case we need them."

"You were just at the construction site?" Sue asked. "You wanted to steal the explosives before the sun came up?"

"No, I did that yesterday," Enrique said.

"We just came back from the compound," Jorge said. "Since we weren't able to see the place where Enrique thought we could compromise the fence before, I wanted to see it for myself, should the need arise to break in."

They looked like guilty kids that'd been caught doing something they weren't supposed to.

Monica's hands were on her hips. "I thought you were going to show Nick and Sue as well."

I wasn't sure why they hadn't informed us as to what they were doing. "And?"

"We didn't mean to not involve you two," Jorge said. "We need to be ready with another plan if we don't hear from Dr. Smith, and we couldn't sleep last night. So ..."

"It's exciting for me," Enrique said.

Monica turned to Sue and me. "They miss doing dangerous things together."

Sue shrugged. "And?"

"I think we could get into the compound undetected there," Jorge said.

I didn't want to sound like I was scolding. "It would've been better if you'd told us what you were up to, in case something happened, so we'd at least have known where to look for you." It was fine if Jorge and his brother-in-law wanted to check out potential options while bonding, but that was no reason to be reckless.

Jorge nodded. "Yes, you're right."

"My fault for being overzealous." Enrique shrugged. "We'll go put the C4 away."

I didn't see a need to know where the explosives were going to be hidden, as I wouldn't know what to do with them anyway.

We left them to it and went to the dining room.

Ivan had gone to lie down for a few hours, having dealt with the time difference in Oslo and worked for most of the night.

Within fifteen minutes Jorge and Enrique had washed up and come to eat breakfast.

"I was thinking." Enrique pulled an *arepa* off a pile on a plate. "I could pose as a homeless person who wants food and shelter and get into the compound. I could gather information from the inside."

Jorge reached for a hardboiled egg. "If anyone is going to try get into the compound, it will be me."

"What about me?" I said. "I should be the one."

Jorge, Enrique, Monica, and Sue all shook their heads.

"Why not? I'm the one most responsible for all of this. I should be the one to take on the most risk."

"For one, we're all in this together and should share the risk." Sue looked across the table. "Except for Enrique and Monica."

"No, no, no," Enrique said. "I want to do it. And I'm local."

"Think of your daughters if anything should happen to you," Sue said.

"It should be me," I said.

"Nick, you're a gringo who doesn't speak Spanish other than ordering a beer," Jorge said. "It can't be you."

"Oh, you have a point there." *Yeah that counts me out.*

▷◁▷◁

"Come here for a minute?" Jorge was sitting in front of the second monitor and used the remote control to rewind the tape in the VCR.

Ivan was too busy concentrating on his work, but Sue and I came over.

"Look who's arrived." Jorge stopped the tape at the point where we could see the passengers' faces in the Mercedes on the road outside.

I was surprised. "That's Carlo Da Silva."

"Yes." Jorge advanced the tape by two frames.

Sue leaned forward. "Yeah, that's him for sure, but I don't recognize the guy beside him."

I stared at the image. The man beside Da Silva was young, blond, and had a round face. "No idea."

Hearing Carlo Da Silva's name must've broken Ivan's concentration, because he came over to the screen. "That looks like Günther Schmidt, Hendrick's younger brother."

"Why would he be here with Da Silva?" I asked no one in particular.

"All the main players are here," Sue said.

A vehicle appeared in the bottom left screen of the live feed monitor showing the front gate.

We all hurried to the front door. Mike had been coming up the hall and joined us.

Within a few seconds a beaten-up Renault Duster parked in the driveway. Out came Lee and Lorraine.

"Bring us up to speed," Lee said by way of greeting.

# INTERLOGUE 10

The only sound in the office was the air conditioner on high, circulating air to combat the afternoon heat.

Hendrick sat at his desk, thinking and worrying. His father had known more than he'd given him credit for. Hendrick had to admit, at least to himself, that this was way beyond him. The research was much more advanced than what he'd learned at Oxford, and he couldn't fake his knowledge as he'd first hoped.

Since Hendrick learned that Dr. Smith had met with Barnes and Popov, all trust was lost. But Dr. Smith was the only person capable of achieving their goals for them. Hendrick hoped that the physical persuasion methods they'd used restored Dr. Smith's loyalty and focus.

Now Carlo Da Silva was arriving, and Hendrick wasn't sure how much he wanted to admit to him. Maybe it hadn't been such a good idea to summon him. Hendrick couldn't show weakness.

Otto escorted two men into the room.

Hendrick stood, his thoughts still forefront in his mind. "Carlo, thank you for coming all this way."

Carlo stepped forward. "No trouble. I've wanted an excuse to come and see the operation."

When Carlo moved, the man behind him came into Hendrick's

view. "Günter, what are you doing here?" Hendrick wasn't happy to see his younger brother.

"Hendrick." Günter gave a slight nod; a bead of sweat formed at his blond hairline and ran down his temple. Standing still in his damp green polo shirt and khaki shorts, he didn't advance to greet his brother.

"I invited him." Carlo sat down on a folding chair and motioned Günter forward. "Come sit, it's cooler here."

Hendrick, for sure, wasn't going to admit weakness to his little brother. He'd always suspected Günter would make a play for power once he was ready, but right now he was only twenty-five and still in school. Günter was following in his brother's, father's, grandfather's, great-grandfather's, and great-great-grandfather's footsteps of being a scientist. He had talent, drive, and was conniving enough, but he didn't have the name, *Hendrick*.

Günter took a seat beside Carlo. "I'm just here to observe your work."

"So you could try take over, perhaps?" There had been no love lost between them ever since they were children and used to beat each other up or pit servants against the other—the younger most often triumphing over the older. Their father outwardly stated he wished they'd gotten along but in secret had relished that his boys were so aggressive.

Günter couldn't hide a sly smile. "No, Hendrick, this is your show."

Carlo already looked annoyed at the sibling rivalry. "So how is everything progressing?"

"It's progressing," Hendrick said. "Would you like a tour of the facility?"

"Of course," Carlo said. "Where is Davis? I thought he'd be here to greet us as well."

"He's taken a turn for the worse today," Hendrick said. "Davis is in the infirmary. His personal physician arrived a few days ago, and Dr. Smith is trying to help, but it's advanced."

Carlo sat up straight. "What's advanced? What are you talking about?"

Carlo didn't know? *Davis hadn't told him.* In that second Hendrick decided to only discuss the positive sides—fortunately, he'd already coached Dr. Smith to do the same. It was only Carlo now that he had to worry about. "I'm surprised Davis didn't tell you he had colon cancer."

"What! Colon cancer? We all were supposed to have been protected. What happened? Could it be another strain?"

"It's the same strain of cancer, and we don't know how he got it." Hendrick had to admit that part. "Further tests need to be run, but we may have to be even more stringent regarding the safe food. Also, Davis admitted that he wasn't as careful as he should've been."

Carlo stood. "I want to see Davis, now."

Günter, who'd been staring at his brother, stood as well. He was an inch taller than Hendrick at five feet nine inches.

"Of course." Hendrick led the way.

Otto came out of nowhere and walked behind them as they left the building. The sun was stifling in the open, so they stuck to the few shade trees as they made their way to the infirmary.

Carlo looked disgusted by the deformed children and scarred adults as they passed. He increased his pace to come up beside Hendrick. "What caused the people to look like that?"

"Direct exposure to glyphosate."

Carlo frowned.

Hendrick thought it was good that Carlo saw firsthand the true power of direct contact with the herbicide.

Inside the windowless infirmary, it smelled of disinfectant. Everything, including the walls and tiled floor, was white. Two rows of fifteen beds lined each side with white curtains separating them;

half were occupied. One man cried in pain, clutching his stomach, the others seemed to be sedated. A man and a woman in lab coats over scrubs rushed over to the patient in distress. Two other medical personnel reviewed charts next to patients.

They walked to the back, and Hendrick opened a door. Inside was a private room filled with medical equipment and monitors. It was much cooler in there. An adjustable bed with side railings was in the center; Davis lay in it, looking upset. A man with a full head of gray hair, wearing a lab coat over a T-shirt and khaki shorts, was standing next to a laptop that rested on a high table.

"Davis, how are you?" Carlo went right to his side. "You never told me you were ill."

"I didn't want to tell anyone." Davis was gaunt and thin under the hospital gown. He looked vulnerable. "I denied it for as long as I could."

"Shouldn't you be back in the States getting treated, not here in the jungle?" Carlo said.

"My doctor is here." Davis motioned with his eyes to the left.

The doctor glanced over his glasses at them and then went back to viewing the screen.

"He's better off here," Hendrick said. "We are getting close to having the cure."

"That's an embellishment of what Dr. Smith told me." Davis clutched the lower part of his abdominal area.

"You're likely going to die anyway," Hendrick said. "You might as well let Dr. Smith test on you. That's your only chance for survival."

"A little tact, please," Carlo raised his voice.

Günter stayed inside the doorway, quiet.

"So what's the procedure?" Carlo asked.

"It's all in my doctor's and Smith's hands," Davis said.

"What about your wife and children?" Carlo asked. "Have you told them?"

"No, not yet."

"How much time is there?" Carlo kept the questions going.

"I'm devoting all my efforts and resources to help Davis." The doctor didn't look up. "This food that you've created should be banned. If people don't stop eating it, there's going to be an epidemic of this strain of colon cancer."

Hendrick, Carlo, and Davis looked at each other. The doctor hadn't been filled in about what was really going on and the big picture.

"I want to speak with Dr. Smith," Carlo said.

"He should be in the lab." Hendrick turned to leave the room. "I'll show you."

🧬

They went out into the heat and walked back across to the building that housed the offices and lab, but this time to an entrance nearer the main gate of the compound.

Carlo was conflicted inside. It was one thing to have the masses that he didn't know or couldn't put a face to dying from disease of their design, but to see Davis suffering the same fate changed things. What if someone in his own family or any of his true friends suffered? What if *he* ended up getting the cancer?

They entered the sterilized coolness of the lab. There were at least ten people in white lab coats working at different stations. They proceeded toward the back where they saw Dr. Smith.

Dr. Smith was reading a chart and looked up. "Mr. Da Silva. I didn't know you were coming to visit us."

Carlo noticed that the skin around Dr. Smith's right eye was black and his cheek swollen with a bandage over a cut. "Dr. Smith. What happened to you?"

Dr. Smith looked from Otto to Hendrick. "I had an accident."

Carlo knew he was lying from the way he looked at the two men and from his tone. *Why would they be harming the man they needed most?* He'd bring it up with Hendrick later. "What's the latest with the cancer cure?"

"I think we've had breakthroughs on both sides in the last few days." When Dr. Smith twisted to place the papers in his hand on the stainless-steel table, he cringed as if protecting his ribs.

Carlo noted that as well. "Tell me."

"The immune-suppressive drugs were not extending patients' lives for more than six months after we removed their colons. The cancer would almost always breach the colon walls and spread into the peritoneum. The patients would be permanently hospitalized, incapacitated, and likely need multiple surgeries."

"Not the results we wanted," Hendrick said. "That's too hard on the medical systems and not enough profit for us."

"With the addition of a new formula of chemotherapy that we've redeveloped, it seems we can substantially slow the cancer spread," Dr. Smith continued, "therefore giving people a better quality of life for I'm hoping our target of three years."

"It would slow the spread by that much?" Carlo wished he knew more about science and medicine.

"I'm pretty sure this could be it," Dr. Smith said. "We're beginning the human trials tomorrow. We'll skip the rodent tests. We have ten people here that have the cancer, and we've removed their colons. I should know how well it's working within two months."

"What about Davis?" Carlo asked.

Dr. Smith leaned against the work bench. "He wouldn't last two months if we were to wait until the initial testing was done."

Carlo took a step toward Dr. Smith. "You're saying if we give him the chemotherapy now, he may survive longer? Perhaps long enough for you to figure out the permanent cure?"

"We've had progress with the immune-enhancing drugs as well." Dr. Smith looked optimistic. "Initially we were using synthetic and genetically engineered properties to boost immune systems. We've switched to an identical natural organic formula, save one herb. The results in mice changed dramatically, within a day, to the point of tumors shrinking. My theory is within time they will disappear. That's the route I propose with Mr. Lovemark and five other patients we have here at similar stages."

"That sounds better." Carlo looked at Hendrick. "Then why did you say you were experiencing challenges when you convinced me to come here?"

"These breakthroughs have only been discovered within the last few days," Hendrick said.

Günter was a few feet behind the other men. "Then isn't it too soon to declare them breakthroughs?"

"Normally we would conduct another, larger test on mice before we went to human testing, but time is of the essence, especially in Mr. Lovemark's case," Dr. Smith said. "We'll remove his colon and the colons of two others. With the other three subjects, we will leave their colons intact. Then all will receive the same intravenous formula. I feel it will work or be close, and then we can make adjustments."

"But if it doesn't work, it'll be too late for Davis?" Carlo wasn't satisfied.

"I feel at worst it could slow the cancer spread enough to keep him alive until we make further adjustments." Dr. Smith still sounded optimistic.

"So ..." Carlo pieced it together. "What you're trying to accomplish is to boost the immune system to the point that the body kills the cancer on its own, right?"

"That's correct," Dr. Smith said.

"It's the only chance Davis has," Hendrick repeated.

That was enlightening for Carlo. "Wouldn't that mean that this could potentially cure all types of diseases?"

Dr. Smith smiled. "Yes."

Carlo looked at Hendrick V. He knew that Hendrick IV hadn't intended on developing such a cure, but it could really help the survivors of the population control plan with all kinds of illnesses. He'd have to make sure Hendrick V saw it that way, and when Günter was ready, that he continued the project. "Good. Hendrick, let's go back to your office."

As they walked down the hall, Hendrick said to Otto, "Why don't you show Günter the cafeteria in the executive quarters." He glanced at Günter. "I'm sure you're hungry and thirsty."

Carlo was all right with that and nodded his consent.

Once in Hendrick's office, he ushered Carlo to a brown couch in the corner. A sweating pitcher of water with glasses sat on the coffee table.

Hendrick opened a small fridge. "Would you like water or a light beer? Beer seems to be the only thing that quenches your thirst out here."

"Water is fine." Carlo sat.

Hendrick took out a beer. "Tell me more about what you're doing regarding the Internet and your progress. I haven't been briefed on that."

Carlo couldn't believe how little Hendrick knew about his work with multiple web layering. That's not what Carlo had come to discuss but liked to take every opportunity to brag about his accomplishments. "To be brief, we've almost completed beta testing with great success on a search-data-gathering engine that works behind regular search engines. For everyone who is on the grid, we can collect all types of information, like where they live, what they do, spending habits, health, money, passwords, et cetera—everything about everyone. We'll have internal access to all computers."

"Is the information meant for sale, to generate money?"

"Information is ultimate power. It's meant for our own affiliate companies, and we'll decide who to share it with." Carlo didn't think Hendrick really got it but didn't much care because it wasn't his forte and he wouldn't be helping in any way.

"So as you can see, we're making progress again with the cancer drugs." Hendrick changed the subject.

"Yes, how things change within only a few short days." Carlo poured himself a glass of water. He preferred it at room temperature.

"These breakthroughs show we've been on the right track for some time." Hendrick sat on the opposite side of the leather couch.

Carlo sensed he wasn't telling the whole truth but couldn't pinpoint the missing part yet. He turned to look at Hendrick straight on. "My main concern is that Davis has the strain of cancer, which means that our safeguards aren't effective, even so early on. Any one of us could suffer the same fate."

Perspiration was forming above Hendrick's upper lip. "Yes, it seems so."

Carlo waited a moment to see if Hendrick would expand his response. That didn't happen, so he said, "I did some investigating before I came, after my own fields were polluted."

"What do you mean about your own fields?"

"Somehow, either intentionally or by some force of nature, two outer rows of grapes next to my high perimeter fence had been poisoned by glyphosate. Also, Naintosa's genetically engineered wheat had been found in my ancient grain field."

Hendrick took a sip of his beer. "Could it have been from a neighbor's farm?"

"There are no neighboring farms," Carlo said. "So I contacted a cross-section of the operations put aside to grow food for the surviving people; the ones that are meant to stay pure and organic. After they tested, four have had genetically engineered seed contamination and three had abnormally high amounts of glyphosate in their ground water."

"I didn't know that."

"How could you *not* know that Naintosa's genetically engineered seed is out of control?" Carlo didn't bother trying to hide his frustration. "Not to mention that glyphosate is showing up in ground water many miles away from where it's being used. It's your fucking company now! That wasn't supposed to happen!"

"I can't fucking know everything that's going on, and this was happening before I took over." Hendrick sat up straight and pointed his finger at Carlo. "You all knew about seed drift and how its spread cannot be controlled. And glyphosate is a cancer-causing herbicide that of course gets into the ground water around where it's sprayed and spreads. You can't be surprised about any of that. You're one of the people who planned it."

"But it's out of control!" Carlo had to take a deep breath, and it felt like the air conditioner had stopped working. "You have to find a way to get it in check, or we're all going to get cancer of the ass and die! That surely is not what we'd planned." Carlo had trusted that Hendrick IV knew what he was doing. Now he realized that he should've asked more questions and learned about the process himself. But he wasn't a scientist.

"How am I supposed to do that?" Hendrick threw his arms up, spilling his beer. "Is that why you brought my brother here? You really want him to take over? He has even less experience than I do."

"I'm hoping he'll be able to help you when he's ready. It's going to take more than just you to get this sorted out." Carlo was lying. He wanted this little prick gone as soon as possible. "It would've been helpful to have your father here." *But you killed him.*

"I never doubted my father's ability." Hendrick placed the bottle on the coffee table. "But he created this mess. And now I see that you and Davis had no clue what was happening."

"We trusted your father."

"And look where that's gotten us."

Carlo took another deep breath. Hendrick was right, but that didn't change anything now. He decided to move onto another subject. "What really happened to Dr. Smith?"

Hendrick looked relieved that they were going to talk about something else. "What do you mean?"

"His face was beat up and his ribs damaged."

Hendrick paused as if trying to figure out what to say.

"The truth."

"We've discovered that Nick Barnes and Dr. Ivan Popov are in Florencia, and that Dr. Smith met with them. So we had to beat his loyalty back into him."

"Hmm. Do you think it worked?"

"Yes, but we aren't letting him out of our sight."

"Do you know what information he gave them?"

"He admitted it was about the seed, glyphosate, and neonicotinoids' uncontrolled spread."

"So you *did* know how bad it was?"

"Not at the levels you told me about. We didn't know that our safe farms have been contaminated." Hendrick chose his words carefully. "It's worse than the data we have."

Carlo's strong jaw was clenched. "Anything else?"

"We are continuing to have difficulty with the Plycite gene in corn."

*What a fucking mess.* "What do we do about Barnes and Popov? How long ago did they meet?"

"Six days ago."

Carlo wasn't normally impulsive, he was more calculating. But in light of what was happening to his friend Davis and the challenges with the plan, he had an urge to lash out at someone. He'd been more tolerant of Barnes and his group than the others; however, now it was time to finally get rid of them. What a better place to disappear people than the Colombian jungle? "Do you know where they are?"

"Not yet."

"Do you know how they communicated?"

"There's a place in Florencia where they leave notes for each other."

"Was there supposed to be another meeting?"

"Yes, Dr. Smith was going to give them information on the cancer drugs."

Carlo rubbed his chin and thought. "Well then, let's set up that meeting."

# CHAPTER 34

*May 30, 2003*

Moving as quietly as I could, so as not to disturb Sue, I sat up and propped my back against the wall. During our meditations since we'd arrived in Florencia, the energy seemed awkward and we'd had trouble getting calm and clearing our minds. I wanted to try on my own.

I focused on my breathing and yawned. I was still sleepy. Breath going in, breath coming out, in and out ...

*Jack went down flat on his face. I ran up to him through the sandy leaf-strewn soil. His Rottweiler, Moose, sniffed Jack's lower leg and whimpered.*

*There was someone beside me; it was Morgan.*

*She took his right shoulder, I took his left, and we pulled him up.*

*"Can you move?" I asked.*

*"It's my ankle." Jack cringed.*

*"They're right behind us," Morgan said. "I can hear them."*

*We wrapped Jack's arms around us and pulled him forward.*

*"Don't think about it, just run," Morgan said with a grunt.*

*Moose stayed right beside us.*

*We pushed forward from the beach to the jungle, where there was shade from the burning heat. Fatigue ran through all of us. Jack looked like he was on the verge of passing out.*

*All of a sudden it was Morgan in the middle, and Jack and I supporting her. Progress was slow through the dense foliage. Sharp branches and plants were scraping at our exposed arms and legs, stinging and bloodying them. We couldn't stop.*

*We stumbled into a clearing where there was a barbed-wire fence around dilapidated buildings. Sue was inside the enclosure, holding a crying baby wrapped in a white cloth. She was staring at us with fear in her eyes. We couldn't see a way in.*

*My right foot caught on a root, and I flipped into a ravine that appeared out of nowhere. I kept rolling until I hit the bottom and stopped.*

*Gunshots rang out.*

*Jack crumpled to the ground.*

*Morgan fell backward over the edge and landed in my arms, dead!*
Thud.

I felt pain in my left shoulder and head as I landed on something hard and cool. I forced my eyes open. I was on the floor. Had I fallen asleep and dreamed, or was that a meditative vision?

Sue looked over the edge of the bed. "What happened?"

"I had a nightmare, fucking awful one." I was shaking.

"What was it about?"

I explained every vivid detail.

"I don't know what to say," Sue said after I'd finished. "That's pretty screwed up."

"I know."

Sue got out of bed. "It's like the past coming to haunt you ... mixed with some possible future."

Everyone was to meet in the living room.

Lee and I were the first ones there.

"How are you doing?" I took a seat on a thick-cushioned chair.

He was looking out the window and turned to me. "You saw that I'm still having trouble moving. I should've waited until I was of more use before I came."

"Well, I don't think you're ready to go out into the jungle," I said. "But it's good that you're here. You can still help."

He nodded.

Ivan came into the room and sat down in another chair. "Lee, is everything in order with Jack's estate?"

With tentative steps, Lee went to a chair and took a seat. "It'll still take a while for everything to be sorted out, but there don't seem to be any real problems. I'm hoping the funds will be released within a few months. I'm still surprised that no one in the Carter family is contesting that you all are benefiting."

"They have enough of their own money," Ivan said.

Sue was going to the couch. "The rich always want more."

"As we thought, Tom Crane is trying to buy Moile R&D," Lee said.

"He wanted it while Jack was alive," I said. "Now that he's passed ..."

"He has to have an ulterior motive," Sue said.

"Or he just wants to shut it down because of his oil and gas interests," Lee said.

"Maybe he wants to use it to test water for extraction," Ivan said. "We all know that clean water is becoming more valuable than oil."

I'd thought of that business use as well, earlier, and had wanted to talk to Jack about it when this was all over.

The rest of the group entered the living room.

I remembered a question I'd forgotten to ask. "Lorraine, did you ever find out who Furyk and Stenson really worked for?"

Lorraine was wearing a thin white sleeveless cotton dress that looked very feminine. "It's confirmed that they are both CIA counterintelligence officers."

"Were you able to find out who was giving them orders?" Jorge asked.

"Unfortunately, no," Lorraine said.

"The reason they may've been posing as FBI is because we're US citizens," Lee said. "CIA can't go after US citizens, but the FBI can."

That made the most sense. "The big question is who is directing them."

Mike stood at the back of the room, holding a beer and saying nothing. He'd been steadily becoming more aloof.

"We still haven't heard from Dr. Smith and don't know if we will ever again," I said. "Lovemark and Da Silva are at the compound with Schmidt V, so something big is going on. I think it's time we plan to get into the compound and see what we can find."

Jorge spoke up. "It would take too long for us to infiltrate the compound as peasants or even as truck drivers. Let's go in through the blind area Enrique found and target the lab and infirmary."

Sue produced a pad and pen. "What else exactly do we need?"

"We need the cancer drug research and formulas." Ivan raised one finger, followed by a second. "I want proof to make sure the Plycite corn is far from being ready for mass distribution." A third finger was raised. "Also, we need photographs of the people who are being used as test subjects, for human-rights crimes. And any charts documenting their conditions would be helpful."

"That could be a tall order for us to achieve all at once," I said.

Enrique brought out the rough sketch of the compound and spread it out on the coffee table.

We all gathered for a closer look.

With a pencil Enrique marked an X at the far corner of the perimeter fence behind the barracks. "We enter here." Then he circled the building in the center of the compound. "The infirmary."

He traced a line and marked a long building at the top of the map. "The lab."

"Have you studied the movements of the guards?" Lee asked.

"Somewhat," Enrique said. "Mainly during the day."

"We watched for an hour the other night," Jorge said. "But I know, Lee, that's not enough, even though we saw minimal movement."

Lee bent closer to the sketch. "I suggest we go tonight and watch their patterns." He pointed at the edges. "We can have observers at different areas of the perimeter and note who goes where and when."

"Even though we may want to, we can't rush this," Lorraine said.

"It'll take a few nights," Lee said.

"Agreed," I said. "We need to use every precaution."

Olga and Esmeralda, who'd been at school, rushed into the room.

"There was a note at the drop-off spot." Esmeralda passed the piece of paper to Ivan.

He unfolded it and read. "Dr. Smith is unable to leave the compound unescorted, because they know he met with us. He has however assembled the cancer drug information and will leave it next to the perimeter fence tonight." There was a second sheet of paper that Ivan held up—a rough drawing of the compound and an arrow pointing to a specific place.

"Does it look like his handwriting?" Jorge asked.

"It's the same as before." Ivan passed the note to Jorge. "His writing has sharp edges."

So for sure they knew we were in Florencia and had been around the compound. It was probably a trap, but could we afford not to go? "I don't think we have a choice."

There was silence in the group for a moment.

"It could be a setup," Sue said.

Ivan looked concerned. "But we need that information ..."

"We'll have to move in and out quickly," Jorge said.

# CHAPTER 35

We'd decided we had to take the chance. Hopefully Dr. Smith would be able to sneak the cancer research information to us. Ivan was the most vocal about how we had to trust Dr. Smith, otherwise why would he have approached us in the first place?

It was agreed that Enrique would go, because of course he knew his way around the area the best; Jorge, because he'd become the security leader; me, because I insisted; Sue, because she insisted even harder; and Lorraine, because she had jungle-combat experience that we'd been unaware of until now.

There was no way Lee would be able to make it to the compound without assistance, so he'd wait at the end of the tunnel with a rifle in case we were followed back.

Of course, Ivan couldn't be risked, as he had to disseminate the research when we returned with it.

Monica and Mike would watch the cameras and monitor communications.

After the decisions were made, people dispersed from the living room.

Enrique and Jorge decided to go out to buy some fresh batteries for the night-vision goggles and see if they could find walkie-talkies or something we could communicate with.

Mike and I were the last ones in the living room, and I wanted to take the opportunity to talk to him.

I approached and patted him on the shoulder. "How you holding up?"

"Fine." He'd tensed when I'd touched him. "I'm fine."

"This is stressful, and we all handle stress in our own way."

Mike took a swig of beer. "This could all go horribly wrong."

"But you know we have to do it." I thought for second. "For me, I know it's worth the risk. There's nothing more important than what we're doing."

Mike stared at the wall.

Maybe if I reminded him how and why he arrived at this point. "What about Summer? She'd be so proud of how far you'd come with the seed bank information and how we've tied it to the population control plan."

His eyes widened, but his gaze remained off to the side.

It'd be best to offer him a way out. "If you want, we can take you to the airport. I'd totally understand, and so would everyone else."

Mike looked at me and then back at the wall. He took a stuttering breath.

"Think about it."

He placed the half-drunk bottle on a small table next to us and wiped his arm across his eyes. As he exhaled, in a quiet voice with determination, he said, "Don't be such a pussy." Then he turned and punched me in the arm. "I'm good. All in. You don't have to worry about me."

Jorge and Enrique were speaking in Spanish when Sue and I entered the dining room. They switched to English as soon as they saw us.

"It's never happened before." Jorge rubbed his stomach.

"Jorge's getting soft," Enrique said to us. "He ate chicken on a stick from a street vender, and now his tummy is sore."

"You had some too," Jorge said to Enrique. "You don't feel anything?"

"No," Enrique said. "Eating United States food must've made your stomach wimpy."

Others filed in for dinner.

Monica brought in a platter of braised pork.

"Sorry, Sis; I need my stomach to settle," Jorge said.

Monica looked to Olga, who was standing next to her. "Please go get your uncle some seltzer tablets and water."

I sat in the living room, in green camouflage pants and shirt, my boots on, the Glock holstered, night-vision goggles in one hand, backpack in the other, waiting to go. We'd made a plan for escape in case it was a setup; however, it was flawed if we were overrun by Naintosa security—we'd have to see them coming. I felt responsible for everyone and didn't want anything to happen to any of them. We'd all come so far.

I noticed that Mike's beer was still sitting on the small table in the corner.

Closing my eyes, I reached deep within. How did I feel? *Nervous.* Were we going to make it through this? *I couldn't tell.* What did I need most? The feeling plowed into my mind—*focus.* I let it solidify and then opened my eyes.

Sue had come over. "You ready?"

"Focus," I said out loud. "Yep. You?"

Sue looked nervous too, and was rubbing her belly in clockwise circles. "As I'll ever be."

I hoped she didn't have the same problem Jorge had. "Your stomach okay?"

"Yeah, why?" She placed her hand down to the side.

Jorge came out of the powder room adjacent to the living room. "Everyone ready?"

Enrique walked past Jorge and sniffed the air coming from the restroom. "Are you sure you can make it?"

Jorge narrowed his eyes. "I'm fine."

It was midnight, and everyone who was going was in the laundry room. The people staying stood around the doorway.

Jorge and Enrique had only been able to find two walkie-talkies that they'd thought could be strong enough to work in the jungle at the required distance; Jorge held one and Lee the other.

Enrique opened the tunnel door, and we filed down one by one with our flashlights on.

It was cool in the tunnel and damp. We went the same way as before, which seemed faster this time. Before long we were out in the thick jungle.

Lee remained at the tunnel entrance with an automatic rifle in hand.

Under the canopy it was pitch black and humid, the warm air dissipating slowly. We could hear nocturnal creatures all around; our flashlight beams came across disembodied eyes watching us.

Enrique led us forward.

Branches and thick leaves kept smacking me everywhere. Something was crawling on the back of my neck, and I went to swat it away. Jorge grabbed whatever it was and threw it off me. I didn't even want to know what it was.

Sue kicked a rock by mistake, making noise. Then I almost stepped on a snake trying to slither away from us.

To add to the inky blackness, we'd entered a bank of low, soupy fog. The ground was muddy and sticky. The flashlight beams were reduced to only about twelve feet.

We switched from flashlights to night-vision goggles, which

worked better.

A thick rubbery leaf that Sue had just ducked under hit me in the face. That made me close my eyes for a second, and when I opened them, I walked right into her. Sue had stopped when Lorraine and Enrique stopped.

I could just make out the fence ahead.

We dropped to our knees and watched for any movement.

After a minute, Enrique whispered, "Wait here while I go get Dr. Smith's information."

I felt Jorge shudder beside me. I pulled off my goggles and looked at his face. He cringed and was obviously in pain.

"I have to go." He was barely audible. "I'll be right back."

It was the worst possible timing, but what good would he be if he shit himself? Tainted street meat could bring down the toughest of men.

The others saw what was going on. Enrique nodded, and Jorge disappeared back into the bush.

"We can't see well from this far back," I whispered. "Let's move in another twenty feet so we can have a better view of the fence line, to make sure you'll be okay."

Enrique nodded and then led us forward, the four of us crouching.

When the fog whitened from the emanating lights within the compound, we stopped.

Enrique looked back at us and then squatted as low as he could and moved forward to the fence.

Sue and Lorraine were on either side of me. We went down on our knees behind a large fern.

There was rustling from behind, which must've been Jorge coming up to join us.

Lorraine tightened on the rifle she was carrying. Sue and I pulled out our revolvers.

Enrique went down on his belly, disappearing from our view.

A beam of light scanned by from inside the compound.

Someone was right behind us. As I turned, I was struck so hard in the back of the head that I hit the dirt face-first. Severe pain engulfed my head as if my skull had been cracked.

I could only open one eye and saw Sue lying next to me.

Another blow ...

# CHAPTER 36

"Don't execute him yet." The voice was rough with a German accent. "We must interrogate them first."

The pain banged between my temples. I was being dragged by someone with their arms through mine, my feet bouncing along the ground. I fought to open my eyes. We were entering the compound. Sue was being pulled next to me, hopefully just unconscious. Enrique was walking behind us, hands clamped behind his neck. Two men were pointing military rifles at him. There was no sign of Lorraine or Jorge.

A man came into my sight line. He was tall, slim, and dressed in black. He walked with a limp. He wore round spectacles and had a gray-and-blond buzz cut above his evil smile. His image reminded me of how an Aryan Nazi would look in a movie. "Hello, Mr. Barnes. It's a pleasure to finally meet you." It was the same voice ordering someone not to execute one of us. "I'm Otto Schilling, head of Schmidt's private security and the one who will inflict excruciating pain on you if you don't do what I say."

The person dragging me had their arms clamped hard under mine. The joints between my shoulders and arms were beginning to ache.

Dr. Smith had sold us out to his employer. Had I actually doubted that he would? The man's guilty conscience wasn't enough to fully turn him to do the right thing. He was probably dead now anyway.

Otto kept walking between the people dragging Sue and me, looking proud, as if we were his trophies. If his words and appearance were meant to scare us, they had a mixed effect on me. Yes, I was scared, but more for the others.

I'd found myself in similar positions in the last three years—this wasn't a new experience. So many people that I cared for had died on this journey that there was little left to lose. What if I'd be beaten and they'd finally kill me? *Stop that thought.* I glanced at Sue. I wanted to live. I didn't want to just be another life snuffed out as they reached their goal of controlling the population. I was surprised at my ability to think that clearly under the circumstances, and the pain between my ears was beginning to subside.

There was concrete under my heels now, and the constant bumping was making my feet hurt inside my boots.

A door opened and we were pulled into a building.

Enrique was close enough for me to see the fear in his eyes. I had to do everything possible for him to make it back to his family.

"What the fuck! Fuck you! Let go!" Sue had gained consciousness. She started squirming so violently that the large man pulling her lost his grip and she fell to the concrete floor.

Otto rushed over and with the butt of his rifle hit Sue square in the stomach, hard. She groaned and went into the fetal position, clutching herself.

"What the fuck are you doing? Don't you dare hurt her!" I struggled to get free but couldn't.

Otto came up to me and pointed his gun at my face, his stare menacing.

Another man came from somewhere and helped lift Sue. They took her by the arms, but she didn't straighten, still holding her stomach.

We moved down a hallway until we entered a windowless room. I was dropped and kicked in the back. That didn't hurt so much.

Someone pulled me up and made me sit on a metal stool. Sue was placed on the chair next to me and Enrique on the other side. Someone sat past Enrique; it was Lorraine. She must've been ahead of us. Thank goodness she was still alive.

I could tell Sue was in a lot of pain but grimacing not to show it. The lap of her pants was wet with something dark.

"Shit, Sue, you're bleeding."

She stared down and then back at me, her eyes trying to look defiant.

Determination poured through me. I had to make sure Sue made it out of here. I breathed deep to force the remaining pain out of my head and think with clarity.

I surveyed our surroundings. The room was square with boxes stacked against one wall, the others bare and gray. Turning my neck as far as I could, I saw a desk against the wall behind us with someone perched on the edge of it.

Otto had left, leaving behind three large guards—one Caucasian and two Latino. We weren't bound in any way; the three guns pointing at us would prevent our escape. I'd have to wait for the right opportunity—one of our captors would slip up.

I glanced at Lorraine, and she appeared to be unharmed; the same with Enrique. Where was Jorge? His diarrhea could've been the best thing that happened. He'd come for us.

The only door to the room opened, and in walked two of the men I hated most—Hendrick Schmidt V and Carlo Da Silva. Then a young man followed who had a resemblance to Schmidt. He'd been the one in the Mercedes with Da Silva, whom Ivan had said was Hendrick's brother, Günter.

Right behind them was Lieutenant Furyk. Now we knew what side he was on. Furyk walked straight back to whoever was perched at the desk.

Where was Lovemark?

Last in was Nazi Schilling. "Leave us," he said to the guards. "Go and see if Villegas has been found."

So, Jorge had gotten away. Also, they wouldn't know about the others back at the house. We had to buy time and make this go as slowly as possible.

"Nick and Sue, we meet at last." Schmidt smirked. "What brings you to our neighborhood? Colombia is a dangerous place; people disappear."

I tried to keep my voice level and matter of fact. "Schmidt Junior, you can't keep going on like your father, ruining the world and controlling the population, without expecting resistance and suffering retribution."

"That's Dr. Schmidt and I'm 'junior' to no one." He took a step toward me, but Da Silva placed a hand on Schmidt's shoulder, stopping him.

"When will you get the point that this is much bigger than you?" Da Silva focused on me. "You lost souls think you're exposing some diabolical plot to destroy the world? We're saving it from all the damage, pollution, and overpopulation. You should be thanking and supporting us."

"The most damage has been caused by you." Sue's breathing was strained. "Your genetically engineered food and pesticides are the worst pollution of all. How can you justify that?"

"Justification is in the eyes of the beholder," Da Silva said.

"We don't need to justify anything to you or anyone else," Schmidt said. "We're the ones who make the rules."

Da Silva continued. "You've never fully grasped what we're doing; this work is for the long-term success of humanity in this world. Our goals have taken generations to implement and will take more time for the results to be achieved. Sometimes it may look like we're creating damage, but we're actually doing good when you see the final result. I'm sure you can appreciate that."

Da Silva looked sincere and seemed to believe the words coming out of his mouth. I would've taken him for his word if I hadn't already known their true intentions—to profit from the diminishing population and fully control the people who survive. "The thing is, we know why you're really doing all this *and* that your long-term plan is going to fail." I made sure to look into Schmidt's and Da Silva's eyes. "You can't pollute the land, the flora, and the fauna to the point it won't be able to recover for thousands of years, and that's what you're doing. You're actually destroying the food system forever, to the point that no one, not even your children, will survive. If you truly wanted to help heal the planet, you'd focus on rebuilding the soil and environment. That's the only way we'll ever fix things."

Schmidt scoffed.

Da Silva looked at me as if having sympathy for my simple mind. "And how can that be achieved when the population is growing at such a rate, wiping out the resources like locusts? We must deal with that issue first."

"We have to cleanse the planet," Schmidt said.

"With your toxic food?" Sue spoke up. "Are you as fucking stupid as you look? Do you not get that you're going about it the wrong way?"

"You can't cull the population." I almost stood. "You need to shift your strategy a hundred and eighty degrees."

I could see Schmidt's eyes light up when I said the word *cull*. He liked it.

"You have to work with the amount of people we have and place your focus on making the world a better, cleaner, and more efficient place." In case they were actually listening and we were getting through to them, I wanted to throw in a compliment to help. "Men of your stature and ability do have the means to change the direction of the whole planet. Why don't you use your power to change the direction of industry to be sustainable? There may still be time."

Schmidt looked over at Otto, and he came up between Sue and me.

"What would you simpletons know?" Schmidt sounded like his father. "Over decades of analysis, we've determined that this is the best way to deal with the situation."

"Well, you're wrong," Sue said.

"How would you know, you little slut?" Schmidt's face had turned red and his voice rose. "All you've done is attempt to sabotage us in your naive ways, trying to scare people. You're tiny fleas. You must accept our decisions and live your meaningless lives ... for however long we allow you to."

That little fucker had a real God complex.

I barely noticed a thin hunched-over man leaning on a cane come into the room. He looked old and frail, his skin a sickly gray. *Oh my god, it's Lovemark.*

"We *have* been going about it the wrong way, Hendrick," Lovemark said.

"Nonsense." Schmidt glared at Lovemark. "Yours was a freak occurrence. You weren't cautious enough ... reckless."

I was watching Da Silva, who seemed to be in the middle of a widening crack, one leg straddling each side. I wasn't sure he really believed what he and Schmidt had been saying to us.

"Why not tell them the truth?" Lovemark's left arm was over his abdomen. "They're going to die anyway. Give them some comfort of knowing the truth and that their work was accurate."

I could feel Sue, Enrique, Lorraine, as well as myself stiffen when Lovemark made the two points—*dying anyway* and *we'd been right.*

"They deserve no comfort," Schmidt said. "And your medication is making you delusional."

"I'm making peace before I die," Lovemark said. "And I blame you, your father, your grandfather, and your great-grandfather for doing this to me. You were all *reckless* and stupid enough to think you could control everything."

*Wow, Lovemark is dying. Does he have colon cancer? Talk about karma.*

"You were supposed to protect us from the diseases you created," Lovemark continued. "Now everyone's at risk, and it's a crapshoot as to who survives. You might be next, Hendrick, or you, Carlo."

Schmidt crossed his arms. "Nonsense, old man."

Da Silva, who'd been quiet since Lovemark entered, spoke up, "All is not lost, Davis. Dr. Smith, as you know, has made great strides as of late, and your physician is one of the best in the world."

That meant Dr. Smith was still alive and had set us up willingly.

"However, this is not the time for that discussion," Da Silva continued. "I would like some information from our guests."

Sue gasped and bent forward, clutching her stomach. More blood had soaked her pants.

I reached for her, but Schilling pulled my arm back to my side. "She needs medical attention."

Schmidt gave a nod to Schilling. I couldn't see Schilling's reaction, because he was behind me.

Lorraine stood and took a step toward Sue.

Schilling moved in front of her with one stride and grabbed her arm. "Sit."

I leaned over and touched Sue's shoulder. "Hang in there."

Sue nodded and grimaced.

"If you answer our questions truthfully, Mr. Barnes, we will get Ms. Clark medical attention," said Schmidt.

I knew he was lying.

# CHAPTER 37

There was a sudden, intense violent shudder of the building and the deafening sound of an explosion. We were all knocked to the ground.

Dust and smoke poured in from the hallway.

An instant of shock stopped everyone, making us disoriented.

My ears were ringing. I saw a large crack form on the interior wall.

Sue was trying to get up, and I went to help. Her breaths were short.

Da Silva pulled Günter out of the room, and they were gone.

Lovemark was down and looked unconscious. Enrique lay next to him on the floor.

Peoples' movements around us looked to be in slow motion due to the dusty haze but were actually fast.

Schilling was going for the doorway but was caught from behind by Lorraine. She flung her arm around his neck and held hard until he came down.

Schmidt Junior was directly in front of Sue and me. He had blood running down his cheek from a cut above his eye.

Automatic gunfire erupted in the hallway. Running could be heard.

"Jorge," I said in Sue's ear.

I helped her up onto one knee, squeezing her clenched body.

Schmidt faced us, looking disoriented. Sue went low and I went high, tackling him before he could get his bearings. As he was falling back, I landed an elbow hard on his face. The bone on the bridge of his nose gave way.

Schmidt screamed when he hit the concrete floor on his back, and blood came gushing from his nostrils.

A guttural grunt came from Schilling as he threw Lorraine off him. He rose to his feet, pulling a revolver from a holster around his ankle.

I was on Schmidt but hesitated.

Schilling leveled his gun at me.

Lorraine had bounced off the wall when Schilling threw her off, and rebounded at him. Her arms ahead of her, she hit his hand with the revolver pushing it down to the right, just as he pulled the trigger.

I didn't have time to duck or even blink.

Schmidt's head snapped to the side and convulsed once.

Sue or I weren't hit, but looking down, Schmidt had gotten the bullet right in the temple.

Schilling screamed in high-pitched, uncontrollable anger and backhanded Lorraine in the face.

Enrique had come to and was trying to get up.

Schilling swung his arm around again to point the gun at me. In that instant his nose and mouth exploded at the same time he pulled the trigger. His eyes were wide, the only features left on his face, as he collapsed to the ground.

Mike was in the doorway, right arm extended, with a smoking gun in his hand. His expression was of both aggression and shock.

I looked over at Sue beside me—she wasn't shot. I hadn't been hit either. At the same time, we turned our heads to the wall. Concrete dust was coming out from the hole where Schilling's bullet had entered. It was right between us, missing us both by inches.

There was movement behind us. I could now see that it was Stenson with Furyk sitting at the back of the room, the whole time doing nothing.

Jorge and Ivan, followed by Lee, came into the room from the hall and pointed their guns at the two CIA agents.

Furyk and Stenson stood up from the edge of the desk and brushed the dust off their matching khaki pants.

"Just observing, ladies and gentlemen," Furyk said. "You don't have to worry about us. We're not going to say anything to anyone."

They casually walked past all of us, sidestepping Schilling's body, and exited the room.

Everyone looked to me to see if I would give the order to stop them. I didn't see the point. Somehow I knew they wouldn't come after us later. I suspected they had some kind of tie to Chief Inspector Plante, and Plante was the connection to Lovemark, Schmidt, and Da Silva.

Lovemark groaned and squirmed but didn't get up.

I helped Sue to her feet.

"What do we do with him?" Lorraine asked.

With effort, Sue walked up to Lovemark, wound up and kicked him in the stomach. "Leave the fucker to die alone. He deserves it."

You could hear Lovemark's breath leave him, and the shell of the merciless man shriveled into the fetal position.

I took Sue's arm and wrapped it around my shoulder for support. "Ivan, can you look at Sue?"

He focused on the blood all over her upper pants. "Were you shot, my dear?"

"No, I was hit by the butt of that Nazi-looking fucker's rifle."

Ivan went to Sue and lifted the front of her shirt, exposing her stomach, revealing a large black, red, and blue bruise on her skin. His eyes went wide, and his face showed concern. "We need to get you to a hospital. It looks serious. You are bleeding from the inside."

Lee was checking the cut on Lorraine's face. He must have gotten here by sheer will power.

As I helped Sue toward the door, I asked Enrique, "Are you okay?"

"*Si*, just a headache."

Mike pointed his revolver into the hall in case there was still anyone out there. As we passed, I placed my free hand on his shoulder. He was trembling, eyes blinking rapidly.

"Thanks, Mike," I said. "You saved us."

"Thank you for coming through," Sue said.

He gave a slow nod, up and down with his head.

Ivan took Sue's other arm.

Jorge, Enrique, and Mike led the way. Lee and Lorraine helped each other. The hallway was filled with smoke. Farther down to the left, flames came out of a doorway. We had to go to the right.

"You used my C4," Enrique said.

"Worked like beans go with rice," Jorge replied.

At the end of the hallway, we found an exit.

Outside, floodlights lit the whole compound. People were everywhere, pouring out of the dorms and either escaping through a hole in the fence or through the front gate. Guards were abandoning the site as well—no one stopped anyone from leaving.

The Mercedes-Benz ML that we'd seen pass by the cameras so many times raced by. The man who looked almost like me was driving, and Da Silva and Günter were in the backseat.

Jorge and Lee aimed their automatic rifles at the SUV, but people crowded behind it after it passed, so they couldn't get a clean shot at it.

Through the chaos, Dr. Smith approached us with his hands over his head. "I'm so sorry this had to happen. They forced me." The skin around his right eye was black, and he had a bandage on his swollen cheek.

"We thought that may have been the case," Ivan said. "You can put your arms down."

"I want to dedicate the rest of my life to work on fixing what they made me create," Dr. Smith said.

"We can work together," Ivan said.

Even if Dr. Smith's conscience made him come to his senses, I wasn't sure he should go unpunished. He'd still spent all that time twisting Dr. Elles's research for negative consequences.

A slim, professional-looking man with gray hair walked up to us with an unarmed guard. "Have any of you seen Davis?"

"This is Davis Lovemark's personal physician," Dr. Smith said.

"He's inside, unconscious," I said.

"And you didn't bring him out?" The doctor seemed flustered.

I shrugged. "He deserves worse."

The doctor, with the guard in tow, ran into the building.

"We really need to get Sue to a hospital." I propped her up as she began to slouch.

Dr. Smith pointed to a row of vehicles. "Take one of those. They leave the keys in the ignitions."

"Enrique, can you drive us?" I asked him. He was standing only a few feet away.

"We need to get the sick out of the infirmary and to the hospital," Dr. Smith said.

We agreed that Enrique would take Sue to the hospital with Ivan and me. The rest would stay and help load the people unable to move on their own onto trucks.

# CHAPTER 38

*May 31, 2003*

As Enrique rushed us to the hospital, three police cars and two fire trucks passed going toward the Naintosa compound and Pharmalin lab.

I held Sue and placed her head against my chest as she complained about the pain becoming more severe.

Being early in the morning, it was quiet at the hospital emergency entrance. I found Sue a wheelchair, while Ivan went to talk to someone in admissions.

Within minutes a doctor who spoke English was there, and they wheeled Sue away to examine her.

As the sun began to rise, buses showed up with the rest of our group and the ill from the compound. Jorge was on the last bus and said the police hadn't detained anyone, just focused on getting everyone out.

I was worried sick about Sue yet wanted to help, so I assisted by finding more wheelchairs and helping people into the emergency staging area.

Enrique had called Monica, and she was on her way.

When I saw the doctor who had been examining Sue approach Ivan, I went over to them.

"She's lost a lot of blood," the doctor said. "She's been taken to surgery to stop the internal bleeding."

"Is she going to be all right?" I asked.

Ivan placed his hand on my shoulder.

"We'll let you know." The doctor turned and went back down the corridor from where he'd come.

Ivan guided me to a chair and then sat down next to me.

"I was hoping they would operate to stop the bleeding right away," he said. "Sue is strong ..."

All the people from the compound had been triaged, and now there was nothing to do but wait. I sat facing the window in a room that contained three rows of eight orange molded-plastic chairs held in place by metal bars. There were two couples at the opposite end, one elderly and one with a child who was quietly coloring over the lines of a book with a pink crayon.

Lorraine walked into the room and sat down next to me. "Any word about Sue yet?"

"I was told the surgery was successful and we'll get more details when she regains consciousness."

"That's good news, right?"

"I think so. Yes." I shrugged. "How are you?"

Lorraine had a bandage over her left eyebrow and the skin around it was a dark purple, almost black. "Just needed a few stitches. Nothing to worry about; I have a hard head."

Monica and her daughters entered and sat down across from us.

"Everyone seems to be in the process of being looked after," Monica said. "Ivan informed me that Sue has been moved from ICU into recovery."

"Yes," I responded.

Olga and Esmeralda gave me encouraging smiles.

"You two don't need to be here," I said to them. "Shouldn't you be at school?"

"It's Saturday," Olga said.

"And we want to be here for Sue," Esmeralda added. "She's a role model for us. Sue's strong, really intelligent, and doesn't hold back her opinions."

"We want to be more like her," Olga said. "And you too, Lorraine; you're amazing. You're beautiful, smart, caring, tactical, and you don't give up ground to any man who's undeserving."

Lorraine blushed. "Thank you."

Monica patted the bare knees of the girl on either side of her.

"I agree." I managed a smile. "Sue and Lorraine are great women to want to be like."

※

It had taken Sue three hours to regain consciousness after her two-and-a-half-hour surgery. Ivan and I were led by a nurse to her private room.

Sue was bleary-eyed and quiet.

"How are you feeling?" I went to her and kissed her on the forehead.

"Tired," Sue said. "I think they have me on painkillers."

"That is expected," Ivan said.

A slim man with black hair graying at the temples and a goatee entered the room. "I am Dr. Jose Rodriguez, the surgeon who performed the operation on Ms. Clark." His accent was strong, but he spoke English well.

"Am I going to be okay?" Sue asked.

"You lost a significant amount of blood, but a transfusion wasn't needed. We've repaired the tears and there's bruising, but within a few days you should be strong enough to leave."

I let out a relieving breath, not noticing until then that I'd been holding it.

"Thank you, doctor." Sue looked consoled.

Dr. Rodriguez took a step closer and stood at the foot of Sue's bed. "Did you know that you were pregnant?"

Sue's facial expression turned to concern. "I was late for my period, and my body was acting a little strange. I thought it was stress."

I took Sue's hand. *She's pregnant. That means she conceived when we were together in Burford. I was the father.*

Ivan looked down at the floor and nodded as if knowing that was the case.

"It was only a month, maybe less," the surgeon said. "You miscarried when you were struck. I'm sorry, there was nothing that could be done. It was too late when we operated and all we could do was repair the area."

There was a delayed reaction as Sue's mouth opened, but no words were uttered. Then her eyes filled with tears and her lips quivered. She began to sob.

The doctor continued to talk, but I'd stopped listening. It felt like someone had punched me in the gut and my legs were going to give way.

I stared at Sue and her at me. "I'm so sorry, my love." I wiped strands of hair from her face and embraced her.

If we'd known Sue was pregnant, she never would've gone to the compound. She'd have been safe. We could've had a baby ... together.

Sue held onto me as hard as I held her, and we cried for our lost child.

# INTERLOGUE 11

*June 1, 2003*

Carlo chose to decant the 1973 Rioja Alavesa from his family cellar. A full glass sat on the wrought iron table in front of him, along with a monogrammed pad of paper, his personalized Mont Blanc Masterpiece pen, a plate of homemade chorizo and cabrales cheese, and a cordless phone. The grapevine-covered trellis provided shade from the afternoon sun. The Mediterranean glistened in the distance below.

His family estate always gave him solace and peace. Carlo needed an inspiring place to think, and this was his favorite. He had everything he required; mind you, a second bottle would likely be needed before all the decisions were made.

He leaned back in his midnight-blue chair and adjusted the yellow cushion under him. Raising his glass, Carlo gazed past the vineyard to the sea. "To Hendrick Junior. You killed your father and ordered Jack Carter's murder. And now you are also dead. Good riddance. I hope your father and Jack find you in hell and seek revenge on your soul."

Carlo had taken Günter and Dale Samson, and they'd left

Colombia on his jet as quickly as they could. He'd learned about Hendrick's death from Chief Inspector Plante when they'd touched down at Heathrow the night before. He'd handed Samson over to Plante. Then he'd shipped Günter back to Oxford, telling him to hurry up and finish his studies; Naintosa and Pharmalin would be there for him when he was ready. From there he'd proceeded home to the safety of Valencia.

Carlo brought the wine to his lips and took a lingering taste. "Mmm." He raised the glass higher for the second toast. "To my soon-to-be-departed friend, Davis: you are a master of transformation, with the ability to manipulate the world to our will. Salute."

The phone rang, and Carlo answered it with his free hand.

"The Colombians are not happy," said Chief Inspector Plante on the other end of the line.

"They'll get over it," Carlo said. "We have copies of all the records. The lab was destroyed and the rest of the compound can be abandoned. Let the Colombian government clean up the mess."

"I'm not the one you should be telling," Plante said.

"I'll make the appropriate call to the president," Carlo said. "You know, your associates didn't help at all. They just stood there and left right after me."

"They weren't supposed to help, only provide information. No one must know of their involvement. That would jeopardize future collaboration with the CIA."

"What involvement?"

"Exactly."

*No, I meant they didn't do anything.* He let it go, not bothering to verbalize his disappointment any further. "And Barnes and his band of rebels?"

"They're still in Florencia. I have local authorities watching their movements, but I don't see that anything more needs to be done."

"Interesting how none of them were killed." Carlo swirled the wine in the glass. "They should've never escaped the compound alive."

There was some static on the line when Plante spoke. "I think that was for the best."

"We must continue to monitor their movement," Carlo said. "Make sure to include Lee Donald. He could want revenge for Jack Carter's death and may not be satisfied when he finds out everyone involved is deceased."

"Yes, agreed."

"Where is Dr. Smith?" Carlo reached for a piece of cheese. "He needs a new lab and must get back to work."

"He was last seen with Barnes's group," Plante said. "Mainly, Dr. Popov."

"Damn." Carlo sighed. "I suspected he was going to change sides."

"How is Davis?" Plante asked.

"Not good but stable," Carlo said. "He and his physician have flown back to New York where he can be with his family."

"What about Schmidt's and Lovemark's companies?" Plante inquired.

"That is what I have to figure out now."

"I'll leave you to it, then."

Carlo put the phone down and reached for some sausage to go with the cheese. He washed the food down by draining the rest of the wine in the glass. Then he poured more.

Taking the pen in hand, he began to write.

Russell Norman, Davis's second in command, would take over the operations of GM Comm until he found a suitable buyer from within the *Club*.

Günter would eventually take over Naintosa and Pharmalin, but realistically that was ten years away. Carlo needed to get interim leaders. He didn't want to do it himself but would be on the board of directors he would form. This time it was probably best to have one CEO per company so as not to overwhelm a single individual.

Ivgeni Svetlov's brother would probably take over Pharmalin, and he had three other potentials for Naintosa. Plus they needed new head scientists. He had a few men in mind and wrote their names down.

It was time to call a special meeting of the *Club*. And maybe Tom Crane could be brought into the fold—he did have a special expertise.

Carlo put the pen down, ate more chorizo and cheese, then took his wine glass in hand and leaned back in his chair. It was up to him to decide what to do with the population control plan. That was the part that would take the most amount of thought ... and drinking.

The focus would have to shift to containment. From now on the main resources would be needed to protect the good seed and undamaged land, and to develop the cancer cure. He'd have the Plycite gene destroyed—it wasn't working anyway, and he didn't want an even bigger mess.

Carlo looked east toward his vineyard and then south down toward the fields. The estate had withstood damage through the Carlist Wars, Spanish Revolution, and two World Wars, yet its biggest threat to date was glyphosate and genetically engineered seed. *Of which I helped facilitate.* The contaminated areas would not grow crops again. The irony was not lost on him.

He felt a sharp stabbing pain in his lower abdomen, like intense gas trapped and needing desperately to escape. Carlo gave the plate of food in front of him an accusing glare and pushed it away.

# CHAPTER 39

*June 4, 2003*

"Here; let me help you get out." I ran around to the passenger side of Enrique's BMW and opened the door for Sue.

"I'm okay. You don't have to be so ..." She cringed when she twisted and grabbed the bandaged area around her midsection.

"Just enjoy the attention while it lasts." I took her free hand and helped her out.

Sue always was beat up worse than the rest of us because of her fearlessness and never holding back. But those qualities endeared me to her, and I'd never want her to change.

While she'd been in the hospital, we'd talked of our grief over the loss of our child that had been growing inside her. The feelings were still raw, and she'd spent long moments in silent contemplation, often crying. I vowed to be there for her.

Ivan and Dr. Smith had pulled up behind us in a rental car. Everyone had been wary about Dr. Smith staying at the house, but his constant reinforcement about dedicating the rest of his life to curing the colon cancer forced us to relent; that and Ivan's reassurance that he trusted Dr. Smith and would watch over him.

Ivan needed his help.

Monica stood by a planter holding a shovel and called Enrique over to help her as soon as we'd arrived.

Mike was outside near the front door having a smoke. He seemed absorbed in thought.

As we approached, Sue said, "I know I've thanked you already, but if you hadn't shot Schilling in that second, Nick and I would both be dead."

"It's hard to explain." There was conflict in Mike's expression. "I'm proud that I was able to pull the trigger and hit who I'd aimed at to save you guys, but still I killed another human."

"I know how you feel," I said. "It goes against our nature. We're writers. People like Jorge, Lorraine, and Lee have been trained for those types of situations; we haven't."

Sue gave Mike a hug, and I placed my hand on his back.

All we could do was keep thanking him, to reinforce that the action shouldn't be something he punished himself for. We hoped that he'd let us be there to help him work through it.

Lee and Lorraine had stuck around the hospital the last few days, just in case anyone from Naintosa's security came to silence us or any of the victims of the experiments. We were fortunate no such encounters had occurred.

Ivan and Dr. Smith had instructed the hospital's doctors on what was wrong with the sick people from the compound and how they could be helped. Specialists were called in from Bogota to study those with tumors, lesions, and various stages of colon cancer. That brought around the authorities, who interviewed Dr. Smith. He fully complied, and even though they knew he wasn't in charge of the operation and wasn't deemed responsible, they still wanted him to stay in Florencia for now.

The victims were treated with compassion, and as word spread that they were at the hospital, we found out that many of them had been kidnapped when relatives came to find them.

We were interviewed by detectives as well. We were honest about trying to get information and getting caught. Jorge and Lee said the fire in the lab and the dead guards happened as a result of them trying to rescue us. Sue and I told them Schilling shot Schmidt by mistake when we were trying to escape, and Mike admitted to shooting Schilling just before he had intended to kill us. They had to have known that something much bigger had been going on and we'd been the catalysts of exposing it. When I tried to explain the population control plan, the detective interviewing me seemed more concerned about when we'd all be leaving Colombia. In the end none of us had been detained, which was somewhat surprising.

The evening after the ordeal at the compound, Enrique and Jorge had snuck back to take a look. They said the place was swarming with military. There was no sign of any inhabitants remaining. The lab had burned to the ground, but the section where the offices were was still intact—that's where we'd been held.

◄▒▒►

"You leave in the morning?" Monica poked her head into the bedroom as I was helping Sue lie down.

"Yes," I said. "Thank you for taking us into your home, and for your hospitality."

Ivan would be staying as long as he felt he was needed, and until the authorities gave permission for Dr. Smith to leave.

Jorge was going to go visit his daughter and parents in Ibague, a four-and-a-half-hour drive away.

The rest of us were flying from Florencia to Bogota and then onto where we were planning to settle.

Sue and I had promised to keep updating the website and

promoting it to the media that would listen. Mike also agreed to write about and share our experiences from his perspective.

We didn't feel security was necessary now, but those of us whose role was protection vowed to be there if ever needed.

With all the experiences we'd shared, separating was emotional for us all. Our bonds would last the rest of our lives.

# EPILOGUE

*June 30, 2003*

This was my favorite part of the day. The sun would soon set over the mountain, and the air was clean and calm. A large raven sat in the nearest tree at the shoreline, as if watching over me. One water skier made turns in the cove, and three boats sped along the open lake to get home before dark. It wasn't quite high season, so there wasn't the amount of activity we were told there would be between mid-July and Labor Day.

I sat in a white plastic folding chair and held an e-mail from that morning that I had printed. We'd set two chairs out when we arrived five days ago and spent a considerable amount of our time on the wharf. The water was still cold, but the days were already plenty warm.

After each going to visit our parents, Sue and I had spent a couple of weeks half-heartedly looking for a place to buy in Seattle. We realized that we didn't feel ready to settle down there yet—eventually, but not now.

During a call with Ivan, he told us that the cabin in Christina Lake, British Columbia, might be available. The couple who owned it were elderly and couldn't climb up and down the stairs anymore. They were the same people who watched over Ivan's home in Nelson when he was away. We decided to make them an offer of renting the cabin for the summer and buying it at the end if we liked it. The couple had agreed.

Sue said she didn't have a problem with the fact that there would be memories for me about spending those winter months there with Morgan. I now welcomed those memories—they were of adventure and discovery. Of course, I still missed Morgan, but so much had happened since she'd passed, and Sue was my future now.

Sue and I had to admit that we'd loved each other for a long time. There was no point in either of us trying to hide or deny it anymore. Plus, with all we'd been through, we had each other to deal with the trauma. Sue and I were meant to be together going forward, baggage and all.

Sue was told after the surgery to stop her internal bleeding that over time she'd still be able to have children. For us, logically, with the potential purge of so many people in the coming years, it didn't seem right to bring more life into the world. But emotionally, the loss of Sue's pregnancy had been devastating and had revealed that, deep down, we wanted a child together. It was good to still have the choice in the future.

I could hear Sue coming down the ramp onto the wharf and turned to her. "Did you check for new e-mails?"

She'd put on a T-shirt and shorts over her bikini. I'd noticed that ever since the surgery she'd absently pull at the bottom of her shirts to make sure the scar was covered, even though it was just below her bikini-line. She passed me a Kootenay Ale before sitting on the other plastic chair. "Rose will arrive in Oslo tomorrow. They're really going to shack up."

I smiled. "That'll make it easier for Ivan. They deserve to be happy together. And he'll have someone to talk to when Dr. Smith is driving him nuts."

"Not to mention her cooking." Sue twisted the cap off the bottle she'd brought for herself.

"But no response from Ivan about the Da Silva e-mail?" I held up the folded sheet of paper.

"Not yet."

Ivan and Dr. Smith had been able to leave Colombia a week after we'd left. They were still in constant contact with the Colombian oncologists who'd set up a ward and lab to help in the pursuit of the colon cancer cure.

Dr. Smith had been welcomed into the Northern European Council for Ethical Farming's lab but watched until they were positive he'd changed sides. Ivan, after spending time with Dr. Smith, had found him challenging and stubborn—he liked having his own way and didn't play well with others.

Sue leaned back in the chair and took a drink of her beer. "I heard from Lorraine as well."

"I wouldn't have guessed that Lorraine and Lee would get together."

"I saw it right away." Sue smiled. "You've always been oblivious to those things."

"I guess."

"Lorraine said that Lee feels he owes it to Jack to find out who hired Bail to kill him."

"Maybe Jorge will help," I said. "He's in Dallas too."

"I'm sure he will."

"If it really was Schmidt V or even Lovemark, he'd be too late."

"I think it's the knowing that's most important." Sue gave a tug down at the end of her shirt.

We hadn't found anything in the media about the death of Schmidt. There had been a few small articles in the Colombian press about a fire at a pesticide lab outside Florencia that had shut it down.

We'd read two days ago that Lovemark had succumbed to cancer and that Russell Norman had taken over operations of GM Comm.

"I think we should go along with Da Silva ... for now." Sue looked out at the lake.

We'd heard that an aggressive environmental group claimed to have sprayed glyphosate on Da Silva's vineyard. We'd been wondering what he was up to, so now that Sam was fully recovered, he and Eugene had volunteered to keep tabs on him. Then Ivan and I had received an e-mail from Da Silva this morning. We were curious as to how he obtained our e-mail addresses, but if anyone could find them, he could. In his message he had assured us that he was going to use his own resources and direct Naintosa to concentrate all of their ability to stop the spread of genetically engineered seed and pesticides. Also, Pharmalin was going to concentrate on the actual cure for colon cancer. He wanted both companies to cooperate with Ivan, Dr. Smith, and the Colombians and pool their research. In return, all he wanted was for us to be silent for a while, and then when there was progress, to report about it. We now knew that the elite were just as susceptible to being culled as the rest of the population, so Da Silva could be being truthful in his offer.

I folded the paper a second time and placed it in my pocket. "Unless Ivan says otherwise, I'll respond to Da Silva tomorrow and say we agree."

"And then we watch him to make sure he's sincere," Sue said.

"Yep."

There had been no contact from Chief Inspector Plante with any of us since we'd left England. I'd expected that he would've been in touch, wanting to question us about what had happened in Colombia. I still had unproven suspicions that he had ties to Schmidt, Lovemark, and Da Silva. We never heard anything from Lieutenant Furyk and Agent Stenson either or had seen the Naintosa men from the Ford again.

It was confirmed that Malcolm Carter was overseeing the sale of Moile R&D to one of Tom Crane's companies. In a news article, Crane stated that he wanted to buy the company because it was his quest to preserve the clean water that was left. That sounded great, but his true intentions were suspect. I also still wondered if Malcolm had been complicit in Jack's murder.

"Still no word from Mike?" Sue asked.

"No, unfortunately." Mike had flown to Seattle with us and said he was going to go visit his mom for a while. Mike bottled up his emotions, so what happened in Florencia could take him a long time to deal with. I'd e-mailed him twice but hadn't heard back. Sue and I both wanted to support him. Hopefully, he'd write about what had happened, even if it was only for his own therapy. "But that's Mike. Remember he disappeared for a year last time. It's just the way he is."

"Okay, I'll try not worry so much about him." Sue sipped her beer.

My publisher had informed me that my initial book sales were going well, and they wanted me to go on a book tour. Sue and I decided to take them up on the offer, as it meant we'd get to go back to Europe in September.

"We need to do some work tomorrow," Sue said.

"By *we*, you mean *me*." I managed a smile.

"This place is inspiring." Sue had written almost every day since we'd arrived. She'd posted her side of our experience and what we'd learned in Colombia on our website. Traffic to the site was steady and increasing. There was also more interest from independent media, and she'd had three phone interviews because of it.

I, on the other hand, had only edited her words and not written any of my own. I hadn't decided if I was going to go the nonfiction route or write a sequel to my first book. I'd start the outline tomorrow and then figure it out. I agreed with Sue that Christina Lake was an inspirational place.

I gazed out over the reflection on the water and sighed. *If only Dr. Elles had lived to see what his work had done to so many lives. Would he have been able to stop it?* He was likely rolling in his grave.

"What are you thinking about?" Sue asked.

"Just remembering Dr. Elles."

Sue reached out and took my hand in hers as we watched the sliver of orange sun disappear over the mountain.

# ACKNOWLEDGEMENTS

I have really enjoyed writing the Dark Seed Trilogy; so much that I left a couple of threads at the end, just in case I want to continue the story at a later date. The characters have become a part of me, and it's hard to let them go.

I would like to thank the following people for their guidance, expertise and encouragement:

Authors Scotty Schrier and Eve Gruschow for their strong suggestions about the direction of the story and characters. There is no way I could have written the trilogy without their help. The countless long Wednesday nights of detailed discussion and banter were informative and fun. Extra thanks to Eve for helping me with the "special scene," and to Scotty for being able to nail each character's accent while reading out loud;

My mother, Kathy Verigin, and my wife, Diana Carrillo, for helping me work out the kinks at the beginning of the story;

Everyone at Promontory Press for their belief in my books and hard work in publishing the trilogy;

Bennett Coles for his sage help, patience, and structural editing;

Karen Brown for her excellent copy editing and advice;

Richard Coles for his detailed proofreading;

Marla Thompson for her fantastic way of capturing the story through cover design;

Cindy Goodman for photography (and I don't like having my picture taken);

Dr. Maria Bautista for all medical terminology and how characters would react when put in harm's way;

Andy Prest for making Sue's article read like a journalist wrote it, because he's a journalist;

Nicola Freestone for advice on British law;

Neetu Shokar and Courtney Harding for help with the title;

My wife Diana Carrillo for traveling with me to all the exotic locations, so I could get a feel for the places;

And most of all, I would like to thank the readers who have enjoyed my books, pushed me to continue writing by wanting to know what happened next, and spreading the word to others about my stories.

# ABOUT THE AUTHOR

Lawrence Verigin is also the author of critically acclaimed and multiple award-winning *DARK SEED* and *SEED OF CONTROL*. His goal is to entertain readers while delving into socially relevant subjects. Lawrence and his wife, Diana, live in Vancouver, Canada.

Contact:
Website: www.lawrenceverigin.com
E-mail: lawrenceverigin@gmail.com
Facebook: Lawrence Verigin
Twitter: @LawrenceVerigin